Coming Home

Holly Kerr

www.threebirdspress.ca

This book is a work of fiction. All names, characters, locations and incidents are products of the author's imagination. Any resemblance to actual persons is entirely coincidental.

ISBN: 978-0-9958045-6-2

Because of the mashed potato fights I had with Kristi

Other Books by Holly Kerr

The Secret Life of Charlotte Dodd
The Missing Files of Charlotte Dodd (ebook)
Unexpecting
Absinthe Doesn't Make the Heart Grow Fonder

The Dragon Under the Mountain (kidlit)

Coming Home

Chapter One

Brenna

There can be no situation in life in which the conversation of my dear sister will not administer some comfort to me.

—Mary Montagu

Brenna Ebans was finalizing the paperwork for a 2.5 billion dollar acquisition for one of her most problematic clients when Kayleigh's call interrupted her train of thought. She looked longingly at the neat file on her desk; she loved her sister but...

Brenna had been surviving on pure adrenaline for the past three days, trying to get the deal done and to everyone's amazement but hers, she'd succeeded. One little loophole and the power was back in her client's hands. She loved her work.

At least, that's what she told herself.

The extension blinked accusingly and Brenna punched it with a sigh. "Kayleigh. Hi."

"You're a tough woman to track down."

"And yet you managed it. What's up?"

Brenna listened to her older sister's gossip with half an ear as her assistant Crystal poked her head into the office. She had a big smile on her face when she dropped off another file with two yellow post-it notes; Call them ASAP with a happy face and I'm leaving in 10 mins with an even bigger happy face.

It was already five thirty on a Monday; Brenna was going to have to cancel yet another dinner with Toby.

At first, Brenna had enjoyed working for the same law firm as her husband. But now it only seemed to create more tension every time she got inundated by work.

Which was becoming almost a daily event.

She wasn't sure how Toby did it. How did he manage time for friends, the gym and fancy dinners? Out of the last six attempts, Brenna managed to make it to one dinner with her husband. One.

As Kayleigh reported on the town gossip with the seriousness of a TMZ reporter, Brenna snapped her fingers to catch Crystal's attention. She covered the handset and motioned to her assistant. "Can you find Toby for me?" Brenna jerked her head towards the paperwork on her desk with a sorrowful expression. "I can't make dinner tonight. I have to finish this."

"I'll tell him," Crystal promised with a distracted smile.

She probably thinks I'm a horrible wife.

Maybe I am.

I should tell him myself.

"Are you coming home for Addison's wedding?" Kayleigh asked, pulling Brenna back to the conversation. "Maggie said you haven't sent your RSVP back."

Addison was getting married? Brenna didn't remember Addison being engaged, let alone planning a wedding. Who was the groom? Rummaging through her inbox, she could swear she hadn't received an invitation. She'd remember a wedding invitation to my own niece's wedding. There was nothing in the work inbox. With a frown, she combed a year's worth of paper out of the inbox marked 'personal.'

"Oh, Kay, work is just so crazy and—"There was the invitation; still unopened with her name written in sparkly green ink, along with a credit card bill and an invitation to join the newest fitness center in the area. "It's been really bad—really busy," she corrected. "I'm doing this deal and no one thought it was going to come together but I managed it and—"

"You're always busy. You work over Christmas and you never take vacations. Look at how late it is and you're still there."

"There's a three hour time difference between Vancouver and Forest Hills," Brenna reminded her. "So, actually, it's not that late."

"It's been years since you've been home, Brenna."

Here it came. Sooner or later, all Brenna's conversations with Kayleigh took a sharp right down Guilt Lane.

Yes, it had been fourteen years since she had left home. Yes, she realized she hadn't been back since.

Brenna rolled her eyes as Kayleigh warmed up. "You never update Facebook, so I don't even know what you look like these days."

"I look like me. Tall. Kind of scrawny. Red hair."

She ran her hand through her hair and remembered she missed her last two salon appointments.

"Brenna..." Kayleigh sighed, her exasperation flying from the tiny town in Northern Ontario to settle heavily on Brenna's shoulders. "Just come home. Please. Addison's wedding is in two weeks. Maggie needs you to be there. It's her oldest daughter. It's Maggie."

Brenna winced in resignation as Kayleigh threw the sucker punch. She knew any mention of Maggie was a sure way for Brenna to feel the maximum guilt.

Their father had abandoned the family when Brenna was three; their mother died ten years later. Eldest sister Maggie had been the rock of stability, taking on the roles of both mother and father to her sisters.

Everyone in the tiny town of Forest Hills knew the five Skatt sisters. Everyone felt sorry for them.

Reluctantly, Brenna ticked off on her fingers what she needed to do if she was going to make the trip back home. Who could cover her cases, how long she could be away from the office, what to tell Toby...?

Toby!

She had to make sure Toby knew she was running

late. The last time she forgot to tell him, he ended up waiting at the restaurant for almost an hour.

"I'll call you back," she told Kayleigh hastily.

"Brenna!"

"I will. I'll see what I can do, I promise. I'll call you back, but really – I have to hang up now. Call you right back-" Brenna hung up with Kayleigh's protests still ringing in her ears and hurried out the door of her tiny little box of an office.

Davis and Daniels Attorneys at Law occupied three floors of a high-rise in downtown Vancouver, and Toby, being next in line for partner, had one of the cushy top floor offices. Brenna headed for the elevator, hoping to catch her husband before he left.

They'd been fighting steadily for weeks – months really – about Brenna's inability to make time for him. They weren't exactly fights; Toby was too passive-aggressive for that. He would make snarky comments that Brenna would pretend to ignore, things would be awkward so Brenna would spend even more time at the office. Last Sunday they had a heated discussion about her choosing to work rather than brunch with him, but Brenna left the condo before resolving anything. Toby hated it when things were left hanging.

He needed things packaged up with a neat little bow.

She used the short trip between floors to respond to an email that Crystal should have taken care of. Brenna realized her assistant wasn't the most efficient, but she was cheerful and friendly and would always bring Brenna a latte when she got one for herself.

Brenna's thumbs flew across her phone, responding to another email as the elevator doors slid open. This should have been done hours ago. What was Crystal thinking?

Crystal had seemed especially smiling that afternoon. Brenna wondered wistfully if there might come a time when the two of them could be more than boss slash assistant. Friends, even. Brenna could ask for advice about Toby and Crystal could tell her about the men she was dating...

Who was she kidding? She couldn't even make time for her husband, let alone someone she could talk to about him.

She checked another email between the elevator and Toby's office, pausing with her fist poised to knock as she skimmed the request. There were texts she hadn't got to –

Toby. Telling him dinner was out of the question.

Brenna couldn't remember if she'd knocked and tentatively pushed open the door. "Toby, I - "

"Brenna!" Toby cried in a strangled voice. He was sitting at his desk by the window.

There was a thump from under his desk.

"Toby? You okay? What was that?"

"What are you doing here?"

"I wanted to tell you -"

And then Crystal crawled out from under Toby's desk. "I was telling him for you," she said with a spiteful gleam in her eyes.

"Thanks...what...?"

It took Brenna a moment to comprehend what she was seeing.

The sight of Toby jumping out from behind his desk, his slim-fitted pants bagged around his ankles, fully exposed and suddenly very flaccid, cemented it.

"Oh, my God!" The cry didn't seem strong enough for the situation. "What the fuck?"

"I can explain," Toby said urgently, pushing Crystal aside. His handsome face was flushed with fear and annoyance, as he fumbled to pull up his pants.

"How can you possibly explain this?"

Inexplicably, the urge to laugh bubbled up and Brenna took a deep breath, swallowing the hysterical giggle. Toby favored an eclectic style of fashion and the image of him wearing a sweater vest, pants around his ankles, and blue and orange argyle socks pulled up was something she wouldn't soon forget.

"Brenna –" Toby proved it was impossible to discretely pull up pants.

"What the hell are you doing?" She noticed how his close-cropped hair had become more silver than brown of late. Toby was seventeen years older than Brenna and getting caught with his pants down—literally—suddenly made him look every day of those fifty years.

"Let me –" His pants were still undone when he stumbled out from behind the desk. Brenna beat a retreat to the door, eager to keep her distance.

"I know what you were doing. You were in her mouth! How do you expect to explain that? And in your office, of all places?"

"Brenna, you know things haven't been great between us."

"This is my fault?"

Crystal snorted as she scrambled to her feet, face flushed with rage rather than remorse. “How can someone so smart be so incredibly stupid? Things are horrible between you two! Everyone knows it but you.” Brenna stared in horror as the girl continued. “You’re a terrible wife! I’ve been taking care of your husband for weeks now and you’re so busy with your head stuck up your ass you haven’t even noticed a thing!”

Brenna flinched at the crassness of Crystal’s attack. “Should I be thanking you for taking care of him, as you so eloquently put it?”

“I’ve done a better job than you ever could!”

One of the straws holding Brenna’s control snapped. “And look where it’s gotten you. I suggest you get your things out of this office because you’re fired. And you,” Brenna turned to a silent Toby. Anger and disappointment raged within her, and as she looked at her husband, disappointment won. “How could you do this to me? With her – here? You know what this job meant to me.”

“You’re upset about a job?” Toby said incredulously.

“No, I’m upset about you. Walking in on you with

my assistant hasn't been the highlight of my day. It's just – how could you do something like that, Toby." She didn't wait for a response. "I can't be married to you anymore."

"Brenna, wait. You're over-reacting."

"I don't think so. I think it's time I do some reacting." She turned to leave but decided a parting shot was necessary. "We're over."

Was that all she had?

"Your penis is pathetic and I've had better sex with my vibrator," she added in a rush. "Plus your socks are stupid and that vest makes you look like a dork. So there."

Brenna swept out of Toby's office with head held high.

Hang on, she told herself, vowing not to break down until she was alone.

How did this happen? How could she have not noticed what was going on?

How stupid was she?

Brenna punched the button for the elevator, praying it would arrive before Toby did. She fully expected her husband to rush out after her.

To fight for her.

Except he didn't.

She held her stomach, sick with disappointment. How could she miss what was going on? Toby and Crystal? How could he?

Brenna remembered how Crystal had always found an excuse to bring in a file or message whenever Toby had been in her office. She laughed at his jokes, listened to his stories.

Tears pricked her eyes and she pushed away from the wall as the elevator arrived.

On her way back to her office, Brenna paused at the pod of desks in the middle of the floor that Crystal shared with three others assistants. One of her client files was open on the desk, paper spread haphazardly, along with a half-empty mug of tea and Crystal's iPhone.

"Can I help you with something, Brenna?" The woman across from Crystal's desk asked, her eyes wide with confusion.

Brenna realized she didn't even know the names of the people she worked with. No wonder she never noticed a cheating husband.

"Did you know she was fucking my husband?" Brenna asked conversationally, carefully tucking the papers back into the file on Crystal's desk.

"What?" The protest was so thoroughly insincere that it left no doubt she and Crystal had spent many hours discussing Toby, Toby and Crystal, Toby and Brenna and her complete and utter ignorance of the affair.

"Could you hold this for a sec?" Brenna asked politely, passing the file over the dividing wall to the woman before picking up Crystal's phone. "Do you think she has pictures of him on here?"

The woman gaped at Brenna, who shrugged and smashed the phone against the corner of the desk.

And again.

"What are you doing?" The fear in her voice was sincere but Brenna saw no need to answer. The phone still looked somewhat functional so she threw it on the floor and crushed the screen with the heel of her shoe, grinding it like a bug.

"Brenna! Stop!"

Looking up, Brenna saw Toby, with a red-faced Crystal right behind him, hurrying down the hall. She snatched Crystal's new hot pink Coach tote bag sitting innocently under her desk and punted it toward them like a football. The contents of the open purse flew out in every direction, pens and tampons flying through the air like miniature Scud missiles.

"Brenna!" Toby shouted. A tube of lipstick hit him in the head.

"I'm calling security," the woman wailed.

Brenna snatched up the mug, which had Be Mine emblazoned in pink and threw it at the PC, the sizzle of wet electronics chasing her down the hall along with Crystal's shrill scream and Toby's shouts, her breath coming in panting gasps.

She locked the door behind her and stood for a minute, with a hand over her eyes, waiting for the tears.

Her phone, still clutched in her hand, rang.

"Kayleigh, I'm coming home."

Chapter Two

Cat

Sisters never quite forgive each other for what happened when they were five.

—Pam Brown

"Cat? You here?"

"What now?" Cat muttered, crawling out from behind the toilet at the sound of her sister's voice. She encouraged a walk-in policy with visitors because the house was so big, it was impossible to hear a knock. The dogs' weren't selective either; they barked at every car that drove down the hill.

Like usual, Kayleigh was doing her best to ignore

the dogs surrounding her at the bottom of the stairs. She wasn't a dog person.

"What are you doing?" Kayleigh gestured to the wrench in Cat's hand.

"The toilet won't stop leaking." Cat gave her forehead an irritable swipe with the back of her hand. "I was trying to turn the water off."

"Can't Mike help?" Kayleigh climbed up a few stairs, the steps creaking ominously.

Another thing to fix.

Cat dropped onto the top step with slumped shoulders. Pictures marched up the wall beside her, a time capsule of the sisters' lives. She reached up and straightened a frame.

"Our brother-in-law is a lot of things but a plumber he ain't. I think I can get Pam's brother to help me, if I can afford it," Cat said, plucking the tuft of dog hair from between the spindles of the banister. Keeping the place clean was almost as much of a chore as the constant repairs.

Cat saw the question in Kayleigh's eyes—why don't we sell it? The solid, three-story old Victorian with the wraparound porch used to be a focal point in Forest Hills. It had been a great house while the sisters were growing up, but those days were long gone.

Cat knew deep down, the house was too big for just her, even with the dogs running around. Even when Grandpa Earl had lived with her, it had been too big, and he had been gone for almost five years now.

She had always insisted she wasn't talented but the truth was Cat could clean a mean house.

The toilets leaked, the porch needed painting, the roof needed replacing, but the kitchen was always spotless and filled with the delicious aromas of fresh bread and chocolate. There were never piles of laundry or papers strewn about. The house frequently exhausted Cat, but it was home. Her home.

The irony of it was that the only way Cat would be able to find the money to fix the house would be to sell it. Every real estate agent in the area had promised her a sweet deal, but it wasn't in the plan.

And then there was the whole mother thing.

Carly Skatt died twenty years ago but Cat was convinced her spirit still lived in the house. Sunshine and warmth would be flooding a room and suddenly Cat would have goosebumps dotting her arms. Or she'd be lying in bed and the scent of lilacs, Carly's favourite flower, would overpower the smell of dogs crowding around her. This would be in January, when the bushes were frozen under at least a foot of snow.

There had never been an actual sighting, nor anything particularly creepy, just the sense something was there in the house. Her sisters scoffed at the idea, but Cat loved it. It made her feel that their mother hadn't really left them.

Besides, their mother had been...difficult...to deal with when she was alive. Handling a ghost was much easier. Volatile and unpredictable, their mother' moods swung widely between irrational obstinacy and loving solicitude. Her fits of temper were as legendary as the dark moods that kept her locked in her room for days on end.

Someday, when things were fixed up, Cat had a plan to turn the house into a bed and breakfast. It would make a perfect B & B. She'd offer a sumptuous breakfast with plates of fresh baking and a selection of her homemade jams. Shivers of excitement tickled her every time she thought about it. Ghost Hills, catering to the eclectic and those who wanted a little spooky mystery with their small–town adventures.

It didn't hurt that she had an actual resident

ghost.

Kayleigh sniffed the air hopefully. “What are you cooking?”

“The cake!” Cat bolted down the stairs to the kitchen, followed by Kayleigh. “Missed the timer because of the stupid toilet.” She pulled the pans from the oven, pressing a finger into the top of the slightly domed cake. The indent filled when she lifted her finger, steam gently rising from their tops. “Another cake for Addison to try.”

“That’s why I’m here,” Kayleigh said excitedly. “I have the best news! I was heading up to Maggie’s and thought I’d stop in to tell you. I just talked to Bee and she’s coming home for Addison’s wedding!”

“Who?” Cat busied herself with placing the cakes on the cooling racks.

“Bee. Brenna. Our sister.”

“I thought you said good news,” Cat muttered, as she turned off the oven.

“Cat! She’s our sister! We haven’t seen her in—”

“Fourteen years. Yes, I can see the importance she places on her family.”

Kayleigh gave her The Look, the same one their mother used, and the same one Maggie had perfected.

What was the point of that? A simple 'fuck off' got to the point a lot quicker than a 'look'. Cat squinted her blue eyes and gave Kayleigh an exaggerated version of the death glare back.

Once upon a time, five Ebans daughters were born to Roger Ebans and Carly Skatt in a tiny village in Northern Ontario so small it never warranted a dot on a map. Smack dab between two monstrous hills, courtesy of the Agawa Canyon, Canada's version of the Grand Canyon, but the community was surrounded with lush forests instead of barren desert. It was a beautiful area of Ontario with towering trees covering the hills and valleys and whole chunks of the Skatt and Ebans families scattered around. Unfortunately, the families often made things a little less beautiful.

Skatt was a horrible name to be stuck with, but even without the name, the family was notorious, usually for the wrong reasons. Most of their cousins were infamous troublemakers, who made Cat look like an angel in comparison.

"So Brenna's coming home." Cat threw down her oven mitt. "Woo hoo."

"I think something must be going on. She sounded like she was crying." Kayleigh made a discrete attempt to check the cookie jar.

"You must have been talking to someone else. Oatmeal raisin cookies."

Kayleigh let the lid drop with disappointment. "You know I don't like raisins."

"You're not the only one who eats my cookies."

"But you love me the best?" Kayleigh smiled widely at her youngest sister.

"What are my choices?"

Kayleigh stuck out her tongue. "Back to Brenna. I think something's wrong. Bee said she was leaving soon...she never leaves work that early."

"It's after six o'clock in Vancouver, Kay. I'm sure that's when most lawyers stop working for the day and do all their non-lawyerly stuff."

"Not Brenna. I don't think she does any non-lawyerly stuff."

"And that's her problem right there."

Cat's gray tabby Sebastian announced his arrival with a wail like a child's cry. He wove three times around her feet and flopped over onto his side on her bare toes.

"That cat is getting fat."

"He's just big boned." Cat affectionately wiggled

her toes against Sebastian's ear. He had a bit of a foot fetish preferring to be scratched by feet rather than hands. Strange, but then again, so was Cat. How many people lived with a ghost?

"Have you ever thought you might have too many pets?" Kayleigh wondered. "Six cats, three dogs..."

"Four cats. Have you ever thought you might be happier with a pet of your own?"

"I am perfectly happy not to be responsible for feeding anyone or anything. Ever think you can't pay for a new toilet because of your vet bills?"

"Naw. Remember I dated that vet in Blind River?" Cat said over her shoulder, searching in the cupboard for a snack for her sister. "He still gives me a discount."

Kayleigh laughed. "Ah, the legendary Skatt charm, still going strong."

"We've all got it—it's just how we chose to use it! Aha!" She unearthed a box of digestive cookies from the back of the cupboard and plunked it in front of Kayleigh.

It was impossible for Cat to be any closer to her sisters, at least the ones who'd stayed in Forest Hills. Maggie and Kayleigh were her favorite people in the world.

Of course most folks were morons.

"So going back to Brenna," Kayleigh began.

"Do we have to?" Cat mock-whined.

"Well, I can tell you're thrilled she's coming home." The crinkle of the plastic sleeve of cookies startled Sebastian who shot back up the stairs. "I just thought I'd let you know before you heard it from anybody else."

"That is a definite possibility around here."

"Why aren't you at work? I stopped in first but they said you called in."

"I feel like crap."

"Are you..." Hope lit up Kayleigh's pretty face.

"No. That's why I feel like crap."

"Oh. I'm sorry, Cat." Sympathy shone on Kayleigh's face and Cat shrugged with irritation.

"I'm not even technically trying so I don't know why I keep getting upset."

"Because you want a baby."

Despite their closeness, Cat refused to show Kayleigh her despair. "I'll probably give up. Mom already had five kids at my age and so did Maggie. Look how long I've been trying. I've been having sex since I was..."She lifted her head and spoke to the ceiling. "Since I'm not going to say how long."

"She can't hear you," Kayleigh said impatiently.

"You don't know that. You don't live here. You won't live here, so you don't know what she can or can't hear."

Kayleigh waved away the mention of their mother with a frown. "It's normal that you're disappointed but..."

"I'll get over it."

"Maybe you should get checked out..."

That was the last direction Cat wanted the conversation to go. "So, Brenna's coming home," she said with fake excitement. "Yay! Break out the marching band! The prodigal daughter returns."

Kayleigh grabbed another cookie with a shake of her head. "I'm going. I just wanted to let you know what's going on. I really think you should give her a chance, Cat. It's been a long time, you're both older now, and Maggie and I are tired of playing referee." Cat rolled her eyes. "For me?"

"That's not fair," Cat grumbled.

"Does Brenna even know?"

"About what?" Cat pretended not to know what

Kayleigh was referring to.

"I think you should tell her. It would be better coming from you."

Cat laughed out loud. "I doubt that!"

"You should," she insisted. "Give her a call. He meant a lot to her."

"Couldn't have meant that much or she would have stayed."

"Come on, Cat, she was a kid! You know what it was like for her. There would have been nothing for her if she'd stayed."

"No? I'm pretty happy, you seem pretty happy here. So does Maggie."

"You're not Bee."

"Thanks for the reminder."

"You know what I mean," Kayleigh sighed. "Just give her a heads up, would you? It's only fair."

"I'll get right on that," Cat said sarcastically.

"Feel better," With a hug for Cat and a handful of cookies, Kayleigh left.

Despite her best efforts, Cat couldn't help but wonder what had happened to Brenna that would bring her home.

Chapter Three

Brenna

I know some sisters who only see each other on Mother's Day and some who will never speak again. But most are like my sister and me... linked by volatile love, best friends who make other best friends ever so slightly less best.

—Patricia Volk

Brenna's tenure at Davis and Daniels ended without fanfare or good-byes. Technically, she wasn't fired; it was suggested a leave of absence would be beneficial because of personal stress.

"I was there five years, made millions for the firm and they got rid of me because I walked in on my husband doing the nasty with my secretary," Brenna told Kayleigh when she called her the next night.

"You should sue them. It's discrimination."

Brenna didn't answer her sister. After being escorted from the office, Brenna had gone home only to gather a few things before calling an Uber to take her to the nearest hotel. There she had spent the evening alone with a bottle of wine and the contents of the mini fridge. It was as if kicking Crystal's new purse across the office had drained her of any will to fight for her job or her husband

"So what's happening to Tony? Did they do anything to him?"

"Toby. His name is Toby."

"I would have remembered his name if I had ever met him."

Brenna remembered the reaction when she returned from a long weekend in Jamaica with Toby and had to tell her sisters they had eloped.

She had apologized, but instead of telling them how much she missed them and wished they'd been there, she had instead side-stepped their hurt feelings by justifying her actions. She never considered what her sisters might have been feeling.

Brenna had graduated at the top of her class in law school, and a year later, the recruiting team for the prestigious and fast-moving firm of Davis and Daniels had come calling to rescue her from her mountain of debt. Better yet, they were located in Vancouver, British Columbia, about as far as she could be from Forest Hills and still remain in Canada.

Toby had been the head of the recruiting team. He wined and dined her and Brenna had been smitten with the older man's intelligence and charm. Toby made her an offer that she couldn't refuse. In hindsight, she wished she had.

A week after settling into her tiny office at Davies and Daniels, she moved into Toby's condo.

And now, almost five years later, Brenna had filed a separation agreement.

"I think it's a moot point now," Brenna sighed. "It's for the b -" She tried for blithe and carefree but the sudden lump in her throat made her sound anything but. "For the best."

"What kind of place do you work in?" Kayleigh demanded. "If these kinds of shenanigans go on."

A welcome burst of laughter bubbled out of Brenna at Kayleigh's self-righteous tone. Compared to their own family's scandalous shenanigans, a quickie in the office was nothing.

"You're laughing?"

The laughter died out and Brenna sighed. "It's either that or cry."

"Oh, Bee. What are you going to do now? You love that job."

It was the use of Brenna's nickname and the gentleness in Kayleigh's voice that started the tears. Brenna gave a heroic sniff and dug her nails into her palms in hopes of preventing the waterworks. Crying wouldn't help her.

"Well, they don't love me. Not anymore. I'll come home for the wedding and then see what happens."

For once, Brenna thought going home might be a good idea. For the first time in her life, her future was uncertain. Nothing was mapped out. There had always been a plan, a goal she was working towards. Now, the future stretched out before her, open and unclear.

It wasn't as frightening as Brenna had thought it would be. At least not yet.

*

Brenna left Vancouver the next evening. She had no job, no husband, and a surprisingly small amount of luggage.

She felt a pang as she flew over the mountains. British Columbia had been her home since she had been eighteen; Brenna had spent her entire adult life there. All the big milestones in her life had taken place there, halfway across the country from her family.

She had left Forest Hills less than a week after she graduated from high school.

She had been the 'smart sister' and she had grown up with the expectation that she'd go on to university. But options were limited in the tiny town. With their fathers' whereabouts unknown, eldest sister Maggie had taken on the guardianship of Cat, Dory and Brenna. It hadn't been easy on the young mother, but Brenna had never heard a word of complaint from Maggie.

Brenna had noticed the lightening of the load when Dory left home and vowed she wouldn't be a burden to her sisters the same way Dory had been. Going away to school was the perfect excuse to leave town.

No one asked her to stay. Quite the opposite–her

sisters did everything they could to encourage her to go.

"Your brain is too big for this place," Maggie would always tell her. Along with Kayleigh, they pooled their money to buy Brenna a plane ticket after graduation. Not only did they want her to leave, they wanted her to leave right away.

Cat had been less subtle. Vividly, Brenna still remembered the day before the graduation ceremony. Her younger sister had stood in the doorway of her room as Brenna tried on her dress.

"What does it matter what you're going to wear?" Cat had asked with the usual sneer on her face.

"I want to look nice." Brenna felt that she had been fighting with Cat their entire lives.

"I don't know why you bother. Nobody cares. You're blowing us off as soon as you walk across that stage with that diploma. You even going to bother kissing Seamus good-bye? You know he's not going to wait for you."

"Don't talk to me about Seamus." Seamus Todd had always been the one constant between the sisters. However unsisterly, the two had been fighting for his attention for as long as Brenna could remember. Cat, with her persistent and aggressive line of attack, had struck first when she was fourteen and claimed four days of Seamus as her boyfriend.

Two weeks after he broke up with her, Seamus became Brenna's boyfriend and stayed that way for over three years.

"Seamus will be better off without you around," Cat had taunted Brenna. "We'll all be better off without you around. No one will miss you. We'll all be so fucking happy you won't be here."

"Go to hell," Brenna snapped.

Apparently happy that her words had hit their mark, Cat had turned with a flounce and left, no doubt, to make plans to console Seamus. Brenna had stayed in front of the mirror, picking at the same piece of thread on her dress, not willing to show her sister how lost and alone and afraid she had felt.

She hadn't spoken to Cat since.

If Brenna had stayed in Forest Hills, she would have married Seamus. Not only had she loved him, but their mothers had planned it from an early age. The whole town had expected an engagement. What would her life have been like if she had stayed?

Instead of the laid-back bustle of Vancouver,

Brenna could have lived in a town of two thousand people, with every one of them knowing her every move. She liked the anonymity of Vancouver. In Forest Hills, Brenna was an Ebans; one of the Skatt sisters. She wasn't the pretty one, like Kayleigh, or the popular, fun one, like Cat. She was the smart sister, the one so focused on a career that she broke Seamus' heart. In Vancouver, she could have been anyone she wanted to be.

She became Brenna the workaholic, with the cheating husband.

It was ten-thirty at night when Brenna filed out of the plane at Toronto's Pearson International Airport with tired tourists and family members giddy to be home.

Which one was she?

Where was Kayleigh? She scanned the crowd. It had been so long; would she even recognize her own sister? Was going home the right thing to do?

"Brenna!" She heard her sister's cry over the noise of the airport and heaved a sigh of relief. The crowds parted and Kayleigh stood arms outstretched, with a huge smile on her face. "Bee."

Brenna took a step toward her, then a little hop

like she was about to run. And then she was on the floor.

"Brenna! Are you OK?"

She had been so focused on Kayleigh she hadn't noticed the little old lady pushing the luggage cart piled high with leopard print suitcases. With a dirty look at Brenna sprawled on the floor, the old lady kept rolling through the airport.

Kayleigh laughed as she helped her sister to her feet. Suitcases were scattered, forcing people to skirt around Brenna with similar scowls on their faces.

"Still a klutz."

"I never even noticed her," Brenna confessed as she stood up. "I only saw you."

Kayleigh's lower lip trembled. "Oh, Bee," she whispered, throwing her arms around her.

Brenna couldn't speak past the lump the size of the Rockies in her throat. She hugged Kayleigh tightly, smelling the lingering hint of her perfume and the faintly unpleasant been-in-a-car-all-day smell, but wasn't about to let go. Her own lip was quivering when they separated.

"Look at you. You haven't changed a bit," Kayleigh sniffled, holding Brenna's shoulders.

"Neither have you." The hug had confirmed what Brenna had noticed in pictures posted on Facebook; there was a lot more of Kayleigh now.

Kayleigh laughed through the tears rolling down her face. "How can you be such a good lawyer if you're such a bad liar?"

Brenna smiled shyly. "You look great." She touched Kayleigh's rounded cheek. "I like the hair." She remembered the rumpled, pageboy cut, which Kayleigh had always cut herself, but her sister's hair was now a more flattering pixie style, highlighting her delicate features and soft blue eyes. The vibrant orange-red color of her hair was beginning to fade, but Kayleigh's face was still unlined, her skin soft and pale.

"I stopped cutting it myself," Kayleigh said. "Erica does it for me now."

"Erica?"

"Anderson. You remember her? We were friends all through high school."

"I thought she got married and moved away."

"She came back but without the husband. Sounds familiar?"

"That Forest Hills is a haven for divorced

women?" Brenna asked ruefully.

"That you can always come home."

They stayed in a hotel near the airport that night.

"Did you want to do anything in the city before we drive back tomorrow? I doubt you get into the city very often," Brenna asked as they checked into the hotel.

Cheerfully, Kayleigh shook her head. "I was here last winter for the craft shows. Cat came with me. We stayed for almost a week–went to a hockey game and got lots of stuff for the store. I come at least once or twice a year now. Erica sometimes comes along as well."

Brenna was surprised that Kayleigh left Forest Hills that often. Her sister had always been a homebody, almost as introverted as Brenna herself was.

Staring at the two double beds in the middle of the hotel room, Brenna felt awkward and shy. It had been years since she had shared a room with anyone besides her husband, even longer than she shared one with Kayleigh. Did Kayleigh still talk in her sleep?

Do I?

"Do you remember the time we all went to

Thunder Bay?" Kayleigh asked, as if she was reading Brenna's mind. "That was the last time we were in a hotel together. So long ago! You and Cat got into a fight about where we would eat and she ended up shoving you off the bed. You were always fighting!"

"I bet no one missed that," Brenna said lightly tossing her suitcase onto the nearest bed.

"You fought about everything and anything. But especially Seamus."

"Why did we go to Thunder Bay again?" Brenna was too full of unanswered questions to talk about Seamus right now. She never wanted to talk about Cat.

"To look for wedding dresses," Kayleigh replied, her voice losing a little of her gaiety. "Maggie never got a nice one so she decided I needed to. Good thing we never found one."

"You were going to marry Trevor Mackey." Brenna found the image of a tall, gangly man-boy hidden away in the archives of her mind. He drove a blue pick-up truck and would let Cat and Brenna ride in the flatbed along the back roads. "But then you didn't. I was thirteen? Or fourteen? It wasn't that long after Mom died. What happened to him?"

"He married Laurel Ellison a few months later. I think he really wanted to get married and when I changed my mind, he went and found someone else. They're still married, have three kids now." Brenna was impressed there was no hint of regret in her sister's voice.

"Are you dating anyone now?" she asked carefully.

Kayleigh shrugged without looking Brenna in the eye. "There's never been much of a dating scene at home," she reminded her. "Besides, you've just proven to me that men are no good. I don't need another Roger Ebans running out on me."

"Not all men are like Toby."

"But enough of them are. Let's have a drink," Kayleigh said, flopping onto one of the beds. The room was more hospitable than the one Brenna had stayed at in Vancouver. "Should we go find someplace...?"

"There's a mini-bar." Brenna opened the fridge. "We can stay here. Rum, vodka or these little cans of beer?"

"Beer," Kayleigh decided.

"Did you eat anything?" Brenna handed the can to Kayleigh, selected a bottle of water for herself. "How was the drive?"

It was awkward. They were sisters, but practically strangers.

"I found a Burger King before I picked you up. One of those rest stops opened up down the highway from us about four years ago. I quite like the Whoppers." Kayleigh drank quickly from the can. "Oops," she giggled as a small belch escaped.

Maybe it was just Brenna who found it awkward.

She sat down on the corner of one of the beds, with Kayleigh settled against the pillows of the other. "How are you?" Brenna asked politely.

"Really?" Kayleigh grimaced. "Brenna, you found your husband with another woman and you're asking me how I am? What's going on? Talk to me!"

Brenna shrugged. "I don't know what to say."

"You're joking! You're a lawyer. That's all they do."

"What have you got against lawyers?"

"That profession took my sister away from me, so I'm not that fond of it. I hate seeing you hurt, Bee."

"I'm OK," she said with a shrug. The last thing Brenna wanted to do was rehash the whole debacle. Or the last few years.

She wanted to leave Brenna, the workaholic, with the cheating husband back in Vancouver.

"No one calls me Bee," she mused.

"Brenna Evelyn Ebans. Or Skatt now?"

"I kept Ebans."

"You haven't changed; still chasing the dream that we had a good father. The only thing he was good for was the gene that gave you the good hair."

Brenna twirled a red strand between her fingers. It was a rich red, streaked with chestnut, and the only thing she loved unconditionally about herself. She had been the only one to inherit their father's true auburn hair, without a tint of orange. Her sisters had all inherited their mother's bright strawberry blonde.

"I don't want to argue about that. I know you don't like to talk about it."

"How is it that you became a lawyer when you hate to argue?"

Brenna had to laugh. Kayleigh was right – she'd always done everything she could to steer clear of conflict. Was that why she buried her head in the sand about Toby? How could she not see what had been going on.

"You can't hide from your problems forever, Bee."

Chapter Four

Cat

Sister to sister we will always be,
A couple of nuts off the family tree.
—Author Unknown

Cat balanced a container on top of the cake box as she gave a quick knock before pushing the door open. The last thing she wanted to do was wake the girls. She loved her nieces, but even their mother admitted they were a handful at times.

A laugh pulled her into the house. Maggie was in the living room, perched on the edge of the couch with a mountain of folded laundry piled around her, a rerun of Friends playing on the TV.

"Hey," Cat greeted her sister. "Kids asleep? I brought cake." Addison's latest wedding cake was red velvet with cream cheese icing – an odd choice but what did Cat know? Her three weddings were hastily arranged without the gardens of flowers and three tiered cake Addison was planning. At least Addison was lucky to have an aunt who not only loved to bake but was pretty good at it. "She's really got to pick one. The wedding is two weeks away."

"Twelve days!" Maggie did a little happy dance with a pair of Strawberry Shortcake underwear.

Setting aside the underwear, Maggie took the cake. Boxes of glittery decorations, towering stacks of wedding magazines and an over-sized seating plan plotted out in pink marker led the way into the kitchen. Maggie was clearly enjoying the wedding planning as much as Addison, if not more.

"Where's Mike?" Cat asked as she filled the kettle. Tea with Maggie was a comfort, predictable. If Cat wasn't working, she would arrive at Maggie's after the girls were in bed, ready for a cup of tea.

"He got a few extra shifts at the farm this week. Helps with...stuff." With five girls, one going off to university in the fall plus a wedding to pay for, Cat was sure there was a lot of stuff that could be helped with.

"What else is there to do?" Wedding planning had spread to the kitchen as well and Cat picked up a stack of neatly printed labels. Addison and Adam June 24, 2017.

"You can take them with you," Maggie said. "Thanks again for the help. The guests are going to love the jam."

The guests had better love them. One hundred and twelve mini mason jars of fresh strawberry and red currant jam with a splash of pinot noir sat on Cat's dining room table waiting for the labels. "She's lucky the strawberries were ready early."

Besides the wedding favours, Cat's contributions for the big day included advising on the menu, agreeing to host the rehearsal dinner and making the wedding cake. All things she was happy to do and none of the arts and craftsy stuff Maggie kept trying to recruit her for.

Despite the bedlam of the living room, the kitchen was as immaculate as always, painted a sunny yellow with a forest of plants surrounding the big window overlooking the back yard. The calendar was filled with appointments and dates of dances and who needed to get six-year old Clare where and at what time. Crayon pictures, party invitations, and wallet-sized photos of what seemed like every child in Forest Hills adorned the fridge in a way that seemed more cozy than cluttered. Cat didn't know how Maggie kept it so neat, with the girls and her plants and the dogs and Mike who, even though he was the best brother-in-law anyone could ask for, was a total slob.

Cat placed the container on the counter beside the cake box. "Cookies for Clare because she doesn't like cake."

"I'm not sure she deserves a cookie." Maggie leaned against the counter with a defeated slump to her shoulders. "Can you believe I got another call from the principal? She was showing everyone her underwear because she thought they were pretty."

"Were they?"

"I don't know! They were underwear! She's in grade one for God's sake."

"Be glad she didn't moon the kids," Cat laughed.

"It's not funny."

"It is, too!" Cat pantomimed flipping up an

imaginary skirt.

A smile broke through Maggie's frown. "Maybe it is a little funny. And the principal is so straight-laced he could barely tell me what she did. What did I do wrong with her? I've already gotten eight calls this year about that little monkey. Most of them because of the swearing—damn Mike. She punched a boy because he pulled her hair, she peed in the sandbox, threw a stuffie at a kid and now this! Stop laughing! It's not funny!"

"It is a little funny. The thing is that she's so cute! I really think she's the cutest of them all. Almost angelic."

"The only time she's angelic is when she's sleeping. Unless she's peeing the bed—intentionally! 'I wanted clean sheets, Mommy, because they feel nice and I thought you'd change them.' Can you imagine the gall of the little bugger? She's not a bugger," Maggie corrected herself.

"She is a bugger. But a cute one. And sweet as sugar when she wants to be."

"I think that makes it worse because she knows she'll always get out of trouble. Geez, now I really need that cake." Maggie flipped the lid on the box and gave an exaggerated sniff. "Mike has been very appreciative of your cake making efforts, you know."

As the kettle began to steam, Cat handed two mugs to Maggie, heavy ones adorned with pictures of the Muppets, rather than Grandma Winifred's delicate cups Maggie had insisted she wanted from the house but never used.

"I never knew weddings were so time consuming to plan," Maggie admitted. "Or maybe it's because my little girl is a wee bit demanding when it comes to getting what she wants, when she wants it. I think poor Adam is about ready to ship her home."

"You love it, though. You've been waiting years for this."

Maggie's infectious smile lit up her entire face, long and horse-like and covered in freckles. She took after the Ebans's side, rather than the more delicate features of Kayleigh, who was the image of their mother. "You're right. I love weddings, and I love my baby and I love Adam and I want them both to be so happy together. And it's fun. I even got Kady to stay home Saturday night and help with the labels."

"I thought Evie was helping you."

"Evie went to a party because she heard Brady

Todd was going to be there. I really wish she'd stop chasing him."

"Don't worry, he won't let himself be caught," Cat said knowingly. She'd witnessed first-hand how Seamus' nephew preferred a more mature woman than her fresh-faced niece.

"I hope you're right. She's leaving for university at the end of the summer and the last thing I want is for her to have another reason to stay home."

"She's too smart for that."

"I hope so." She sighed, a mother's worry weighing heavily on her, and reached for the now boiling kettle. "Did Kayleigh tell you Brenna's coming back?"

Cat grimaced. She would rather have continued to talk about her nieces than her sister.

"She went into Toronto to pick her up. They'll be back tomorrow. You coming over? I know Brenna won't want a big party because she hates parties but there's lots of people who want to see her, so I'll just do an open house with burgers and some salads. Do you think that'll be OK? I think—"

"I have to work."

Maggie raised an eyebrow at the no-nonsense

tone of Cat's words. "How old are you again? You've got to get over this feud with Brenna someday, you know."

"Already got the lecture from Kayleigh, thanks," Cat muttered.

"Are you sure you can't take an hour off and stop by to see her? She is your sister."

"I know she's my sister!" Cat snapped, unable to soften her voice even as Maggie gave her The Look. "That's all I've been hearing. 'Your sister's coming home! Your sister's coming back! Aren't you happy to see your sister?' You know what? No, I won't be glad to see her. I'm not looking forward to her being home! I don't give a shit if I never see her again!"

"Are you sure?" Maggie asked, remaining calm in the face of the outburst and handing her a mug of steaming tea, sweetened with the perfect amount of honey.

"Yes. No. I don't know," Cat said sullenly. "She left us, not the other way around. Just like Dad and Dory and Mom and Al—I'm fine without them. I'm OK. Brenna'll mess things up if she comes back."

"You know that's not what happened. We're the ones who told her to go," Maggie reminded her gently.

"It's different than it was with Dad or Dory or Mom. And Alex, too." Maggie caught Cat's slip. "I know you miss them."

Cat blew on her tea before answering. "I don't miss our father. Or Dory. I haven't figured out about Brenna yet."

"Well, all I'm asking is for you to give her a chance." Maggie tried again with the patience only a mother of five could have. "Before you get your back up and start in with the fighting, just give her a chance. It's been a long time, and she's grown up. You both have. You're not teenagers fighting over Seamus. That's not what this is about, is it?"

"No."

Maggie sighed again. "She still doesn't know, does she? I was looking forward to her coming home. Now I'm not too sure."

"And you're blaming me for this? Jesus, she's not even back but already I'm the bad guy. Nothing ever changes." Cat took a sip of tea, burnt her tongue and thumped her mug of tea onto the counter with frustration. "Dammit, I didn't come to fight with you, Maggie. Enjoy the cake."

"Stop it," Maggie ordered before Cat took a step

towards the door. “Just stop it. I only want all of us to get along.”

“Well, you’ve got three out of five, so you should be happy about that.” She held Maggie’s gaze until Maggie shook her head and reached into the drawer to pull out a knife.

“Thanks to you, I’m going to eat this cake now. I might even eat the whole thing. What kind of cake is it, anyway?”

Cat held her gaze for a moment and then grinned. “What she asked for. Red velvet.”

“Too red.”

“That’s what I thought. I don’t know if you’ve noticed, but your daughter is a wee bit stubborn. Not to mention a wee bit demanding.”

“Think she’s like anyone else we know?”

“Oh, I don’t know—maybe all of us?” She watched as Maggie carefully cut a huge slice of dark red cake adorned with a thick layer of sweet frosting. “That’s really too red for a wedding.”

“I think so, too but you’ll give it another try, won’t you?”

The question was too complicated to answer.

Chapter Five

Brenna

Big sisters are the crab grass in the lawn of life.
-Charles M. Schulz

"Brenna? Ready to go home?"

Kayleigh had wanted to get any early start; it was a nine hour drive from Toronto to the tiny village of Forest Hills, smack dab between Sudbury and Sault Ste. Marie and almost on the Michigan/Ontario border. Home.

Brenna was a morning person, but with the time difference, six a.m. in Toronto was the middle of the night in Vancouver. She was still disoriented with eyes that felt like sand had been rubbed in them and a queasy stomach from lack of sleep.

Or maybe because of a lack of food. Brenna wasn't sure the last time she had had a full meal.

"I'm good." Brenna shoved her phone into her purse. She had been checking emails, texts, iMessenger while Kayleigh had showered, but had found nothing. With the exception of a quick question about one of her cases, there had been complete radio silence from the law form.

They were no longer her cases. All the work she'd accomplished for her clients, the cases won, that last big acquisition finalized. It was over, like someone else had done it. She would get no credit, no accolades. From now on she'd only be a topic of gossip around the office coffee maker – 'Did you hear what happened to...'

There would be no preconceptions about how she would be judged; she had lost control, trashed Crystal's work station, caused a scene in an office that was still ruled by the old boys' club. It wasn't fair that Toby would get the sympathy from the partners and most of the associates, while Brenna would be viewed as the unstable problem he was lucky to be rid of, but that's how it was in the Davis and Daniels firm. Toby was considered a more valuable resource than she was.

It was frustrating, but it no longer made her angry. Funny how she thought she'd miss it. Instead she felt light. Almost happy. Like the stereotypical weight on her shoulders was lifted.

Every day, for the last fourteen years, she had been working, studying, fighting, and now suddenly her days stretched endlessly before her. It was unsettling but somehow freeing...

There had been no word from Toby.

She hadn't spoken to her husband since he had agreed to her suggestion to a separation.

Brenna didn't want to admit she felt relief about that, too.

The sun rose, turning the sky from a rosy pink to a beautiful clear blue. She watched as the busy highways of Toronto segued into the suburbs, letting Kayleigh's steady stream of chatter wash over her. Her mind raced in circles. What was waiting for her? Could she still call Forest Hills home? Did she want to?

Did she have a choice?

The Egg McMuffin Kayleigh bought for her sat

like a stone in Brenna's stomach as Kayleigh regaled her with the exploits of old high school acquaintances. Would she be talked about like this? The residents of the tiny town were close-knit and loose lipped; she expected her sisters to have reported on her success in her career, her marriage.

She glanced at her sister. Crammed behind the steering wheel in the light of day and without of the haze of a five hour plane trip, Brenna realized her sister's weight gain was more considerable than what she first envisioned

Had Kayleigh told everyone what had happened? Did everyone know she had walked in on her husband with her assistant? Brenna wasn't sure if she could live that down.

As they passed from the four-laned mega highways to the slower two-laned roads, Kayleigh began to run out of gossip. Resting her head against the cool glass, Brenna tried to let go of her worries and absorb the scenery. She'd always loved the Canadian Shield with boulders the size of small cars, rock walls as high as an office building, towering pine trees. The mountains of British Columbia were spectacular, but the rocky hills of Northern Ontario had their own splendor. Lulled by the comforting familiarity of the landscape, the monotonous rhythm of the tires, Brenna began to drift off.

"Why did you leave?"

Brenna snapped to attention, banging her head painfully against the window. "What?" She stretched out her arms, the lure of sleep still pulling at her. "I told you all that. Because I found Toby with my assistant. Not really in the mood to talk about it." Visions of broken phones, smashing the cup against the computer screen and kicking the purse at Toby filled her mind.

No, she did not want to talk about Toby.

"No, I meant, why did you leave us?"

Brenna gave her puzzled smile. "To go to school. I wanted to be a lawyer. Again, you know all that."

"Yes, but you could have gone to school in Thunder Bay or Toronto or even Winnipeg. Why did you have to go so far away?"

Brenna found she couldn't answer.

"Did you have fun?" Kayleigh asked skeptically.

"Not really," she admitted. She could have lied, said her years away had been the best of my life, but this was Kayleigh, who used to know her better than anyone. "There were some...fun...times."

Kayleigh smiled. "You didn't go away because of fun times. You were never the party girl. That was Cat. And Maggie, until she did had one party too many."

"I could party!"

"Oh, you could drink," Kayleigh conceded. "You would sit in a corner all night, after calculating the amount of alcohol you could drink based on what you'd eaten that day. You spent all of high school reading and studying and if it wasn't for Seamus and Missy dragging you out, I doubt you would have had any social life. Not that there's anything wrong with being quiet and studious. I like my alone time as well. But I'll bet University Brenna was pretty close to High School Brenna, sitting in the corner with her bottle of rum." Kayleigh glanced over with a frown. "I know you, and I know you didn't go for the fun."

Brenna turned to the window. I left because you didn't want me. Because it would be easier for all of you if I wasn't around. One less sister to worry about.

The sisters had made a promise to one another – to look out for the family. To take care of each other. Leaving was Brenna's way of fulfilling her vow.

But then there was the other reason she'd never

told anyone about.

It had been a long time since she'd even admitted the truth to herself. "I always wondered what was over the hills."

"I remember you asking Mom if the hills were so big because they were hiding something. I remembered you asking Dad something like that too, before he—"

"I tried to find him," Brenna interrupted in a rush. "I thought if I left, I might find him, find out why he left. That's why Dory left. Dory and I, we always wanted to know where he went."

She had spent years reading names in phonebooks, scanning the faces in coffee shops, malls, restaurants, always with the hope she might someday stumble across her father. Where did he go? Who was more important than they were?

Brenna glanced at Kayleigh. The sister had always been split on the subject of their father; Maggie, Kayleigh and Cat taking their mother's side with their hearts hardened against him. Only Brenna and Dory had defended their father. He had a good reason for leaving them. Didn't he?

Doubt crept in, and she banged the lid shut on it.

Her father, like Toby, like her fears, was a Pandora's box she had no desire to open right now.

Apparently Kayleigh didn't feel the same way.

"Is that what Dory said?" Kayleigh's hands tightened on the steering wheel, her voice tinged with anger. "He left us, Brenna. He left us with Mom when he knew what she was like. He could have stayed and we could have figured out how to make her better."

"She wasn't going to get any better. It couldn't it have been easy for him. She was never a loving wife. Sometimes -"

"She loved you, Bee."

"She had a funny way of showing it."

"I hate that you defend him. You were a baby; you don't remember what he was like. You have this romanticized vision of him in your head, same as Dory did. It's bullshit, is what it is." Brenna puffed a sigh as a reply; best to be silent in the face of Kayleigh's anger. Her sister had been ten years old when Roger left; unlike Brenna, Kayleigh had known their father. She had memories of him, where Brenna only had pictures.

Kayleigh hadn't finished her attack. "So you left us to go on a wild goose chase. Was it worth it? Did you find him?"

"It wasn't the only reason. C'mon Kayleigh, you wanted me to go" Brenna snapped. "You'd been pushing me out for years. You all said it was the best thing to go away to school."

"Because it was! You were too smart for us, Brenna. You would have been miserable if you stayed. But you didn't have to go so far away! And now I find out it was because of him?"

"I stopped looking." It had taken years before Brenna admitted she was searching for a stranger, a figment of her imagination, a father who would have protected her from her mother's indifference. Years of pain of finding an address for Roger Ebans, only to discover he had moved onto another city, another country.

"Good," Kayleigh said shortly. "He doesn't deserve to be found."

That was the end of that conversation. Brenna sat quietly until she managed to fall asleep.

*

"Almost there."

Brenna tried to stretch her cramped legs to no avail. “You said that twenty minutes ago.”

“No, you were sleeping twenty minutes ago. I mean it this time. Last hill.”

Reaching out with her arms to push against the dashboard, Brenna stretched her shoulders, felt the welcoming crack in her neck. “You sound like Mom.”

“Alive Mom or dead Mom?”

“So she’s still there?”

Kayleigh shrugged. “Apparently.”

Brenna caught her breath as the van crested the hill. Forest Hills.

Brenna had always related to the valley; the hills were awe-inspiring and provided so much to the scenic area, that they diminished anything else.

Just like her growing up with four sisters.

The tiny town was still as beautiful as she remembered it, but seemed smaller. There were a few roads winding into the woods leading to clearings; popular places for bush parties when she was a teen. She had gone with Seamus. Did the kids still party out there?

The first hill was covered with the ‘downtown district’ with eight or nine stores hunkered down on the left side of the road and the older, larger homes of the village facing them. Most were big, Victorian style houses—some brick but most painted in pastel shades like yellow and lavender—and all with beautiful front porches. All with well-manicured lawns and since it was the middle of June, beautiful flowerbeds. No one would question Forest Hills was a picturesque little spot.

"General Store's still there," Brenna murmured to herself as they cruised through the town. "The Source; that's new. Sara's Sandwich Shoppe – still there."

"Cat makes cakes for her -" Kayleigh began but Brenna cut her off with a squeal of excitement.

"There's your store!"

"The Hills of Christmas – everything you'd want to celebrate your holidays, and even more you didn't," Kayleigh told her with a proud smile. "Used to be the appliance store."

Brenna noticed a few other quaint, touristy places had popped up. No wonder it had turned into a popular weekend getaway from the city.

"Forest Hills United," Kayleigh pointed out the church, set back two thirds the way down the hill. "With the Reverend Macleod still presiding over his flock."

The road led them into the valley, over the bridge, with the winding river flowing through the valley into the more commercial section of the historic old town.

"Look, there's Seamus' Mom," Brenna cried and before Kayleigh could stop her, she leaned over and hit the horn, all the while waving madly at the motherly-looking woman with her arms laden with bags coming down the steps of the Co-op. Too late, Brenna remembered how no one honked coming down the hill unless they were out of control and in danger of taking someone out. When she heard the horn, Fiona Todd panicked and with a look of horror on her face, dropped one of her bags and jumped back up the steps.

"Oops." Brenna's wave froze in mid-air. "Shit." She turned in her seat to watch a man leaving the store stop and help Fiona pick up her groceries.

"Don't swear in front of Maggie's kids," Kayleigh warned. "Mike said 'fuck a duck' last week and Clare's been repeating it ever since. She's got quite the potty mouth for a six-year old."

"That's the youngest, right?"

Kayleigh rolled her eyes. "You are the worst sister,

you know."

"But better than Dory, right?" she asked with a winsome smile.

"Barely." Brenna saw the hint of a smile. "You haven't asked about Seamus, you know."

"What's there to say?" Feigning disinterest was better than peppering Kayleigh with questions.

No one knew about the letters Seamus sent, pleading with her to come back. He had called her, late one night; she could tell from his voice he'd been drinking.

"I want you to come home," he began, speaking slowly and carefully. "I should have told you years ago. I want you here, with me. I don't want you to be gone anymore."

"Seamus..."

"You did the school thing – I get that. But it's time to come home. Our mothers – you know what they wanted for us, Brenna."

"That's not a valid reason for me to come home." Her heart had leapt when he made his declaration, but there had been no follow up – no I love you. I need you. No, I want you here because I can't live without you. There was just Seamus with his feeble fight to get what he thought he wanted.

Brenna was never sure what her response would have been if he had put up a more serious struggle to get her to come back home. Seamus never asked again and six weeks later she received an invitation to his wedding; she was sure it had been sent out of spite by his bride-to-be.

Down in the valley, they passed the wide expanse of green space, with the baseball diamond, the soccer field, and the playground, filled with children. The road curved as they headed out of town, and Brenna wrinkled her nose when she spotted a new subdivision perched on the side of river. Taupe-coloured houses filled the old meadow, marching all the way down to the banks where she'd fished for trout with her sisters. Up the hill, older houses were scattered on either side of the road, smaller than the ones downtown but still just as nicely tended with multi-colored impatiens decorating the flowerbeds. At the top of the second hill was the mushroom farm on one side and the Ebans Estate, with its stables and horse track set back from the road.

What had it been like for her father to grow up there? High on the hill with his father, Marcus Ebans, lording it over the rest of the town.

Kayleigh turned at the third driveway, pulling up beside a small bungalow with a huge addition on the back, kids' toys and bikes littering the yard.

Maggie's house. The lump in Brenna's throat grew as she thought about seeing her sister.

Kayleigh glanced at Brenna as she turned off the van. "Maggie said to deliver you to her place straight away. She said you'll stay with her. Seeing as Cat has Mom's place."

Brenna had avoided looking at the rambling old Victorian across from the church; the huge, three-storied white house, with wrap-around porch filled with spots to curl up with a book. Where she and Cayleigh would carve pumpkins for Halloween. The porch where there had been countless goodnight kisses from Seamus in front of the door.

Her sister Cat lived there now, along with the ghost of their mother.

"You're going to have to see her, you know." For a minute Brenna thought Kayleigh was referring to their mother rather than Cat.

"I'm counting the minutes."

"In the meantime, you'll have to deal with the

party Maggie set up. Not really a party," Kayleigh explained, as Brenna blanched.

"A party?" She had noticed cars parked haphazardly around the house and on the side of the road, but thought the neighbours...

"Just a few people who wanted to stop in, say hello. You know Maggie, still the social butterfly. I'm sure it'll be over soon."

"It'll never be over," Brenna muttered darkly.

"Don't forget you have to deal with Maggie first," Kayleigh said as she got out of the van.

"What do you mean?" Brenna's hand froze on the door handle.

"Fourteen years is a long time to go without a visit, you know." Kayleigh laughed. "You're right to be worried."

The front door burst open before Brenna made it up the stairs and her knees quaked at the furious expression on Maggie's face.

Chapter Six

Cat

"Children of the same family, the same blood, with the same first associations and habits, have some means of enjoyment in their power, which no subsequent connections can supply..."

—Jane Austen, Mansfield Park, 1814

Cat was changing in her room when the dogs burst into action downstairs. Dashing madly up and down the hallway, their paws and claws skittered on the floor while they barked a welcome. As she pulled on her work shirt, she heard a voice.

"Aunt Cat?"

Not only did her sisters walk straight in her home but Maggie's daughters' did as well.

Poking her head into the hallway, Cat recognized Evie's red hair at the bottom of the stairs crouching in the middle of the pack of excited dogs. "Just push them off," Cat called. "Be right there."

"Mom asked me to pick up whatever you made for the party," Evie said apologetically when she saw Cat was wearing her black jeans and Woody's T-shirt.

"I was coming to drop it off," Cat told her, her steps light on the stairs. Her niece followed her into the kitchen as she rummaged through her containers for something Evie could carry the squares she had made—brownies, blondies, and Nanaimo bars.

Evie's hand was in the cookie jar before Cat could turn around.

"I tried the latest cake," Evie said through a mouth filled with cookie. "It's so good, but too red for a wedding."

"That's what I thought." Cat popped a broken brownie in her mouth. Even after being in the kitchen for most of the day, she had forgotten to eat lunch.

"Addison loved the color. She's saying that's the one. I don't know..."

"We both know you can't tell that sister of yours what to do. If she likes the red, she'll want the red. But I've got one more for her to try. I ran out of time to make it today."

Evie gazed at the plates of sweets covering the table. "I guess so."

The plates were the only evidence of Cat's baking marathon. The kitchen had been tidied to its usual state of cleanliness. It helped that Cat had a bank of cupboards and drawers and unlike Maggie, didn't collect much clutter. A few plants, pictures of her nieces on the fridge were the only added colour to the all-white cabinetry.

"How'd it go with Brady the other night?" Cat asked as she swiftly packed the sweets into plastic containers.

"How'd you know about that?" Every time Cat saw Evie, she wondered how Mike and Maggie had produced her. Luckily, she was too preoccupied with school to pay much mind to the attention from the boys of Forest Hills, or Mike would have had a full head of gray hair by now.

"Your mom said something about a party," Cat said. "You know Brady Todd is too old for you, right?"

The only man Evie paid attention to was the only one he couldn't have. Just like her aunt.

"He's only twenty-one."

"Twenty-two. You're eighteen – just. And he likes his ladies a little long in the tooth."

"Yeah. I've heard...things." Evie said sadly. "He doesn't know I exist, so it doesn't matter."

"He's an idiot if he doesn't know you exist, and whatever I can say about the boy is that he's no idiot. That's the problem." Cat sighed. "I've been there, Evie. I know what it feels like. If someone had given me the heads up when I was your age..." She trailed off, laughing as she listened to her words. "Forget it. I remember what I was like and I wouldn't have listened either."

"Why, what were you like at my age?" Evie asked coyly.

"Forget I said anything." She slid the containers across the counter to her niece. "There you go. Enjoy."

"You couldn't have been that bad. All you did was get married. A few times," she teased.

"Yeah," Cat said morosely.

"What did I say?" Evie's green eyes widened. "I thought..."

Cat gave a wave of her hand. “It’s nothing. Look, I’d better get to work.” She had suffered years of teasing comments and outright concerns about her various marriages and it never got any easier.

“Aren’t you coming over later?” It was sweet that Evie wanted to include her; despite the years between them, Cat’s relationship with Evie was more of a friend than aunt slash niece. “Aunt Brenna’s coming home!”

Will Brenna take away Evie too?

“Yes, I’ve heard that. I’m sure everyone will be able to fall all over her just fine without me being there.” Cat pushed away from the counter, Evie following her to the front door.

“Did you know she left her husband because he was cheating and quit her job because he worked there,” Evie said, watching Cat pull on her boots.

“Oh?”

“Apparently he did it with all the women in the office and Aunt Brenna never knew a thing. But when she found out, she went ballistic and threatened to burn the building down. They had to call the police on her.”

“Who said that?” Cat scoffed. “I doubt it.”

"I heard about her husband from Mom, but a kid at school told me his mother heard about the cops."

Cat shook her head. "Don't believe everything you hear, especially around here."

"So I shouldn't believe what I hear about Brady?" Evie asked with a winsome smile.

"Ha ha. Sneaky. No, you believe that and more if that's what it takes to get that boy out of your head."

"I like him being in my head," she admitted.

Cat smiled ruefully. "Just so you know, Seamus would skin Brady alive if he hurt you."

*

Seamus followed Cat into the back office at Woody's. The bar was practically her second home; Fiona Todd had hired her as soon she was old enough to serve alcohol. Seamus had now taken over the family business from his mother.

"When were you going to tell me Brenna was coming home?" Seamus demanded as Cat hung her jean jacket on her hook.

"I figured you'd hear from someone." He needed a haircut, Cat decided. How was it that a man could have the same style since he was twelve? Slightly shaggy around the ears, the ends curled when it got too long. Cat liked Seamus' hair short, liked to dance her fingers along his bare neck...

"Rather it'd been you to tell me," Seamus said mildly.

Brenna and Cat were barely thirteen months apart in age and competed for everything, starting with a yellow hand-me down dress from Kayleigh when Cat was four. Sports, grades, attention—everything had been a competition.

Seamus had been the top prize.

And she won him first. Cat knew it hadn't been a good sister move to steal Seamus from Brenna when she had been fourteen, but in her defense Brenna and Seamus hadn't technically been together. Cat had lost her virginity to him when sixteen-year-old Seamus drank too much at a party. His intoxicated state was the only reason she had managed to seduce him, not one of Cat's finest moments.

And it hadn't even worked, hadn't brought them together. It wasn't until years later, with Brenna long gone and Seamus' marriage ending that Cat had finally got the timing right.

They'd been together for three years now.

"Next time," Cat promised. "I'm sure she won't be hanging around too long."

"Is that what she said?"

Did Seamus have to sound so interested?

"I didn't talk to her. Nor do I want to."

"Cat..."

"Please don't start lecturing me. I've heard it from both Cayleigh and Maggie and I've had enough. End of story."

"You should go to Maggie's thing tonight," Seamus said as if Cat hadn't spoken.

"Are you going?" she demanded. She hadn't realized she was facing him with hands balled into fists until she caught sight of herself in the mirror.

"I'm not family. You are. Pam could cover your shift for an hour or so."

"It's Wednesday, it's dart night. You need me here."

"True, but we'd manage."

"I'll work. It's fine." Her words were clipped and cold and Seamus sighed. "Don't start," Cat warned.

He raised his hands. "She's your sister."

"What does that have to do with anything?"

"You're not worried about -"

"Should I be?"

Seamus sighed again as he moved against her, sliding his hands around her slim waist. Cat's arms instinctively, encircled his shoulders, her body relaxing enough to drop her head against him. Cat was a tall woman, Seamus only a few inches taller but she'd always thought their bodies fit together perfectly.

"You shouldn't worry about anything. I love you."

"I know."

Seamus' arms tightened around her. "What else is going on, if it's not Brenna? You've been moping around for a couple of days."

"No, I haven't." Seamus was sweet and kind, a great boyfriend, but not always the most observant of her moods.

"You kind of have. I didn't want to say anything the other night because I figured it was because of Brenna but -"

"I want to have a baby," Cat blurted.

"Because Brenna's coming home?" He sounded bewildered.

Cat sucked in her breath, attempted to draw away. "No. The two have nothing to do with each other.

Forget I said anything."

She had wanted to tell him for weeks now, but knowing his reaction, hadn't wanted to bring it up. To blurt it out now, with the ghost of Brenna hanging between them...

I have the worst timing ever.

Seamus' hands tightened against her waist. "Hang on, Cat...I know you want kids but we talked about this. Later, after we get married..."

"I don't want to get married." Her voice was muffled against his shoulders and she hoped it would take away the sting of her words.

"Later, I know. We'll give things a little more time..."

"I don't want to marry you. Now or later. But I want to have your baby. I'm not getting any younger and -"

His silence interrupted her. Cat changed tactics, rushing the words, trying to fill the angry silence. "I love you, too. We'd still be together but I just can't be married again. I've done it three times already!"

Seamus pulled back, his warm brown eyes searching her face. "We've talked about this. It doesn't matter to me. Four's a lucky number." He looked so earnest, hopeful and Cat felt her heart sink. She loved him so much, but she just couldn't take the chance of hurting him.

"It's not," Cat said miserably. "I've been divorced twice, Seamus. I'm not good at being married. And Alex -"

"Did not end in a divorce."

"No. He died," Cat snapped. She took a deep breath. "Look, I-"

"Are you sure this has nothing to do with Brenna? We ended years ago. You know that, right?"

"This has nothing to do with Brenna," Cat lied. "I just want to have a baby. I thought it might happen by itself but -"

"You're not on the pill?" She could see a muscle clench in his jaw, the only outward sign of his anger. Seamus had a long, slow fuse, but when he got upset...

"No." She regretted the admission as soon as the word left her mouth.

There was a long pause and Seamus slowly stepped away from her.

"I'd marry you if you got pregnant. You know that."

"I'd say no."

"You'd say no," he said flatly. Another pause but longer this time as he moved behind the desk, tapping his fingers on the invoices and order forms that littered the surface. "What the hell gives you the right to be so selfish?"

Cat tried not to wince at his shout. Seamus was so easy going and relaxed. She was the one who fought with raised voice and harsh words – not Seamus.

"And when were you going to tell me all this?"

"Now?" she suggested.

Seamus gave a bark of humorless laughter. "You had to bring this up now, here? How hard were you actually trying to get pregnant? Like, are you doing the ovulation thing?"

"I have a kit, yes, but there haven't been too many times when it worked out."

"I see. I don't know what to say. This really…it pisses me off."

"I can tell."

"Fuck! I love you, Cat. I want to get married and start a family. You know that. And now you're telling me no?" His voice cracked with frustration and underlying anger and her belly twisted with guilt. "I want a chance to get it right – with you."

"We'd still do it right, just differently."

"You want different?" he asked angrily.

"Seamus..." Fear added to the guilt. What had she done?

"I've got to get back to work." Without another word, Seamus stormed out of the tiny office. The mirror on the wall trembled as he slammed the door.

Chapter Seven

Brenna

"Help one another, is part of the religion of sisterhood."

—Louisa May Alcott

"Brenna Evelyn Skatt!" Maggie let the door slam behind her. She swelled like a balloon ready to pop as she stalked towards Brenna. "I cannot believe you haven't been home in almost fourteen years."

Brenna cringed as Maggie punctuated each syllable with an increase in volume so that by the end of the sentence she was shouting. Taking a giant step back led her right into Kayleigh. Trapped; flattened like a slapped mosquito. Maybe coming home wasn't such a good idea after all.

But then Maggie grabbed her in a hug.

And caught in Maggie's embrace, Brenna couldn't help but notice that, like Kayleigh, there was a lot more of Maggie to wrap her arms around.

"Hi." Her voice was muffled from being squished into Maggie's shoulder. She sniffled, blinking away the pool of tears in her eyes.

"Oh, Bee," Maggie sighed. "It's about time."

"I know."

Releasing her, Maggie smoothed Brenna's cheek with a soft hand. "You look tired."

"Long drive," Brenna said, shocked at how Maggie had aged. Fine lines surrounded the blue eyes, the once fiery red hair had faded, now streaked with gray.

Well, what had she expected? Fourteen years had left their mark, especially on her.

"Kayleigh told me about-"

"Not now," Brenna pleaded. She couldn't go into what happened now, not with the unknown waiting for her on the other side of the door. She was exhausted, her feelings so close to the surface she didn't think she could handle anything more, least of all a discussion about the state of her marriage.

Maggie nodded. "You did good coming home."

I didn't have anywhere else to go.

Warily, she trailed Maggie through the front door, not looking forward to being the center of interest and wishing Kayleigh had given her more notice about what to expect.

"Look who finally came home!" Maggie cried. Brenna sucked in her breath at the wave of noise that hit her in the face like a sucker punch. Apparently the cars surrounding the house didn't belong to the neighbours after all; it seems like half the town was there. They couldn't all be there to see her; they came for Maggie.

Because they loved Maggie...everyone loved Maggie.

Brenna opened her mouth to reply but nothing came out. Distinctly uncomfortable, she managed a smile and a wave, which seemed adequate considering the racket made normal conversation impossible.

A small ball of red hair rushed past her and launched herself on Kayleigh. "Aunt Kay-Kay!"

"Hi, Clare-bear!" Kayleigh said, swinging the child into her arms. "Say hi to Aunt Brenna."

The curly haired moppet with Maggie's bright

blue eyes stared at Brenna intently. “I don’t know her.”

“You’ll get to know her,” Kayleigh smile was warm and welcoming. “She’s home now. You’ve got plenty of time.”

Six laughing teenagers clustered around a table groaning under platters of cookies and sweets, hands diving into bags of Doritos spilling chip crumbs everywhere. Brenna’s brother-in-law stood back from the melee, a bottle of beer in his hand and a big smile on his ruddy face.

A genuine smile bloomed across her face. “Mike.”

“Well, hey, there.” Two steps and strong arms wrapped around her. Mike’s fists pressed against her back as he squeezed her tightly. Mike had taught Brenna how to throw a ball, how to ride a bike. He’d held her hand at the funeral, kept her safe.

Could he do the same for her now?

Brenna clung to Mike, hiding her face against his shoulder so no one could see the film of tears.

“Good ta see ya, Bee.”

With a final squeezc, she unwrapped her arms from his neck. The years had thickened his waist and raised his hairline, but he was the same old Mike.

"You, too." Her smile was shaky, but indisputable.

Beside them, Maggie had tears coursing down her cheeks. "I can't believe you're finally here!"

"Me neither." Pressing her lips together, Brenna stared unseeing at the Doritos bag until she was sure could hold back the tears. She prided herself on never breaking down, but being home was playing havoc with her emotions.

Mike laughed and threw an arm around her shoulder. "I know, there's a lot of us. I'll get you a drink."

"Dirty Martini, extra olives," Brenna said automatically, practically tasting the cool gin sliding down her throat.

"'Fraid you'll have to make do with a beer. Beertender! Evie, will you grab your aunt a cold one?"

Brenna hadn't known what to expect, but it wasn't this. So many kids, talking, laughing , fighting for control of the television. Wasn't anyone bothered by the noise?

She felt like an intruder.

Brenna gaped in amazement as a slim, redheaded girl handed her a bottle of beer. "Thanks. You can't be Evie."

"I am. You're going to tell me the last time you saw me, I was this high." Her niece lowered her hand to her knee and smiled. She had Mike's smile and Maggie's freckles across her nose.

"Maybe not as tall and definitely not as gorgeous." She looked like Cat, Brenna decided. More Cat than Maggie, with Kayleigh's sweetness.

A perfect mixture of all of them.

As the evening wore on, Maggie would suddenly appear at her side. Brenna wasn't sure if it was to show her off, or to rescue, as if she could sense how overwhelmed she was. The constant moving and talking to people made it impossible for Brenna to do more than pick at her food. But after the guests had put a dent in the mountain of casseroles, meatballs and spinach dip, Maggie led her to the door where Mike was holding a jacket.

"You look like you could use some air. Missy told me to send you over to Woody's as soon as I could." Maggie brushed a strand of hair out of Brenna's eyes, making Brenna feel like a ten year old. "Get out of here, go see your friends."

Even though she wanted nothing more than to crawl into a bed, Brenna agreed and Mike bundled her out of the chaos of his home as if he had gotten a death row reprieve.

The night air was cool and blessedly quiet. “That was…fun…” Brenna said, as they left the laughter behind, starting down the hill towards Woody’s Bar and Restaurant.

Mike snorted. “Your sister can always find a reason for a party. This wedding is gonna be her biggest one yet.” He gave her a sideways smile. “She’s happy you came back for it.”

“Me too.”

Mike cleared his throat. “This husband thing…you need me to do anything?”

Brenna felt a rush of warmth at his words. “Thanks, but I took care of it.”

“Thatta girl!”

Mike’s attention diverted to the sound of a crack of a bat and the cheers erupting as they walked past the baseball diamond. “You’re still playing?” Brenna asked.

“They’ll have to carry me off the field.” Mike began a commentary about the teams he coached, how impressive a player his girls were, allowing Brenna to collect her thoughts.

Seamus ran Woody's; the family business.

Did Cat still work there?

Her stomach tight with a mixture of dread and fear and a lack of food, she took a deep breath as Mike pushed open the door.

For a moment, Brenna stood frozen at the door. Then Mike kept moving and left her wide open as everyone's eyes focused on her.

She imagined the whispering.

"Hey, Mike!" A voice cut across the noise; Brenna would know it anywhere.

"Seamus," she whispered nervously, meeting his gaze. A moment later Seamus had ducked through the opening in the bar and she was lifted off her feet with the force of his hug.

The memory of how she fit in his arms, the smell of him...Brenna laughed with relief into his shoulder.

"'Bout time you came back," he said into her hair. She'd been hugged more in the last twenty-four hours than she had in years, but this one was special.

"I know. Kayleigh's been giving me the guilt trip since I told her I was coming."

"Good girl. She was always my favorite sister."

The conversation took place as they remained

locked together and Brenna had no intention of letting go. But suddenly Seamus pulled back and took a good look at her, his gaze traveling from her hair to turquoise painted toenails. “Nice toes. You look good, Bren,” he said admiringly.

He reached out a hand and Brenna thought he was going to touch her face or hair, but he stopped himself and settled for her elbow, giving it a tight squeeze.

Her heart leaped at his touch. Suddenly it didn’t matter what anyone else thought. Seamus was glad to see her.

“Thanks. You too.” Brenna looked away before she could embarrass herself.

“You staying at Maggie’s?”

“For now.”

“There’s always my couch if it gets too crazy there. Sometimes Mike is worse than all those girls!”

Mike guffawed beside him but Brenna was stunned at Seamus’ quick invitation. What did it mean? He wanted her to stay with him? He must have known she was married and therefore heard of the breakup. Did he really want her to sleep on his couch? Did that mean...?

"My mom said to say hi." Seamus seemed unaware of Brenna's heart leaping like a fish at his offer.

"I saw her when we drove down. Outside the store." Brenna found herself with her hand in her hair, a nervous trait.

"She thought you might be the crazy who honked."

"Oops."

Seamus laughed. "We're packed tonight, so I gotta get back to the bar, but I'll come find you later?" Brenna managed a nod, and Seamus gave her one last quick, fierce hug. "It's real good to see you, Bren."

"You too." Nostalgia was quick to wash over her as Brenna watched him go. Seamus was the man who'd taken her virginity. And her sister's too.

That image completely ruined her warm and fuzzy reminiscences.

"You weren't worried about seeing him, were you?"

Brenna pulled her gaze away to find Mike watching her with a teasing grin.

"Not too much."

He laughed and threw an arm around her

shoulders. “You were missed, you know that, Bren? A lot.”

She was still basking in Mike’s affection when she saw Cat.

Brenna had geared herself up to see her youngest sister, but it was still a shock when it finally happened.

They stared at each other. Brenna couldn’t read her expression, but a lifetime of memories flashed across her mind. She had spent most of her teenage years, and a good part of her childhood being mad at Cat for one reason or another. There had been happy times full of sisterly affection, but for the most part, they were eclipsed by the conflicts.

But whatever had happened between them, whatever they had done or said to each other, Cat was still her younger sister. Brenna may not have liked her much, but she did love her. She was family.

She opened her mouth to call out when Cat gave her a brusque nod and went about loading her tray with bottles of Blue and pints of Canadian.

Obviously, it hadn’t been much of a moment for her.

Mike settled her at a high table on the edge of the bar before saying something about his dart team. It was too loud for her to fully comprehend, or maybe she was too befuddled between seeing Seamus and then Cat, so Brenna nodded and let him disappear. She looked around with curiosity; not much had changed. The walls were a different color, with new tables and chairs, but the atmosphere was the same. Casual, friendly, with the smell of beer, melted cheese and chicken wings permeating everything.

If she let herself, Brenna could pretend she was back in high school, waiting for Seamus after baseball practice. Nursing a Coke and a basket of fries, Brenna would sit at a table away from the boisterous dart players with her textbooks while Seamus helped his mother.

And then he would take her to their spot, a dead-end road with a view of the valley. They would talk, and plan…and kiss.

Brenna sighed as she caught sight of Seamus laughing with a customer behind the bar. That had been a long time ago. Once, she'd believed they'd be together forever.

Didn't seem to work out for either of them.

Over the years, she had consciously stopped herself from asking Kayleigh about him. Finding out about his marriage was difficult; it was better that she didn't know about his life, who he shared it with after his divorce. It had made it easier for her to pretend there was a chance they still might end up together.

But as she watched him, she couldn't help wondering if there was someone else sitting at the bar waiting for Seamus to finish work?

Caught up in memories, it took Brenna a while to notice she was being watched from the corner of the long counter.

He was young. He was pretty. The curve of a well-defined bicep peeked out from underneath his shirtsleeve. And most unbelievably, he seemed to be smiling at her.

There must be someone behind her. Brenna twisted to look over her shoulder, then turned back with a quizzical expression on her face.

He was still smiling. At her. And then he wiggled his eyebrows in a way that made Brenna smile back.

"Dirty Martini, extra olives."

Brenna was jolted back into reality to see Cat standing before her with tired eyes, red hair tied back in a pony tail. Cat placed a glass in front of Brenna. "I heard that's what you were into these days."

She stared at the shimmering gin and vermouth with wonder. “Thanks.”

Cat just shrugged and with a hint of a smile, walked away.

Chapter Eight

Cat

"We acquire friends and we make enemies, but our sisters come with the territory."

—Evelyn Loeb

Cat could tell the exact moment Brenna walked into Woody's.

She could have pretended it was a second sense, but in reality, she was serving Trevor Mackey and heard him turn to his buddy and hiss. "Jesus, it's Brenna Skatt. Lookit—she's all growed up."

The admiration in his voice pissed her off. Truth be told, Kayleigh had always been the prettiest of them all. But Brenna? Since when did Brenna warrant comments from bar patrons, even if it was only Trevor Mackey?

Looking up, Cat had to stifle a gasp at her first glimpse of her sister. The years had been good to Brenna. Instead of tall and skinny, she was long and lean and her jeans fit her like a second skin—flattering all of her curves and lines without being too obvious. And Cat loved Brenna's purple shirt. Brenna looked expensive. Successful. Sophisticated. And not at all like the teenage Brenna she remembered.

As Seamus rushed up to Brenna, wrapping his arms around her, Cat's heart sank like her plumber's wrench. She steeled herself, pasting a smile on her face, wishing she could wipe the smile off his.

What was Brenna doing hanging onto him like that?

Maybe telling him she didn't want to get married hadn't been the smartest thing to do.

When Cat glanced back, Seamus was gone and her sister was staring at her. Envy swelled inside Cat. She managed a curt nod and looked away to Mike approaching with a big smile on his face.

"Maggie's pissed you didn't stop by," he said,

elbowing up to the bar.

"I knew Brenna couldn't stay away from Seamus," Cat retorted bitterly.

"Ah, Cat," Mike sighed. "Don't do this. It's ancient history. Can't you two get over it?"

She shrugged.

"Give the guy a little credit, will you? He's with you now, so why make a big fuss about her? She's your sister, so just try and be happy to see her. Maggie'd appreciate it," he added with his wide grin. "And not having to hear about how the two of you won't stop fighting would be pretty good for me, too."

"I'll try for you," Cat promised reluctantly.

"She drinks Martinis now," Mike told her in a low voice. "Dirty, I think she said, something about olives. Might be a nice welcome home present." With a smile, he moved away, his stocky build giving him a lumbering gait.

Pam slipped behind the bar to pour a couple of beers. "I saw Brenna. She's really changed."

"I didn't notice."

Pam knew Cat well enough to pick up her tone and changed the subject. "My brother said to tell you he'd be happy to help out with whatever you need at the house."

"Really? I'd really like to get the porch painted and the shutters but that's beyond me. I didn't know anyone else I could afford." Cat hated being reminded about the poor state of her finances, but anything was better than talking about Brenna.

"He can definitely take care of that, plus stuff inside the house if you want. He said he'll call in the next day or so."

"Oh, Pam, that's great. The place is so tired looking and maybe..."

"It'll be a kick in the butt to get your B&B finally set up and running."

Pam was one of the few people Cat had confessed her plans to. She had come up with the idea of converting it to a bed and breakfast a few years ago after Kayleigh's Christmas store started to take off but there was so much she needed to do and only so much money in the bank account. Cat wouldn't ask Kayleigh or Maggie to help, so she had been quietly saving everything she could. And her Cat's Cakes business hadn't hurt.

About four years ago, Kayleigh had taken her to talk to the woman who owned the Sandwich Shoppe and a partnership was born. Cat now supplied all the baked goods for the shop. Along with that, she sold a few cakes a week, for weddings or big parties. Getting paid to do something she loved was a treat.

If she was careful with who she hired, the savings from her entrepreneurial activities would be able to pay for the new paint job on the porch and the bedrooms, plus the conversion of one of the rooms to a new bathroom. Champagne bubbles of anticipation rose in her belly. Maybe in another year or so...

“I can help out.” Cat glanced up to see Brady Todd leaning over the bar, eavesdropping on her conversation with Pam. His brown eyes were deep and dark and smiling. “In lots of ways.”

“No thanks, Brady.” The boy was too cute for his own good and Cat hoped Evie would take her advice and stay away.

“No, seriously, Cat. I’ve seen you pushing that ancient mower and I really think you’re going to hurt yourself.”

“Thanks for your concern. I’m fine.”

“C’mon, I’ll give you a good deal.” Brady wheedled, his dimples out in full force. “We can come up with a mutually beneficial agreement that would make both of us very happy."

"I'm sure your uncle would love to hear all about that." Cat said firmly.

"Aunt Cat!" Brady actually attempted a pout. "What do you take me for?"

"I'm not your aunt, little boy.

Brady grinned at Pam. "Not so little, right?" Cat snapped her head to Pam, eyebrows raised. A ha! The flush on Pam's cheeks confirmed her suspicion. The two had hooked up last winter. Brady turned his attention back to Cat. Keeping his eyes on her over the rim of the glass, he licked the foam off his lips and winked.

Cat rolled her eyes, even though deep down she had to admit it was flattering to have someone ten years younger flirt with her. "You never learn, do you?"

"It wouldn't be as much fun if he did," Pam said, taking her tray with a knowing laugh.

Brady's gaze followed Pam as she headed out onto the floor before returning to Cat. "You can teach me whatever you like. Whenever." He wiggled his eyebrows suggestively.

Cat laughed. "You haven't changed one bit!"

Brady smiled again, his brown eyes full of mischief. “Seriously, Cat, let me do your lawn. You can pay me in beer and cookies. Or...whatever...”

“Really?”

“Really. I’m open to whatever.”

“Brady...” she warned and he shrugged his shoulders innocently.

“Can you blame me for trying? How about a free pitcher of beer every time I come in and all the cookies I can eat?”

“You eat a lot of cookies. One free beer when you come in and cookies once a week for cutting my lawn. That’s it. Final offer.”

“Throw in some muffins and a cake every year for my birthday and it’s a deal. It’s a big lawn.” He offered his hand. It didn’t seem necessary for Cat to mention she already made him a cake for his birthday every year. It was a pretty good deal. She hated cutting the grass.

“Will you look after the flowerbeds for me, too?” Cat asked as Brady held her hand a little longer than he needed to.

“For extra cookies, I’ll look after whatever you want,” he leered and she laughed again.

"You're trouble."

Brady gave her a wink. "Don't you know it. Hey, was that your sister who just walked in?"

Cat's smile faded.

Chapter Nine

Brenna

"Having a sister is like having a best friend you can't get rid of. You know whatever you do, they'll still be there."

—Amy Li

"Brenna!"

Brenna whipped her head around from where she was smiling at Bar Boy to find Missy and Colin had arrived at her little table. Almost falling off the high stool with eagerness and guilt for being caught staring, she threw herself into the arms of her best friend.

"I didn't get a hug like that." Mike joined them

and smiled at the intensity of Brenna's embrace.

"That's because you're just the brother-in-law. I'm the BFF." Missy pressed her head against Brenna's cheek. "God, I missed you!"

Inseparable since kindergarten, Missy had been by her side through school and Seamus, cried when Brenna's mother died and had been furious when she left home. Missy had been so angry at being left behind, she broke off all communication with Brenna; no letters, phone calls, or funny cards during the first three years Brenna was away.

Then Colin had asked her to marry him.

"You were the first one I wanted to tell," Missy had told her over the phone, tears in her voice.

And like no time had passed, they were best friends again, with letters and phone calls, and eventually emails and the odd FaceTime call keeping them connected. It wasn't the same as being there every day for each other, but it was enough for Brenna.

"Well, lookee here!" Colin all but howled, pulling her out of Missy's warm embrace into his much bonier one.

"How's my half-brother?" Brenna asked as his

arms circled her like a vise.

Colin grimaced. "Don't spoil it for me." He gave her a quick peck on the lips as he released her. "I'm reliving the two best days of my life."

In high school, Colin had been the only boy to distract Brenna from her feelings for Seamus. She and Colin had two days of French-kissing behind the school before his mother had caught them. The humiliation was brief compared to the bombshell Mrs. Farrell dropped – she had had an affair with Brenna's father, the result of which was Colin.

In less than three days, Colin had gone from being Brenna's boyfriend to her half-brother, forever tarnishing her image of her father.

Missy rolled her eyes, and hoisted herself onto the stool. "You better remember who you're married to or this will be the *last* day of your life. Now go away so we can talk about you."

Colin adjusted the stool for Brenna, made a gallant effort to help her sit down. "You're still as pretty as the day you kissed me behind the school. Almost as beautiful as my lovely wife." Colin blew a kiss to Missy as Mike dragged him away.

Missy watched them go with an affectionate smile.

"Mike's been great to him, took Colin under his wing when we got married, like a real brother."

"Half or whole, Colin's the only brother we have, so he's real enough."

She leaned over the table. "You never told me – did you ever find your father? *Colin's* father?"

Brenna sipped at her Martini. She should have known that coming home would bring up emotions she'd tried hard to push down; thoughts of her father, the pain of his abandonment, the frustration of never understanding *why* he had left them.

It must have been just as bad for Colin, never knowing his biological father.

"No," Brenna said as she fished an olive out of her glass. "I never found him."

"Too bad." She watched Brenna take another sip, somehow knowing Brenna didn't want to talk about her father. "How can you drink those things?"

"They're good. It's an acquired taste." There was a lot she could say about her sister, but had to admit Cat made a good Martini.

"Like wine. I bet you drink buckets of wine, and fancy champagne, all *la di da.*" She threw her blonde curls over her shoulder, nose stuck firmly in the air.

Brenna laughed even as she shook her head. “I don’t know what you think my life is life. There’s no buckets, no fancy. No *la di da*.”

Missy turned serious even before her hair fell back into place. “That’s the thing. I don’t know anything about your life. No one does. Like your husband. What happened to your husband, the one I’ve never met?”

“What husband?” For a moment Brenna wished she could pretend there was no Toby, that she had spent the last five years alone. She took another sip of her drink and then another. “So, you - kids. Lots of kids. With Colin, so I guess they’re my...”

“Nieces and nephew. Yep. They keep me busy. What with running after the girls, even though two are in school now and the baby’s going to be starting solid food soon—I hope I can get his poop figured out because he’s all bunged up right now. But—you don’t want to hear about that. And obviously you don’t want to talk about your marriage.” She took a breath and looked at Brenna searchingly.

Brenna had forgotten how relentless Missy was when she wanted to know something, like a dog with a bone. “There’s just not a lot I want to talk about,” she said reluctantly. "I thought I'd come home for Addison's wedding."

"Ten days early?"

"I needed a vacation."

Missy shook her head. "Well, that hasn't changed. You were always horrible when it came to talking about stuff."

"You're a good friend, Miss," Brenna appeased her.

"I'm not just a friend anymore, I'm *family*. Something that you'd remember if you cared enough to come home for my wedding." Missy said with a smile that took the bite out of her words.

"Which I will regret to the end of time, but I just couldn't afford the ticket. I was working three jobs to pay for school."

"I know, and I'm so proud of how well you've done. A lawyer. You always said that's what you wanted to be and you went and did it! You were always so determined."

"Which made me very poor." Brenna drained the last of the gin, thankful to have diverted her friend from the Toby topic. Without thinking, she reached across the table and squeezed Missy's hand on the table. "I've missed you."

"I know. How could you not? Plus, I'm your sister-in-law now and speaking of sisters..." Missy nodded at someone behind her.

Brenna turned to see Cat approach, holding the stem of a Martini glass by two fingers, a disdainful smile on her face. "Thought you might need a refill."

"Thanks." Brenna glanced warily at her.

"So where's this brother-in-law of mine?" Cat began, setting the drink on the table and cocking her fist on her hip.

"Mike's over there somewhere," Brenna said blithely, popping the last olive in her mouth before taking a sip of the fresh Martini.

"I meant the Vancouver one."

"Back in Vancouver."

"That didn't last long."

Brenna recognized the smug look on Cat's face. Things hadn't changed at all. "You should know a thing or two about quick marriages," she said in a low voice.

"At least I invited you to my wedding."

"Which one? Number four or five?"

Cat's eyes narrowed. "At least I didn't try and hide

the fact I got married. Maggie was so proud it took you two weeks to tell her. What's the matter – ashamed of him?"

"It took us that long to get out of bed." The lie wasn't even believable. It had been a long time since Brenna spent the day in bed with anything but a bad cough and a box of Kleenex, but Cat didn't need to know that.

"Nice. You always were one to kiss and tell."

"If my memory serves correctly, there weren't so many to tell about. Unlike you..." Brenna pretended to count on her fingers.

"This is a nice reunion. Nice to see nothing has changed between the two of you," Missy interjected.

"She's turned into an even bigger bitch." With a scowl, Cat turned on her heel and walked away.

"I'm not a bitch," Brenna said to Cat's retreating back.

"Whatever you are, that wasn't pretty," Missy said mildly.

"She started it." Brenna scowled into the Martini.

"Absence hasn't made the heart grow fonder then?" Missy asked with a rueful grin.

"It's obvious she feels the same way."

Brenna sipped her drink and listened as Missy told her every single detail about her kids, the more shocking town gossip for the last few years. As Brenna sat quietly and listened, she finished her Martini in short order.

When Colin ordered her a third drink she accepted it without complaint.

Brenna watched Cat talking with the patrons at the bar, smiling with tired eyes. What did she have in her life to be tired about? She shrugged. Who cared? Cat obviously didn't.

"I'm going to find the ladies' room." Brenna slid off her chair and headed for the washroom.

Dart night was a popular draw at Woody's. Brenna threaded her way through an obstacle course of bodies and beer, smiling apologetically at those she bumped into, avoiding the eyes of those she didn't. She almost made it unscathed, but as an enthusiastic dart player stepped into her path, his face red with drink and laughter, a quick sidestep sent her careening into a tall, broad back.

The man glanced over his shoulder with a scowl. "You spilled my beer."

Brenna had had a long, exhausting day. "You

should learn to hold on your precious beer," she snapped. "I just brushed you." She flicked his arm with her fingers as a demonstration.

He turned around and looked her up and down with narrow eyes. "Don't they teach manners where you come from?" he drawled.

"Don't they teach you how to treat ladies where you're from?" Seeing Cat had put her in the mood for a fight, but she sucked in her breath at the full sight of him.

Picking a fight with someone whose three-button shirts fit snug against his broad chest with the sleeves rolled up to show muscular arms the width of her legs was never the best idea.

"Show me a lady and I'll show you how nice I'll treat her." The overhead lights reflected off his bald head. She noticed the edge of a tattoo peeking out from under his shirt.

"I doubt that," she shot back. "And I'm more than enough lady for you."

"'Fraid not, sweetheart. You're all big city swank. You don't belong here."

Brenna's anger dissipated in a rush, leaving a hollow feeling in its wake. "You're right," she said sadly. “I don’t belong here anymore.” She turned away before he saw the sudden wetness in her eyes.

“What did I say?” His hand gripped her arm gently, like one might hold a kitten.

“The truth.”

Bafflement replaced condescending. “Hang on a sec - who are you?”

“Brenna. Brenna Ebans.”

Realization dawned in his blue eyes, and then regret. “Ebans...Cat’s sister. Look, I - ”

She shrugged out of his grasp and tried to ignore the sinking feeling of disappointment. “Everyone knows Cat,” she said bitterly. “That’s never changed. Just me.” And without another word, she stepped around him to continue on to the ladies’ room.

“Well, hello.” Just as she was about to snap, Brenna recognized the smile of Bar Boy.

“Hi.” Seeing him again, closer up, Brenna thought he looked vaguely familiar. She probably knew his mother, or gone to school with a sister but she wasn’t in the mood to figure out who he was.

She suddenly wished no one knew who she was.

“You look a little lost.” He smiled warmly at her, a sharp contrast from the patronizing scowl of Cat’s friend. Big city swank rang in her ears.

"That obvious?"

"Only to someone with a keen eye for observation." He was only an inch or two taller than Brenna, tanned skin the color of a soothing cup of hot chocolate after the whipped cream was mixed in. He stepped closer, the heady scent of cologne mixed with beer surrounding her. Brenna leaned back, suddenly uncomfortable with his closeness, but hemmed in by a group of dart players. "Can I buy you a drink, help you find your way?"

"I don't think I need another drink." She could have smiled, should have stepped away from him, but there was something about him… "Are you trying to pick me up?"

"No, why? Do you want me to pick you up?" Before she could react, he stepped even closer, put his hands around her waist, and easily lifted her off the floor. One of her flip-flops fell off and she couldn't help but laugh with embarrassed delight.

"Please put me down!"

"But I thought you wanted me to pick you up?" His grin was irresistible. No one had smiled at her like that since Seamus.

"I didn't say that," Brenna floundered as her feet returned to the floor and she shuffled her foot into the sandal before it got stepped on. "Not that like. I just asked..."

"Would you like me to buy you a drink?" He hadn't moved his hands from her waist and she held her breath, to make her waist as small as possible.

"Well, I...um...I don't..."

"Yes or no. Simple question, really. I don't like anything too complicated." That smile, with his warm brown eyes and a few days stubble that covered his chin, made him quite appealing.

What was she doing?

It had been only days since Brenna had broken things off with Toby. She didn't come home to meet men in bars. She didn't want to meet men anywhere. She didn't do that sort of thing. She never had.

But an image of Crystal rising up from under the desk flashed through her mind.

"Yes. Please," Brenna answered, ignoring the flutter in her stomach. But she couldn't ignore everything. Her more pressing need was becoming uncomfortable and she really needed to duck into the ladies room. "But could you—would you mind..."

Suddenly the smile vanished and Bar Boy's hands whipped from her waist so fast she had friction burn. "I gotta go."

"Okay?" What else was she supposed to say? "But..."

"I'll take a rain check, okay?" And then he was gone, disappearing among the throng of bodies by the bar.

"Not really," Brenna said with bewilderment. If that's how easily she scared off men, there was no hope for her. She turned to see the giant of a man staring at her, still with a scowl on his face. With a flounce of the hair move copied from Cat, she stormed into the ladies room.

One of the lights was burnt out but the washroom was blessedly quiet after the raucous sounds of the bar. Brenna's shoulders slumped as she gazed at her reflection in the mirror.

What was she thinking coming back here?

Cat's friend had been right. Brenna didn't belong there. She never had.

She wanted nothing more than to go home and crawl into bed. But it wasn't her bed. It would be her niece's bed. She didn't have a bed. She didn't have a home.

She pushed into the stall as desolation threatened to overwhelm her. She swayed, caught herself before she fell over.

One minute she felt the relief from being able to release her bladder and the next moment she was asleep.

"Brenna, are you in here?" Brenna jerked awake at the sound of Missy's shout.

"Shh," Brenna managed after finding some saliva for her mouth.

The metal wall she was leaning on was blissfully cool on her cheek. The toilet seat didn't feel as nice.

Missy's head popped out from under the divider like a curly blonde Jack-in-the-box. "What the hell are you doing?" she screeched.

Brenna's head felt strange, like she had walked through a wall of fog. "I don't know. I think maybe I fell asleep."

"You passed out, you dumbass. Now, unlock the door because I sure as hell can't slide under the door."

Brenna hastily pulled up her pants before unlocking the door. Missy laughed as she swung it open. "Get up! We thought you went back to Maggie's and Mike went home to check. It'll serve you right if you wake up with a nasty hangover."

"It's been a long day. I was tired."

Missy heard the snap of Brenna's voice and backed out of the stall.

"I'm just here to help, you know," Missy said to Brenna's reflection in the mirror as she washed her hands.

Brenna saw the care and concern in Missy's face and knew she wasn't talking about waking her up. "I know. Thanks."

"It's pretty shitty that you didn't come home, but I forgave you. I know you were trying to make a life for yourself, but I wished you'd remember you have a life here, too." The smiling, ever cheerful Missy was serious, her big blue eyes solemn.

"It was hard to remember what I had here," Brenna confessed in a low voice.

"And we didn't help, did we?"

For a moment, Brenna felt dizzy, didn't think she'd be able to hold back the tears. She had always taken the blame for the distance between her sisters, but the truth was that they hadn't made an effort to see her either. Busy with their lives, Kayleigh and

Maggie had assumed letters and phone calls were enough. Never once had they realized what Brenna needed, what she craved was the warmth and love of their physical presence. To have Missy admit she was to blame as well was almost too much for her already overwrought emotions to handle.

Her control was about to crumble when Cat burst through the door. “You find her?”

Brenna grabbed hold of herself with all the willpower she could manage.

“She was asleep,” Missy said, tucking an arm around Brenna’s waist. Brenna refused to look at her sister as Cat held the door open.

“Passed out, you mean,” Cat snorted.

Woody’s had cleared out but a small group waited for her.

“There she is!” Colin cried. “I knew you wouldn’t leave without a good-bye kiss.”

Brenna tried to smile but her face was hot with embarrassment.

“Everything OK?” Seamus asked with concern.

“She’s had a really long day.” Missy’s arm remained firm around Brenna’s waist, comforting and protective.

"I told Mike you'd drive her home," Cat said, appearing over Seamus shoulder.

Brenna couldn't decipher the glance between them. "If you say so," Seamus said, getting up from the table.

"You don't have to," Brenna protested. "I'm fine."

"Fine or not, you're not walking home." Missy's arm slid away, leaving Brenna suddenly feeling cold.

"I saw you talking to Brady," Cat interrupted.

"Who?" She'd seen so many people tonight...which one was Brady? Her brain was full of fog.

She shouldn't have had the third drink.

"Brady. You need to stay away from him."

"Who's going to make me?" Despite not knowing who Cat was talking about, Brenna's response to Cat was automatic and drew a groan from the others.

Seamus grabbed her arm and started for the door. "Enough squabbling for the night. Let's get you home."

It felt surreal to climb into Seamus' truck. Brenna knew it wasn't the same truck that had driven her home countless times in the past, where she had sat close to him, with his warm hand on her thigh; it wasn't the same truck where she had laid in Seamus' arms in the back, looking at the stars, but it felt like only yesterday she had been with him.

She sat, stiff and uncomfortable, trying to push away the memories as Seamus pulled out of the parking lot.

It wasn't yesterday. It was years – a lifetime ago.

Seamus turned down the country music that filled the cab. "Are you really okay?" he asked solicitously. "Missy was worried. She didn't know..."

"I'm fine." Brenna's voice was curt. She stared out the window; like with Missy in the washroom, she was afraid Seamus' concern would push her over the edge. There was so many things she wanted to say to Seamus, but couldn't. She didn't know where to begin, where it would end.

The headlights soon illuminated Maggie's house as Seamus pulled into the drive. "Well, here we are."

It wasn't planned. Brenna never even thought about it, just slid across the seat and Seamus opened his arms.

"I never forgot you," she whispered, breathing in the still-familiar scent.

He gave a rumble in his throat that might have

been a laugh. “I couldn’t forget you. You Skatt girls are unforgettable.”

Sitting in his truck, Seamus’ arms around her, Brenna wasn’t able to push away the memories. She leaned in and brushed her lips against his.

Seamus pulled away, his head slamming against the window. “Hey, hey, Bren...maybe this isn’t...not a good idea.”

“No. Okay.” Brenna scuttled away from him.

“You’re still married and now you’re back and you and Cat aren’t talking yet...”

“What’s Cat have to do with this?”

“It’s just—”

“Never mind.” The chill of the night air cooled her face as she opened the door. “Thanks for the ride.”

“Bren.” Seamus’ shoulders slumped.

She couldn’t believe she had kissed him. This night needed to be over because Brenna didn’t think she could take much more.

She hopped out of the truck too quickly and lost her footing as she hit the ground.

“You OK?” Seamus called as Brenna stumbled to her knees.

“I’m fine, “she mumbled, pulling herself to her

feet. Managing to hold her head up high, despite the tears that threatened, Brenna made it to the door. Seamus waited for her to step inside before flashing his headlights like he used to.

But nothing was like it used to be.

Chapter Ten

Cat

"Sisters are different flowers from the same garden."

—Author Unknown

Cat knew it took four minutes to drive from the parking lot at Woody's to Maggie's. When twelve minutes had passed, and Seamus still hadn't returned, the slow simmer of anger turned to a low boil.

She wasn't sure exactly who she was angry with—Brenna for requiring the ride home; or Seamus for jumping to her rescue like some sort of stupid white knight vowing to save the queen at all costs.

She conveniently forgot it was her who told him to

take Brenna home.

Getting pissed at Seamus probably wasn't the smartest idea, seeing as how Seamus was probably still upset with Cat.

She was also mad at Missy for letting Brenna drink so much; Kayleigh for bringing her back home; Mike for leaving her at the bar and even Brenna's shitty husband because if it wasn't for his dickhead behavior she wouldn't have come home in the first place. No one escaped Cat's wrath as she banged glasses into the dishwasher behind the bar and swiped at the puddles of beer on the counter.

"I see your sister finally came home."Cat glanced

up with a scowl to see ex-husband number one with his elbows on the bar, narrowly missing a puddle she hadn't wiped up.

"She did." She wasn't in the mood to deal with Tommy during the best of times and tonight wasn't one of those.

"Didn't take her long to take up with Seamus again." That had been the basis of their relationship—they would needle each other mercilessly until one of them would snap and start a fight, most times resulting in a physical altercation, and would invariably end up in bed.

It hadn't been healthy relationship.

It had been ten years since Cat had gotten rid of him, and he still knew which buttons to push. "Fuck off, Tommy."

"Hit a soft spot, did I?"

"There's no soft spots with Seamus and I, unlike there was with you."

Tommy guffawed. "Ah, Cat. Lots of good memories."

"Like the time you pushed me down the stairs?"

Anger flashed in his dark eyes. "Seems I recall you giving as much as you got."

"I'm going, Tommy," one of his friends called out. "You want a lift or what?"

"Go home to your *wife*, Tommy," Cat spat out the word.

"She's a better wife than you ever were. Not so good with the marriage thing, are you? Seamus'll figure that out soon enough."

"Fuck off!"

With a humorless laugh, Tommy pushed away from the bar. "Always a pleasure talking to you, Cat. Still the biggest bitch in town."

Tommy moved away as Cat was about to leap across the counter at him. Their four years together had been some of the worst in her life.

Cat had worked up a really good mad when Seamus finally walked through the door.

"She pass out in your truck?" Cat called nastily. There were still a few stragglers grouped around the bar but she took no notice of them. "Took you long enough to drop her off."

Seamus ignored her as he rang the bell hanging over the draft taps. "Last call, boys! Time to go home to bed."

"So you took her to Maggie's?" she persisted.

"Why? Did you think I tucked her into bed at my place?"

"I would hope you had more sense than that."

"Sometimes I wonder about my sense. Would you rather I took her to your place?"

"No! I'm not dealing with her."

Seamus looked Cat in the eye. "She just broke up with her husband. You of all people should have some sympathy."

"What's that supposed to mean?"

"It means that since you insist on your past

marriages being so important, I think they should be included in every conversation we have from now on."

Cat's mouth gaped open. "I'd prefer not being reminded about them." A few of the stragglers who had been making lame attempts at leaving stopped and watched with interest.

"So would I, and yet you continue to bring them up every chance you get," Seamus retorted. "Been there, done that, not gonna do it again."

"I didn't say that!"

"Sounded like it to me. You know, maybe you should wait til you're asked before you kick the guy to the curb."

Cat's face burned hot with rage and embarrassment as Seamus turned his back and walked away.

"Don't walk away from me!"

"Trouble in paradise?"

She glanced up, half-expecting to see Tommy grinning meanly. Instead it was Joss Ryan with his bald head and a rueful expression. He took a dramatic step back when he saw her scowl. "Sorry I asked. Jeez, you're scary when you get pissed."

"You look like this all the time!" Cat felt the edge

of her anger soften.

“Yeah, but I’m prettier than you so it’s not as bad.”

“You’re not prettier than me.” She had always found the tall, big and brawny types attractive. Joss was one of the good guys, a good friend.

“I’m definitely not as dumb,” Joss leaned over the bar, his blue eyes accusing. “You shouldn’t go after your boy like that. He doesn’t deserve it.”

“No one asked you.” Cat turned her back on Joss, wished he would leave. She didn’t need him acting as her conscious.

“Which is why I’m telling you.”

“I didn’t ‘go after’ him. Whatever that means,” she said defensively. “Besides, why do you care?”

“Because he’s a good guy. Almost as good as me.”

“He’s better,” Cat admitted, under her breath.

“Which is why he doesn’t deserve it. Now, go make nice. Go clean the bathroom for him. That’s women’s work, isn’t it?” But he grinned as he said it.

“‘Night, Cat,” a straggling patron called.

“So popular with the boys,” Joss noted, watching him to the door. “He’s here more than me. “What does his wife think of this being his second home?”

“No one sees much of her. He almost married my sister, you know. Kayleigh.”

“Well, I didn’t think it was Maggie. I had the pleasure of meeting the other one tonight. She come in to see you?”

“No.”

It always came back to Brenna. Cat heaved a sigh at Joss’ questioning glance. “I’m waiting for you to give me your opinion on her being back. Everyone has one. How good it is to see her, how long it’s been since she’s been home, how good she looks, what did she say about Seamus and me?”

“She’s kind of cute.”

Cat rolled her eyes.

“Not my type though,” he continued. “Too nervy looking, like some pure bred dog that’s going to freak out whenever there’s a thunderstorm.”

“You’re comparing my sister to a dog?” Cat couldn’t hide her smile.

“Not in a bad way. Why would she say something about you and Seamus?”

“I forget, you’re not from around here. There’s some...history...with me and Seamus and Brenna.”

“You mean something like a threesome? You Skatt

girls—"

"No!" Cat snapped. "God, no. Back when we were kids, I was with Seamus, and then Brenna stole him from me—"

"He's a person, you know. Can't be stolen."

"Well, she did." Cat knew she sounded like a pissed off child but couldn't help it. "Go home, Joss. I don't want to talk to you anymore."

"Because I'm right and you're being silly. She's your sister and you haven't seen her for years. Go be nice to her. She looked pretty lost coming in here. Sort of shell-shocked, like a refugee with nowhere to go. I saw it in the war."

Cat suspected a lot of Joss's crotchetiness had to do with his two tours in Afghanistan. "She's got lots of people wanting to take care of her. She'll be fine."

"I'm sensing she's somehow the source of the squabble between you and Seamus."

"There's no squabble."

Joss raised his eyebrow. "Someone's not getting lucky tonight because someone's cleaning the bathroom all by his lonesome."

"I'll do the women's. I always do."

"He started with that one."

Cat cursed under her breath. Seamus must have been really mad.

As Cat locked the door behind Joss, Seamus appeared with her beat-up denim jacket in his hand. “You might as well head out,” he said, tossing it in her direction. “I’ll be here a while longer.”

They usually left together, Seamus staying the night at Cat’s. “Oh. Okay. I’ll leave the porch light on.”

“I think I’ll stay at my place.”

He hadn’t been over in three days. Something was very wrong.

“That’s a good idea,” Cat bluffed. “I’m going to Elliott Lake early in the morning anyway.”

Anger kept her warm as she walked home alone.

Chapter Eleven

Brenna

"Sisters remember things you would rather forget, in graphic detail...With proof."
—Unknown

Mike met Brenna at the door with a worried expression on his face.

"I fell asleep." she said automatically. "I didn't mean for you to worry."

As soon as the door shut behind her, Mike grabbed her in a tight hug. "It's OK, Bren, it's just—first night back and I already lost you? Glad Maggie slept through it or I'd never hear the end of it."

"I don't want you to get into trouble. I won't do it

again." She had been humiliated enough for one night; Brenna doubted she would want to leave the house again at all. Could anything else have gone wrong? All she wanted was to go to bed and forget everything that had happened that night.

"Naw, it's OK. You're a big girl now; you can take care of yourself."

"I've been doing it for long enough." Brenna spoke without thinking and was rewarded by an injured expression on Mike's face. "I didn't mean it like that. Look, I'm going to go to bed. It's been a long day."

"Night," Mike said as she turned from him.

Evie was softly snoring as Brenna tiptoed into the room. She would have preferred her own room, but beggars couldn't be choosers and Addison had happily given up her bed to stay at her fiancé's.

Brenna hadn't considered living arrangements when she left Vancouver. Most people ran away from home, not toward it.

The room gently spun as she lay in Addison's bed and tried to sort out her thoughts.

She didn't realize her face was wet with tears until she rolled over.

Coming home wasn't supposed to be like this.

For years she buried her feelings under a mountain of work. It hurt to be away from her sisters; it wasn't good for her. She was like a rose cut from a blooming bush, able to exist for a time, looking pretty and smelling sweet but fading and withering in time. She had missed them desperately, even Cat. And Seamus. She had missed Seamus so much that for years, she lived with a steady pain in her stomach, like a knot in a necklace impossible to detangle.

Coming home should have been easy and simple, but nothing had gone right.

How could she have *kissed* him?

He was her childhood love, but Brenna was a thirty-three year old *married* woman who should not be making out in pickup trucks.

The humiliation of Seamus pulling away, Toby's easy rejection of their marriage and Cat's reaction crashed over her like a bucket of cold water, washing away the warmth of Mike and Maggie's welcome.

"You're all big city swank, sweetheart. You don't belong here."

But where did she belong?

Curled up in a ball, her pillow damp with tears, Brenna lay awake for a long time.

*

A buzzing snarl from outside woke her. She tried to ignore the irritating noise, burrowing her head under the pillow. When the distant noise, moved closer, she couldn't ignore it any longer.

The thin curtains on the window did nothing to block the bright sunlight streaming into the room. What time was it anyway? It took Brenna a full minute until the events of the previous night rushed back, adding to the unsettled feeling in her stomach. Pounding head, sticky, dry mouth and queasiness. Classic hangover.

As she pulled herself up on unsteady legs, she realized the house was quiet as a tomb, the chaos from the party last night blessedly silent. It was evident where her nieces had divided the room; a corkboard with a calendar, lists and a few pictures hung on the wall on Evie's side while Addison's side was papered with pictures torn out of magazines. Inches from Brenna's face was a family picture of the Kardashians.

The buzzing noise began again, and Brenna stumbled to the window in time to see a red lawn mower being pushed by a smooth, tanned back disappear around the corner of the house next door.

With a minty fresh mouth and two Advils to sustain her, she headed for the kitchen, where the aroma of coffee greeted her along with two dogs of questionable breeding. She gave a prayer of thanks there was some left for her as she poured a brimming cup.

The room looked different in the bright light of the morning. The mountain of food had disappeared with only a box of cereal standing open on the counter, a few dishes in the sink. A plastic cup had been left lonely on the table, still half filled with juice. Brenna carried it to the sink.

How did Maggie do it? It was Friday; the girls were at school, Maggie already left for work. Brenna had somehow slept through the morning exodus.

Her sister was obviously some sort of super woman. There was nothing she couldn't do, even keeping excitable children from waking her.

Her Coach wallet had been left on the counter, and Brenna grabbed for her phone inside.

Zero text messages.

But there was an email from Toby.

Wrapping herself in a cotton throw blanket, she

made her way to the back deck with her phone, a mug of coffee and Maggie's dogs.

> You seemed to want this settled in order to move on so I had the separation agreement drawn up. Please advise on any changes and I will courier original to you.
> Please advise of forwarding address.

Sinking into a plastic lawn chair, Brenna re-read the email as the dogs chased each other around the yard. The sun was warm, the air smelled like freshly cut grass and she was reading the proposed separation agreement for the dissolution of her marriage.

This was what she wanted.

The irony didn't escape her.

The sight of Krystal crawling out from under his desk...the anger rose within her, as foul as the queasiness in her stomach. How *could* he humiliate her like that?

He didn't want her. Four years of marriage, over, simply because she had gone to his office to tell him she couldn't make it for dinner.

How long had the affair been going on? Was it an affair, or just a one-time thing? Had there been others? Just how many other office assistants had he seduced in that big corner office of his?

The thoughts upset her stomach more than the alcohol from last night.

The bare back pushing the lawn mower had circled the neighbour's house and was coming into view again. The dogs bounded over to him.

Caught in her thoughts, it took a moment for Brenna to realize the man was shouting at her.

"What?" She was conscious that the blanket around her shoulders didn't do a great job hiding her thin nightshirt, which wasn't at all suitable for walking across the lawn.

He cut the engine with a gurgle that sounded like the mower would never start again. "Can you put the dogs in?"

"Oh. Sure." Brenna drew a blank at the names of the dogs. "Dogs," she tried. "Here, dogs."

The man crouched down to pet the dogs, sending them into a frenzy of tail wagging. With a scowl, Brenna pulled the blanket tightly around her, and headed over to collect them.

"I guess I didn't think they would – hey," Brenna faltered as she drew close enough to see his face.

"Hey!" Recognition swept his face at the same time and he smiled widely, dimples on full display.

It was Bar Boy from last night.

"What are you doing here?" she asked with a self-conscious smile, stepping carefully over the flowerbed separating the two properties.

He looked down at the ancient red mower and then back at Brenna.

"Oh. I just thought – it's a little early to be cutting the grass, isn't it?" she stumbled over her words.

"Most people around here don't sleep in past ten. I guess I woke you up."

"Maybe a little," Brenna admitted, conscious of the dark eyes, gazing at her with a mixture of amusement and admiration.

The ball of loneliness in her belly loosened a tiny bit.

"Just a little? I can wake you up all the way?" he asked. "I know a *really* nice way to do it..."

"Oh." She couldn't get her trained legal mind to come up with a coherent response and dropped her eyes to his bare chest.

Big mistake.

"Sorry about the noise," he said. Brenna wrenched

her eyes back to his face, to be met with an expression that told her he knew exactly what she was thinking about.

What was she thinking about?

“I don’t suppose you could keep it down?” she asked weakly.

“I don’t think I can keep it down at all.” His raised eyebrow turned Brenna’s simple act of inhaling into a cough. “You okay there?” He patted her gently on the back, his hand warm through the thin blanket.

“Fine,” Brenna muttered, backing away from his touch. “Work - I’ll let you do it – let you do your work. Go back to work.”She wished she could hide in the blanket as her face flamed.

“Why? You seem much more interesting. Going back to bed?”

“No,” Brenna cried with dismay.

“Too bad. You’ve got some grass on your blanky.”

Grass cutting decorated the edge of the blanket and as she yanked it up, it slid off her shoulder, exposing the thin straps of her nightgown.

Then as Brenna backed away, trying to keep her eyes off his bare chest, she tripped over one of the flowerbeds and landed in the marigolds with a small shriek.

Smirking, he hauled Brenna to her feet. As soon as she was upright, she snatched back her hand and clutched at the blanket. Flustered, she held it tightly closed with one hand while trying to brush off the dirt and flower petals with the other. “It’s really hot out here,” he called as she practically ran back over the grass. “I sure could use a drink!”

Snatching her phone from the deck, she heard his laugh even after she slammed the door, resisting the urge to lean against it like some romantic heroine swept off her feet by the brooding hero.

The mower started with a roar.

“Just stop it,” Brenna said aloud. “He’s cutting the grass. He’s being nice. Flirting. People do that.”

Just not with her.

Her phone buzzed as she held it and she couldn’t stop the leap of her heart as she saw the text from Toby.

> What do you want me to do with your shoes?

Did he want her gone that badly? Was he already moving Crystal into the condo?

Brenna was tempted to tell him where to shove them.

Tiny blades of fresh cut grass were caught between her bare toes. What did she need shoes for? Pushing aside the kitchen curtains, Brenna peered out of the window, watching Bar Boy until he vanished around the house again. He was cute , too cute. She wouldn't know what to do with so much cute.

Oh, yes, she would. She'd know exactly what to do.

She dropped the curtain with a sigh. This wasn't her.

She fantasized about work and clients and closing the deal, not cute guys who cut the grass.

That had been her problem with Toby. She had been getting excited about work, and he was getting excited at work with Crystal, and who knew who else.

Crystal had taken advantage of the situation with Toby – lonely married man, pretty available woman who knew the right thing to say, to wear to attract him. She would take advantage of *this* situation if she was here.

So would Cat.

Then Brenna noticed the sudden quiet. The

lawnmower had shut off.

He was probably finished and getting ready to leave. Brenna stood frozen in Maggie's kitchen, back against the wall, thoughts racing as much as her heart rate.

Toby was going to throw out her shoes.

There was a separation agreement on her phone waiting for her approval.

'Big city swank.'

"Screw you," she said, just as the polite knock sounded at the back door. With a deep breath, and then another, she opened it. The dogs burst in, with wagging tails and panting tongues, and headed for their water dish in the kitchen.

"Oh!" She'd been so flustered she'd forgotten to bring them in.

"It's really hot out there," he said with a smile, leaning against the door jam. Perspiration covered his bare torso like the sheen of wax. "And I brought the dogs back for you."

She made a little sighing sound, a little louder than she meant to. "Thanks. I'll get you a drink."

He leaned against the counter, looking at her with a suggestive smile. Brenna caught her breath; it was the very same expression she had seen on Seamus' face so many times.

She didn't want to be reminded of Seamus. Or Toby.

"Here you go." She handed him a glass, trying to avoid looking at him directly.

"You're not going to join me?"

Looking around for her coffee, Brenna realized she had forgotten it outside.

He smiled over the edge of his glass. "You don't seem like the Kool-Aid type to me."

"What type do I seem like?" Her voice was hesitant, nervous. Why couldn't she talk to men as easily as Cat did?

"You seem like my type."

"I—really?"

"Sexy, smart...well, except for letting a stranger into the house. In my case it's okay, but I wouldn't make a habit of it."

She laughed uneasily. "I don't make a habit of doing anything like this."

"Now, that's a shame. Pretty girl like you...looking all cute in her pajamas."

Brenna flushed. "I should get dressed."

“Please don’t. You’re over-dressed as it is.”

In a fluid move, he set his glass down and stepped toward her. She stepped away.

Maybe that was why Toby got bored of her—because she kept stepping away.

“I’m not going to hurt you,” he whispered. He reached out a hand to stroke her arm like she was a nervous puppy.

“I don’t do things like this,” she confessed in a whisper. “Ever. And here...”

“Whad’ya thinks going to happen here?”

Brenna froze, her insides clenching with humiliation at misreading him, misreading the whole situation. “Oh. I -”

“I know what *I* want to happen,” he continued, stepping closer, snaking his arm around her waist.

She was so relieved that she let herself be backed against the counter, pinned by his unyielding body.

His warm, sexy body...

The blanket slid to the floor.

“I thought you were so hot last night,” he said in a husky voice. His warm fingers were dancing on her arm with a mesmerizing distraction. They moved over her shoulder, down her back, flicking aside the straps of her nightdress. “You look even better in this.”

Brenna held her breath as he kissed her. Her stomach fluttered as he dropped soft, light kisses on her cheek, the corners of her mouth. Her stomach flipped over when his hands slid under her nightshirt to cup her bottom.

There was a moment of clarity when he pushed himself against her. *What am I doing?* But then his lips found hers with none of the awkwardness of past first kisses.

It was a good kiss. Brenna sighed, and told herself to enjoy it.

And then she didn’t have to tell herself.

Hands and lips, fingers and mouths, moving faster than she ever imagined. There, and there...and *there*. Right *there.*

I shouldn’t be doing this in the kitchen! What if someone knocks on the door?

Why didn’t Toby and I ever do this in the kitchen?

Thoughts of her husband sealed the deal. What was he doing now? Was he curled up with Crystal, in the bed *she* once shared with him?

Why shouldn’t Brenna have a few moments of pleasure with an attractive boy – man? He was old enough to be called a man.

Maybe more than a few moments.

He was *definitely* a man.

*

"Good, huh?"

Brenna awkwardly pulled up her panties, which had pooled around one of her ankles. Her body tingled with satisfaction, but her mind reeled with confusion.

Did he want a compliment?

"I know women like you are all reading those *Fifty Shade of Sex* books so I try and make like the fantasy," he said with a smirk, zipping up his jeans.

"Fantasy? Women like *me*?"

"Y'all like it rough. I get it." His grin widened, became even cockier. "Man in control, demanding. I got that."

"I don't know what you're talking about." The feeling of satisfaction was fading with every word he spoke. "I've never read those books."

"Really? Maybe you should. Broaden your horizons, things like that. Chicks your age, you know—"

"How old do you think I am?" Brenna demanded. She tried to regain her poise and composure but it was difficult to do when standing in a kitchen in a nightgown with a man who had just tucked himself back into his pants.

"You're the same age as Seamus, aren't you?"

"Seamus?"

"He's my uncle."

Chapter Twelve

Cat

If sisters were free to express how they really feel, parents would hear this: "Give me all the attention and all the toys and send Rebecca to live with Grandma."

—Linda Sunshine

Cat woke to the sound of soft snoring. She smiled, still with her eyes closed and reached for Seamus beside her.

Instead, her hand found the fur-covered folds of the bulldog, spread out beside her.

"Connery, get down!" she snapped. The dog jerked awake and without glance at her angry face, made a running jump off the bed, his stumpy legs tangling beneath him on the dismount.

He knew he wasn't allowed to sleep on her bed and if Seamus had been with her, Connery wouldn't have dared. But Seamus wasn't here; he was in his own bed, probably spread-eagled on his back, arms tucked under his head.

Seamus took up a lot of room in the bed, even more than the dogs.

Even forced to a tiny corner of the bed, Cat liked waking up with him. Being alone in the bed brought back the remnants of her bad mood last night, even though she was a little unsure of whom she was supposed to be angry with. She had a nasty feeling it was herself.

She could have handled things better with Seamus.

Her sister had come home alone and vulnerable, her marriage seemingly over—why wouldn't she run straight to Seamus? It's what Cat herself would do.

It's exactly what she did, or what she tried to do.

When Cat broke up with Tommy, it was Seamus who she had run to, but he was already with Bec. And so Cat married Perry MacLeod.

Perry and Tommy were as different as night and day. Perry had loved her since they'd finger-painted each other's faces in kindergarten. He would have been happy spending the rest of his life taking care of her, if she had only let him.

After her marriage with Perry ended, Cat left town to for a hospitality course at the college in Sault Ste. Marie, a hundred kilometers away. When she met Alex, her planned nine-month stay lasted three years.

When she returned, she went straight to Seamus. They'd been together ever since.

It was no wonder she was worried about Brenna doing the same thing.

Cat forced her mind away from Alex, from Seamus, by taking the dogs for a walk through the woods behind the house, taking a moment to stroke Connery's soft ears, her version of apologizing to him.

There was no point worrying about Brenna and her connection to Seamus. What they had had was childish, juvenile. Yes, everyone expected them to marry, but they had been teenagers. Cat was a woman, mature and experienced...

Experienced in failed marriages.

"Stop it," she told herself. With a questioning

whine, Connery looked up from where he was nose deep in an old log. "Not you."

If it came down to sister against sister with Seamus, Cat was sure she'd win.

Pretty sure.

But there was no point in worrying about it today. Addison's big day was in less than two weeks and Cat had a wedding cake to prepare. A new pan, some good white chocolate, and the painting supplies from Home Depot...Cat had the list in her head as she set off.

Closer to Michigan than the rest of Ontario, the village of Forest Hills lay between Sudbury and Sault Ste. Marie, a quick skip north of the Trans-Canada Highway. Elliott Lake was the nearest big town and Cat headed directly to the little cooking store in the downtown area and spent long minutes browsing among baking pans and utensils before heading to the Home Depot.

She was browsing in the paint aisle, dreaming over designer colours when she heard a familiar voice. Ralph. She'd forgotten her cousin worked here.

"Hey, Kitty Cat," Ralph cried, his voice, booming through the painting aisle. "Long time, no see. What are you doing in this neck of the woods?"

He'd seen her. Cat sighed and turned around, hiding her irritation behind a fake smile. "Hi, Ralph." Ralph had been calling her Kitty-Cat and meowing at her since she could walk.

"I heard Brenna's back."

Cat nodded, fighting the urge to run away. *Always Brenna – BrennaBrennaBrenna!*

"Mom said we should have you all over for supper, to see what she's been up to. She really a lawyer?" He scratched his head, calling attention to the unnatural, Donald Trump-like blonde hair.

"Yep." She couldn't stop staring at the tuft of yellow hair, but he took no notice.

"Dad says we should get her working on Uncle Jerry's case. Said, what's the point of a fancy education if she don't help out family?" Ralph's face was an expression of delight. Cat wasn't sure if it was because of seeing her, the thought of Brenna or the possibility of their uncle getting out of jail.

"You should definitely give Brenna a call, ask her about that," she said, feeling like the wicked witch of the west and not a bit sorry about it. "I'm sure she'd *love* to help, make up for all the time she's been away."

"I'll tell Dad," Ralph said with excitement.

"I'll let you get back to work. I've just got to pick up some paint."

"What are you painting?"

Cat explained the projects and Ralph helped her pick out the paint. "Is your mom still hanging around the house?" he asked, swinging two gallons of paint by the handles. She jumped aside to avoid a nasty bruise.

"Yep."

"She's like, what, haunting the place?"

"I wouldn't call it haunting, no."

"What do you call it?"

"Hanging around," she said flippantly. "Can you mix that paint for me, Ralph? I've got to get back. I've got—"

"You really shouldn't believe that ghost nonsense, you know."

The voice came from behind Cat, icy cold with more than a hint of rudeness. She turned, wishing she had gone to the Canadian Tire instead of Home Depot.

"This is just a *great* day for family," Cat said, her tongue tipped with sarcasm. Despite her flippant remark, seeing her paternal uncle was unsettling.

Pictures showed her father had looked like his older brother, almost like twins.

Was this what her father would look like now? Red hair faded to white, deep lines etched into his tanned skin?

Peter Ebans glanced at her with cold eyes. "Your sister is back."

"No, really? I had no idea."

"Still continuing your childish fight with her, I see."

"That's really none of your business. Neither is any other part of my life, or any of my sisters' lives."

"I really wish all of you thought that."

"What's that supposed to mean?"

Peter gave Cat a knowing smile. "Apparently the Skatt sisters aren't as close as everyone thinks."

"What's *that* supposed to mean?"

"It means not all of your sisters want to keep to themselves. My father is tired of hearing about you and your problems."

"What problems? Who's talking to Granddad? Marcus, I mean. He's no grandfather to us."

With a shrug of his shoulders, Peter walked away, leaving Cat fuming and bewildered. When their father had abandoned them, his father Marcus Ebans had severed all ties, even refusing to attend his daughter-in-law's funeral.

Cat forced herself to take a deep breath, and ignored Peter's words. Maggie or Kayleigh would never contact Marcus Ebans. Maybe Brenna had.

She hadn't been home in years, had probably forgotten about the feud. She'd always kept a soft spot for their father, as well. It would be just like her to go behind their backs.

Ralph staring thumped her paint cans on the counter. "I've never liked him," he muttered.

"Makes two of us," Cat agreed.

Chapter Thirteen

Brenna

If your sister is in a tearing hurry to go out and cannot catch your eye, she's wearing your best sweater.

—Pam Brown

"He's my uncle."

Once she knew the connection, it was easy to figure out her Bar Boy was none other than Brady Todd, the eldest son of Seamus' brother.

She had babysat him when she was fifteen, remembering him as a shy, funny looking boy with a larger than normal sized head and short legs. Not the type who would easily seduce a woman ten years his senior in the kitchen.

She leaned against the door after Brady left, head in her hands. *What had she done?*

Yes, she had enjoyed it; both physically and because in her mind, it was a way of getting revenge on Toby. But what was the point of revenge if Toby didn't know, nor care where she was, or who she was with?

Sex with Seamus' *nephew*? What had she been thinking?

It had been a long time...Brenna could justify her actions, rationalize why the idea of morning sex with a virtual stranger was a good idea, but it didn't change the fact it had been just plain stupid.

He *spanked* her.

Brenna shook her head with disbelief as she heard Brady's truck bounce out of the neighbor's driveway. *Spanked* her.

She needed more coffee and headed back to the kitchen to retrieve her cup from the back deck. It was cold, with a dead fly floating in the top. She threw the liquid over the railing.

Why did it have to be him? Why couldn't it have been *anyone* else?

"Arrrgghhh!" Brenna growled, yelled it, as she stepped back into in the quiet kitchen.

"Are you okay, Aunt Brenna?"

Brenna jumped in horror to see Evie by the door with her knapsack in her hand, looking impossibly pretty and school-girlish.

"What are you doing home?" Her stomach seized, her heart stopped.

What if she had come home ten minutes earlier?

Brenna had never felt such disgust, shame...even destroying the office property had been better behaviour. Could she tell? Did they leave any evidence?

"I only had first period at school today," Evie was saying. "Aunt Kayleigh said she'd take me to town. Want to come with?"

Where was the condom?

Glancing wildly around, Brenna couldn't see the foil wrapper. Had Brady taken it with him? What if - ?

"Are you all right, Aunt Brenna?" Evie asked.

"Why?"

"You're acting kind of weird."

Brenna realized she was peering into the garbage. "I don't know what I did with something," she explained.

"Do you want me to help you look?"

"No! No, that's fine. I'm sure it got taken care of. I should have a shower, I think," she said in a rush. "That would be good."

"OK." Evie looked quizzically at her. "Do you want to come with us to Elliott Lake?"

"Sure, fine," she stammered. "That would be good—nice. I'd like that." Brenna took a deep breath and smiled at Evie. "Sounds good."

The wrapper was right on top, partially covered by the condom and its contents. Brenna ran to check as soon as Evie left the room. With a handful of paper towels and a plastic bag, she shoved the evidence deeper into the bag, and washed the Kool-Aid cups, all the while still shaking her head over what had happened with Brady.

No one could ever find out how stupid she'd been.

*

"It seems the only thing I'm doing is spending time with you in the car," Brenna told Kayleigh as they headed south to Elliott Lake. She'd managed to calm her heart–rate; unsure of the increase was due to Brady or Evie's sudden appearance.

Evie was texting in the back seat next to her sister Kady, both oblivious to what had gone on in their kitchen only a short time ago.

Hopefully, they would remain oblivious.

"Sorry I wasn't up to going with you last night," Kayleigh said.

"I wish *I* hadn't gone to Woody's last night," Brenna admitted in a low voice.

"I bet."

"What did you hear?" Brenna's heart stopped at the thought of Kayleigh knowing about Brady in the kitchen.

Kayleigh's smirk became a wide smile. "I just heard that you had a little nap. In the ladies' room!"

"Oh, that." She couldn't stop the sound of relief in her voice.

"Why, what else happened?"

"Nothing, just...nothing."

"Bee! What happened?" Kayleigh demanded. "There's something you're not telling."

"Nothing," she said, trying to sound convincing. "I saw Missy and Colin and some other folks. Yes, I fell asleep but I didn't pass out, no matter what anyone said. I fell asleep. It was a really long day, especially with the time change and the flight."

"I'm sure it was," Kayleigh said with a laugh. "Other than your little impromptu nap, did you have a good time? Was it nice seeing everyone?"

"It was great seeing Missy and Colin." An image of Brady flashed through her mind and was swiftly set aside.

"That's what true friendship is. Of course, friends usually don't let that much time go by without seeing each other..."

"Thanks for bringing that up. Again."

"Just want to make sure you remember that so you won't stay away so long next time." Kayleigh grinned as she crested another big hill, the sensation sending tingles deep into Brenna's stomach. Driving the roads was like riding a roller coaster.

"I just got here and now you're talking about me leaving?"

"Are you planning on staying?" Kayleigh asked, turning with surprise and hope in her eyes.

"I don't know, Kay." Brenna sighed. "I don't know much about anything these days. Everything's happened so fast."

They both glanced in the backseat. Kady stared out the window, ears blocked by the sounds of music, but Evie glanced up from her texting and smiled. Brenna could tell Kayleigh was bursting to ask her about Toby, but after her morning, Brenna wanted nothing to do with men.

"Well, maybe you'll find something to keep you here," Kayleigh said cheerfully. "Meet anyone interesting last night?"

Brenna's heart jumped again. "Why? What did you hear?"

"Just that you were seen chatting to Joss Ryan."

"Who's that? Why would I want to talk to anyone? I'm married! I don't want to be meeting anyone new and younger...or older!"

Kayleigh's expression was similar to Evie's earlier in the kitchen. "I thought you were getting a divorce?"

"I am." She didn't want to tell Kayleigh about the email from Toby; talking about it would make it real and possibility lead to an admission of her time in the kitchen with Brady.

"You OK, Bee?"

Brenna took a deep breath, and then another. "I'm fine," she said with difficulty. "It's just been a lot to deal with."

"Things with Toby or coming home?"

"Both." She gave her sister a shy smile. "It's been a long time to be away. I'm realizing just how long."

Brenna turned back to the window, wishing she could confide in Kayleigh. There was so much on her mind, so many questions. She felt like a wire stretching to the breaking point; one quick move and she'd snap.

She'd always thought sex was supposed to be relaxing. It had been more calming dealing with multi-million dollar contracts and clients feeling entitled to those millions.

Maybe shopping would help. Something to take her mind off the mess her life had become.

Maybe she needed to find another job. At least then she wouldn't be home alone the next time a sexy nephew stopped by.

In Elliott Lake, Brenna trailed after the ever-complaining Kady as she fought with Evie about which stores to look at. She imagined her nieces loose in the stores on Robson Street in Vancouver.

They could come and visit me.

"They fight all the time," Kayleigh confided as she fingered through the racks of a little boutique. "Remind you of anyone?"

"I can see a little bit of Cat in Kady," Brenna admitted.

"I think she's more like Dory," Cayleigh grumbled.

"And yet you still want to spend time with her?"

"You should try this on, Aunt Brenna," Evie called, holding up a rust colored skirt. "And this." Both the skirt and the tunic-style shirt were loose and flowing.

"It's not really my style," Brenna said, taking a closer look. Most of her clothes were professional suits, in no-nonsense gray, black, and navy, with conservative blouses and shoes to match. "But pretty. I guess I need something for Addison's wedding."

Once the girls had an objective, the squabbling ceased as they focused all their efforts on outfitting Brenna, rather than annoying each other. And they were relentless, charging into every store they came across. Brenna was exhausted long before Kayleigh called it a day. It made for a pleasant, albeit expensive, afternoon as she was soon weighed down with bags full of new clothes.

Their last stop was the drugstore, where Brenna discovered Kady standing in front of the boxes of Clairol and L'Oreal hair colorant.

"I don't think you should color your hair," Brenna told her.

"It's not permanent," she argued. "Wouldn't I look better as a blonde?"

Brenna took a handful of her niece's long red hair in her fist. "Do you realize this particular red has come all the way from Ireland? Do you know how many women beg their colorists to give them this color? Don't you realize that this red hair is what truly marks you as a Skatt woman?"

"But I'm a Monroe, not a Skatt."

She frowned. "You're a Skatt. You've got the temper, the hair, and you're feistier than your Aunt Cat. Besides, only one Skatt woman ever colored her hair, and you know what happened to her?"

"No, who was it? What happened?"

"My sister Dory. And no one knows..." Brenna

widened her eyes at her niece.

Dory was born to create conflict. A colicky baby, she spent her days being passed around from arms to arms as all of Forest Hills tried to comfort her. By the time she was a teenager, she hated to be held, had problems with authority. Rebelling against the world, Dory had dyed her red hair black, pierced everything she could and came home from Toronto with tattoos. There were constant arguments with their mother and Maggie, breaking curfew, drunken stumbling up the stairs, shoplifting from the General Store, and getting picked up by the police in Sudbury for panhandling. Brenna remembered the desperate phone calls from Dory's teachers – asking how to control her, that she was wasting her potential, she needed to be tested to see if she's gifted, she may have ADHD.

No one had known what to do with Dory. No one had understood her.

And now no one knew a thing about her.

"You're full of shit," Kady laughed nervously.

"And you've got a potty mouth."

"Yes, but I'm a Skatt, so it's OK."

Kady didn't buy the hair dye. The last stop was the LCBO and Brenna bought half a dozen bottles of wine, one of Hendricks gin and one of vermouth.

She liked her Martinis.

"Ugh, wine?" Kady cried as she helped Brenna carry her bags to the car. "At least get something half decent, like Malibu or peach schnapps."

"And how old are you?"

"Fourteen."

"How do you know what's decent to drink?"

"Will you let me try it?"

"No, of course not."

"I bet Evie's going to drink at her graduation party," Kady needled in an annoying younger sister voice.

"And Evie's a lot older than you. So – a party." Brenna met Evie's eyes in the rearview mirror. "Anyone interesting going to be there?"

"She likes Braa-dy," Kady's voice chimed in from the backseat.

"Brady who?" she asked, before the realization hit her like a sledgehammer. "Brady Todd? You can't like him!"

"You remember him, do you?" Kayleigh laughed. "Seamus' nephew. Real cutie-patootie these days."

"It's true. He's totally hot," Kady chimed in. "But

he won't look twice at Evie."

She forced herself to turn around and noticed Evie's pink cheeks. It was a small town, there could only be one Brady Todd.

"You really like Brady?" she asked weakly.

Chapter Fourteen

Cat

Sisters annoy, interfere, criticize. Indulge in monumental sulks, in huffs, in snide remarks. Borrow. Break. Monopolize the bathroom. Are always underfoot. But if catastrophe should strike, sisters are there. Defending you against all comers.

-Pam Brown

Before heading home, Cat stopped at the I.G.A at the bottom of the hill to talk to Maggie.

"Peter Ebans is an ass and Brenna's been running to Marcus with our problems," Cat announced as she caught sight of Maggie loading a bin with warm baguettes.

Heads swiveled in Cat's direction.

"Why don't you come in the back and talk instead of sharing dirty laundry with the entire store?" Maggie invited, a quick flick of her eye the only warning of her anger.

Cat trotted after her, almost bouncing with rage.

"What did Peter say?" Maggie asked as she led Cat through the employee door deep into the bakery department. Fragrant scents assaulted Cat as she paused to inspect a cake, comparing it smugly with her own.

"He said—I saw him in Home Depot and he said something nasty about Mom and I told him to mind his own business and he said he would but we kept coming to them with problems so I thought it was probably Brenna because—"

"I asked our grandfather for a loan." Maggie pulled a pan of muffins from a huge oven.

"—she would be the only one stupid enough to do that, but maybe...What?" Cat had to be hearing things. "What did you say?"

"I asked Marcus for a loan," Maggie explained, her face red from the heat. "For Evie's school tuition."

"You...Why?"

Maggie swiped her hair off her forehead with an angry arm. “Because I need the money, Cat,” she said with an exasperated shrug. “Why do you think? I didn’t want to, but it seemed easier than going to the bank.”

Why didn’t she come to me? Cat immediately felt betrayed but a rational thought quickly replaced it. *I wouldn’t have been able to help her.*

“I don’t understand.”

“It’s not that difficult.”

“I mean, why would you go to him? How much do you need?” Cat said in a low voice, this time conscious of others within hearing distance. “Why haven’t you said anything to me?”

“Because this is something between me and Mike. I can take care of my own kids, Cat. I took care of you and Brenna and Dory and I can take care of my kids too.” Maggie’s lips were tight with frustration. “This isn’t something I’m proud of, so the fewer people that know, the better. Damn Peter for saying anything.”

“But, Maggie...”

“Sending Evie to school is going to cost everything we’ve got. Add in Addison’s wedding and we’re tapped out. She’s got a student loan, but it won’t be enough. I thought Marcus might help, like he did for Brenna."

"He *what*?"

"He helped Brenna with school," Maggie sighed. "And he's going to help Evie."

"But...really?"

"Really. He's been a godsend, Cat. I know you don't think much of him, but Marcus is nothing like Peter. He's totally mellowed. He's a good man."

"Who paid for Brenna's school. Jeezus. She really does get everything!"

Maggie rolled her eyes. "Why do you make everything about Brenna? This has nothing to do with her."

"She always makes it about herself. I can't believe you went to him - he did nothing to help us when Mom died!"

"That was a long time ago. He's changed. And I don't think he's well. He's trying to make amends."

"By paying you off?" Cat knew that was the wrong thing to say as soon as the words tumbled out of her mouth. "I didn't mean that."

"No, I'm sure you did. I went to him for help, because there was no one else. What would you have me do? Tell Evie she can't go to school? Addison can't have the wedding she's always dreamed about? What about Kady and McKenna? And Clare? What will they have to give up just because Mike and I can't make enough money to give them everything they want?"

Cat blinked at Maggie's tone. She and Mike had married at seventeen; Maggie took an extra two years to finish high school. She had already taken over parenting the sisters when Roger left, so there had been no teenage years full of angst and first loves for her, no free and easy twenty-something like Cat had because Maggie always had responsibilities and dependents heaped on her.

Cat had never heard her sister complain about her situation.

"Kayleigh doesn't know anything about this, and neither does Brenna so I would appreciate you keeping it to yourself." Cat had never heard Maggie sound so exhausted.

"Yeah, but...are you and Mike okay? Financially, now if he's helping?" It wasn't possible for Maggie and Mike not to be okay; they were peanut butter and raspberry jam – so good apart but even better together.

"Money's always going to be tight," Maggie said

simply. "Five kids cost a lot of money."

"But...Maggie, I could..."

All Cat could think of was the house. Selling the house would solve some of Maggie's financial worries.

How could she not help her sister?

"I don't need your help, Cat. You've got enough on your plate. All those animals," Maggie said with an affectionate smile.

"I could sell the house." Her brain froze with the thought, but she had to say it, had to offer, even if she couldn't imagine how to begin.

"You want to open a bed and breakfast. Why would you want to sell it?" Maggie turned to another over, pulling out a sheet cake.

"For you. To give you money. It's partly yours, you know."

Maggie sighed. "Actually, it's not."

"Why not?"

"It's our father's house, Cat. It's the marital home. They never divorced before Mom died. She didn't have a will—it's still his house. Where ever he is." Maggie's voice was a mixture of disgust and defeat, which shocked Cat more than her words.

"No...That can't be right."

In the heated bustle of the I.G.A bakery, Maggie looked older than her forty-three years. “It is. Unfortunately. So even if you wanted to sell it, which I know you don’t, you can’t. And if I were to let you, which I wouldn’t. None of us can sell it, unless we find our father and get him to sign it over to us.”

Chapter Fifteen

Brenna

"I know my older sister loves me because she gives me all her old clothes and has to go out and buy new ones."

—Author unknown, attributed to a 4-year-old named Lauren

Kayleigh dropped Brenna off at Maggie's just as their sister drove in with a load of groceries. She and Evie carried the bags in as Kady scampered away with a feeble excuse.

Brenna surreptitiously avoided the part of the counter Brady had pushed her against and worried that Maggie would somehow sense what she had done. But her sister seemed preoccupied, no doubt tired from the long day at work

It had been bad enough Brady was Seamus' nephew, but now he was suddenly the boy Evie liked, too? Liked? Loved? Were they dating?

"So how was shopping?" Maggie asked as she stored a big box of *Frosted Flakes* in a high cupboard. "Clare isn't supposed to eat these."

"Duly noted. It was fun. I liked getting to know the girls."

"They grow up so quick," Maggie mused. "Evie was four, I think, when you left. And I was pregnant with Kady. You being gone doesn't seem that long when you look at it that way." She placed a few cans of Alpha-ghetti beside Brenna and pointed to another cupboard. "They go there."

"It never seemed that long to me." Brenna stacked the pasta beside cans of ravioli. "I really didn't mean to let so much time go by, Maggie. There was always school, and then in the summer I was working all the time to pay for it. I hardly had time to go out—"

"I doubt that." Maggie laughed, trying to find room in the fridge for a bag of apples. "Young girl away from her family for the first time..."

"Yes, it was one big party." Maggie must have

picked up on Brenna's sarcasm because she poked her head out of the fridge.

"What are you saying, Bee? Were you okay? Were you lonely?"

Brenna smiled sadly at her astonishment."I was fine."

Maggie shut the fridge with more force than necessary. "You forget who you're talking to. How bad was it, really?"

Brenna shrugged her shoulders, unwilling to disclose how unhappy she had been. But Maggie seemed to sense what she wasn't telling her.

"Bee, I'm sorry. Getting out of this place was the best thing for you. You were so smart and capable, I never imagined you'd have problems being on your own. I never thought to worry about you. I figured you'd take over the world if we gave you the chance."

"Haven't really gotten to that yet."

Maggie slapped her hands on the counter. "You were my responsibility after Mom died. I let you go without a thought as to how you would make out. You were Brenna, the strong and smart one, so things were going to be easy for you, like they always had been."

"Things were never easy for me," Brenna told her

wryly. "I think you're mistaking me for Cat."

"Bee, you always got everything you wanted. You were so smart at school—"

"I worked for those grades."

"—you had Seamus. Who you..." There was a very pregnant pause until Maggie came up with the appropriate word, "...you *acquired* from Cat."

"She took him from me first."

"He wasn't anyone's to take."

"Exactly. He made his own decision to break up with her. Why does everyone still blame me?"

"Bee, he didn't have a chance. Cat could never compete with you."

Brenna stared at Maggie, still holding a box of spaghetti. "Are you kidding? That's all Cat ever did. She tried to take everything from me. Everything—boys, clothes, your attention, Mom's love."

"Brenna, Cat *worshipped* you! You were her big sister and she just wanted to be like you. Can't you see that?"

"No. No, I can't," Brenna said flatly. "I think you've got the wrong sister."

Their conversation was interrupted by McKenna and Clare bursting through the door like a Molotov cocktail, followed by a harried Mike. It was clear the girls were in the midst of a major argument.

"Enough," Maggie ordered, waving a box of *Kraft Dinner* at her daughters like a baton as the screams became incoherent. "We do not come through the door like that. Simmer down, the both of you!"

"She started it!" The accusation shot from their mouths almost in unison.

"I don't care who started what, only that it stops *now*!" Maggie raised her voice only once but that was all it took. "McKenna, go to your room and make sure your homework is done. Clare, go get the dogs in and feed them. Quietly, both of you, and without any fighting."

With foul expressions directed at each other, the girls separated. Mike stopped hovering by the door and came over to Brenna with a chastened grin.

"They were like that when I picked them up," he told Maggie. "Couldn't do a thing with them."

"Maybe if you weren't such a teddy bear around them, they might understand that you mean it when you get mad at them," Maggie admonished him. But she said it so affectionately that Brenna's heart melted a little. For them to still be together, in love with each other—to still *like* each other—was downright awe-inspiring. She smiled at them with admiration.

"What?" Mike asked with real concern. "Do I have lunch still on me? It was a meatball sub and it was plenty messy."

"No, you're fine." Brenna laughed, happy to be finished with the conversation about Cat. "I just think you both are amazing parents."

"Of course we are," Mike said, throwing an arm around Maggie. "We're fuckin' awesome! Shit," he hissed, glancing around to make sure the girls weren't in earshot. Maggie playfully pushed him away with a shake of her head.

"I've never really seen what a good marriage is like," Brenna mused. "Dad was gone before I could - "

"That wasn't a good marriage."

"They had to love each other."

"Roger Ebans loved himself and that's about it," Maggie said with real venom in her voice.

"Let's get off *that* topic," Mike muttered. "Need a beer, Bren? Mag?"

"I wish you remembered him the way he really was," Maggie continued, ignoring Mike's offer. "You idolized him and he didn't deserve it. He didn't deserve it at all. Grandpa Earl was a much better father to us than he ever was."

"What, in between suicide attempts?"

Earl Skatt had continued the notoriety of his family with his nineteen suicide attempts; none of them successful. Fortunately, he'd never injured anyone beside himself. He died after driving into the side of the bank while trying to avoid hitting a squirrel.

"You were *three,* Brenna, when he left us. He *left* us—a family of five girls with a mother who could barely take care of herself, let alone her children. Cat was two, you were three, Dory was almost seven—"

"I know how old we were!"

"You don't remember what it was like! Cat wouldn't stop crying and Dory kept getting in trouble in school—I had to go visit the principal for my little sister because Mom had locked herself in her room! I was fourteen!" She shook the box of granola bars in her hand.

"I guess I never thought about what it was like for you," Brenna said, echoing Maggie's own words.

Maggie dropped the box and pulled her close. "I'm not fighting with you," she said into Brenna's hair. "I don't know how long you're here and I'm not wasting any time fighting over something as worthless as the container of sperm who impregnated our mother."

Brenna stood locked in Maggie's embrace for long minutes. She smoothed her hand over Maggie's back, silently communicating her apologies. She would never be able to replay her sister's devotion. Sorry didn't even come close.

The phone rang, starting them out of their embrace. Thrusting a bottle of beer into Brenna's hands, Mike, jumped to answer it. "Hey, Cat."

Maggie released Brenna who twisted open the cap on the beer and gave it to her.

"I'm sorry I jumped on you, Bee. I had a crappy day. And the girls fighting never helps."

"I'm sure having me here isn't helping either."

"What are you talking about?" She seemed surprised at the comment. "I love having you here! Why wouldn't I want you here?"

Mike waved to catch their attention. "Really? Let me check with the boss." Without moving the phone away from his mouth, Mike called to Maggie. "What's Evie doing tonight?"

"Working. Why?"

Mike's eyes lit on Brenna. "Bren," he cried. "You can still play, can't you?"

"Play what?"

"Baseball, what else. We've got a big game tonight."

Chapter Sixteen

Cat

"Sisters are probably the most competitive relationship within the family, but once the sisters are grown, it becomes the strongest relationship."

—Margaret Mead

Cat watched her family tumble out of Maggie's old green van. McKenna argued with Kady, both as feisty as their flaming hair color; little Clare clung to Kayleigh's hand, even as she struggled in vain to get out of her car seat. Maggie, calm and relaxed, and Mike, as smiling and stalwart as ever, happy be playing ball.

And Brenna, in a pair of tight black Capri pants and dwarfed by one of Mike's old baseball shirts, glanced around nervously.

Mike led Brenna over to Cat with little Clare tagging along. "Here she is," he cried jovially. "Our star player for the night."

"Please don't put that kind of pressure on me," Brenna begged. "I haven't played in years."

"I'll be the star player," Clare announced, throwing her arms wide.

"In a few years, you betcha you will be," Mike told his daughter, pulling at the red pigtails.

"You used to be OK," Cat conceded. Showing support for the team was the responsibility of the manager, even if the player was unwanted by the team manager. "But you're not playing," she said to Clare.

"When I'm big like you I will," Clare replied with the utter confidence only a six-year-old could have.

"Only if you're lucky and listen to everything your Daddy tells you."

"I already do that."

"Clare, don't you have something to say to Aunt Cat," Mike prompted.

"Thank you for bringing me cookies, Aunt Cat,"

she said, sounding as sweet and angelic as she appeared. "They were some good shit."

"Clare!"

"That's what you said about them, Daddy," she said with an innocent expression, then turned to Cat, who was trying hard not to laugh. "You told me to listen to him!"

"Go sit with your mother," Mike said in a strangled voice. "And no swearing!" With a guileless grin, Clare skipped away. "Fuck a duck, she's going to be the death of me because Maggie's gonna fucking kill me!" His hands covered his head like he was warding off a blow when he realized what he'd said. "Jesus, I've got to stop using that language in front of her."

Cat couldn't contain her laughter. Glancing at Brenna, she saw her sister's face light up with an amused smile.

Cat was torn on how that made her feel.

"You're going to have big trouble with her," she said to Mike with a nod of her chin towards Clare scampering up the bleachers to Maggie.

"You're telling me. She's worse than the rest put together. Just give me a boy, I kept telling Maggie. But did she listen?"

"I think that might be on you," Brenna ventured. "Sex is determined by the male."

"So it's my fucking fault," Mike groaned. "Now I've got all these girls with their hormones and monthly friends and pigtails and Dora fucking the Explorer—"

"I think you might be watching the wrong movies if she's doing that," Cat said with a laugh.

"Baseball! I need to focus on baseball, not my potty-mouth kindergartener or the next freak attack Addison is going to pull over this wedding."

"Baseball," Cat agreed, giving Mike a pat on the shoulder. "It'll be OK. You'll get through this. And then you can have a beer."

"It's no wonder I drink so much," he mumbled.

"Why don't you go warm up?" Cat suggested to Brenna, looking for a way to have her sister stop the nervous hovering. "Missy'll play catch with you."

Brenna nodded and headed out to the field, Evie's glove dangling by her hand.

"She'll be okay," Mike said. Cat wasn't sure if he was trying to convince her or himself.

"Probably," she admitted. After her talk with

Maggie, Cat looked at Mike differently. He had been twenty when Maggie got pregnant and there had been no hesitation in his reaction. He picked marriage and a family, even if it meant giving up the possibility of a career in baseball.

And it had been more than a possibility. When Maggie found out she was expecting, Mike had just been recruited by the Barrie Baycats, a semi-professional team. Coaches and scouts watched his every move, with excited talk about him going to the next level.

When Maggie told him about the baby, Mike made the eight hour drive back to Forest Hills and never finished the season.

“Get under it, Pam,” Mike called as she missed an easy catch.

“You’re a good coach,” Cat told him affectionately.

“What?” He turned to her with confusion.

“Nothing. Let’s play ball.”

Cat was torn when the game began; she hadn’t wanted Brenna to be brought in as a backup player because she was afraid she would be better than Cat. She had been good during high school – she might have continued playing in university. She might have been captain of the team and how would Cat look playing beside that?

But as co-coach of the team, Cat didn't want Brenna to be bad either, because that wasn't good for the team.

The first few innings were uneventful, except for Mike's beautiful three run home run. Cat watched him round the bases gracefully, a huge grin on his face, looking younger than his forty-six years. Brenna didn't do anything to call attention to herself and Cat was happy.

"Pam, you're up, Joss and Brenna on deck," Cat called at the top of the fourth inning. Brenna dutifully went over to where a tangle of aluminum and wooden bats were propped up against the fence. She ducked out of the way of Joss as he took mighty practice swings, the width of his chest and sizeable biceps stretching the thin cotton of the shirt to its limit.

But either Joss didn't have the sense to avoid Brenna or she wasn't paying attention because when she finally picked up a bat and swung it, she almost hit him in the head.

"Jesus!" he cried, bouncing off the screen in an effort to move away. "Watch it!"

"You watch it," she retorted with more spirit than Cat had heard from her since she had been back. "I stayed out of your way."

"Not enough," he muttered.

The crack of the bat signaled Pam had hit safely to first. Cat glanced over to see Brenna watching as Joss step up to the plate. "Looks pretty good, doesn't he?"

"Not really my type," Brenna replied coolly.

"Probably not," Cat agreed. "He doesn't seem to like you, either."

She folded her fingers into the metal screen and silently watched Joss swing at the first two pitches. Brenna stood beside her.

"How were you feeling this morning?" Cat asked with a smirk.

"What? Why?" she asked nervously.

"Toilet time last night?"

"I didn't pass out," she said firmly. "It was a long day. I fell asleep."

"Must have been *really* tired to fall asleep on the john."

"I was. It was a long flight, a long drive." Brenna paused and Cat thought she was finished. "It was a bad week at home. In Vancouver."

Cat couldn't keep Seamus' remonstrations of last night echoing in her head. *She just broke up with her husband. You of all people should have some sympathy for her.*

"Are you okay?" she asked.

Brenna glanced over, her expression wary. "I'll be fine."

Cat was annoyed at the dismissive tone in Brenna's voice. Kayleigh and Maggie had asked her to make an effort, and here was Brenna blowing her off, just like she always did. Why didn't they make Brenna try? "Always have to handle everything yourself, don't you?" she muttered.

"Who else is supposed to handle it?" Brenna shot back, sounding just as irritated. "I've been on my own for years."

"Wasn't my decision to stay away so long."

"Stop being such a martyr," she snapped. "I never once saw you trying to get a hold of me. In fourteen years, all I got from you were wedding invitations. You made no secret that you were happy I left. How long did it take you to go after Seamus once I was gone?"

"Who says I had to go after him?" Cat drawled. "You're up to bat."

Without another word, Brenna stepped up to the plate and hit a hard line drive that shot straight into the glove of Brady on third.

"Hey, there, thanks," Brady called to Brenna, as he tossed the ball back to Mike. "You woke me up this time."

The smile vanished from Cat's face when she noticed how Brady was grinning at Brenna.

"Brady's hitting on you already," Missy said to Brenna as she sat down on the bench. "The boy works fast."

"No, he's—it's nothing. I can't believe he's all grown up." Her laugh sounded nervous and Cat moved closer to listen.

"And grown up in such a nice way," Missy laughed. "Yummy. There's lots to tell you about that bad boy."

"Maybe I shouldn't hear it. I just found out Evie likes him." Cat heard the odd catch in Brenna's voice and was reminded of years ago, when Brenna confessed to her that Seamus was now her boyfriend.

"You knew I liked him!" Cat had cried with frustration. She had known the day would come, when Seamus and Brenna would become Seamus-

and-Brenna but never expected it to hurt so much.

"But I love him." Guilt and regret and what might have been sympathy had mixed in Brenna's voice, creating a concoction that had done nothing to ease Cat's rage. She had leaped across the bed at her sister, forcing Kayleigh to break up the fight.

It hadn't been until the next day that Cat had realized Brenna had not thrown a punch or a slap to defend herself.

"You Skatt girls can't get enough of the Todd boys, can you?" Cat heard Colin say to Brenna with a guffaw.

I'm the only one with a Todd boy and it's going to stay that way, Cat vowed as she stepped up to the plate.

She was satisfied to hit the ball right over Brady's head.

Still a better ball player than Brenna.

Chapter Seventeen

Brenna

"If you don't understand how a woman could both love her sister dearly and want to wring her neck at the same time, then you were probably an only child."

—Linda Sunshine

When Brenna arrived with the rest of the team at Woody's after the game, she found Brady waiting for her outside the ladies' room.

Brenna had been so nervous about playing that she hadn't noticed Brady on third base until he caught her line drive. After that, he had seemed to be everywhere—hitting the ball straight to her, heckling her when she was up to bat, and teasing her mercilessly the one time she managed to get on base.

"Why didn't you tell me you were playing?" Brady asked with a big smile as Brenna wiped her hands on her pants to dry them. Brady spoke loudly over the laughter and music; tonight the Tragically Hip had been replaced by the electronic drumbeats of 90s dance music.

Brady would have been a gawky little boy when this song was first released.

"Why didn't you tell me you only sleep with women over thirty?" Brenna shot back. Missy had told her stories of Brady's pursuit of the women of Forest Hills.

Brady's grin widened. "Aw, c'mon now, you're telling me you're not twenty-nine? Besides, I didn't do any sleeping." He winked.

She remembered the warmth of his hands against her that morning, holding her up against the counter. Swallowing audibly, her entire body felt like it was heating up.

"So," Brady leaned in closer, putting his arm against the wall behind her, effectively boxing her in.

He smelled of sweat and beer and Axe body spray.

"No."

"No...what...?"

"Whatever you're going to suggest. You're Seamus' nephew and Evie..."

"What about Evie?"

He *smirked.*

"Nothing. No. Just no." She put her hand on his chest and was about to push him away when a growly voice interrupted.

"You not learn your lesson about bothering women?"

Brady jerked his arm away like she was on fire. Brenna saw the glowering expression of Joss Ryan over Brady's shoulder as his face transformed into a kid caught cheating by the teacher, complete with sullen expression, pouty mouth and defiant up thrust jaw. He looked young. And not at all appealing.

"Whatever," he spat at Joss. "Later, Brenna," he added, and that was the last she saw of Brady.

Brenna glanced from Brady's retreating back to Joss scowling after him. "What was that all about?" she declared. "He wasn't bothering me, and even if he was, I can take care of myself."

"He was bothering *me*," he said.

Brenna wondered if Joss had any other expressions other than irritable. He had to be one of the most unpleasant men she'd ever met.

Why wasn't she walking away then?

"Why is that my problem?"

"He should stick to playing with kids his own age."

As Joss stormed off, Brenna caught sight of Cat standing by the bar with a smirk on her face.

"Are you always such an asshole?" Brenna called, hoping it was loud enough for Joss to hear.

Joss stopped and looked over his shoulder. "Pardon me?"

"You heard me." Only the Skatt temper would make Brenna insult someone who towered over her by a foot and looked like he was a card-carrying member of the Hells Angels motorcycle gang.

With measured steps, Joss returned to stand in front of her. "I'd like you to repeat that." He crossed his arms, his baseball shirt straining to contain his biceps.

Brenna flicked her gaze; Cat was still watching.

"I asked if you were always such an asshole,"

Brenna said in her best litigator's voice.

"Only when someone brings it out of me."

"So this is my fault." Brenna felt something break loose inside her, allowing every emotion she'd pushed down deep to come flooding into her chest, and spew out with ugly words. "I'm fucking sick of it!"

Joss looked surprised at her outburst.

She'd had enough of the blame, the guilt, of always feeling the need to apologize. Brenna hated apologizing. "I'm sick of everything always being *my* fault. There's no way in hell I'm the only one who does anything wrong."

"Well, the way you're acting -"

"Don't tell me what to do," Brenna snapped. "Do you appreciate being told what to do?"

She didn't wait for an answer.

"All this bullshit about how I never came home. Did anyone bother to ask *why* I never came home? No one gave me a reason to! They didn't need me. No one wanted me here! They were happy with their lives, content to go about their business without me. No one needed me here. If it wasn't for the gossip Kayleigh gave them, I'm sure this place would have forgotten I existed."

Brenna stopped for a quick breath, her voice rising in volume and strength as she continued her tirade. She had no idea where it was coming from, why she was directing her anger at Joss, but it felt good. Really good.

"They all thought I was the smart one, the responsible one, but it's no *fun* being alone halfway across the country! What do they want from me? *You* made it clear I don't belong here. I don't, because I've changed. I'm not the same old Brenna but no one sees that! They all expect me to be the same old Brenna, all bookish and boring. Well, I'm not. I don't want to be. I don't know who I am but it's about time I had some fun because God knows I haven't had a lot lately! And I'm allowed to have fun. I deserve it, because I've had a pretty shitty week!" Despite the quake in her knees, her chin jutted out defiantly.

There was a long, indeterminate pause. Brenna stared at Joss, waiting for his response until she realized what had burst out of her and she deflated like a balloon. "Oh, God, I shouldn't have -"

"Would you like a tissue for your issue?" Joss asked slowly, his face expressionless.

"What?"

"My problem," he said, crossing his arms across his chest. "Is with Brady Todd. I don't like how he treats women. I caught him making a huge play for my sister. She's married with two little kids at home and he thought he had a chance with her." Joss shook his head. "I don't think much of him or his morals and frankly, it pisses me off to see him play with women the way he does. But if that's someone you're interested in, if you're looking to have some *fun* because you're mad at the world and your family and that husband of yours for obviously treating you like shit, then Brady is your guy."

Brenna's shoulders hunched as Joss continued.

"But I'm not sorry I got him away from you, and I'm sure I'll accept your apology when you realize that he's not the fun little boy toy you think he is. You seem like a nice woman, smart and as cute as hell so why would I want to let *him* get his hands on you when you seem to be someone *I'd* like to get to know?"

"He's not," Brenna said quietly. "I made a mistake."

Did he really say she was cute?

Joss gave a brisk nod. His face relaxed, the scowl vanishing , turning him into an surprisingly attractive man."Everyone's entitled to make a mistake."

"Just one?" Brenna gave a bark of laughter, surprising them both. "I've made tons and that's just since I've been back."

"I don't think you're doing too badly. This is a tough place to break into." Joss' face seemed to soften even more, and Brenna noticed the brilliant blue of his eyes. "Need to get anything else off your chest?"

She dropped her head as her cheeks flamed. "No. I shouldn't have said all those things to you. I didn't mean -"

"No worries." They stood awkwardly and as embarrassed as she was, Brenna didn't want to walk away. "I apologize for interrupting," Joss finally said.

"I wasn't aware of Brady's reputation when I...when I met him the other night," Brenna admitted. "I just thought—I used to babysit him. How bad could he be?"

"People change. You said so yourself." Joss searched Brenna's face but she found she didn't mind the scrutiny.

"I did?" she managed.

"I thought you were supposed to be the smart one."

Joss' mouth curled up with a ghost of a smile. He turned away, throwing a last comment over his shoulder. "And, by the way, I would have never forgotten you existed."

Chapter Eighteen

Cat

More than Santa Claus, your sister knows when you've been bad and good.

—Linda Sunshine

"You ready to go?" Seamus asked. Woody's had cleared out and Cat had cleaned the ladies room like she usually did. There had been no chance for her to talk to Seamus during the day, and truthfully, she didn't have the inclination to get into things again. What could she say; that she was worried her sister was going to steal her boyfriend? Cat felt like she was back in high school.

But she had seen the way Joss Ryan had been

watching Brenna all night, and the way Brenna avoided looking at him. Maybe she didn't have to worry about Brenna and Seamus after all.

"You just giving me a ride home or are you coming in?" she asked Seamus with bated breath. She hadn't talked to him all day and now, when things seemed calm between them, was afraid of saying the wrong thing.

"Thought I'd come with you." His lopsided smile still melted Cat's heart. "That okay?"

"Sure." She turned so he wouldn't see her own smile. "No problem."

Taylor Swift's latest song played during the short ride back to the house. Cat thought about all the boy problems the poor girl had and how she had the courage to tell the whole world about them in her songs. Maybe it made things easier putting it all out there.

She doubted it.

They were going to have to talk about the baby issue. Seamus seemed to have gotten over his anger with her – or maybe he was mad and doing a good job of hiding it.

She couldn't tell. But she knew she hated fighting

with him and wasn't in the mood to rehash things. She wanted a baby. So did he, but he thought marriage needed to be involved. Seamus was determined, but no one was as stubborn as Cat.

They were going to have to talk and try and resolve it and –

"I don't want to talk about the baby stuff tonight," Seamus said, interrupting her thoughts. "I know we have to, but I got pretty upset and now I'm not and I'd like to stay that way for at least tonight. Maybe we can talk about it tomorrow."

"Or maybe the next day," Cat suggested, hiding her smile of relief.

The dogs greeted Seamus eagerly at the door and he spent a few minutes with them. Cat was happy that he liked her dogs since she didn't think she could be with someone who wasn't an animal person. That had been the only common thread in all the men she had been involved with.

"I heard something in the bar tonight that I didn't like," Seamus said, following her the kitchen and eyeing the two cakes she had baked earlier.

"Don't even think it," Cat warned. "They're for Addison. But if you go over with me she'll give you a piece."

"What kind are they?" He poked a finger into the icing of the nearest before she could stop him.

"Hummingbird—pecan, pineapple and banana—and that one is vanilla chai. They both have cream cheese frosting."

"I know," he said, his eyes bright and a finger in his mouth. "Yum."

Cat loved him so much.

Would marrying him really be that bad?

Seamus must have been encouraged by her expression because he slid his arms around her waist. "What else have you got for me?"

"What do you want?" She felt his warm breath on the side of her neck and arched to give him better access as he dropped a kiss on the exposed skin.

"You." His hands traveled up to caress her breasts under the Woody's baseball shirt. Cat was conscious of being sweaty and smelling like beer and wings.

"I have to let the dogs out."

"Already done." His lips trailed kisses along the side of her neck, always a favorite spot.

"I have to let them back in." She was finding it difficult to concentrate.

"They can wait. It's a nice night." He turned her to face him then and there were no more excuses as he kissed her. Not that she wanted an excuse. Being in Seamus' arms like this, kissing him—there was no place she'd rather be.

Or maybe there was. "Here?" Cat squeaked as he pulled off her T-shirt. Living on her own in such a big house meant that everywhere was fair game and she and Seamus had certainly explored the various rooms, but never in the kitchen. "I cook in here."

"You better turn off the smoke detector then," Seamus laughed as he undid her jeans. "'Cause I'm going to set you on fire."

"That's awful!"

"I thought it was pretty good," he argued as her jeans followed the shirt onto the floor.

"You need new lines if you're going to be picking up women."

"No plans to do that." Cat felt his fingers unclasp her bra.

"In the kitchen though?"

"You want me to stop?" He lifted his head and dropped his hands.

"No!" Cat gasped. "Forget I said anything."

"Didn't hear a thing. You cleaned your floor didn't you?" he asked, as he pulled her down. She couldn't find the energy to protest even if she wanted to.

Afterwards, Seamus made pillows out of their clothes and they lay together on the cool floor. He smoothed Cat's hair where it stuck to her cheek.

"You make me very happy," she whispered.

"Even when I piss you off by hugging your sister?"

Cat wanted to talk about Brenna even less than she wanted to talk about the baby issue. She raised her eyebrows. "Do you think now is best time to talk about this?"

Seamus laughed. "Probably not." He was curled beside her, one arm thrown across her belly and snaked his fingers along her side. "But I want to make sure we're cool. I love you, Cat. You. Not Brenna. Brenna is a friend, the same way I care about Maggie and Kayleigh."

"What about Dory?" Cat tested him.

"Eh," he shrugged. "I haven't had much use for her since she tried to kiss me when I was ten."

"You never told me that!" she cried, throwing off his arm and sitting up.

"It's nothing I'm proud of," Seamus pulled her back. "She was what, thirteen or something and even if I had liked girls then, I was too scared of her to kiss back. She laughed at me," he confessed. "Called me a little boy."

"The bitch!"

"Which is why I never said anything. I don't need to be another reason for conflict between the sisters."

"You're not the reason," Cat told him, feeling guilty. "Well, not the *only* reason."

"Well, I wish I wasn't any of the reason."

"It's not our fault you find all the Skatt women irresistible," she teased.

"Yep, I'm just counting the minutes until Kayleigh gives me the green light. You are so gone, then," he joked.

Cat laughed, thinking about how both Maggie and Kayleigh had always been like big sisters to Seamus and his brothers. "I wish Kayleigh was happy."

Seamus looked at her strangely. "Cat, you know your sister is—that she doesn't like men, right?" he asked tentatively.

"She's never admitted it, but I know that's what everyone thinks."

"Well, because it's true. She's been with Erica Anderson for years now."

"Erica! They're friends—they have been since high school."

"I think they're more than friends now."

"No! Really? She's never said anything..." Cat raised herself on her elbows to look at him with disbelief.

"She's never said anything about it? Have you ever asked her?"

"No, I just thought she tell us when she was ready."

"Maybe she's waiting for you to be ready."

Cat mulled the thought over as she lay back down, comfortable even if the floor was hard and becoming a bit cold. "Really? Kayleigh and Erica?"

"I always see them at Erica's place." Erica lived across the road from Seamus.

"They hang out. They're friends."

"Do friends hang out until after midnight most nights?" he wanted to know.

"You do."

"Because I'm usually in bed with you at that time."

"Oh. Wow. Way to go Kayleigh," Cat mused.

"You're...okay...with this?"

"Why wouldn't I be?" she demanded. "Aren't you?"

"Hey, I love Kayleigh as much as the rest of you do and I want her to be happy. But there must be a reason she hasn't told any of you."

"I can't think of any. Maggie would be fine...I couldn't care less who she's doing as long as she's getting some. Except for you." She narrowed her eyes at Seamus, recalling his earlier comment. "I don't want you to be doing her."

"I don't want to be doing anyone but you," he told me, kissing her shoulder. "Can we get up now?"

"Hey, you're the one who insisted on the floor." Cat let him help her to her feet.

"You weren't complaining. You complained about the counter..."

"Only for a moment," she said, putting her arms around his waist. They stood there for a minute, naked and wrapped in each other's arms.

"This is nice." Seamus rested his chin on the top of her head. "It could be nice all the time."

"Seamus..." Cat tried to push away, but he held firm, his arms tightening around her.

"I'm not asking, but will you at least think about it? I love you, Cat and I don't care about your past. It doesn't even bother me to see Tommy in the bar anymore."

"It bothered you?" She craned her neck to see his face. "You never told me that."

"I'm not the jealous type," he assured her. "Never have been. But the guy can be a dick. Knowing you were with him..."

"I made a mistake. I can admit that."

"I don't want this to be another one. Letting go of us, just because you're afraid -"

"I'm not afraid." She managed to break free of his embrace this time, but stood shivering, her arms wrapped around herself.

"Then what are you? Not many women would choose to be a single mother when they already have a man who loves them. And can provide for them. And who wants to be a dad to their kid."

"I thought we weren't going to talk about this tonight?" Cat said sullenly. She didn't want a heated discussion now. She wanted simple and happy and being able to slide into bed with Seamus tonight. She didn't have the energy to argue with him.

Seamus threw up his hands and stepped back. “End of discussion. I’m just asking you to think about it. We both want the same thing, Cat. And we love each other. We’re good together. Think about it? Please?”

How could she say no? It was a simple request, she wasn’t promising anything. Giving a quick nod, she caught the smile of relief on his face before bending to grab her shirt off the floor.

“Was that stuff about Kayleigh what you wanted to tell me before?” she asked to change the subject. “You said you heard something in the bar.”

“Oh, yeah. Your underwear is on the stove,” he pointed out. “Good thing it was off or the smoke alarm really would have gone off.”

Cat pulled on her jeans, stuffing her panties in the pocket. “You’re going to burn my house down because you want to try new positions,” she grumbled, happy to be off the baby subject.

“Same position, new room,” he corrected, pulling on his own pants, also commando. “So, about what I heard tonight. I don’t think you’ll like it. It’s about Brenna.”

“I don’t like most things about her these days,”

she said with mock cheerfulness.

"Yes, well, people are saying she hooked up with someone."

"She's been here, what? Two days? How could she hook up with someone? Who was it supposed to be?" Cat asked, curious despite the disbelief.

"Brady."

"No!"

"This morning apparently," Seamus said, checking the clock on the stove. "Or rather yesterday morning. Friday. At Maggie's."

"You're joking! Please be joking." Cat implored him. What was Brenna thinking? Brady was cute and sexy but he's a *kid*."

How did she...? If Cat was being honest, she'd say part of her was jealous.

The other part wanted to run and hide from what was certainly going to be nuclear-size fallout when the news broke to Maggie.

"I hope it's not true," Seamus said bleakly. "If it was, it was probably a revenge thing, getting back at her husband. But Evie..."

"Is totally in love with Brady," she moaned, scrubbing at her forehead, and worried about Evie's reaction. "Brenna wouldn't - that bitch! How could she do that to Evie?"

"She probably doesn't even know Evie likes him."

"How could she not? Everybody knows!"

"Brenna hasn't been home in years. Evie's probably liked a dozen boys since then, so how would Brenna have a clue."

"I have a very bad feeling about this," Cat breathed. "Maggie's going to *kill* her."

Chapter Nineteen

Brenna

Never let an angry sister comb your hair.
—Unknown

The next morning, Brenna was woken by the cheerful giggles and screams of small children. The warmth of the bright sun bled through the curtains, adding to Brenna's contentment. Despite the noise, for the first time she was glad she had come home.

Previous Saturdays had involved her saying good-bye to Toby as he met friends for a run, or a bike ride, or game of squash. Then she would head to the office to enjoy the weekend quiet as she waded through her cases.

What would have happened if, just once, she had spent a weekend going for a bike ride with her husband inside of rushing to work? Would she still be here, snuggled into Addison's bed?

A new voice joined the others in the kitchen. Brenna lifted her head to listen. Missy? She sat up and swung her legs over the edge, suddenly anxious to get up. Saturday morning coffee with her family and oldest friend; what a great way to start the day.

"Morning," she said, heading into the kitchen with a cheerful smile. "Mmm. Coffee smells -"

Maggie swooped across the room like a bird diving for prey, grabbing Brenna by the arm and propelling Brenna ahead of her. "What happened?" Brenna gasped, backpedaling back up the stairs to the bedroom. "What's wrong?"

"What's *wrong*?" Maggie's face was red with anger, chest heaving as she paced through the tiny bedroom. "Like you don't know:"

"I don't!"

"What is going on with you and Brady Todd?" Maggie's clenched jaw made the words stiff and unyielding.

"Oh." Her heart sank quicker than a cannonball

into the pool. "How...?"

"You're not denying it?" Maggie cried.

"I don't know what to deny." Her legs gave out and she sank onto the bed, still unmade, the imprint of her head on the pillow.

Maggie loomed before Brenna, blocking her escape, with hands balled on ample hips. Her mouth twisted into an ugly slash. "Give it a shot."

Brenna gaped at her sister, speechless. There was no way to escape. No response that could smooth Maggie's thunderous expression. As though Brenna's silence had lit a fuse, Maggie exploded.

"Jesus Christ, Brenna! You *knew* Evie liked him! And you *slept* with him! Sex, Brenna! With *Brady*! You *fucked* him. Doesn't Evie mean anything to you?"

"She does..." Brenna bunched the pillow into her lap; something, anything to protect her from the onslaught of fury from Maggie, the flood of guilt and shame from herself.

"He's a *boy*!" Maggie shouted. "You *babysat* him! You should be ashamed of yourself! What kind of person have you become?"

"I didn't know..." Tears pricked her eyes and she blinked them away. She wanted to explain, defend herself, but Maggie's rage hit her with the force of a tidal wave. It knocked her down, kept pushing her down.

"To bring him and your disgusting behavior into *my* house—any of the kids could have come home to find him in bed with you...Evie's room, no less! How *could* you?"

Brenna had never seen Maggie so disgusted, not even when Dory got caught shoplifting. "Not Evie's room."

She regretted the words as soon as they left her mouth.

Maggie sucked in the air from the room, swelling like a bubble about to burst. "*What*?"

"Maggie, listen -"

"I'm not listening to a *word* you have to say. How could you? I just don't understand. You come into my house, you drink too much and *pass out*, cause fights with Cat, and now this! What are you? First you steal Seamus from Cat, then Brady—I suppose Toby had a girlfriend when you met him?"

"No—"

"You're a—a *home-wrecker*, Brenna!"

Brenna's tears fell fast and furious as her heart

split into pieces. *Maggie* was saying these things? Maggie, her...Maggie. Brenna had never felt so ashamed.

"Don't you cry!" Maggie pointed an accusing finger at her. "You've never been a crier so don't start now! You don't deserve any sympathy from me!"

"I didn't know," she stammered, swiping the wetness from her cheeks. "Maggie..."

Maggie turned away as Missy appeared in the doorway, an expression of sympathy on her face.

"I didn't know." Brenna appealed to her friend. "I really didn't."

"Brady's telling people," Missy explained, shutting the door behind her. "Colin told me he heard about it last night. You have to remember it's a small town...people talk. Brady, obviously, talks."

"You're responsible for breaking my little girl's heart," Maggie said with the self-righteous air of a mother facing the enemy of her child.

Brenna stared at her sister. "I'm so sorry, Maggie," she implored. "I didn't know. I found out later, after... that she liked him but I didn't think...I didn't think he'd say anything! I didn't want anyone to find out."

"You're another notch on his belt," Missy said matter-of-factly. "The first Skatt sister. Of course he's going to want to tell everyone about that."

"I just didn't think. After I found out about Toby...it messed me up." She knew it was a lame excuse but it was the only one she had. "I didn't even know who he was. I met him at the bar and -"

"You didn't -?" Maggie threw up her arms. "That makes it even worse! I don't know what to say to you but know I want you out of my house right now. Right now!" She stomped her foot with emphasis. "I don't want you to stay here one more day. One more minute! Out!"

"Maggie - "

"I'm serious, Brenna. Even if Evie forgives you, which I doubt she ever will, I can't have you here. I've got kids and if any of them had come home to find you like that—what if Evie had come home and found you with him?"

Brenna didn't want to remember how close it had come to happening.

"And why did it have to be *him*? I get that you're a single woman now, but you can't do that here. I can't have it. Clare picks up on *everything*, Brenna!

Everything! She's six. And McKenna and Kady..."

"It won't ever happen again!"

"I can't take that chance. Go to Kayleigh's, if she'll have you. Or Cat's."

Brenna nodded, unable to speak past the lump in her throat.

"You'll understand when you have kids," Maggie said. For a moment something akin to regret for her harsh words flashed across her face and Brenna held her breath, hoping she would relent, let her stay, but Maggie's expression hardened again. "I won't let you hurt my kids."

Brenna shook her head furiously. "I wouldn't."

"*You did.*" With that, Maggie stormed out of the room. The slamming of the door shook the room.

Missy blew out a breath. "Wow. That was bad. You okay?"

Brenna was shaking, face wet with tears, nose running. She'd never seen Maggie like that before.

Missy handed her a box of Kleenex. The bed creaked as she sat down beside Brenna, and threw an arm around her shoulder. "She'll cool off soon, sweetie. You hurt her baby, is all. I'll talk to Evie for you."

"I didn't know." Her lament sounded pathetic even to her own ears, but it was the truth. If she had known who Brady was...

She buried her face in her hands. It didn't matter. Either way, she'd had sex with a stranger. In her sister's kitchen. There was nothing redeeming in her behaviour, no matter how she looked at it.

"You should have told me what happened. We could have made up some story."

"I didn't think he'd say anything! It was just one time! Why should anyone care what I do? It was a good way to get back at Toby and Brady was cute and-" Brenna looked imploringly at her. "I only found out *after* that Evie liked him. I'd never hurt her."

"I know, chickie," Missy patted her knee. "I'm sure she'll forgive you. It's not like Brady was her boyfriend or anything. She's just liked him for a long time."

"Does everyone know that she likes him?"

Missy paused. "It's a small place. People talk."

Missy helped her pack her things; there wasn't much. The sight of the clothes Brenna had bought with the girls the day before, still folded in the plastic bags, caused the lump in her throat to expand. The picture of Evie and her friends pinned to her corkboard made her lip quiver.

She never meant to hurt anyone. But she had and now Maggie wanted her to leave – again.

Maggie had taken the girls out so Brenna wouldn't have a chance to say good-bye. Tears filled her eyes as she glanced at the wedding preparations piled neatly in the corner of the living room, the line of tiny running shoes by the door.

Did they know what she had done?

"Where to?" Missy asked after Brenna's belongings were tucked between the car seats in the back of Missy's car. "I wish you could stay with me, but there's just no room now with the baby."

"I couldn't ask that," Brenna said, and heaved a deep breath. How much worse could it be at Cat's? Having to deal with her might be a suitable punishment for her. "Take me to Cat's, I guess. I doubt Kayleigh would have room for me either."

It took less than three minutes for Missy to drive down the hill to Cat's. Brenna stared warily at the huge, white Victorian house, like a kitten eyeing a kitty carrier.

"You're not going back to Vancouver, are you?"

Missy asked.

Less than an hour ago, the decision to come home had seemed like such a good idea. Now, as exhausted and forlorn as she had been when she arrived, she doubted anything was a good idea. "Maybe. I don't know. I don't know what to do."

It was quick work to unload her things and Brenna waved sadly as Missy backed out of the driveway. In a daze, she stood alone at the door. The paint on the front porch was faded and peeling but painting supplies were piled optimistically beside one of the old chairs where Grandpa Earl used to sit out in the evenings, the smoke from his hand- rolled cigarettes keeping the bugs away.

This was a bad idea. Maybe sleeping on Kayleigh's couch was better than dealing with Cat.

She knocked timidly at the door. Instantly, a chorus of barking responded to her solid thump on the peeling paint.

Cat appeared with a smirk on her pretty face and a pack of dogs milling around her legs. There was no welcoming expression as she looked Brenna up and down. "We usually dress to go visiting around here. Wandering around in pajamas is seen as bad manners."

Brenna glanced down, horrified she was still wearing her nightgown. "I didn't have time to get dressed."

Cat stared at her expectantly. "So? Just dropped by for a visit? With all your stuff?"

"No."

Cat's green eyes were cool and calculating, her expression unwelcoming. "What are you doing here, then?"

Dammit, was she going to make her say it? The way her body barricaded the door convinced Brenna she was. "I've come to stay in my old room," Brenna said through gritted teeth.

"I thought you were staying at Maggie's." Cat's tiny smile told her how much she was enjoying this.

"I was."

"What happened?" she asked sweetly, her eyes still cool.

"You know damn well what happened!" Brenna burst out. "I can tell by your face."

"Well, I know you fucked Brady Todd, the one guy Evie is in love with," Cat said, making the act sound as crass as she could. "I'm guessing that put a little damper on you staying at Maggie's. Or did you fuck up in some other way that I haven't heard about yet?"

Brenna stared past Cat into the house. "In my defense-"

"Spoken like a true lawyer."

"I *am* a lawyer."

"And that's something to be proud of?"

"At least I made something of my life."

"And you were *so* successful that you came running back here with your tail between your legs as soon as things got rough. Nowhere else to go? No one else to run to?" Cat stepped aside with a grimace. "And now I have to put up with you. Thanks a helluva lot."

Brenna didn't respond as she stepped inside, Cat waiting until Brenna's shoulder brushed her before moving aside. "Yeah, well, make yourself at home. Everything's pretty well the way Mom left it, but then, it's been so long since you were here, I doubt you remember."

Brenna glanced down the hall. "I don't remember dogs."

"You don't like dogs? You don't have to stay here."

"Dogs are fine," she said stiffly, bending to pat the

nearest one.

"That's Connery, that's Cassie and the shy one is Chuck."

"Good dogs. You're painting the porch."

"It needs it."

Brenna straightened up and looked around, not mentioning that the whole place needed work. Cat watched her carry her things inside, without lifting one of her bitten nails to help.

She cast an eye over Brenna's suitcases and bent to check out the bottles of wine. "You've got expensive taste. We're still at the wine-in-a-box phase here."

"I've noticed." Brenna hefted the box and carried it into the kitchen, Cat following close behind.

"You might as well use your old bedroom. I was going to fix it up for a gym but never got around to it."

"I suppose you moved into Mom's room?" Brenna asked returned to grab hold of her suitcases to lug upstairs.

"Why would I do that?" Cat retorted sharply. "I've got stuff to do." Without another word, she pushed past Brenna to the stairs.

"So welcoming," she mumbled to herself. Cat overheard.

"Well, what do you expect? You want me to roll out the red carpet for you? Just stay out of my way, I'll keep out of yours!"

Chapter Twenty

Cat

Sisters don't need words. They have perfected a language of snarls and smiles and frowns and winks—expressions of shocked surprise and incredulity and disbelief. Sniffs and snorts and gasps and sighs—that can undermine any tale you're telling.

—Pam Brown

Cat watched Brenna lug her suitcase upstairs, stopping once to adjust a picture of Cat that she brushed against.

What was she supposed to do with her? This was Cat's home, one she didn't appreciate sharing. Not even Seamus lived with her. Admittedly, it was his choice. When she'd suggested he move in, he was quick to decline.

She shrugged the thought away. Now wasn't the time to worry about why he'd said no.

Cat brushed away the thought as she stomped into the kitchen. As she thumped her battered Kitchen Aid mixer onto the counter, her rage against her sister grew. She had her weekly order for the Sandwich Shoppe to fill, which was normally a process that never failed to relax her, but now, with Brenna there, in her house...

She banged the bag of flour on the counter with a satisfying thud, knocking against one of the eggs, which began a slow roll towards the edge.

"Dammit!" Grabbing for the egg, she missed and it landed on the floor, cracking gooey yolk where she had laid with Seamus last night

Cat felt her irritation multiplying like mould within her as she wiped up the mess. Soon, every part of her seethed. She could hear Brenna's footsteps upstairs, the hesitant tread of the unwelcome guest.

"I hope she's uncomfortable. She should be, invading my space like this," Cat muttered, her words inaudible as she switched on the mixer. “Why come here? Why did she bother coming home anyway? So her hubby cheated? Big deal. She should have ploughed him one and gone on with her day. Would have made my life easier.”

A flicker of guilt eased into Cat’s irritation. Despite her bravado, she knew first-hand the end of a marriage was a big deal.

A crash vibrated through the house and Cat paused the mixer, listening first for the tell-tale whimper of one of the dogs, and then for cries that Brenna might need help.

Nothing. With an annoyed shake of her head, she continued mixing.

It wasn’t until she slid the first of the cakes into the oven that Maggie called.

“Did you know?” Maggie demanded.

Cat tucked the receiver under her chin and added cocoa powder into the second round of batter. “No. Well, Seamus told me last night.”

“And why didn’t you think to let me know what she had done?”

“Well, since it was late and me and Seamus were naked in the kitchen, I didn’t think it was the best time to call and tattle on Brenna."

Maggie's huff of exasperation blew through the phone. "Why is everyone having sex? I'm too bloody tired to get any, worrying about this wedding and Evie getting ready to leave for school. Now this -"

"I'll deal with Brady," Cat promised. "And really, it's for the best."

"You're kidding -" Maggie practically growled the word and Cat was quick to jump in.

"You know what he's like, and now Evie does, too. It'll get him out of her life, once and for all. I knew something like this would happen. I just never thought it would be Brenna..." Cat gazed at the footsteps still sounding above her. How did Brenna...Brenna and Brady Todd...?

A frisson of admiration joined with the disgust Cat felt.

"So, what happened?" Cat asked, leaning against the counter, her hand toying with the switch of the mixer. She needed to finish the cakes but it was best that she heard the story first hand from Maggie. Rumours would be flying by the time she got to work that afternoon, and she wanted the full story to be able to react accordingly.

To defend Brenna?

Why would she do that? Her sister had never taken her side about anything. But as she listened to Maggie, she grudgingly concluded Brenna wasn't to blame.

"She didn't know Evie liked him," Cat surprised herself by saying.

"Don't you take her side on this," Maggie warned.

"Believe me, I'm not, but think about it – Brenna just met Evie, what, two days ago? How is she going to know who Evie has a crush on?"

Cat knew her arguments were reasonable, but it felt wrong, unsettling, to be defending Brenna about anything. Brenna had been her nemesis all of her life, their relationship full of conflict and competition. Cat had never once felt like defending her sister.

Why now?

"She had sex in my house!" Maggie exploded. "And I don't even know where they did it."

"Do you really want to know?"Cat laughed. "Sorry, but look at this from her side – she just got dumped and this hot guy was coming on to her. And you know as well as I do, that Brady is hot and comes on pretty strong. She probably hasn't had any action in months, so who's going to say no to him? Plus, pretty sweet revenge."

"Shut up, Cat!"

"Shutting up, but just think about it. Yes, Evie got hurt but I don't think Brenna can be blamed for that. This is on Brady. And this is me saying this – I can find a way to blame Brenna for just about anything."

"You just want me to forgive her so I'll let her come back."

"That sounds good to me. I don't want her here."

A noise made Cat look up. Brenna stood in the doorway of the kitchen.

From the stony expression on Brenna's face, Cat suspected she had at least heard her last comment but nothing else. Of course. "Look, Maggie, I gotta run. These cakes won't make themselves."

"Don't you hang up on me! You're taking her side!"

Cat expected Brenna to leave, but she stood her ground in the doorway. She had showered and changed into Capris and a polo shirt so white and pristine Cat thought it would be perfect for center court at Wimbledon.

The whiteness of the shirt irritated Cat.

"Why on earth would I be on Brenna's side for anything?" Cat drawled, watching for a reaction on Brenna's face.

Her sister blanched, mouth tightened. But then her chin lifted defiantly.

"I'll call you back, Mag." Maggie was still spluttering protests as Cat hung up the phone. "What do you want?"

"Nothing from you," Brenna snapped back. "I should have known you'd grow up to be an even bigger bitch than you already were."

"Four years of law school and that's all you got?" With a derisive sneer, Cat flicked the switch and the mixer whirred into life.

"You're so childish!" Brenna shouted over the noise.

"And you're such a frigid bitch. Oops." Cat clapped a hand against her cheek. "Not anymore, not since Brady defrosted you."

Brenna's face turned red and Cat grinned at her evident frustration.

"I know you don't want me here, and believe me, this isn't my first choice," Brenna began. "But this is my house, too. I have every right to be here."

"What? I can't hear you?" Cat mocked, holding her hand to her ear. "Mixer's too loud." She increased the speed, the beaters twisting frantically, the scent of chocolate batter adding to the smell of the cakes baking in the oven.

With an expression of disgust, Brenna turned and Cat silently crowed a sense of victory.

But then Brenna spun back to face her. "I don't believe you," she spat, crossing the kitchen with angry strides to loom across the island from Cat. "Don't you feel guilty about taking this house away from Maggie and Kayleigh? Maggie has absolutely no room with all those kids. But no, selfish Cat had to have this great big house all to herself and to hell with anyone else! Well, you can just keep it. I'll be gone soon enough. Keep all this," she waved her arms, knocking over the bag of flour.

White powder billowed out and settled over the counter, but Brenna ignored the mess. "Keep it all to yourself. You may not like me, you may think I'm horrible for what I did, but at least I made something of my life! I had a life I was proud of, that you know nothing about. What do you have? Nothing but your dogs and your cakes and the memories of your failed marriages!"

An icy cold rage descended on Cat as she shut off the KitchenAid. She dipped a finger in the batter to taste, before sliding around the island to stand before her sister, noticing for the first time that they were the exact same height.

Brenna stood her ground, lips clenched, breathing deeply, wearing that white shirt like a badge of honour.

Cat's fingers flexed, once, twice. "Fuck off." She slammed both hands on Brenna's chest and gave her a hard shove.

"You're kidding." Brenna stumbled back. "This is how you want to do it?"

"Why not?" Cat took a step forward and gave her another push, noticing the spot of chocolate on the white shirt with satisfaction.

This time Brenna was ready and didn't budge. "Do you really want to fight me? We're grown women."

"But you just called me childish." Cat hadn't expected to hit her, but her hand was fisted and felt like it needed to fly out and punch Brenna.

A nice left jab, right in the corner of her mouth.

"You hit me!" Brenna cried, slapping a hand to

her mouth.

"What are you going to do about it?" And then Cat hit her again.

It wasn't the first time Cat and Brenna had gotten into a physical altercation, but Cat had never expected it to happen again, at this age, with cakes baking in the oven. Even in her fury, Cat expected to Brenna to run away in tears.

She forgot her sister never backed away from a fight.

The blow was a shock; an uppercut to Cat's belly pushing out the air with a whoosh. While she was doubled over, Brenna smashed a left hook into her chin.

"Fuck," Cat cried, holding her jaw. With a harsh cry, Cat loosened years of sibling resentment, ramming her shoulder into Brenna's stomach.

The two crashed onto the kitchen floor with a resounding thud. The dogs swarmed around them like this was some sort of fun game, preventing Cat from getting in another punch.

Brenna scrambled to her feet. "Why did you always have to be such a bitch?" She darted away, using the kitchen island as a shield. "You never let me have anything for myself. You stole my clothes, tried to get my room. Not even Seamus! You couldn't stand it, had to have Seamus first when you knew I liked him!"

"I hope that drives you crazy," Cat snarled, pushing the dogs away before clambering to her feet. "That I had him first!"

She stalked towards her sister, fists clenched. She saw Brenna's eyes flick to the counter, grab at the measuring cups, still held together with the plastic ring.

"Still can't throw worth shit," Cat taunted, easily dodging the projectile as she rounded the corner of the island.

With a scream, Brenna scooped a handful of cake batter from the bowl and flung it.

Chocolate spattered against Cat's shoulder, her stomach, her cheek as Brenna found her target. "People have to eat that!" Cat shouted as she snatched the fallen bag of flour and threw it at Brenna, hitting her square in the face and covering them both in white dust.

Cat lunged at Brenna but slipped on the mess, landing on her bum. Brenna rounded the island, heading for the door. The dogs barked wildly, assumed the sisters were in the middle of an elaborate play session. They gamboled around Brenna's legs, preventing her escape. Cat scrambled to her feet and lunged at Brenna.

"He loves me more than he ever loved you!" Cat shrieked, knocking Brenna to her hands and knees with a flying tackle. As soon as Brenna flipped over, Cat aimed for her head, her shoulder, but the dogs blocked her every move, practically standing on top of Brenna, barking wildly like they were cheering them on.

Brenna managed to retaliate, bringing her knees up and lashing out with her legs, kicking Cat in the stomach. One of the dogs let out a yelp as Cat landed on them.

Brenna pushed off the dogs and jumped to her feet, rushing into the hallway. Shoes began flying into the kitchen; Cat got to her feet, arms protecting her head as she discovered Brenna had a much better aim with a heavier object.

The border collie leapt into the air to snatch a shoe.

"Couldn't you have thrown like that last night?"

she shouted. Reaching Brenna, Cat grabbed her by the arm and swung her into the screen door, which opened, depositing Brenna onto the porch, and knocking over one of the chairs.

"Fuck you!" Cat leapt on Brenna, straddling her. Fists flew from both of them, a few connecting with a curse but most bouncing off painlessly. With a heave, Brenna finally managed to throw Cat off of her, and scooted crab-like away. But she didn't realize the steps were so close and bumped her way down the three porch steps. She rolled out of the way just before Cat jumped on her.

"No, fuck you!"

They were so consumed with hitting each that neither one of them heard the screech of tires as the car pulled into the driveway. Suddenly, Cat was jerked off of Brenna, coming face to face with yet another angry sister.

"Look at the two of you!" Kayleigh shouted. "Grown women rolling around the ground like animals. Have a little respect for yourself. Everyone's watching you behave like idiots."

Breathing hard, Cat looked across the road to where Kayleigh pointed. There was indeed a group of people watching the action with expressions of delighted horror on their faces.

"What the hell do you think you're doing?" Kayleigh raged, holding Brenna by the back of her not so pristine white shirt.

"Catching up," Brenna said in a flat voice. She looked at Cat, covered in flour and dirt and chocolate, and started to laugh.

"What the -?"

Brenna's hair was pure white from the flour. Cat wiped a hand through the chocolate on her face, and grinned.

"You're both fucking idiots," Kayleigh growled and shoved Brenna toward the porch. Cat followed, unable to hold in her laughter. "Get in the house." she demanded as she stomped after them.

"You have chocolate in your nose!" Brenna gasped as the door swung closed after them.

"You threw it in my face!" Cat chortled, reaching out to pull her hair. "Your hair's completely white."

"The flour's down my shirt!" Brenna pulled at the front of her shirt.

"My kitchen!" Cat wailed, catching a glimpse of the mess.

"I'll help you clean it up," Brenna promised.

Kayleigh's head swiveled from Cat to Brenna with an expression of astonishment. "I'll never understand the two of you!" When there was no sign of the laughter stopping, she threw up her hands and stormed out again.

It was another few minutes until the humour faded and Cat found herself alone with her sister.

"I think I need a beer," Cat said slowly.

"I have wine," Brenna offered, shyly.

"We can drink your wine next time," Cat grinned wickedly, even though the smile hurt her face.

Brenna paled underneath the flour. "There's going to be a next time?"

"Jesus, I hope not."

Chapter Twenty-One

Brenna

Brothers and sisters are as close as hands and feet.

—Vietnamese Proverb

"That was an interesting welcome," Brenna said as Cat handed her a cold beer.

She had helped Cat clean up the kitchen, vacuumed up piles of flour, scraped chocolate from every available surface. Hid her smile when she remembered the look on Cat's face when she threw the cake batter.

It had been a good shot.

Clearly, both had a few good shots with their fists. Once the kitchen was restored back to its natural order, Cat passed Brenna a bag of frozen peas, took one for herself and pressed it against her chin. "Here. You'll probably get a few bruises."

"So will you." The cold was a shock against the heat of the already-swelling contusion around her eye.

"Yeah..." Cat stretched her jaw and winced. "You hit harder now."

"You've clearly had some practice." Even with the bag of peas settled against her eye, Brenna could see the slow bloom of a bruise on Cat's lower face and hid her smug smile.

"Yeah," Cat mused, flexing her hand gingerly. "I broke two fingers when I was married to Tommy."

"He hit you?" Brenna was amazed; not only about her marriage, but that she had volunteered the information. Sibling rivalry had never led them to true confessions.

"I usually hit him first." With one hand holding the bag of peas, Cat moved around the kitchen with confidence, measuring flour and baking powder into the mixer. "It wasn't the healthiest of relationships."

"Did he cheat on you?" Brenna watched open-mouthed as Cat added cocoa powder and gave the bowl a quick stir before cracking eggs into a separate bowl. This was a side of Cat she never seen, or expected to.

"No...that was me, too. He did too, but only after I started it." She looked ruefully at Brenna. "Doesn't feel nice, does it?"

"No."

Cat nodded, dumping eggs whisked with sugar into the larger bowl, and gave the mixture a stir. "This is going to get loud," she said with a sheepish grin, her hand hovering over the switch.

Brenna set her empty beer bottle on the counter, keeping the peas pressed against her eye. "I'm going to go have another shower, try to get the flour out of...everywhere."

Cat's laughter followed her from the kitchen.

As she headed upstairs, Brenna glanced at the pictures on the wall. Her childhood was documented in school pictures; the ugly green sweater she wore in the Grade One photo, the bad haircut Kayleigh gave her when she was twelve. Every frame was between a picture of Cat and one of Dory, set there like a barrier. Cat and Dory never fought, never argued. It had been as if they had an unspoken agreement to ignore each other.

There hadn't been such a barrier between Cat and Brenna.

How would they fare under the same roof again?

She had to admit the fight had cleared away the immediate tension, but she wasn't keen on resorting to physical violence to sort out the rest of their issues.

And years of issues to wade through. There weren't enough bags of peas to soothe those bruises.

Brenna stood in front of the mirror in her room. She looked a mess. Leaning closer, she fingered the part in her hair. Most of the flour had shaken loose in the kitchen, the grayish-white were her roots showing. A bruise was beginning to blossom under her eye, matching the one on her chin.

Cat had a nasty punch. Brenna remembered her ex-husband Tommy being tall and strong and thought grudgingly that her sister wouldn't have had any trouble holding her own against him. Three marriages, two ending in divorce and one – what was his name?

Alex.

Alex had died, Brenna recalled with a twinge of

guilt. Cat had been widowed and the only thing Brenna had done was send her a generic sympathy card.

In her defense, Cat hadn't even told her she'd remarried. Kayleigh had told her, as usual.

After her shower, Brenna spent time in her room, unpacking the essentials, hanging a few of her new clothes in the closet. She left most of her things in the suitcase, unsure of how long she would be there, wary of being thrown out again.

Walking into her room was like going back in time. She hadn't taken much when she left, so it was as if she'd stepped back in time. Movie posters from *Erin Brockovich, Billy Elliott* and *Gladiator* hung on the walls; Johnny Depp's countenance held the prime position directly over her bed. It was surreal.

Opening a dresser drawer, Brenna found a yellowed packet of pictures, photos of her and Missy in high school. Seamus with his arms around her. She stood for long minutes looking through the past until she was forced to brush the wetness from under her eyes.

She'd left her CD player behind, assuming Cat would lay claim to it, but it still sat on her desk under the window, surprisingly clear of dust.

Her room was...tidier... than she'd expected it to be after all this time. All that was needed was an open window to air out the staleness and fresh sheets on the bed.

It was like Cat had kept it clean.

Out of curiousity, Brenna checked if there was a CD in the player. Dixie Chicks' *Home.*

How fitting.

As Brenna cued up *Landslides,* the scratching of feet in the hall drew attention. Two of the three dogs panted in the doorway, looking like they were waiting to be invited in.

"Good dogs." At her words, they bounded forward, the black and white border collie leaping straight onto the bed. "Is this why Cat cleaned up in here? Is this where you hang out?"

The dog opened his mouth in a smiling pant before turning a circle and settling down with a sigh.

Brenna left him curled up on the bed, the bulldog sitting on the floor with a forlorn expression on his face. She assumed it was because his legs were too short to jump up.

It was the same bed that she'd had since she was

nine years old; a double bed with an ornate white iron headboard. It had been Maggie's until she moved in with Mike. The door hadn't shut behind Maggie before Brenna had moved out of the room she shared with Cat, and claimed Maggie's room for herself.

She sat down and bounced on the bed, smiling at the memory. She'd dressed her Barbies in their best outfits and arranged them on the dresser, piled her books on the shelf and hung her favourite posters before collapsing on the bed with a happy giggle.

But the conflicts hadn't stopped once they'd gotten their own rooms. The day she moved into her own room, Cat had spoiled the day by stealing her favourite Barbie, slathering peanut butter on it and giving it to the dogs to gnaw on.

Brenna had retaliated by taking her grandfather's wire cutters and sniping every other spoke on Cat's bike, carefully enough that it wasn't noticeable until the wheel had collapsed when Cat was riding it.

How were they possibly going to live with each other?

"How do *you* live with her?" she asked the dog on the bed. Ears perked, he watched her every move.

At least Brenna wouldn't be here forever.

But where was she supposed to go?

Carefully, she lowered herself to the edge of the bed – her body was beginning to ache, especially her tailbone from where she'd bumped down the steps. The dog wriggled closer, nudging her hand to be petted.

"Good thing I like dogs."

Did Cat spend her time talking to the dogs as well? The house was too big for one person. At least they wouldn't be falling over each other. It would be easy for Brenna to hide.

Is that what Brenna wanted – to come back home only to hide away from her sisters and her mistakes?

Her marriage to Toby was over – that had been clear, even before she caught him with Krystal. What kind of wife preferred working to spending time with her husband? Brenna was good at being a lawyer because failure wasn't ever a choice for her. Neither was giving up. She had set her mind on being a successful, high-priced corporate lawyer because it was the one career she couldn't have in Forest Hills.

But now she was back at home, adrift in the chaos of her formerly calm life, and she didn't know what to do.

She sat on her bed for long minutes, considering her options, listening to the bluegrass sounds of the Dixie Chicks, and petting the dog, who was now crowded onto her lap. A breeze blew in through the window, and Brenna wondered if it might rain, since the room was noticeably cooler.

Suddenly with a whine, the dog bounded off the bed and out the room. "What did I do?" Brenna called after him. The bulldog jumped up and followed.

A step in the hall and Cat appeared in the doorway. "Do you want a list?"

Brenna smiled even though she wasn't sure Cat was joking.

"So this is where the dogs were. You're staying in here?" Cat asked awkwardly, glancing at the suitcases still unpacked.

"Do you have another suggestion? Maybe the old shed in the backyard? I remember you locking me in there once."

"Ha ha, that. The raccoons took over the shed a few years ago, so maybe not. Look, I've got to – I'm heading -" She paused with a perplexed look on her face. "I'm not used to telling someone what I'm doing."

"Don't mind me," Brenna said lightly.

"I just thought, if you were looking for me. I'm going to the store for a second. I – do you need anything?"

"No, I'm fine thanks. I've got everything..."

She had nothing. No food, the bare essentials for toiletries, just a case of wine and bottle of gin.

"I guess I'd better go to the store myself," she admitted.

Cat gave a wave as she backed away. "You do the shopping next week."

"Okay, thanks. Sheets?" she called.

"Linen closet in the hall by Mom's room."

Brenna waited until she heard the door slam behind Cat before heading in search of bedding. Poking her head into Dory's room, she noticed it had been stripped of everything personal. The bed was still covered by one of the quilts Grandma Winifred made for each of them when they were born. Brenna peered in dresser drawers and found rolling papers and old make-up, dried into nothing but colored powder.

Cat must have cleared it out since Dory had left in the middle of the night with barely a knapsack of clothes.

Brenna paused outside her mother's room and took a deep breath before pushing open the door. Other than the faint covering of dust, it was just like Brenna's bedroom—everything remained as if her mother had just left. The bed was made, the covers tucked neatly over the pillows and smelled fresh, with a faint floral tinge.

Her fingers left trails in the dust as she reverently stroked the jewelry box on the dresser. When she opened the box, she found a heart pendant sparkling with tiny diamonds and a pair of amethyst earrings.

Why had no one taken them?

Her mother had died on Brenna's thirteenth birthday.

Brenna shivered, willing the memories away. But one kept returning. She'd huddled beside Cat on the bed, as the sisters sat miserably on their mother's bed the day after the funeral.

"What are we supposed to do?" Kayleigh had whispered as they huddled on the bed, careful not to muss up the spread. All of them had been drawn to their mother's room, which had previously been barred to them.

Dory motioned to Cat and Brenna, sitting silently

at the end of the bed, both dry-eyed and for once not fighting. "We can't let them take the girls.

"No one is taking anyone," Kayleigh had retorted staunchly.

"They're still minors, Kayleigh, and now they're orphans. So am I. Grandpa Earl is here but..." She didn't have to finish. Grandpa was in the hospital in Elliott Lake, recovering from his latest suicide attempt. "I think you and Kayleigh should become their guardians."

The swell of Maggie's latest pregnancy was visible under her shirt as she looked at Dory.

"Why do we need to do that?" Kayleigh had asked. "We're sisters; we'll take care of each other."

"So they don't split us up," Dory had insisted. "This is our home. If they think we can't care for them—"

"Who's they?" Cat had wanted to know. Brenna had wondered herself, but no one bothered to explain.

Maybe their father would come back, take care of them. Maybe he had been waiting, maybe their mother wouldn't let him come back.

"No one is taking anyone," Maggie had vowed.

"We'll take care of each other. Promise?" She looked around, meeting each pair of eyes – blue, green, green, hazel. "Do you all promise? That we'll always be there to help each other?"

"I promise," Cat had said solemnly, Brenna repeating the vow.

"That's not enough," Dory had insisted. "What if some family takes Brenna and Cat away to live somewhere else?"

"I won't let them," Maggie told her. "We stay together as a family. Always. The five of us will always be together."

A chill had raced up Brenna arms. Glancing at Cat, she noticed her bare arms were covered in goosebumps too. "What's that?" Cat asked in alarm. "Can you smell it?"

"Why is it so cold in here?" Maggie wondered nervously.

"I smell lilacs," Dory had said with wonder. "I smell Mom." Their mother had loved lilacs and would bring in armfuls of boughs when the trees were in bloom so that the house was filled with a heady, spring-like aroma.

"She died," Kayleigh had said flatly.

"Can't you feel it? Can't you feel her?" Dory jumped off the bed. "Mom? Are you here?" She whirled around the room, searching the closet, the corners. "Are you here? Don't leave us! Please! Don't go..."

Maggie's eyes filled with tears.

"Dory." Kayleigh reached for her, but Dory dodged and weaved throughout the room. "Dory, stop. She's gone."

Brenna had seen her mother in her coffin earlier that day; saw her laid in the ground and dirt shoveled over it. She knew their mother was dead, so why was Dory...

"It's her ghost!" Dory had said excitedly.

"A ghost?" Cat asked with interest.

"Stop it. There's no ghost."

It had been an on-going argument right up until Brenna left. Who believed what, who experienced what. Dory claimed she had felt the spirit of their mother several times; so had Cat. Maggie and Kayleigh denied it.

Brenna had never felt her mother's presence. Like when she was alive, her mother had had her reasons for staying away from Brenna.

Brenna picked up her mother's Christmas brooch, a green enamel holly leaf with glittering red berries in the bottom of the jewelry box. It would appear the first of December every year and remain on the well-worn winter coat until the end of January.

Brenna held the pin tight in her palm and felt the prick of the sharp edges.

Dust motes swirled in the sunlight as the room suddenly chilled, like the air conditioning had been turned on and she was standing right on top of a vent. The hairs on her arms stood up as a gust of air reached the back of her neck.

The smell - *lilacs*.

She stood frozen, still clutching the holly pin. Was this it? Was their mother finally paying attention to her, after all these years?

It took her three tries to form the word. "Mom?"

A tear trickled slowly down her cheek as she felt the whisper of a touch on her shoulder.

Chapter Twenty-Two

Cat

Whatever you do they will love you; even if they don't love you they are connected to you till you die. You can be boring and tedious with sisters, whereas you have to put on a good face with friends.

—Deborah Moggach

Cat was spreading vanilla custard along the top of the cake when she heard footsteps on the stairs. Slow at first, then rushing down the last few stairs.

Brenna appeared in the kitchen, hazel eyes as big as saucers.

"Saw Mom, did you?" Cat laughed.

"She's here. Somehow..."

Somehow their mother's spirit had remained in the house she had lived in all her life. Cat didn't understand how it came to be, or why. She preferred to believe their mother had chosen to remain, rather than she was somehow trapped within the walls.

"I don't understand it." Cat placed the second layer carefully on the custard and began skimming a layer of frosting around the side.

"She's been here the whole time?"

"She never left."

"Kayleigh said she was still here but I never...I thought she might be but not that I would *see* her. You know, *feel* her. She was in the room with me. She was *there*!"

Cat smiled as she finished icing the cake. Brenna stalked through the kitchen, hand pulling at her hair.

It was refreshing to see her sister freaked out about something.

She cleared the counter before pulling out a package of cold meat, cheese and mustard from the fridge. She couldn't help but notice Brenna's face already bore purplish swelling around her eye, along her jaw.

She had seen herself in the mirror. Brenna had left her mark on her as well.

Talk about the fight had already begun at the General Store when she ran in. Things moved fast in Forest Hills.

Without asking, Cat sliced two extra pieces of bread. "So where were you?"

Brenna stopped her pacing, chewing her lip nervously as she leaned against the counter across from Cat."Her room. It was...strange...I didn't see anything, but it was like I could sense her. She was *there*."

I've never really *seen* her. Gets pretty chilly, doesn't it?" Cat asked as she spread mustard on the bread. "I remember once just after Kayleigh moved out there was this big storm - "

"You never liked thunder."

Of course Brenna would remember that.

"It had only been about week since I'd been on my own, and the thunder was so loud I couldn't sleep. And Mom kept, I don't know, *checking* on me. Totally freaked me out."

Brenna's wide eyed expression hadn't changed.

"It takes a little getting used to," Cat told her. "It's

strongest in her room. I think that's where she must hang out. The dogs won't ever go in there. Once in a while she'll wander around, especially if she knows I'm upset about something."

"Hang out? How do you—I don't understand how you can talk about it so casually," Brenna laughed nervously. "You live with a ghost. That's not normal. Even for here."

"Yeah, well, nothing ever seems to be 'normal' with this family."

"That's true." Brenna stared out the window, at the huge lilac tree in the backyard its buds only beginning to bloom. "It never happened before. There was that time, in her room after the funeral, but Kayleigh said..."

Brenna trailed off and Cat knew she was filled with the same image; the five sisters clinging to each with grief, alone and afraid, and promising to take care of each other. They promised to be there for each other.

How had that promise turned out?

"Kayleigh doesn't get it. Neither does Maggie." Cat pushed aside the memory. It made her heart catch to remember the weeks following the funeral.

"But you do. And Dory did."

"I think it's the only thing we had in common. She was into the Goth stuff then, probably thought it was cool to have a ghost around."

In a family where there were no shortages of issues and drama, Dory was the undisputed queen of conflict. She had left home in the middle of the night; clearing out wallets and piggy banks and taking with her Kirby Conlin, Cat's secret crush.

Cat never forgave Dory for taking Kirby with her.

"You see her," Brenna murmured. "And I know Dory did. But never me."

Cat placed the shaved turkey on the mustard and added a slice of ham as well. Cheese, a bit of avocado, a crisp leaf of lettuce. She concentrated on making the sandwiches because Brenna looked like she was ready to cry and Cat wasn't ready to deal with that.

They had beaten the crap out of each other a couple of hours ago and then shared a beer. Cat thought that was enough sisterly sharing for one day.

She pulled a plate from the cupboard, slapped one of the sandwiches on it, and slid it across the counter in Brenna's direction.

"What's that?"

"What does it look like? I'm hungry." To emphasize, she took a huge bite of the other sandwich.

"You made me a sandwich?" Brenna's voice was incredulous, suggesting Cat had given her something more precious than mere meat and bread.

"It's not that big a deal," Cat muttered through a mouthful of turkey and ham.

"Thanks." Lifting off the top slice of bread, Brenna plucked off the cheese. "I think I'm lactose-intolerant."

"You could have stopped me from putting it in." Cat reached over and snagged it from her plate.

"I didn't think you were making one for me."

"Do you think I'd be so rude as to eat in front of you?" She cocked her head to the side and grinned. "Actually I would."

Brenna took a tentative bite. "Sure you didn't put anything weird in it?"

"You were standing right here watching me." Cat took two cans of Pepsi from the refrigerator and slid one across the counter.

"Wouldn't put it past you."

They stood companionably in the kitchen, with the warm sun pouring through the windows, the fragrant scent of the cakes filling the room, and ate the sandwiches.

Cat couldn't remember ever sharing a moment like that with Brenna. Not only were they not at each other's throats, but it was...peaceful.

She shook her head and wondered how long it would last.

"This is good." Brenna chewed carefully. "What kind of bread is this?"

"Multi-grain sourdough. I made it," Cat said. It would have sounded arrogant had she not spoken through a mouthful of food.

"You bake." She gestured to the cake. "That's new."

"I like to cook." Cat said defensively. "I like to bake."

"Mom used to..."

"Yeah. It's kind of like she helps me." She paused. "I know that sounds weird."

"Surprisingly, no," Brenna shook her head. "She always helped you. She was never on my side for anything."

The bruises were still fresh and the resentment had already returned.

But for once, Cat didn't feel like going on the attack.

"You still bitter about that? You were too much like Dad for her to deal with."

Brenna chewed thoughtfully. "That's what Maggie told me. She said I was a constant reminder of him. But how do you know? You were two years old when he left."

"Seamus' mother told me. She said you looked like him; he was super smart like you. Mom couldn't relate to you, the brains made you intimidating."

Brenna cocked and eyebrow. "You were intimidated by me?"

"I ain't afraid of anyone," Cat said with false bravado.

"Right. Except the Mom ghost when she first showed up. You just about ran from the room!" Brenna smiled Cat heard the na-na-nanh in her voice.

"That's because it was the first ghost I'd ever seen! It freaked you out too!"

"Not as much as it did Kayleigh."

"Or Maggie! She wouldn't believe it was possible. 'She's dead', she kept saying." It was easier to bring humour into the memories of that day, than focus on the sadness.

"No, that was Kayleigh. Maggie just kept saying there was no such thing as ghosts."

Brenna glanced around. "It must be tough with the upkeep of this place."

"I manage," Cat said shortly. The timer on the oven chimed and she pulled out pans, the scent of chocolate cake overpowering everything. "There's a lot to do. I'm getting the porch painted, and one of the bedrooms. I'd like to start a bed and breakfast."

Cat couldn't believe she had blurted out her plan to Brenna, of all people.

"That's a great idea. But what about the ghost thing?"

Cat glanced warily at her sister. Brenna seemed to be interested…"It could be a selling feature for some. 'Come stay in a haunted house.' Besides, she's not a bad ghost. She doesn't do any damage. She doesn't scare people." Cat suddenly laughed at a memory. "I had a guy over years ago and Mom made an appearance. Totally freaked him out. He ran around bare-assed, yelled at me that I never told him the house was haunted."

Brenna laughed. "Who was it?"

Cat smiled smugly. “Kirby Conlin.”

Chapter Twenty-Three

Brenna

You keep your past by having sisters. As you get older they're the only ones who don't get bored when you talk about your memories

—Deborah Moggach

Brenna swallowed the last bit of her sandwich. The truce was a nice change but any more time spent with Cat might be pushing her luck. They seemed to be getting along, but Brenna was sure it was only a matter of time until they resumed the status quo.

It was a nice spring day, she thought as she carried her plate to the dishwasher. She'd go out for a walk. Give Cat some space. Besides, she needed some privacy to sort out what had happened with Maggie.

She decided to go for a walk in the forest behind the house. At this time, Brenna would take the swarm of blackflies over the prying but well-meaning townspeople. Grabbing a sweater and a fresh can of Deep Woods Off, she set off.

The woods were full of pathways that would wind through the trees; everything from faint trails used by dogs chasing squirrels to major conduits for ATVing and snowmobiling; bike paths, hiking trails, none marked but memorized and well-traveled by the people of Forest Hills.

Brenna recognized the path she used to take to Seamus'.

She turned in the other direction, past a swampy pond surrounded by tall reeds and pussy willows with water as dark and murky as her thoughts.

Her mother was a ghost.

Her sister was...Cat wasn't as bad as she'd expected.

Brenna's heart ached thinking about Maggie's anger, Evie's confusion and hurt. If only Brenna could speak to Evie, explain it to her herself.

Damn the mouth of Brady Todd. He might have been a talented kisser, but he clearly didn't know when to keep his mouth shut.

Brenna hoped Evie would forgive her. Until then, there was no real reason for her to stay in Forest Hills. Addison's wedding was in a week; maybe it would be better if she took the bus into Toronto, stay there for a few days, while she figured out a plan.

Surprisingly, the thought of leaving left her with a hollow feeling. She snorted and a squirrel nibbling a nut in a nearby tree trilled a warning. Brenna had been pummeled by her sister; why wasn't she hotfooting it out of town before the next round?

Living in Vancouver, Brenna had convinced herself she had everything she wanted – an amazing job, a husband who...

How would she describe Toby? He wasn't an incredible husband... Suitable? Convenient?

He should have been someone else's husband.

And the amazing career? Why didn't she miss the work if it was so amazing?

Brenna's thoughts unraveled as she walked, as she sorted and plotted and tried to figure out a plan. She liked plans and she liked lists and as she followed the path, she wished she had a pen and paper, or at least her phone to organize some of her ideas.

So caught up in her thoughts, she didn't realize her calves were burning from the uphill climb until the land began to level out, and the trees thinned. The speckled light of the forest brightened and a distant motorized whine replaced the chatter of birds and woodland creatures.

When she reached the cedar fence, she found she had walked to the very top of the hill. She was in a field at Ebans Stables.

Her father had grown up on this farm. He had brought her here once; sat her on a horse for the first time. Brenna remembered clutching the coarse mane of hair, her father's smile as he walked beside her, his hand supporting her back.

She still loved riding.

She had felt safe, then. Loved. Like a little girl should feel.

He left them soon after.

Brenna leaned on the fence, lost in the memories.

Where did he go? Why did he leave? She'd given up the search years ago, but the unanswered questions continued to haunt her.

Rows of stubby green plants stretched as far as she could see. Staying along the edge of the field, Brenna headed for the barn in the distance.

Since she had found her way up the hill, the least she could do was stop in and see her grandfather.

She had never told her sisters how Marcus Ebans had secretly helped pay for her education. It wasn't something she'd asked for; wire transfers began appearing in her bank account when she moved to British Columbia. Before that, there had been an odd scholarship that she won when she graduated from high school.

Brenna had traced the transfers and discovered her grandfather had been her mysterious benefactor. Her letter of gratitude had begun a tentative correspondence that still continued with yearly Christmas cards.

As she crossed the field to the red barn, she realized with a pang that the horses were gone. Sold long ago, the track overrun with weeds and gopher holes. The barn only held bales of hay and a cat, who raced away as she tried to coax it towards her.

"Can I help you?" The male voice came from inside the barn, deep and no-nonsense.

She took a tentative step closer to the open door. "It's Brenna..." she said hesitantly. "Brenna Ebans."

"Brenna? Hi." She was surprised when her cousin Jamie stepped from the barn. "I'd heard you were back."

Despite being the same age, Brenna had always kept a friendly distance from Jamie in school, knowing how little his father thought of her family. Short and wiry, his Ebans red hair was now faded to a rusty brown.

To Brenna, Jamie looked a lot like the pictures of her father at that age.

"I got here a couple of days ago." Brenna was unsure of the proper greeting. Hug? Handshake? In the end, she did nothing but smile.

"Just here for a visit?"

"I felt like a bit of a walk, so I started up the hill and...oh. You meant why am I here, in Forest Hills. Addison's wedding. I'm not sure how long I'm going to be staying."

"Ah." There was an awkward pause; both aware of their family history.

"I should- "

"D'you want some coffee?" Jamie asked in a rush.

"Or a glass of water?"

"You're working. I don't want to intrude. I should just – hey..."

Joss Ryan emerged from the barn, with a smile instead of a scowl. "I didn't know we had visitors."

"What are you doing here?" Brenna demanded.

"I could ask the same thing. Your father was looking for you a while back," Joss said, looking at Jamie. "He was headed for the back field."

"I should go see what he needs," Jamie said, reluctantly. "You know what Dad's like if he's kept waiting. It was good to see you, Brenna. You should stop by, see Granddad."

"I was planning to." Brenna spoke to Jamie but was conscious of the tall form of Joss looming beside her.

Was it only last night that she verbally attacked him in Woody's, throwing all of her hurt and loneliness onto him? Her face flushed with embarrassment, and she had difficulty focusing on what her cousin was saying.

"He'd like it. Granddad's getting old. He still has everything in working order, but he's getting up there."

Brenna waved as Jamie walked away. She bounced on her heels a few times then turned to face Joss.

He hooked his arm around a post and grinned down at her. "So. You planning on yelling at me again?"

"Do you deserve to be yelled at?" A smile threatened at the corners of her lips.

"I'm sure you'll decide I've done something wrong. Even though you were the one who spilled my beer in the first place."

"It was an accident!"

"See? You're just about to yelling level and I haven't done a thing." The smile transformed his face, made him much less intimidating.

It also produced a strange fluttering sensation in the pit of Brenna's stomach.

"What brings you up to this neck of the woods?" Joss asked.

"For a walk." She craned her neck to look up at him. Tall and broad, with a bald head so shiny she was tempted to run her hand over the dome.

She wanted to touch his head? What had gotten into her?

"It's a pretty big hill to get up, just to go for a walk."

"I like the exercise. I used to do the Grouse Grind, in B.C. It's this hike up the mountain in Vancouver." She wasn't sure why she told him that, why she had a need to talk to him at all. It was like Joss opened the floodgates, forcing her to say things she had no intention of saying.

It was either talk or stand foolishly staring into his blue eyes.

He called her cute. Said she looked like someone he'd like to get to know.

It was much more complimentary than 'Big city swank.'

"I've heard of it," Joss told her. "I've spent some time out there. That's where you've been hiding all these years?"

"I wasn't hiding."

"Uh huh. You're close to yelling again."

"I am not. What are you doing here?" Brenna demanded, trying to catch her sense of balance. Why was she so unsettled around him?

"I work for your uncle. Jamie is married to my sister," he explained. "After I was discharged, a summer in the country sounded like a good idea. I never left."

"You were in the army."

"I was." Joss' face tightened, the smile toying with the corners of his mouth quickly vanishing. It was the same expression he wore last night.

"I better go," Brenna said abruptly.

Surprise raised his eyebrows. "That's too bad," he said lazily. "You're nice to talk to when you're not yelling at me."

"I didn't yell at you!" Brenna protested, a little louder that she intended.

"See?" Joss grinned and Brenna's face relaxed.

"But I really should go," she repeated, this time with obvious reluctance. The last thing she wanted was to have her uncle return and find her there.

"Cara said you and your sisters don't really get along with Jamie's dad."

She raised her eyebrows.

Joss shrugged at her unasked question. "I asked."

"You asked about me?"

"Seemed the thing to do."

He asked about her? What did that mean? She didn't have the mental energy to figure it out now.

Better to just... "I've got to go."

"That's what you keep saying."

After another uncomfortable pause, Brenna turned and walked away without a word. If she turned around, she knew Joss would be watching her walk away. She hoped Joss couldn't see the lopsided smile on her face.

Eager to put distance between them, she quickened her steps around the barn and saw the old red-bricked farmhouse. She hurried across the yard and climbed the steps to the porch. Heavy clumping footsteps responded to her knock.

"Brenna Evelyn Ebans!" Her granddad smiled as he held the door open. "Look at you. I'd heard you were back, getting into all sorts of trouble, just like when you were young. I wondered when you'd show your face. But first you'd best tell me what happened to your pretty face."

"I—uh," Brenna stammered, feeling like a child being reprimanded. "Cat. But it wasn't my fault! She started it!"

His laughter boomed through the house, startling her. The man at the door was not the grandfather of her childhood. Marcus Ebans had been straight backed and strong with an unsmiling, unchanging forbidding expression, frightening children and adults alike. There were never smiles when she saw him in town, definitely no laughter.

"Haven't changed much, have you, you and Cat?" Marcus asked over his shoulder as she followed him into the kitchen. "Still squabbling like a pair of puppies over the last bone. Well, come in, have some tea with us."

Brenna followed him to the kitchen, noticing the house was neat and tidy for an older man living alone. She wondered -

"Hello, Brenna."

Her mouth gaped at the sight of Seamus' mother, soft and round with Seamus' cheerful smile. "Mrs. Todd?"

She had been their mother's best friend since birth. Growing up, she had always been there for the sisters, making sure they ate when their mother locked herself in her room. When Brenna was fifteen and madly in love with Seamus, Mrs. Todd had welcomed Brenna into her family like a daughter.

Her hug felt like home.

"I've known you since you were a baby, Bee. I

think, after all this time, you can call me Fiona."

"It's nice to see you. Here." Brenna couldn't fathom a reason where Fiona Todd would be visiting Marcus Ebans.

And then Marcus did the unthinkable and tucked Fiona under his arm. "These days Fiona spends a fair amount of time here. I've been trying to convince her to move in with me, but she keeps saying no."

Her jaw dropped. "Really? But you—"

You hated each other. Brenna had heard Fiona cursing the Ebans' name on more than one occasion when she was young.

"A lot of time has passed, Brenna, and we've done a lot of growing up. Especially your grandfather," Fiona said with a twinkle in her eye. "Come, sit and have some tea. We want to hear all about your life in Vancouver."

Brenna couldn't contain her shock of seeing Fiona here. It felt like the two sides of her world had collided. "I think it's a lot less interesting than what's going on around here," Brenna said weakly, as she sat at the butcher block table.

Despite her correspondence with Marcus, this was the first time she had been in the house. Bright and airy, with plants and flowers covering windowsills. Comfortable and warm, and not what she expected.

"What were you and your sister fighting about?" Marcus asked as he settled at the table. His expression was stern but there was a hint of a smile at the corners of his mouth. This was not the man who used to stalk through the valley, instilling fear in everyone he passed.

"It just happened. How did you—?"

"You fighting with your sister was something this town hadn't heard about for a bit. I think you had quite the audience. I heard it from at least three people," Fiona teased. "At least it was a nice change from the other rumors floating around." She looked pointedly at Brenna.

"People here need a life," Brenna said firmly to hide her embarrassment.

"I suppose you're right," Marcus mused.

Brenna turned to Fiona in amazement. "What did you do to him?"

"It's nice, isn't it?" She smiled at Marcus. "The feud seems to be over."

Brenna stayed longer than she intended. Marcus seemed interested in her law career and Fiona excused herself while they chatted about a few of her cases.

Brenna took that time to ask him directly. “Seamus’ mom? How did that come about?”

“Fiona’s a good woman,” Marcus said.

“You don’t have to tell me that. She was my mother’s best friend.”

Marcus sipped his tea. “Brenna, I find that I made a lot of mistakes when it came to your mother. I blamed her for things that weren’t her fault. And I know I realized too late but I’ve been trying to make up for it.”

“By paying for my school?”

He nodded. “That was partly the reason. And the other was because I couldn’t bear to see a granddaughter of mine waste her intelligence here. You deserved more than what this place had to offer, even though it may have pissed off Fiona that you didn’t stay to marry her boy. I was glad to help with that. I’m proud of how you turned out,” he added gruffly, not meeting her eyes.

Brenna dropped her head so he wouldn’t see the wetness in her own eyes. Only Maggie and Kayleigh had ever expressed pride in her accomplishments.

"I'm helping out young Evie as well," he continued. "She seems to be taking after you in wanting to leave. I don't think she has plans to go as far, or stay away as long though."

Brenna rotated her tea cup, again. "Thank you," she managed.

"You've thanked me enough." His hand briefly touched hers. "You're my granddaughter. I only wish I had done more."

"You changed my life," Brenna told him in a rush of emotion. "And that you're doing it for Evie – thank you."

"She's a good girl," Marcus said with smile.

"She is. We'll – Maggie will miss her, but it will be good for her, just like it was for me."

Marcus nodded, studying her intently. "You're a lot like your father," he said carefully. "This place was always too small for him."

Brenna caught her breath. "Why did he leave?"

Marcus sighed heavily, looking every day of his seventy-nine years.

"Do you know why he left? Because that's all I've ever wanted to know!" The words tumbled out, somersaulting over each other in her haste. "I tried to find him, for years, so I could ask. Was it us—the fact there was so many of us? It couldn't have been easy. Or was it Mom and the way she was, the mood swings and the dark stuff?"

"Oh, Brenna. You mustn't blame yourself." Marcus reached for her hand, and Brenna clutched his age-spotted fingers, feeling the strength that remained.

"But I do. We all do."

Marcus shook his head, leaning away, as if he wanted to distance himself. "That's not right. Brenna, I'm so sorry. Roger didn't leave because of you, any of you. He left because of me."

"Did you have some sort of fight, some falling out?"

"He left because I told him to."

"I don't understand."

Marcus appeared to choose his words carefully. "At first, Roger took up with Carly because I was against it. He knew it would anger me, and it did. I never had much patience for your mother's family, and I afraid I never had much patience for your father, either. Roger would get himself into heaps of trouble, but then he'd smile and find his way out of it.

He was a rascal, a scamp, and he never did grow out of that."

"But why -?"

"The first time he was unfaithful to your mother was two days after the wedding. When she was in the hospital, giving birth to your sister Maggie, Roger was at Woody's with one of her cousins draped all over him. When she took to her bed because of pregnancy – I think that was your sister, Dory – he moved in with Margery Frew. You know about Amelia Farrell. There were so many women." Marcus hung his head, shamed by his son's behaviour.

"I've never heard – why didn't anyone tell me any of this?" Brenna demanded. "The whole town must have known."

"And wanted to spare you and your sisters. Maggie was old enough to know what was going on. Kayleigh as well. But you three..." He tapped his teacup with a fingernail.

"What else?" she asked in a cold voice. "What else did he do?"

"There were a few incidents while he'd been drinking. There were drugs – he liked the fast life, he had money and all sorts of unsavory types flocked to him. He killed a man from Blind River -"

"What? Killed someone?" All the hopes and dreams Brenna had had about her father vanished with a sharp tang of bitterness. Who was this man she had thought of as her father? Who was Roger Ebans? Kayleigh and Maggie had been right – he was a stranger to her.

"An accident, but still. And, to my regret, Peter and I covered it up. Your father should have taken responsibility for his actions. He used those women like he used the drugs, made me ashamed how he turned out. He had no care that he humiliated your mother, our family. I finally had enough and told him to go. Told him to leave." Marcus' expression was stoic and unyielding, the face of the man Brenna remembered.

"I don't understand. You made him leave?"

"Yes," Marcus admitted, his voice steady.

"He left – you made him leave because he was cheating on Mom – on my mother?" Wasn't that her decision to make?"

"Would you rather he left your mama for another woman in town?" Marcus asked. "Living right under your nose, with a new family?"

"That was my father," Brenna said incredulously. She didn't realize she was standing until she was backed away from the table, wanting to put distance between her and her grandfather. Never, in all her speculations on why he left, did she ever consider someone—his own father—had driven him away.

"Brenna, you don't know what he was like." Again, Marcus reached for her hand. She shook him off.

"And that's because of you! You took my father away so I never knew him! How could you – how did you? How did you make him leave?"

"I told him I'd cut him out of the will." Marcus dropped his eyes.

"You told him -" Her mind reeling, she looked everywhere but at the old man sitting beside her. "And that's why you helped with my school. Because you felt guilty. Well, you should! How dare you? That was my father!"

"He wasn't a good man. He may have been my son, but I wasn't proud of him. I'm sorry, Brenna, for how I raised him and what he did to you and your sisters."

Marcus' apology fell on deaf ears. Without another word, Brenna walked out of the house.

She ignored the voices calling after her, heading for the road, heading for home.

Home. She laughed at the irony.

It was Cat's home, not hers.

It was no longer her father's home.

Brenna used to imagine what it would be like if he came back. Of course there would be accusations, but he'd explain himself. He'd been away saving the world from evil warlords, or searching for a cure for their mother's illness - the reasons changed each time Brenna imagined the scenario. But never had she contemplated Roger had left because of his own father thought him selfish and childish, unable to fulfill his role or provide for his family.

He killed someone.

Brenna was almost at the road when the motorcycle pulled up beside her, covering her in grit and dust. She jumped to the side, the long grasses scratching her bare legs.

"I thought maybe – what's wrong?" Joss insisted when he caught sight of her face.

"My father," Brenna said simply. She hadn't realized there were tears until she pushed her hair out of her face and found her cheeks damp.

"But I thought – ah." An expression of sympathy replaced the usual scowl as he handed her a helmet. "Get on. I'll take you home."

She had never been on a motorcycle before, but sliding on the machine, her arms wrapped around Joss' unyielding torso as they sped down the hill was more of a comfort than Brenna could ever have imagined.

Chapter Twenty-Four

Cat

The mildest, drowsiest sister has been known to turn tiger if her sibling is in trouble.

—Clara Ortega

"Please tell me those bruises aren't because you told her about us," Seamus asked when he caught sight of Cat's bruises when she reported for her shift at Woody's that evening. Cupping her face, he smoothed his thumb along her cheekbone, one of the few spots that hadn't been a recipient of Brenna's fists.

Cat had kept the bag of frozen peas pressed to her eye as long as she could, but the bruise had bloomed, purplish-blue, as vivid as a flower. The heel marks where Brenna had kicked her stomach looked worse. But nothing felt as bad as the sudden lurch in her stomach. “I kinda haven’t told her.”

“What do you mean?”

Cat dropped her eyes from his questioning gaze. “I haven’t exactly told her we were together.”

“Cat -”

“I’m sure she knows!”

“What if she doesn’t?” Seamus pulled her aside, farther away from the regulars already propping up the bar.

“Somebody would have told her. Missy, or Kayleigh...”

“*You* should have told her. She’s your sister for God’s sake.”

“Well, I didn’t.” She hated the expression of disappointment on his face, her uncertainty that Brenna probably didn’t know about her and Seamus. It’s not like it would have come out while they were rolling around the kitchen. “Look, I’ll mention it to her next time I see her. Okay?”

“She’s been in town since Thursday.”

“Which is why I’m sure someone already told

her," Cat lied.

"I don't think anyone did." Now Seamus was the one with shifting eyes.

"What happened?" Her voice was quick to snap, like a lizard catching a bug.

"Nothing," he said quickly. "It was nothing. The other night -"

"When you drove her home? What did she do?"

"Cat, she didn't know."

"She kissed you, didn't she?" Cat breathed deeply through her nose, doing her best to calm the rage that instantly welled up at the thought of her *sister* and Seamus.

"Right," she said, closing her eyes, still fighting for control. She backed away from Seamus and he caught her arm.

"It wasn't anything, didn't mean anything and I stopped it right away."

Cat couldn't say anything.

"What are you going to do?"

She exhaled once, twice, pushing the image of Brenna and Seamus wrapped in each other's arms down, down deep, only to be brought out in times when she wanted to be depressed, or angry with

Seamus. “Nothing.”

“Nothing...?”

Smiling grimly, Cat touched his chest. “You still love me, don’t you? Despite everything?”

He grabbed her hand with his own. “Don’t be stupid.”

She shook her head, gave a humourless laugh. She wasn’t stupid, but some of her choices definitely were. This time, she wouldn’t make the same mistake. She knew Seamus – he wouldn’t want her to feel insecure or jealous. “I would have done the same thing.”

Seamus’ laugh sounded relieved. Crisis averted. “So what was the fight about?”

Cat leaned in and kissed him, even though her cut lip made it painful. “We cleared the air,” she told him, heading for the bar. “Things needed to be said and it got physical.” Other than the fight with Brenna, she’d had a productive day in the kitchen and had delivered three cakes and a tray of pastries to the Sandwich Shoppe before work.

And even though Brenna had ruined her first batch of chocolate batter, it had been refreshing to see the side of her sister that was capable of losing control. She wasn’t always perfect after all.

"Is Brenna OK?" he asked hesitantly.

Cat refused to let jealousy rear up again. Seamus loved *her*. "She was fine last time I saw her. She went for a walk."

"I meant..."Seamus gestured to his face.

"I gave her a nice shiner. Hey, she started it!" Cat protested at the disapproving look. "Well, maybe not. She hit back though. Hard."

"That's more like it." Seamus led the way to the bar at the back of the restaurant.

They passed a family seated at a corner table having an early supper. The exhausted looking mother tried to catch a little girl crawling under the table, and two boys rolled, pushing and shoving on the floor, not unlike what she and Brenna had done earlier. The father stared intently at his phone, ignoring the chaos around him.

For the first time, Cat had a twinge of apprehension about her baby plan. How could she control a child when she couldn't even control her own temper?

Seamus would...

Cat stared at the back of Seamus' head as he grabbed a glass, holding it under the tap as beer trickled out.

In her plan, Seamus *wouldn't* because he wouldn't be around.

Cat pasted on a smile as she greeted a few of the locals already elbowed up at the bar, pushing her dark thoughts farther back in her mind.

"Nice to know the Skatt-fights aren't a thing of the past," Tommy called to her. Cat gave her ex a tight-lipped smile, refusing to be baited.

"I think the two of you look even more alike with the matching bruises," another regular guffawed.

"She's gotten feistier in her old age," Cat said, tying her apron around her waist. "And she's still got the temper."

"I didn't think that would go away," Seamus grunted, as he checked on the lines connecting the beer kegs to the taps. "The keg needs to be changed."

"I can do that. How did you hear about the *brawl* anyway?"

"Kayleigh. Well, she was the first one to tell me, but there's been a few since. Main story about town."

"Aren't I always?"

"You shouldn't be in this good of a mood," Seamus said with a worried frown. "You're scaring me."

"Why?" Cat moved behind him and slid her arms around his waist, pressing her body against him. One of the regulars, sitting opposite them, gave a hoot. The town knew they were together, but displays of affection were usually kept private.

She felt Seamus tense and knew it was more than her public display that caused it. Leaning around his shoulder, she watched Brady Todd walk in with his usual cocky grin.

Cat unwound her arms from Seamus, the smile of contentment vanishing.

"Cat, I'll handle it," Seamus tried, reaching for her.

She ducked past him. "I've got this."

"Hey, Kitty Cat, where's my cookies!" Brady called as she met him halfway towards the bar. Brady's grin quickly disappeared at the sight of the thundercloud distorting Cat's face. He took a step back toward the door, but she grabbed his shirtfront before he could make a run for it.

"How dare you!" Cat began in a low voice.

"She wanted it!" Brady bleated like a frightened sheep.

"I don't care." Stepping closer, she poked a hard finger into his chest. "You are never, ever to lay another finger on another member of my family ever again. Do you understand?"

"I didn't—she wanted it -"

"How could you do that to Evie?" Brady winced as she raised her voice.

"Cat," Seamus called a warning.

Gripping Brady's shirt in her fist, Cat leaned closer. "You *know* she likes you, Brady Todd! And for you to do that with Brenna—her *aunt*? How could you be such a jerk? Such an asshole—such a disappointment." Her voice dropped and she was gratified to see the first show of remorse cross his face.

"Cat, I didn't think..."

"No, you were thinking with your dick instead of your head like usual." She flicked her fist against his lower stomach, refusing to let Brady see how much the gentle tap hurt her hand. "And then to tell everyone about Brenna—to *brag* about? You're nothing more than a childish, immature little ass of a boy. I can't believe you!"

"Cat..."

She held up her hand. "No. You screwed up big this time. Your smiles aren't getting you out of this. I'm done with you. So disappointed in you, Brady. You stay clear of Evie, and Brenna and the rest of my family. If I ever hear of you pulling shit like this again, there'll be hell to pay. Now, get out. You're not welcome here tonight."

"Hey, c'mon, I just want a beer," he cajoled. "I've been working all day..." The pleading smile was full of charm, full of admiration.

Full of shit.

The smile wasn't about to get him anywhere that night. "If you sit your ass at that bar tonight, if I have to serve you a beer, it's going to be over your head. And then I'm going to have to clean it up. And if you think I'm pissed off now, you haven't seen anything yet."

"C'mon Cat..."

She had to give him credit for being persistent. "Listen up, Brady, I heard all about your little tryst with Pam last winter. If you don't want the whole town to know about your pathetic little Christian Gray spanking episode, you'll leave now. And trust me, every woman in town will know that being spanked by a silly little boy is about as sexy as the time I spanked *you* after you threw a ball at my window when you were four years old. Got it? You think you're the only one who can tell stories."

Brady's tan had suddenly vanished, leaving his face pale and frightened, without a hint of adolescent defiance.

Cat's mouth curved in a smile as she danced back towards the bar. Nobody messed with her family.

Chapter Twenty-Five

Brenna

She is your mirror, shining back at you with a world of possibilities. She is your witness, who sees you at your worst and best, and loves you anyway. She is your partner in crime, your midnight companion, someone who knows when you are smiling, even in the dark. She is your teacher, your defense attorney, your personal press agent, even your shrink. Some days, she's the reason you wish you were an only child.

—Barbara Alpert

Brenna's legs were shaking when Joss pulled up in front of the house. She kept her arms wrapped around him until she was positive the motorcycle wasn't going to move again.

"You can let go now," he told her, a hint of amusement in his voice.

After being pressed against the warmth of Joss during the ride from the farm, Brenna's chest felt cold when she scrambled off the bike. "Thank you," she said stiffly, raising her voice over the throaty growl of the engine.

He frowned. "You should never wear shorts on the back of a bike. Make sure you have pants on for the next ride. Jeans, preferably."

"Next time?" The question escaped in a squeak, producing a laugh from Joss.

"You don't like bikes?"

"I've never given it much thought." At the moment, Brenna was too busy noticing how attractive Joss was when he laughed. His blue eyes shone, full lips curved up...

"You should think about it." He smiled at her as something long forgotten in the pit of her belly slowly woke up and stretched.

Brenna fumbled with the helmet. "Here." But when she tried to hand it to him, Joss shook his head.

"Keep it for now."

The flutter of apprehension at the thought of getting back on the machine fought with the twinge of pleasure that Joss wanted to see her again.

He gunned the engine with a grin. “You should lay off your sister,” he called over the noise.

“Why?”

Joss’ finger waved in the direction of her bruised face. “If you look like that, I can only imagine that Cat looks worse. Your sister’s a feisty one, but my money’s on you.” With a blinding smile and a wink, Joss roared out of the driveway, leaving Brenna standing there holding the helmet with a silly smile on her face.

She was still shaking her head when she headed to the porch and turned the doorknob.

The door was locked. Brenna gave it a firm tug and hammered on the door with her fist. A crescendo of barking answered.

If Cat was in the house, there was no way she would miss someone at the door with that racket. She waited another minute and knocked again.

Cat obviously wasn’t there. Either that or she was crouched inside, having a good laugh at Brenna’s expense.

Brenna checked the time, assuming Cat had

already left for work.

"Dammit." Brenna could tell from the ever-fading roar of the engine that Joss was halfway back up the hill. Not that he could have done anything but drive her to Woody's to pick up Cat's key.

She could walk over herself, but the thought of asking her sister for anything wasn't appealing.

How did Dory used to get in the house?

Ten minutes later, Brenna had wriggled triumphantly through a window that led into a pantry at the back of the kitchen. All these years, and the latch on the window still wasn't fixed.

She soon found herself back on the porch, this time with the door propped open, with dinner consisting of an apple, a pot of yogurt and a large glass of wine. The dogs had apparently decided to keep her company or offer protection, whichever they felt she needed.

Brenna stretched out her legs and leaned her head back, grateful for the silence of the evening. Her conversation with her grandfather rose, unbidden, and she blinked away the sudden tears. How could her father have left them for money? The threat of losing his inheritance was more important than his wife and children. A tear escaped, trickling down her cheek. She'd given him the benefit of the doubt and now to find out the truth...

Nothing had ever hurt so much.

She felt hollow, emptied out. Numb. The anger would come eventually. But now she sat in the chair like an orphan. Abandoned and alone.

The first stars were beginning to show themselves when Brenna finally took the dogs inside. Half a bottle of wine hadn't helped the whirlpool of her thoughts.

"Enough," she told the dogs. "Time to put everything to bed."

She climbed the stairs and fell into bed with one of the dogs on guard beside the bed. Despite the early hour, Brenna's exhaustion was stronger than the thoughts still mingling in her mind.

A man's laugh intruded into her dream.

"Toby?" she mumbled.

Toby was in Vancouver. Brenna was home, in the old house, in the bed grew up in, and there were voices in the hall. She recognized her sister's voice.

The least Cat could do was keep it down.

Pulling the quilt around her shoulders, Brenna opened her door and poked her head into the hall.

Cat in the arms of a man. They were kissing; he had her pressed up against the wall. Brenna blinked, once, twice. It looked like –

"Seamus?"

Still entwined, both Cat and Seamus turned.

"Oops," Cat said. Even in the dimness of the hall, Cat's face clearly showed the evidence of their earlier blows.

"Hey," Seamus slowly backed away from Cat, guilt evident on his face.

"What are you...?" Brenna blinked, shook her head. "Never mind, it's obvious." She swayed with the surprise of it, grabbing the wall to steady herself. Seamus...and Cat.

It made sense. Cat had always wanted him. But still, to find out like *this*?

"Sorry to wake you," Cat said.

"Sorry to *wake* me?" This was Toby all over again, apologizing for being found out, never the act itself. This was another betrayal, and the pain of it seared through her, as if Cat's fist had punched her straight in the heart.

"Bren, look -" Seamus began, heading towards her.

"Don't!" Brenna threw up her hands, nearly clipping Seamus on the chin. "Just don't."

"I never wanted you to find out like this," he pleaded.

"Find out...This isn't a...it's...you're...When?" It took Brenna three tries to get the words out and finally she gave up.

This wasn't a *thing*. This was a together.

Seamus dropped his head.

"What does it matter? You left," Cat said.

"You're together." Brenna breathed through her nose. She had left. It had been years since she and Seamus...

Cat and Seamus?

"It was after my marriage busted up. It just...happened," Seamus explained apologetically.

"Everyone knows? And no one thought to tell me?"

It was like Brenna was seeing Seamus for the first time. She had known it was over between them, that they had both moved on, but there had always been that last shred of hope that he still loved her.

Brenna desperately needed someone to still love her.

"I thought you knew." Cat's voice was flat, expressionless.

But when Brenna looked at her, she thought she saw the hint of a smile in her green eyes. Cat knew she'd won.

Anger, anguish, frustration rose within Brenna like hot lava of a volcano. "I can't do this." She back away from Seamus, suddenly gasping for breath. "It's too much. You – everything...coming home..." With sobs choking her, she turned and ran for her room.

"Brenna!" Seamus called.

Slamming the door, Brenna leaned against it, hand pressed against her mouth to hold in both the swell of nausea and the hateful words she longed to spew. She needed to fight, to attack...to hurt...

The door vibrated as Seamus pounded his fist against it. "Brenna, let me in."

"Why?" The word began as a moan, a whimper. "Why would I want to let you anywhere?"

She yanked open the door so quickly that Seamus practically tumbled inside. "Why did I think it would be a good idea to come back here?" she cried, blocking the door. Seamus shrank back from the violence in her voice. "I didn't know the two of you were together.

No one thought to tell me. Just like no one thought to tell me it was Granddad who made our father leave us. And how the hell was I supposed to know who Evie liked – no one told me! No one thinks to tell me anything! No one thinks of me at all! No one visits, no one calls -"

"That's what happens when you leave and stay away for fourteen years!" Cat spat out, leaning over Seamus' shoulder like a bird circling its prey. "All this feeling sorry for yourself – it's your own damn fault!"

The anger deflated with a shaky breath, leaving a vast wasteland within her. Brenna stared at Cat, noticing for the first time how like looking in a mirror it was. She swallowed, not wanting to cry, not wanting to cry in front of Cat.

"Cat, go." Seamus pushed Brenna aside and stepped into the room. "You're not helping."

"She can help herself," Cat sneered, immovable as a rock. "It's what she's used to doing. She already told me."

"Enough." He shut the door gently in her face, reached for Brenna.

"No." Moving away from him again, Brenna backed into the bed, sat down hard.

"Stop being so stubborn." His voice was gentle, his body warm as he sat beside her. "I'm sorry. I thought you knew. I just assumed after all these years that you'd be okay with it."

"I don't care," she muttered. Heat rose in her throat, scalding her, the pain announcing the oncoming tears. "It doesn't matter. It's not that." Her hands hid her face, trying to staunch the heaving sobs that threatened. "It's everything."

She couldn't stop the rush of tears, bringing with them a sweet sense of release. Somehow Brenna was cradled in Seamus' arms, crying so hard she felt her body was trying to turn itself inside out. It felt like she was ridding herself of her grief, long minutes of weeping, wailing, of cleansing herself. Of clinging to Seamus like a lifeline.

But then she quieted, there were no more tears. And somehow two dogs were with her, cold noses pressed against her bare legs.

Seamus waited to speak until her sobs had turned into hiccups. "Are you okay?"

"I -" Brenna heaved a deep breath and sat up, wiping her cheeks with the blanket still clutched around her shoulders. "I think so."

"That was – wow."

Somehow she found a smile. "You always hated seeing me cry."

Seamus shuddered. "Couldn't stand it. Still can't."

"I haven't cried in a long time." She looked everywhere but at Seamus. The only light in the room came from the ever-widening crack where the dogs had pushed past the door. The basset hound lay at her feet with a sigh, as the collie pushed his nose into Brenna's lap. She stroked his soft ears.

Seamus stirred beside her. "Was that all because of me? Me and...Cat...?"

"No." Brenna chuckled softly. "You were just the last straw."

Chapter Twenty-Six

Cat

When sisters stand shoulder to shoulder, who stands a chance against us?

—Pam Brown

Cat sat on the porch, the front door open behind her to let Seamus know she was outside. The screen door squeaked as he pushed it open and stepped out.

"Well?" she demanded.

"It wasn't just seeing us together that set her off," he said, settling into the chair beside her.

"Just? What do you mean, just? What else could it have been?" Cat's stomach twisted with guilt. She'd done plenty she wasn't proud of over the years, some that could even be called unforgivable. Cheating on Perry. Not telling Seamus she'd stopped taking birth control. But this was a new level of remorse. She'd broken her sister's heart. They weren't kids anymore and she could see the result of her actions. Or lack of actions.

"She's got a lot going on," Seamus said. "It couldn't have been easy finding out like that. You should have told her."

"You could have told her!"

"One of us should have made sure she knew," he agreed, his voice as heavy as hers.

Cat stared at the stars, Seamus silent beside her.

"She's gone back to bed," he finally said. "I think I might head back to my place."

"Might be a good idea." Cat knew she wouldn't be comfortable being in bed with Seamus when a tear-streaked Brenna lay alone down the hall. She kissed him good-night, watched his truck pull out of the drive before heading upstairs to bed.

As Cat passed Brenna's room, she paused, listening. The door was open a crack, but no sound came from within. She rested her fingers against the door.

"I'm sorry," she whispered.

*

When she woke up Sunday morning, Cat found Brenna's door open, bed made, the room empty. Last night left Cat in the unfamiliar territory of feeling sympathy for her sister. The lack of sleep hadn't helped the feelings of guilt.

If she hurried, she could be in time for church, the tried and true spot guaranteed to make her feel better.

As Cat crept into the Forest Hills United Church, aiming for the Skatt pew three rows from the back on the left side—she was shocked to see Brenna already seated there, head bowed.

Relief swelled within Cat, releasing some the ache in her belly. She slid along the smooth wood, bumping Brenna with her shoulder.

"What are you doing here?" Brenna demanded with a scowl.

"It's Sunday. I go to church," Cat said defensively. As Brenna slid further down the pew to make room for Cat, the haunting sounds of the organ began.

"You're late."

"I'm right on time." Cat swallowed and leaned closer to Brenna. "I thought you had left."

"Sorry you didn't get your wish."

"Didn't want you to leave on my account." Cat did her best to sound sincere. It was surprisingly easy. She caught her breath at the revelation. She wanted Brenna to stay.

Brenna's mouth tightened skeptically before she turned and grabbed the hymn book.

It was a small church and more than two thirds full this morning. Cat's former father-in-law, Reverend Macleod still preached from the pulpit and Cat cringed when she met his unforgiving gaze. Perry might have forgiven Cat for all the hurt and trouble she had caused him in their brief marriage, and maybe God had too, but Reverend Macleod definitely hadn't.

Brenna sat stiff as a statue beside Cat in the pew. Church service in Forest Hill was a casual event. A few of the older ladies wore their Sunday finest but the norm was pants and a clean shirt, or at least one without any visible stains. Brenna stood out in the crowd, looking expensive and lawyerly in her blazer and slim-fitting pants.

Except for the shoes; when Cat glanced down she noticed the hot pink sandals.

Cat wiggled her toes in her Birkenstocks sandals. At least her toenail polish wasn't too chipped. "Nice shoes."

Brenna replied with the same eyebrow raise Maggie had perfected, the one that assured she didn't believe a word Cat was saying. "Thanks." She turned her attention back to the hymnbook but curiosity got the best of her. "What are you doing here?"

"I go to church," Cat said defensively.

"Since when?"

"Since I was baptized when I was four months old. You were there—they did you at the same time. Ever wonder why we didn't get our own baptism? All the others did."

"At least they didn't make you wait an extra year."

This conversation occurred in whispered tones but even then, Mrs. Patton, who sat in the pew in front of them, turned with a finger to her lips. Cat had never liked Mrs. Patton, who had once complained about the sweetness of her icing. She stuck her tongue out at the back of Mrs. Patton's head, and caught Brenna trying to hide a smile. "Why are you here?"

"I go to church almost every Sunday," Brenna admitted.

"Really? Why?"

"Why do you go?"

"I don't go every week," Cat admitted. "Just -"

"Just when you feel guilty about not telling your sister you took up with her ex-boyfriend as soon as she left home? Did you at least actually wait until my plane was in the air?"

"It was about four years ago," Cat hissed. "He got married, did you forget? And so did you! C'mon – it's been fourteen years!"

"I've been here since Thursday!" Brenna whispered. Cat had never heard a whisper sound so angry. "Didn't anyone think to tell me?"

"I thought you'd figure it out sooner or later."

"Yes, by seeing the two of you making out right outside my bedroom!"

"I had to watch the two of you make out lots of times!"

"And how did it make you feel?"

"Not great," Cat conceded. "What do you want me to say? I'm sorry you were too stuck in your own world to figure it out? The great genius Brenna can't see what's in front of her eyes? Just like you didn't know your husband was getting jerked off by your friend?"

Anger flashed from Brenna's eyes. "She was not my friend," she said, a little too loudly for Mrs. Patton, who turned around again.

"Girls," she warned.

Brenna ignored her. "I can't believe you would say that! Have you cheated on so many husbands that you can't have any sympathy for what it feels like to be cheated on?"

"I never cheated on Alex," Cat muttered.

"Who's Alex?"

"You don't even know the names of my husband's?"

"Well, you had quite a few!"

"At least I knew how to keep them happy in the bedroom so they wouldn't screw around!"

"You're such a... bitch!" Brenna hissed, dropping her voice at the last word.

"All that education and that's all you got?"

"Fucking bitch!" Brenna was obviously beyond caring if she was overheard.

"Girls, enough!" Mrs. Patton whipped around

again. "We are in church! This isn't appropriate at all."

"And I'm sure God's been waiting just as long as I have for my sister to apologize so would you please stop interrupting and mind your own business?" Brenna said, her voice dripping with insincere politeness.

Cat tried to stifle her shocked gasp but it turned into a laugh at the outraged expression on Mrs. Patton's face.

"Skatts," Mrs. Patton mouthed, face twisted into a disapproving frown.

"I heard stories of your daughter being pretty hung up on one of our handsome Skatt cousins so I'd watch yourself there. We might just end up related some day," Cat said with a cheerful smile.

By that time, those in the pews around them were more interested in their conversation than what the Reverend was saying. "We should be quiet," Brenna murmured. "It's inappropriate."

"Why? We're Skatts," Cat managed a perfect imitation of Mrs. Patton's disapproving tone. "We're supposed to be inappropriate."

Neither Cat and Brenna could prevent another outbreak of giggles, which was thankfully muffled by the booming of the organ.

The knot in Cat's stomach loosened with the laughter.

Chapter Twenty-Seven

Brenna

What's the good of news if you haven't a sister to share it?

—Jenny DeVries

After church, Brenna stayed in town to pick up a few things at the store, needing some distance between her and Cat. Sure, they'd ending up having fun in church but the tough ball of hurt and disappointment still lingered. It wasn't that Brenna expected Seamus to want her back. Far from it. But coming home, seeing Seamus had opened the door a crack for her, leaving a what if?

Now the what if was what if Cat married him? The door to Seamus had been slammed shut and padlocked without Brenna even getting a peek at what was on the other side.

After browsing in the General Store, Brenna was heading back to Cat's when she paused outside the Sandwich Shoppe. Enticing aromas wafted out but what caught Brenna's attention was the sight of her niece, Evie.

Evie worked at the café. If she could get a minute with her, apologize...

Brenna swung open the door to the Sandwich Shoppe with her hip, her arms filled with the brown paper bags that the General Store still used to bag groceries. The café

was filled with the low buzz of conversation from the after church crowd. Brenna's stomach growled as she was surrounded by the scent of mouthwatering aromas.

She hadn't eaten since her solo pity party on the front porch yesterday.

"Brenna, hello! Nice to see you after so long." Sara, a middle-aged woman with a sweet, mother-like smile and the best raspberry pie in the province, stepped over to greet her. She swept an arm in the direction of the few empty tables. "Where can I put you today?"

"Actually, I just need a minute with Evie. Um...You still making the raspberry pie?"

"Just took one out of the oven."

"Maybe I have time for a slice?"

"I'll bring you out a piece," Sara promised. "But first a bowl of soup? And maybe a sandwich. We've got a grilled cheese on special, made with some of your sister's wonderful bread. Just sit yourself down where ever you can."

Brenna had a flash of spreading Wonder bread thickly with butter, her mother dropping them into the frying pan before adding the plastic-wrapped Kraft cheese slices.

It had been the one thing they did together.

"That sounds great," Brenna said.

Sara bustled back into the kitchen as Brenna found a seat in the corner and settled the bags on the floor around her, nodding at the people at the table next to her.

She couldn't help wondering if they were whispering about her, what she had done with Brady.

Or about the fight with Cat. Or that she fell asleep in the bathroom at Woody's. Or that she only came home because her husband cheated on her.

The list was long and getting longer.

"Aunt Brenna?" Evie seemed paler than usual with her red hair hanging over her cheeks, framing her face. Against the black pants and a white shirt, the apron Sara still insisted her staff wear made the waitresses look like candy stripers.

"Do you have a second?" Brenna asked. "I really need to apologize to you."

Evie shrugged without meeting Brenna's eyes and filled the water glass on the table. "There's no need."

"There is. I'm so sorry you were hurt." Brenna touched her arm. "I had no idea you had feelings for Brady. I wouldn't have...well, you know. If I'd known. I wouldn't have gone near him."

Evie nodded and studied her feet. "It's okay."

"It's really not." Brenna leaned closer. "My behaviour was inexcusable. To show such a lack of respect...in a bizarre way, I thought would be a good way to get back at Toby," she admitted in a whisper. "That's all. He cheated on me, so I thought..."

"I understand. Really," Evie said with a small

smile. "And it kind of helped. Aunt Cat's always telling me not to go near him -"

"She's right."

"It sounds strange to have you agreeing with her. Especially..." she waved a finger at the bruises evident on Brenna's face.

"Ah. That." Brenna glanced around her, noticing once again she was the object of interest. "We cleared a few things up."

"Maybe try talking first, next time?"

Brenna laughed, relieved Evie understood, forgave her. "That might be a good idea."

"Now you can move back into our place," Evie said eagerly. "I'm sure Mom's over being mad at you."

"I'll give her a little more time. But I think I'll stick it out with Cat. She hasn't killed me—yet," she said with a tentative touched of her chin. "Who knows what'll happen? But as soon as your mom gives me the OK, I'll be back to see you all."

"Are you sure you'll be OK staying with Aunt Cat?"

"I think it's all out of our system now." Brenna stood and gave her niece a hug. "Is everything OK for the wedding next weekend?"

"Mom's stressed and Addison's unbearable, so pretty normal."

"Maybe you should come and stay with Cat and I," Brenna suggested, but instantly shook her head as Evie's eyes lit up. "Forget I said anything. Your mom would be furious with me. I'm going to get you into enough trouble if you don't get back to work. Go on. I'll talk to you soon. And I'm really sorry about everything."

Evie gave her a shy smile. "On a good note, I think it did help me get over him," she offered.

"You're just saying that so I'll stop feeling so guilty."

"Kind of. But I don't like him as much as I did, now."

"Well, that's one good thing."

With a smile that warmed Brenna's heart, Evie returned to the kitchen as Sara brought out a steaming bowl of broccoli soup dotted with slivers of cheddar and a sandwich, melted cheese oozing out the side. Brenna was scrambling in her purse for a Lacteeze pill before Sara made it across the floor.

Brenna barely thanked her before diving in.

Cat might be the creator of the bread, perfectly

crunchy with a soft inside, but it was the cheese that was the star of Brenna's lunch. Melted white cheddar, with a slice of Swiss. She tasted the scraping of apple jelly with the cheese and let out a soft moan of delight.

Cheese was not her friend, but she still loved it.

Both the plate and bowl were empty when Sara brought out a slice of pie and two cups of coffee. "That looks wonderful," Brenna enthused, salivating at the slice of pie oozing raspberries, with chocolate drizzled on the plate.

Sara smirked, her focus behind Brenna. When she glanced over her shoulder, Joss Ryan was standing behind her, with a smile on his face.

Her stomach did a little flip at the sight of him. "You again."

"And you have pie."

"What are you doing here?"

"Same thing you are, I imagine."

Brenna thought of Evie. "I doubt that."

Sara set the coffee on the table, along with the pie. "Enjoy," she sang over her shoulder.

"You're not here to eat some pie?" Joss looked fixedly at Brenna's plate, before sitting down facing her. "Sure, don't mind if I do. You were going to ask me to sit down, weren't you?" He took the fork out of Brenna's hand. "And to share your pie?"

"No!" She reached for the fork, but Joss already had a mouthful. "I've waited years for that pie."

"Sharing is the polite thing to do, isn't it?"

"I've never been good at sharing."

"I've heard that about you. We'll have to work on that." With a shake of his bald head, Joss cut off a corner of the pie and popped it into Brenna's open mouth. "You're such a nice, sweet girl," he added sarcastically. "I'm sure you would have offered. Been in anymore fights recently?"

The tartness of the berries blended well with the scrape of chocolate on the fork. "No. I don't -" She swallowed before finishing. "It's not something I tend to do."

"Good thing. It's too pretty a face to let it get all messed up. I saw the bruises on Cat's face. You're pretty good with your fists."

Brenna caught her breath at his offhanded words, tried to keep her cool even though the smile threatened to streak across her face. "You should see what happens when someone steals my pie."

"We're sharing." He forked up another mouthful

for Brenna before she could respond.

Quickly, quietly, Joss shared her slice of pie, evenly distributing it between both. She took the time to watch him, wondering why he was here, sharing her table. Like their previous meetings, it could be a coincidence that he was in Sara's at the same time, but there was no need for him to sit with her.

And share her pie.

Brenna didn't invite him to sit. She didn't encourage. He just sat, intimidating her with the width of his shoulders, the obvious strength of his arms. The size of his bald head alone, the lights of the café reflecting off it, seemed massive.

The way his mouth moved under the beard, flashing glimpses of white teeth when he grinned at her.

Joss overflowed with masculinity and Brenna couldn't help compare his maleness to her husband. Toby had always been overly concerned with his attire, taking more time than Brenna fixing his hair. Always ready to shop, visit a spa. Pamper himself.

Joss looked like he didn't know the meaning of pamper.

If he wasn't her type, why had her body clenched

when he sat down, tightened even more every time he placed the fork against her lips?

Brenna craned her head to look around. "People are staring."

"Why?"

"I don't know!"

"Must be cuz you look uptight." Joss appeared anything but uptight as he leaned back in his chair, his forearm resting on the table. A dragon was inked on the inside of his arm.

Brenna had never spent time with a man with tattoos.

"I'm not uptight," she snapped.

"And here I was just trying to make polite conversation...What's gotten into you today? Someone special or just your own thoughts? That's the problem with girls like you. You always over-think things."

"I don't over-think."

"No? What happened—did someone look at you the wrong way and now you think no one likes you?"

"No. I was thinking about how my husband didn't like me much."

Joss leaned forward, his arm sliding across the table. "Throughout the whole marriage or just at the end?"

"I'm not sure. Definitely near the end."

"And you're trying to figure out if that was your fault?" He nodded to himself.

"Why—how did you know?" Brenna gasped.

"'Cause I have a sister who I listen to, plus I'm pretty good friends with your sister. I like to think I've got a fairly decent understanding of women."

"Because of Cat?" Her voice cooled at the mention of her sister.

"No, my years and years of experience as one of the good guys."

"I don't think I'll ever understand men."

Joss smiled and forked another piece of pie into Brenna's mouth."Why not? We're an open book."

"Well, it's one I don't know how to read."

"Must be the only one you don't. I heard you were one smart cookie."

"Are cookies really that smart?"

"They keep getting eaten, so no, I guess not."

Brenna burst out laughing, spewing crumbs of pastry from her mouth. "You keep hearing things about me. Is my life an open book around here or is it just speculation and rumors?"

"You tell me. What's real and what's rumor about Brenna Skatt?"

"Ebans. I don't know what's being said."

"Why are you Ebans, and Cat and Kayleigh go by Skatt?" Joss asked with a frown. Brenna watched as his lips pulled every bit of berry off the fork, and then cut into the pie with the same fork, offering it to her.

It felt as intimate as a kiss.

"No one's ever asked me that." Brenna wrenched her mind away from the image of kissing Joss.

"You're stalling. You don't like to talk about yourself, do you?"

"Do you?"

"Sure. I'm a cool guy.

"Cool guys don't steal pie."

"I'm sharing your pie," Joss corrected as he held the fork to her mouth again. "Besides, how many guys have you known that are as cool as me? Why are you glaring at me?"

"I'm trying to decide if you're trying to be overly-arrogant or this is just who you are."

Brenna rescued the forkful, as Joss spread his long arms wide and looked like a bird ready to take flight. "This is who I am."

"Mm hmm." She didn't want to let him know that his attitude, arrogant or not, was very refreshing. He was so different from Toby, who epitomized charm and control at all times. The one time Brenna had seen him out of control was when she interrupted him in his office.

That image was still difficult for her to shake.

"Why do you shave your head?" Brenna asked to change the subject.

"I shaved my head twelve years ago." He swept a hand over his bald pate. "When my best friend was diagnosed with breast cancer and started chemo. There were four of us who did it."

"Your best friend was a woman?"

"It is possible, you know. Are you saying you've never been just friends with a man?"

"Actually, no, not for a long time. Friends of either sex have been sort of few and far between in the last little while." Brenna smiled ruefully. "That makes me sound pathetic, doesn't it?"

"There's anything pathetic about you. I think you've closed yourself off from people, probably because you've been hurt. Seems a shame." Her mouth dropped open at his gentle tone. "So, no, Rick wasn't a women. Unfortunately, men do get breast cancer. He was a great guy. We'd been friends since we were little kids. All he ever wanted to do was join the army and he was so happy when I finally let him talk me into it. We served in Afghanistan together. Made it a little easier that I was there with him."

"You don't often hear about men with breast cancer."

"Trying being diagnosed while you're in the military."

"Did he make it?" There was such genuine affection in Joss's tone when he spoke of his friend.

He gave a quick shake of his head. "Made it through the first round of chemo but then they found it had spread to his lymph nodes. They gave him six months and he lasted almost a year but..." He kept his eyes on the table.

"I'm sorry." Brenna reached out to touch his hand.

"Yeah, well, so am I," he said roughly.

There was a pause.

"That pie's not going to finish itself," she said softly.

Joss looked at her and smiled. Something deep inside her heart flipped over, leaving her suddenly breathless.

"How long were you in the military?" she asked, frantic to change the subject, not to dwell on why the smile elicited such a reaction.

Joss shook his head again, his face losing the haunted expression. "Nope. You got your question, now it's my turn. Why'd you keep your dad's last name when your sisters can't stand to mention his very existence?"

Brenna didn't realize she was pleating the white tablecloth hanging over her lap, over and over, into tiny folds that would be impossible to get out with an iron. "I never got along with my mother," she admitted finally. "My father left when I was three, so I didn't really know him but I had this romanticized image of him, that never really went away. I remember my father telling me he loved me. I don't remember my mother ever saying that." Joss opened his mouth as if to speak. "You're going to say, 'Of course she loved you', aren't you?"

Joss cocked his head. "You don't think she did, though."

Brenna gave a quick shake. "She was—she had problems. I don't know what they say about her these days, but I think she must have been bi-polar. She wasn't an easy person to live with."

"I hadn't heard that, no. I heard she had mood swings."

"That was the polite way of explaining it."

"Is this separation thing a good thing?"

The change of subject startled her. "Me and Toby? I think so. Why?"

"What happened?"

"He—you already had your one question."

"I'm asking nicely for another." There was that smile again.

Brenna shut her eyes to avoid being drawn in. "I caught him with my assistant at work," she blurted.

"Really?" Joss blinked, the only evidence of surprise.

"I'm not sure why I told you. I've only admitted it to my sisters." He fed her the last piece of pie. It was the strangest experience Brenna had had with a man, and yet one of the most pleasant.

"It's easier with me. You don't know me that well. Besides, closed-mouth folks are the best listeners."

"I don't think I'm a good listener."

"There's always time to learn. Like trying to listen

when the whole town was trying to tell you about Seamus and your sister."

"Yeah. I kind of missed the boat on that one. Does everyone know my business?"

"First thing I learned when I moved here—your business is not your own."

"No, I guess not." Brenna noticed only a few crumbs remained on the plate. "You ate all my pie."

"I think you got your fair share." He lifted his cup of coffee to her. "You going to want to share this, too?"

"It was my pie!"

Joss chuckled before his face turned serious again. "So. You're separated. How long should I give you before I start coming around?"

"Excuse me?" He held Brenna's gaze with those blue eyes, a hint of a smile curving up the corners of his lips until she felt heat creeping up her cheeks.

"Are you opposed to me coming around?"

"Coming around - are you asking me out?"

"No. I'm trying to see how much time you need to get over your husband."

"Oh. I don't know..."

Joss swallowed, looking vulnerable for the first time since she had met him. "Take what time you need and if..."

Brenna stared at the man sitting across from her, the stranger she already knew so much about. Who seemed to know her so well.

"Would it be bad if I said I don't think I need a lot?"

Chapter Twenty-Eight

Cat

Sibling relationships—and 80 percent of Americans have at least one—outlast marriages, survive the death of parents, resurface after quarrels that would sink any friendship. They flourish in a thousand incarnations of closeness and distance, warmth, loyalty and distrust.

—Erica E. Goode, "The Secret World of Siblings," U.S. News & World Report, 10 January 1994

Cat found Brenna on the balcony outside Dory's old room that night, the same place Cat herself often escaped to. To get out of the house at night, Dory used to dangle from the edge, dropping down onto the picnic table. To this day, Cat still didn't know how she got back inside.

She hesitated in the doorway of the room, watching Brenna on the floor, leaning back on her arms, with her legs between the balusters of the railing, the same position Cat liked to sit in.

A loose floorboard creaked under Cat, startling Brenna. When she turned and saw Cat, Brenna raised her glass of wine as a greeting.

"Careful you don't end up with splinters," Cat said, stepping onto the balcony. "It needs some work up here."

"It was always my favorite spot," Brenna admitted, staring into the sky. "Dory used to bring me out here with her when she had a cigarette. She taught me how to smoke."

"I didn't think that was something that needed to be taught." Leaning on the railing, Cat brought her bottle of beer to her lips.

"When you cough as much as I did, it was obvious you need to be taught. The first time I had a joint was worse."

"When was that?"

"I think I was sixteen. With Kayleigh, if you can believe it. Out here, after Dory left."

"Kayleigh smokes all the time," Cat said.

"Really? Well, I guess everyone needs their vice. I have mine." Brenna swirled her red wine in one of their mother's old crystal glasses Cat never used. Those glasses were for sitting in the china cabinet in the dining room and looking pretty. She rarely used the dining room either.

"Me too." Cat leaned down and clinked her bottle against Brenna's glass. "I come out here sometimes for a drink."

"It's pretty with the moon coming up behind the trees. Peaceful. Do you want—should I go?" she asked carefully. "I don't want to be in your way."

"It's okay." Cat settled on the floor beside her sister, smelling wine and coconut-scented shampoo. The night was mild; the chirp of crickets, a rustling in the woods behind the house and the screaming of six-month old Tyler Macklin next door were the only sounds.

"I don't know if I could handle a kid screaming like that all the time," Brenna confessed, staring at the neighbouring house with a frown.

"He's usually pretty good – I watch him for Ellie sometimes. She says he's got a cold."

"Do you want kids?" Brenna asked hesitantly. "Did you ever think... you and Seamus?"

Cat wondered if it bothered her to ask, if it felt like the sharp stab of pain she used to feel when people assumed Brenna would eventually come home and marry Seamus.

"Are you getting married?" Brenna added in a rush. "It's none of my business, I know, but...I got married. He can too."

"But to me?" Cat glanced over, at the forlorn expression on her face.

"I'm dealing with that." She gave a humourless laugh, took a big drink of wine. "Give me some time. This is all new to me."

"What did you think would happen when you came back?" Cat asked. Did she really want to know if Brenna had hoped to find love again with Seamus? Was she just asking for trouble?

Brenna sighed, staring off into the trees. "I don't know. I didn't expect anything. I was just—things with Toby were never great. I always had thought of

Seamus as an example of what a good man was. Sort of like the ideal boyfriend."

"He's a pretty good boyfriend." For once there was no smugness to her reply. She had Seamus now, but Brenna had loved him once. Things could have been different.

"Yes, he was." In unison, they laughed, a comfortable companionable laugh despite the conversation. "How bad is it that we both, you know—the same guy?"

"Pretty bad," Cat winced. "There should be a sister rule, like the best friend rule."

"What's the best friend rule?" Brenna wondered.

"You know. You're not allowed to be interested in the same guy as your BFF."

"Oh. I guess finding out Colin was a half-brother fixed that little problem for Missy and me."

"I guess. Ugh—can't believe you made out with our brother!"

"Half-brother, please. It's bad enough that he's half."

A bat flew across the sky, causing Cat to instinctively duck her head. A car started up the hill, engine laboring, muffler sounding like it had a hole in it. She sighed quietly, thinking how much she had missed the tranquility of Forest Hills when she had moved to the city for school. Had Brenna felt the same way?

"This sounds horrible," Cat admitted with a guilty smile, "but I don't even know what you took at university. I know you're a lawyer..."

"I took my bachelor of commerce at University of Victoria in British Columbia and went to law school there," Brenna told her. "I took a double program and got my law degree and my Masters of Business. After I passed the bar, I moved to Vancouver, and went to the University of British Columbia and got my Masters of Law, specializing in international business. I've been thinking about getting my PhD in law as well."

"Wow." Cat had known Brenna was smart but she hadn't realized her sister was *that* smart, that educated. Even more amazing, was the fact she didn't feel jealous of her sister's accomplishments. Brenna's life was one Cat had never wanted for herself.

"And I did co-op terms in Austria and Taiwan for my undergrad and master's degrees."

"You *lived* there? What about the language?"

"Most people spoke English where I worked in Taiwan, but I managed to pick up a little of the language. I spoke pretty good German by the time I left Austria, but everyone spoke English there, too."

"I didn't know any of this," Cat confessed. "Kayleigh would try and tell me things about you but..."

"You didn't want to hear it." Brenna shrugged, and drained her glass. "I didn't know the name of one of your husbands, so I guess we're even."

Cat was confused by how she felt about learning about Brenna's life. It wasn't jealousy—Cat was used to that emotion—but she wasn't sure...

Maybe, possibly...could Cat be *proud* of Brenna?

"So with the schoolwork and co-op work and living overseas, I didn't date much," Brenna continued as Cat sat stunned from her realization. "I didn't have time for much other than studying. I had a couple of part-time jobs to pay for everything. There wasn't a lot of time for guys. There was a guy when I was in law school...we were together for a few months and he moved into my apartment for a while. I think it was mainly because his place was a dump."

"What happened with him?" Cat finished her beer, set the bottle by the door and leaned back on her arms. Clouds scuttled across the moon, darkening the night. Brenna was only a shadow beside her.

"I came home one day and all his stuff was gone." She reached around for the bottle and Cat smelled the berry scent of the wine as she refilled her glass. "I didn't bring another glass," she said apologetically.

"Is it red? I have no problem drinking out of the bottle." Brenna passed her the bottle, and Cat smiled her thanks before taking a mouthful. "So, he left? Just like that?"

"Yeah, just like that. He wasn't the best boyfriend. He was really selfish. I wasn't that upset he moved out—I was at first, but then I got busy with a mock trial I was leading and...I haven't had a lot of luck with men."

"Well, at least you didn't keep getting married, over and over again" Cat said ruefully. "Tommy was such a dick, but amazing in bed. We figured if the sex was that good everything else would work out."

"But it didn't."

“Not in the least.” She washed away the grimace with a mouthful of wine, full and fruity with an almost chocolate aftertaste. “This is good. Perry was sweet.”

“I remember he was always such a nice guy. What happened with the two of you?”

“I lost a baby. I lost one with Tommy, too. He threw me down the stairs and I miscarried; I hadn’t even realized I was pregnant. I left him after that.”

“I can’t imagine anyone treating you like that!” Cat heard the astonishment in Brenna’s voice.

“We had some wicked fights. We fought over everything and most of the time it got physical. I was as much to blame as he was.”

“But he shouldn’t have...”

“No, he shouldn’t have, but I wasn’t a victim. It was my fault, too. I broke his nose once. I threw a plate at him, too. Cut his cheek and he had to get stitches. We’d always make up in bed, though. Maggie was beside herself the whole time. We’ve both grown up a lot since we were together. He’s married to Tanya Raymond now and apparently they’re very happy together. But back to Perry. After I lost that baby, I went a little crazy and kind of cheated on him.”

“What does *kind of cheated* mean exactly?”

"Means I cheated on him." Cat took another mouthful of wine.

"You cheated on the minister's son?" Brenna's eyes widened in horror. "You're going to hell for that, you know!"

"Oh, probably. Poor Perry. He was too good to me...or for me."

"And the third husband?" Brenna asked, leaning forward.

Cat was silent for a moment, watching the clouds skidding before the moon. It was almost fully dark, the baby next door finally quiet. "Alex," she said finally. "I met him in Sault Ste. Marie when I moved there to take a hospitality course. He was...he died. Of cystic fibrosis."

"That's..." Even in the dark, Cat could tell Brenna was searching for the definition. "That affects the lungs, doesn't it? It's hereditary?"

"Cystic fibrosis is a genetic disorder that affects the lungs and digestive system and makes you more vulnerable to lung infection," Cat recited, like she had done so many times. "He died of a lung infection. He was twenty-eight."

"I didn't know that. I'm...so sorry."

"I met him just before I finished the course and stayed in the city with him…I really loved him. We got married a few weeks before he died. Other than Seamus, Alex was it for me. If he hadn't died, I might not have come back."

"I didn't know any of that," Brenna said sadly.

"I don't talk about it much. Maggie tries to get me to open up, but…" Cat leaned in, clinked the half-empty wine bottle against Brenna's glass. "So I don't have the best luck with men either. Maybe it runs in the family. But I loved him. Them, all of them. Alex and Tommy—at least I did at first. Perry…I just can't make it work with a guy, no matter what I do. I'm not sure if I can marry Seamus," Cat suddenly confessed. "I cheated on Perry and Tommy too, and basically everyone I've ever been in a relationship with. Alex was the only one I was ever faithful to. With Seamus, I'm afraid I'll end up screwing up and hurting him."

"That doesn't mean you're going to be unfaithful to Seamus. You said you don't want to hurt him—that should be enough for you to keep your pants on."

"I don't want to risk it. I've been tempted…when Joss moved into town…"

Cat heard Brenna's sudden intake. "Please tell me you and Joss are just friends?"

"Why?" Cat demanded in a teasing voice. "You enjoy your pie this afternoon?

Brenna drained her glass without answering. "Well, I'm finished with my wine and I think I'll go to bed. Seamus—will Seamus be here tonight? Not that it's any of my business..."

"No. He's working, he'll go home after."

"I just—it's better to know. So I don't, you know, interrupt anything."

"Okay."

"I think I can be happy for you," Brenna admitted into the darkness. "It might take a little bit, but I'm trying."

"That means a lot," Cat said. "I'm sorry, I guess, for not telling you."

"It was a bit of a shock. But I should have guessed. I should have known he'd be with someone. Why not you? It makes sense."

"I still should have said something."

They sat in silence, lost in their thoughts. "It doesn't seem right, fighting over a man," Cat finally said.

"I'm not fighting."

"No. But we did. For a long time."

"We did. It was always something, but most of the time it was Seamus. Have you ever done anything to hurt Maggie or Kayleigh?" Brenna asked suddenly.

"Of course not! Why would I?"

"Because you love them and, more importantly, you care about them. They're really important to you, so of course you would never want to hurt them. That's how you should look at Seamus. Not just like another man, like Tommy or Perry. You didn't care about them as much as you should, so you had no problem cheating on them. People are tempted all the time, but if you're with someone you shouldn't be, or who you really don't care about, you can let yourself act on the temptation. If you care, if you love them, you won't cheat or hurt them. That's what I think. But what do I know," she finished with a laugh. "I'm just the cheatee, not the cheater."

"Makes sense," Cat admitted. "So you don't think I'd really cheat on Seamus?"

"It's not for me to say, but I can't see you hurting him intentionally. Do you think," she asked slowly, "that if it wasn't for him, we would have gotten along like normal sisters?"

Cat only thought about it for a moment. "Naw," she said with a laugh. "Neither one of us are normal."

Chapter Twenty-Nine

Brenna

Sisters function as safety nets in a chaotic world simply by being there for each other.

—Carol Saline

Brenna woke up with a smile on her face. She stretched languidly, her toes escaping from under the quilt. This was a new feeling for her, waking up feeling refreshed and ready to take on the world.

There were no ex-boyfriends disturbing her sleep, no angry sisters to wake up to. Just the peaceful sounds of birds and the soft panting of a dog asleep beside the bed.

She stroked the head of the bulldog beside her,

never expecting to enjoy sharing her bed with a dog, never expecting Cat to be the type to have dogs. Brenna had been the animal lover growing up, making friends with squirrels and neighbours' pets. She'd always yearned for on, but their mother had put her foot down. "The only animals in this house are humans," she used to say.

That must be why Cat had so many. Maggie, too; she recalled the dogs dancing around Brady as he cut the grass that fateful morning.

Everything happened for a reason, Brenna decided, pulling herself out of bed. As soon as she moved, the dog scurried away, as if he expected trouble. If she hadn't messed around with Brady, she'd still be at Maggie's house. She and Cat wouldn't have connected. For the first time in their entire lives, things were peaceful between them. They were getting to know each other.

Maybe, with time, they might even become friends.

Cat's room was still in silence when Brenna passed by after her shower. She paused, realized if she stayed in town, she'd have to get used to the thought of Seamus sleeping beside her sister.

There would be no more fighting over him. She and Cat had agreed on that much last night. It would take time before she stopped feeling awkward around them. Brenna had known Seamus better than she'd known another person; had shared the most intimate part of herself with him. But that was a long time ago, and it felt good to let it go. She felt lighter, like she was full of helium.

Brenna was about to head downstairs when the faint chime of her cell phone, stuffed deep in her purse, stopped her. Without checking the name, she jammed it to her ear.

"Brenna? It's your husband."

With a gasp of surprise, she sat down on the freshly made bed. She closed her eyes as a rush of emotions threatened to overwhelm her – anger, frustration, guilt and then most unexpectedly, longing. The sound of his laughter, how he smiled at her when she rolled out of bed in the morning, how it felt to hold his hand. She missed him.

She missed him? No. No way.

"I thought we were separated," Brenna said coolly, pushing her revelation aside. "I read the agreement, gave you an address where to send the papers Do you really think you should be referring to yourself as my husband anymore?"

"I don't think I want to know what you've been referring to me as." Toby chuckled, easing the tension.

Brenna laughed dryly. "No, you probably don't. What do you want, Toby?"

Despite her disappointment at how their marriage had ended, Brenna was surprised at the wave of emotions sweeping over her. She had been comfortable with Toby, content. There was no great passion, but there had been friendship and love.

"Just checking in, I guess," Toby said. "How are you?"

It was Monday, a week since she'd discovered his infidelity, six days since she had fled Vancouver. Other than his email about the separation papers, this was their first contact.

"I'm – good." In the past, Brenna's response to the question had always been that she was busy, or some hyperbole for the word. "You didn't need to check on me. You gave up that right when you let Krystal crawl under your desk."

"I didn't know where you went." Toby ignored the remark about Krystal.

"I came home. I sent you my new address last week."

"I guess it's obvious how little I know you because I never would have expected you to go back to Ontario."

Where else would she have gone? Brenna had a sinking feeling in her stomach – if she hadn't been talking to Kayleigh on the phone that day, would Forest Hills have been her first choice? Would she have stayed in Vancouver, apologized for her outburst and tried to salvage her job? Would she have kept her head down, and worked even longer hours to make everyone forget what happened?

If she hadn't come home, she wouldn't have made the mistake with Brady. She still would have the childhood dream that she would somehow end up with Seamus.

She and Cat wouldn't have fought, and made up.

She wouldn't have met Joss.

How did he make the list?

"I came home," Brenna said firmly, quieting the questions in her head. "And I'm good, so you can give up any thoughts of being responsible for me."

"It's not that – I was worried about you. You took

things harder than I expected."

"Well, catching you with Krystal wasn't what I ever expected. But once I was out of the situation, back with my family, I could see our marriage for what it was."

"Which was?"

"Convenience, for both of us. Both workaholics – me more than you. I loved you, but you can admit we weren't made for each other."

"I was happy with you." Toby's protest sounded weak to Brenna's ears. "Before you lost yourself in work."

"You knew what I was like before you married me. You told me you hired me because of my work ethic, so what did you expect?"

Toby huffed with exasperation. "I didn't call to argue with you."

"Which leads me to my original question, Toby – what do you want?"

"I have the separation papers in front of me. I want to make sure this is really what you want, Brenna. Because if it's not..."

Did she want him back, with everything that entailed? She thought of the small thrill she'd felt when she picked up the phone and for a brief, impossible second, felt tempted. But no. Seamus wasn't the only person who belonged in her past.

She took a deep breath. "No. I don't know what I want out of life, but I don't think it's you. I could never trust you again, Toby," Brenna told him honestly. "I think we can both agree I wasn't the wife you wanted, or hoped for, but that was no reason to treat me with such disrespect. To have an affair is one thing—to do it at work, right under my nose, with my assistant? That was uncalled for. It was horrible!" The humiliation she felt at the discovery of Toby and Krystal together welled up and bubbled over. "It was just shitty, Toby. How long had it been going on? How long has everyone been laughing at me behind my back?"

"No one was laughing at you."

"If I had seen myself kick a purse across the room, I would have laughed."

Toby chuckled wryly. "That was unexpected."

"So was finding Krystal under your desk!"

"Again, I am sorry about that."

"Me too."

A pause filled with regret caught both of them by

surprise. Toby cleared his throat, breaking the silence. "As well as wanting to check on you, I called with something you might be interested in. I talked to an associate of mine in Vienna. They're looking for a senior associate with expertise in Canadian, American and international trade, a knowledge of tax laws and a willingness to relocate. Speaking German would be an asset. I think you'd be perfect for it."

"Austria?"

Nostalgia stole her breath as Brenna remembered walking along the cobbled streets, exploring the Schloss Belvedere and Hofburg Palace, gasping with amazement at the beauty of the city from atop the Riesenrad. The city was steeped in history and traditions, unlike any place she'd ever visited. She loved the time she spent there. The opportunity to go back...

Her mind swam with possibilities. Could she do it? Could she seize the opportunity for a fresh start. A week ago, she would have jumped at the chance.

But now...

"You don't have to decide now," Toby said before he hung up. "But at least email them, find out more."

"It wouldn't hurt," Brenna mused.

What an opportunity.

Brenna had never expected to return to Vienna, but she hadn't considered staying in Forest Hills either. Her sisters were here, but what else did the town have to offer her? She needed to work and jobs for lawyers with her experience in international tax law were in short supply in this area. She would have to leave to get her career back on track, so why not Austria?

But there was an uneasy feeling in her stomach as she sent a quick email to Toby's contact.

Heading downstairs, Brenna heard noises and music from the kitchen. She paused on the bottom stair. Last night was the first time she and Cat had really communicated about anything. Should she tell her about the phone call? Sisters were supposed to confide in each other. Friends were supposed to do that as well. Is that what they were becoming? Was it possible for Brenna to finally become friends with her sister?

Cat looked up as she entered the kitchen. The counter was covered with bowls, and bags and flour and other baking ingredients. "I'm making a cake," she explained, with a relaxed expression on her face that Brenna had rarely seen.

“I can see that.” She stood awkwardly at the counter, watching Cat pour flour into a measuring cup, tap to settle it.

Cat raised an eyebrow as the flour met the rest of the dry ingredients in the mixing bowl. “What’s going on?”

“I just talked to Toby. He thinks he’s found me a job.”

Cat’s eyes widened and Brenna couldn’t tell if it was surprise or satisfaction at the thought of her leaving. “I didn’t know you were looking for a job. What about the one you had?”

Did Kayleigh not tell Cat what had happened? “I don’t think it would be a comfortable workplace for me anymore” she said stiffly.

“I heard you caught him with the girl there. He should leave, not you.”

Brenna shrugged.

He must feel guilty, finding you a job after all that.”

“No...I don’t know,” Brenna said thoughtfully. “Do you think that’s why?”

“He gets caught with his dick in some girl’s

mouth, and you get fired for it? Of course he feels guilty! Unless he's a complete ass. Which, hey, guess what? He is."

"He's not. Not really." Brenna toyed with the spatula lying on the counter. Cat was there, ready to listen, perhaps even sympathize. What was she waiting for?

Cat had never been open for confidences. But now, after everything they'd gone through?

She took a deep breath. "He said it was mainly my fault that he cheated. That I pushed him away." The words came out in a rush, but they were out there.

Cat snorted, adding eggs to a bowl of sugar. "You didn't push him in that direction, so that one's on him."

"He said I push everyone away. That I have abandonment issues."

She whisked the eggs and sugar together. "Makes sense."

Brenna's mouth fell open. She had expected scorn or maybe even anger towards Toby in her behalf. "It does?"

"Sure. Probably the same reason I messed up my marriages. Dad screwed us up royally when he left."

Relief flooded through Brenna at Cat's easy explanation. Brenna wasn't the type to blame others for her problems. Even assuming she was partly responsible for Toby's infidelity felt natural. "And Mom – when she died. That wasn't good for us."

"I'd say no, it wasn't. And Dory leaving didn't help either. You expected Toby to leave so you pushed him away first. End of story. End of marriage. So, what about this job?"

"The job..." Brenna felt dizzy at the ease of which Cat had justified the end of her marriage, removing the heavy weight of blame. "The job's in Vienna."

"Vienna..."

"Austria."

"And you're taking it." It wasn't a question. Brenna had never seen Cat's eyes grow so cold so quickly and she quickly stepped back from the counter, out of throwing range.

On the wall, the old-fashioned phone rang, breaking the silence.

Chapter Thirty

Cat

Our brothers and sisters are there with us from the dawn of our personal stories to the inevitable dusk.

—Susan Scarf Merrell

Cat gently hung up the phone, feeling sick with dread.

"What's wrong?" Brenna demanded.

"Marcus...that was Fiona. They took him to the hospital last night. He had a heart attack." Cat moved automatically, turning off the stove, putting the milk and eggs back in the fridge. The batter would be ruined, but she would make more when she got back.

Brenna's eyes were wide, hand over her mouth. "Oh, no."

"He's—he's not waking up yet and I...I need to go." She looked around, suddenly dazed.

"I'm coming with you. Give me your keys."

"What's the speed limit in British Columbia?" Cat asked as the car flew down the hill towards Blind River. For a moment, she wished she hadn't been so quick to hand over her keys. "I never expected you to drive so fast over these hills."

"I'm used to mountains," Brenna said grimly. "These are nothing."

"Did you know Marcus was helping Evie go to university?"

Brenna nodded, her face set. "He helped me, too. I never would have got through without him. I just couldn't come up with that much money on my own. If you look closely at the course you took in Sault Ste. Marie, I bet he somehow paid for some of it."

The semester she swore she hadn't paid for, but the admissions office showed as fully paid. She thought the school had made a mistake.

"He felt guilty about our father leaving," Brenna

added bitterly.

"Maybe he was trying to be a grandfather."

"It takes more than money to be a grandfather."

Cat was silent for the rest of the way to the hospital, caught up in her memories. Her maternal grandfather Earl had died five years ago, but his death had been easier, since he spoke about dying so much.

Marcus wasn't going to die.

It was her mother's funeral Cat remembered, the suffocating pain in her chest when she thought of her mother's body in the casket, being lowered into the ground. How she refused to hang on to Maggie's hand, instead biting her fingernails to the quick to stop herself from crying. The loss, the loneliness...

Cat stared at the trees flashing by. Marcus Ebans hadn't bothered to show up for the funeral. Was the guilt the reason why he started paying for their education?

"How much did he pay for?"

"Not everything is a competition, Cat."

"I know."

At the hospital, their cousin Jamie was the first person they saw, sitting hunched in a chair in the Intensive Care Unit.

“How is he?” Cat asked.

Purple smudges shadowed Jamie’s eyes. “They think he might be coming around. Dad’s in there now, with Fiona.”

“What happened?”

“Thank God for Fiona. I know Dad’s had his issues with her, but she saved his life. If she hadn’t been there—she did CPR right away and—she saved his life.”

“It wasn’t as dramatic as that, Jamie,” a soft voice behind them said. Cat turned to see Seamus’ mother, still in her flannel pajamas and robe with a wan smile on her haggard face.

Brenna flew into her arms. “Brenna,” Fiona crooned. “I’m so glad you came.” She reached out and touched Cat’s face. “And Cat. I knew you’d come.”

“Is he going to be okay?” Brenna demanded.

“He’s waking up now. Jamie, why don’t you go in now and then we’ll take the girls. Maybe seeing them together will bring him around.”

“It might give him another heart attack,” Cat choked, but her words made Jamie smile as he hurried down the hall.

“Marcus will love to see you both. Brenna, he was

so happy you stopped in on Saturday and he felt horrible you left so upset…" she trailed off as Brenna's expression changed to one of horror.

"Did I do this? Is this my fault?"

"Of course not," Fiona soothed, drawing her back into motherly arms. "I know what went on with him and your father. I believe Marcus did the right thing in telling Roger to leave."

Cat couldn't have heard correctly. "What are you talking about?"

Brenna pulled back. "Even after seeing what it did to us? Growing up with just our mother?"

Fiona touched Brenna's face, her eyes full of warmth and sympathy. "I think it would have been much, much worse for you had he stayed. He wasn't meant to be a father, as much as he might have thought he wanted to be."

"What the hell is all this about?"

Brenna turned to Cat, sorrow and anger written on her face. "Our grandfather is the one who forced our father, his son, to leave town. To leave us."

Cat looked at Fiona for confirmation.

"It was complicated," Fiona said, sounding as exhausted as she appeared.

"Not really," Brenna interrupted. "Apparently, Dad did some bad things and Granddad didn't think he was good enough to raise us and told him to get out of town or he'd disown him."

"That's not how it was, Brenna."

"That's basically what he told me. I left out the part where Granddad felt really, really bad about it." Brenna closed her eyes. "How can I be so absolutely furious with someone and yet be praying for them to be all right?"

"Is she serious about this?" Cat demanded.

Fiona closed her eyes as well. "Roger Ebans was a bad father, an even worse husband and very few would call him a good man. Marcus believed—and still does—that he would have been a destructive influence on your life and he suggested—"

"Suggested?"

"—told him to leave."

"Or he'd be cut out of the will," Brenna finished.

"So he took the money and ran," Cat said slowly. "He picked a piece of the pie over us. That's pretty shitty. Even you, with your weird sense of daddy-love, can see that."

"Maybe so, but I don't think it was Marcus'

decision to make," Brenna said firmly.

Cat's mind spun. Imagine a father kicking out his son because of how he treated his wife and family.

"How bad was he?" she wondered.

"You don't want to know," Fiona said heavily.

*

They kept a vigil at the hospital for the day.

Uncle Peter refused to speak to Brenna or Cat, reserving only the most cursory comments for Fiona.

"He should be out soon," Fiona said late in the afternoon. Cat had only a brief glance at their grandfather before he was rushed into emergency bypass surgery. There had been no chance to ask him anything, to tell him...

What did she want to tell him?

Thank him if he helped pay for her course. Curse him for sending away their father. Demand to know why, what reasons, what right he thought he had.

Thank him for freeing them from the weight such a man would put on them?

Soon after Marcus was wheeled into the operating room, Fiona pulled Cat and Brenna aside on the pretense of getting coffee. In the halls of the hospital, watched by the glow of the vending machines, Fiona had told them about their father.

More than anything, Cat felt as if her anger with Roger Ebans had been justified.

Brenna had fallen asleep against Cat's shoulders. She stirred at the sound of Fiona's voice, pulling away from Cat. "Sorry," she mumbled, eyes still heavy with sleep.

"You're getting good at falling asleep wherever you sit," Cat told her.

"Shut up," Brenna retorted with an embarrassed half-grin.

"At least I'm not saying you passed out anymore."

"I heard about that," Jamie spoke up from across the room. "You fell asleep on the toilet? Really?"

"It was a long day." Brenna stretched out her arms, rotated her neck with a resounding crack. "The flight, the drive and then Cat made these wickedly strong drinks for me..."

"You didn't have to drink that many."

"You didn't have to keep bringing them."

Cat grinned at her sister. They were together, without the fights, without the competition. Why did it take something like Marcus' collapse to make things normal between them? What had they missed out on all these years?

Fiona smiled fondly at Cat and Brenna. "Should you call your sisters, do you think? Wouldn't they want to be here?"

Brenna glanced at Cat. "It might be hard for them to get away," Cat said diplomatically. "With the kids and the store -"

"I called Roger," Peter interrupted. "Last night. After it happened."

"You called our father?" Cat breathed.

"Where is he?" Brenna demanded in a strangled voice.

"Toronto. He lives in Toronto now," Peter said brusquely. "He was leaving first thing in the morning. He should be here in an hour or so."

Cat's mouth had lost all moisture. She stared at Peter with dismay, frustration and with anticipation at war within her. "Why didn't you say anything?"

"I just did."

That was all Peter would say about the matter even though Brenna peppered him with questions until he stormed out of the waiting area.

"He hates the whole business," Jamie confessed in a low voice after his father left.

"What, the whole business of keeping our father's whereabouts from us?" Cat said bitterly.

"Your father made his own decision to leave," Fiona interjected as gently as she could.

"No, not really," Brenna said, her voice cool. "He had some help."

"This isn't the best time for this," Jamie interjected. "We don't know -"

Cat was still reeling. "I don't want to see him," she said abruptly, jumping to her feet. "We're going home."

"We can't! How can you not want to see him?" Brenna protested.

"He's never wanted to see us!"

Brenna sat with her shoulders slumped. "You can go if you want, but I'm staying here. I've waited too long for this." She stubbornly leaned back in the chair as if daring Cat to move her.

"Your granddad will be out of surgery soon. Why don't you stick around until then?" Fiona suggested.

"I need to call Seamus," Cat said abruptly, stalking out of the waiting room. A helpful nurse pointed out the exit for her. It was late afternoon, and cars sped past the hospital. Everyone was on their way home.

Including her father.

She leaned against the wall of the building and called Seamus. "How's Marcus?" he asked immediately.

"He's had surgery; he should be out soon. They called our father! He's coming home." Normally the sound of Seamus' voice would calm her mood, but the tension in her body was increasing the closer it got to his arrival.

She was going to see her father again.

"You're kidding!" Seamus exclaimed.

"He's been in Toronto all along. Or—I don't know. Bee's freaking out, but I—I don't want to see him. She does."

"It wouldn't kill you to see him, you know. It might even help." The suggestion sounded practical, and was the last thing Cat wanted to hear.

"Help with what?"

"I don't know. Questions you might have, stuff like that."

"Like where the fuck he's been for the past 30 years?"

"Yeah. But maybe say it a little differently."

"You're not helping!"

"I don't know how to! Jesus, Cat, I've never heard you mention him more than a few times which, for you, means it's still a sore spot. So here's your chance to find out stuff. Even to just see what he looks like. Say hello. Hug him."

"I'm not hugging him."

"So don't hug him. I don't know what you want me to say."

Cat shrugged miserably. She didn't know either.

Chapter Thirty-One

Brenna

Sisters share the scent and smells—the feel of a common childhood.

—Pam Brown

"How is he?"

Brenna started at the new voice, taking in the man who strode into the room like he owned it bringing a welcome cool cologne scent into the tiny waiting room. Tall, handsome, dressed in dark pants and a striped polo shirt, looking like he stepped out of a country club.

The red hair was faded, lines creased the tanned

face but it only took a moment for her to recognize her father.

All the air seemed to be forced out of her lungs. Her father was standing right in front of her.

"Roger." Fiona didn't stand but spoke with an obvious attempt at civility.

Brenna arranged her face into an expectant smile, told herself to keep the accusations out of her voice until she could find out his side, and waited for her father to welcome her into his life.

He turned to Fiona and his eyes slid unseeingly past Brenna in the chair. Like she wasn't there, like she didn't exist.

He didn't even see her.

Brenna opened her mouth; she had to say something.

"What are you doing here?" Roger barked at Fiona, his gaze skirting her bedraggled appearance, still wearing the pajamas and robe she had on when she arrived with Marcus in the ambulance. Without waiting for a response, Roger stepped towards Jamie. "How's my father?"

Brenna watched Jamie look between Fiona and Roger like he was a spectator at a tennis match. The struggle for loyalty was evident in his face.

"He's still in surgery. Dad went to talk to the doctor. Uh, I'm Jamie, Peter's son..."

"I know who you are."

The rudeness in his voice sets Brenna back; she could only gape at him with disbelief. This was her father?

"Your father and I have been dating for almost ten years now." Fiona stood up, her eyes turning cold. Despite her small stature and flannel robe, she was a formidable opponent. "As you would know if you bothered to stay in touch."

Brenna noticed Roger's jaw clench at Fiona's words. Where were the smiles, the warm greetings? He hadn't even looked in her direction. This wasn't the laughing, caring man she remembered, the man who hugged her without abandon, who tickled and kissed and loved her.

"How convenient for you," Roger sneered. "I can only imagine what you've been telling him about me."

"I've never interfered - "

This was the man who picked money over his family. Disappointment fell with a sickening thud in the pit of her stomach. She couldn't believe all the years she'd wasted.

"Dad."

The word felt foreign on her tongue, unwanted, unexpected.

Fiona reached for her hand as Brenna stood, joining the circle with a pale face, stunned from the sight of him as well as his rude behaviour.

Roger looked over his shoulder, gaping at Brenna as if he'd seen a ghost. His emotions flew across his face; like Maggie's, so easy to read. Annoyance, confusion, acceptance. "Catherine," he said with a hint of a smile.

Her heart shattered as he called her by her sister's name. "Brenna," she corrected.

"I'm Catherine. Cat." Cat slipped her hand into Brenna's, her eyes a steely green.

Brenna hadn't noticed Cat slide into the room, but knowing she was there, made Brenna straighten her spine rather than cower back into her chair.

"It's good to see you both," Roger said after an awkward pause. Brenna waited for him to make a move, to hug them, but nothing.

Nothing.

"My dad went to talk to someone." Jamie cleared

his throat.

It was as if the walls were closing in on them. Brenna couldn't take her eyes off her father.

"Granddad should have been out of surgery by now," Jamie continued, staring at the floor like he wished it would open and swallow him up.

"So, why -?" Cat began.

"What have -?" Brenna demanded at the same time.

"What happened with my father?" Roger asked Jamie.

And that was it. That was all the attention they received from their father. The big emotional reunion Brenna had been waiting for, dreaming about for years.

Roger immediately left with Jamie to find the doctor. Brenna couldn't find her voice. Her father had been here, in the same room as she had been and he just walked away.

Brenna sank back into her chair, feeling physically nauseous. "What just happened?" she asked faintly.

"What an asshole." Cat stared out the door where Roger had disappeared, fists clenched at her sides.

"He's upset," Fiona said in a low voice. "He's had

a long drive and anxious to find out about Marcus. Just give him time."

"How can you say that after how he treated you?" Brenna's eyes stung with unshed tears. She blinked furiously, refusing to cry over such a man.

"I couldn't believe that. I've seen you rip new assholes in people," Cat added. "You just stood there and took it? Why"

"He's your father." Fiona spoke the word through gritted teeth.

"He didn't even know who we were." The bitterness dripped from Cat's voice.

"It's been thirty years," Brenna said, feeling hollow from her grief and disappointment. That had been moment she had been waiting her whole life for?

She'd never felt so cheated.

"Are you defending him? It's his own fault!" Cat's shout echoed through the room.

"Cat." Fiona reached for her, but Cat batted away her hand.

"What do you expect me to do? He didn't even recognize you, Bee! We're his children and he could have walked right by us on the street!"

"He thought I was you." The pain ripped through

Brenna and she clutched her stomach, as though she had been slashed with razor-tipped claws.

"You spent years looking for him and this is what you get for it?"

"Ms. Todd? And—" A man entered, wearing scrubs and looked questioningly at Brenna and Cat.

"These are Marcus's granddaughters."

"Where is Mr. Ebans?" The doctor was young, hesitant. Suddenly Brenna was afraid to hear what he had to say.

"Here. I'm here" Roger strode into the room in front of Peter and Jamie. "How is my father?"

It was only then Brenna noticed the sympathetic expression on the doctor's face and heard Fiona's quiet sob.

"I'm very sorry..."

Chapter Thirty-Two

Cat

Between sisters, often the child's cry never dies down. "Never leave me" it says; "do not abandon me."

—Louise Bernikow

As Cat listened to the doctor detail the cause of Marcus' heart attack, all she could think about was how much she had missed out. She had so many questions, things she needed to know.

And now that she knew the truth about everything, it was too late.

"...I'm so sorry for your loss..."

Cat had always considered her uncle Peter a cold,

rude man. He'd never showed the least bit of interest or charity towards his nieces, even when their mother had died and they needed it the most. But now, seeing the grief etched on his face, at the tears running unchecked down his cheeks, Cat's heart softened. As the doctor spoke, he clung to Jamie, as if he was trying to gather strength from his son.

There was little outward reaction from Roger.

"What's the next step?" Roger demanded, stepping in front of Cat as if she was invisible. The Ebans men closed ranks, like pioneers keeping the wagons in a circle, protecting what was theirs. They pushed Fiona aside, taking no notice of the tears; ignoring Brenna who stood stunned, but dry-eyed, and Cat, who was ready to lash out at someone, anyone.

"Girls," Fiona said. "It's time to go." She was a heartbreaking sight, standing so proudly with tears dripping silently down her face.

"No," Cat protested, reaching out to touch the older woman's elbow. "You need to be here for him."

Roger turned to Fiona. "I think it's best if you leave. I'll be staying at the house while I'm here. Could you see that your belongings are out of the way?"

"I'll let you know about the arrangements," Jamie said quietly with an apologetic glance at Cat.

Fiona dashed the tears off her cheeks, raised her chin. "Just so you know, Roger, we weren't living together. And I'm nothing like the gold-digging whore you seem to think I am. I loved your father very much. He wanted to marry me."

"I doubt that. And I never called you a whore."

"You're not half the man your father was. And I think it's a miracle that with your arrogance and selfishness and patronizing ways that your daughters turned out to be such wonderful women. They are a credit to their mother – not you. Girls." Without another word, Fiona swept out of the room.

Brenna hesitated for a split second, but Cat took her hand and pulled her after Fiona.

In that moment, blood was not thicker than water.

Since Fiona had ridden to the hospital in the ambulance with Marcus, Cat offered to drive her back to Forest Hills. Driving would be a welcome distraction, give her something to concentrate on other than that shit show she just went through.

Who did Roger Ebans think he was? He didn't deserve the title of father.

Her fury towards him only grew as the car sped away from the hospital, but she kept quiet, conscious of Fiona's grief, of Brenna sitting frozen in the backseat, staring out the window.

"I can't believe he's gone," Cat said, finding it necessary to interrupt the silence. The car labored up the last hill. They could see the lights from the farm as they approached.

They didn't shine as bright as they usually did.

"He was a good man." Fiona spoke firmly, despite the tears still streaming down her face. "Whatever you may think of how he dealt with your father, Marcus was a good man."

"Our father wasn't a good man." It was the only words Brenna had spoke since they left Blind River.

"No. He wasn't." Fiona heaved a sigh when Cat turned into the long driveway of the farm. "I need to go to the house, please."

"Jamie said you...you were there?" Brenna asked from the back seat. "You found him?"

"I had stayed the night before and when he woke up, he told me he wasn't feeling well. I told him to stay in bed and I was bringing him some tea...they said his heart just stopped."

"It's my fault," Brenna murmured.

Cat stopped the car in front of the house. No one reached for the door handles.

"He never had any heart problems." Fiona said, shifting in her seat to look at Brenna. "It's not your fault. It had nothing to do with you."

"Why would it have anything to do with you?" Cat demanded.

"I went to see him the other day," Brenna admitted. "That's when I found out about our fath – Roger. Marcus was upset -"

"Because you were upset. He felt guilty. That would not have brought on a heart attack. Brenna," Fiona warned, when Brenna resumed her stony-faced silence. "It had nothing to do with you. Just like you had nothing to do with your mother's death."

"Why...?" Cat remembered the funeral vividly, recalled her mother being sick. But that day, the day she had died had been locked away for so long. Carefully, like picking a shard of glass out of a finger, Cat sifted through her memories.

"Please go see Doctor Bennett," Maggie had pleaded, on her knees before the locked door of their mother's room. Carly had barricaded herself inside days ago, but something about this time felt different. They all had felt it; something was seriously wrong. The five sisters had met in the hall, desperate for one of them to be able to get their mother out of her room.

"You're our mother!" Kayleigh had screamed, startling them all. She was usually so quiet and level-headed; to see her so close to losing control had scared Cat. "You have to take care of us!"

"We don't have anyone else," Dory had added. "She's so selfish."

Cat had stood quietly beside Brenna. It had been Brenna's thirteenth birthday, but no celebration had been planned. Cat had made her a cake, an uncommon sign of sister solidarity and had planned-

"The cake!" The smell of acrid burning had drifted up the stairs as the piercing ring of the smoke alarm confirmed her cry.

Moments of chaos as they ran for the kitchen. Cat had hoped the noise would bring their mother out of her room, but the door remained closed. It wasn't until after Maggie had pulled the blackened cake out of the oven, Dory had opened windows and waved at the smoke with a dishtowel and Kayleigh climbed on a chair to yank the smoke alarm off the ceiling that Cat had realized Brenna wasn't in the kitchen.

"Where is she?" Kayleigh had asked with a worried glance at Maggie.

"You're the one who found her." Cat met Brenna's eyes in the rear-view mirror, her throat suddenly desert dry . "I forgot. I can't believe I'd forget that."

"I went outside when you were all in the kitchen and climbed up the tree," Brenna said in a voice that sounded nothing like her. "I saw her on the bed, just lying there. I banged on the window, but she never looked up. I kept banging...she wouldn't look at me..."

"Oh, Brenna," Fiona said sorrowfully. "You never told me that."

"The window broke," Brenna continued as Cat stared at her sister with horror. "I guess I smashed it, pushed the screen in. I climbed in - "

"You cut yourself," Cat remembered suddenly. "There was blood everywhere."

"She was dead." Brenna's voice was expressionless, but Cat could see her face was white in the dim light. "She was lying there, dead."

Cat was stunned. How could she have forgotten it had been Brenna who had found their mother?

"How did she die?" she asked after minutes of

silence. "Have I forgotten that too?"

Fiona heaved a sigh. "Your mother was very stubborn. And she had a fear of doctors. I've never seen anything like it. Your grandfather Earl refused to have an autopsy done, but I knew one of the doctors, talked to him. Carly had cancer; we knew that. It was stomach cancer. She never got treatment. What you may not know, is that Carly had something called pernicious anemia. She also had diabetes."

"I never knew that," Cat said quietly.

"Again, she never got treatment. I doubt she even knew what was wrong with her."

"Could that have caused the...her other issues?" Brenna wanted to know.

"Carly was bi-polar," Fiona said frankly. "The only thing it had to do with her medical issues was that it might have prevented her from getting help. The anemia and diabetes – she could have easily dealt with them. Left untreated, both have a risk of gastric cancer..."

"And that's what killed her?" Brenna asked.

Fiona turned in the seat, looked back at Brenna again. "Her body just gave out. It couldn't take anymore."

"But she could have...she didn't have to die. She didn't have to leave us." Cat had never heard her sister sound so cold.

"It's possible the depression was more serious than anyone thought," Fiona said, raising her hands helplessly. "Her father was suicidal. Maybe she just wanted to die."

Cat leaned back against the seat. Marcus' death had opened up areas of Cat's life she had spent years hiding from. Her mother's death, her father leaving them...

"This family is fucked," she said bitterly.

Chapter Thirty-Three

Brenna

One the best things about being an adult is the realization that you can share with your sister and still have plenty for yourself.

—Betsy Cohen

The lump in Brenna's throat grew as she followed Fiona into the house.

While Fiona was throwing clothes and books in a bag, Brenna helped Cat clean up the mugs of tea that lay broken on the floor where Fiona had dropped them.

"Well, that's the last time we'll be up here," Cat muttered as she shut the door behind Fiona. Brenna helped carry the bags to the car.

"Marcus was a good man," Fiona said again. "I know you may not believe me right now, but he was. He was very kind, generous. Caring. I wish you had the chance to get to know him better."

Brenna couldn't think of how to respond.

Her mind whirled, trying to sort out the events of the day. Marcus' death, while tragic, seemed to be catalyst for the more emotional trials. Seeing her father again...what kind of man he had become...

Maybe he had always been like that. Brenna had a three-year old's memory of her father; all little girls believed their fathers were heroes, and she was no exception. To her, Roger Ebans had been a big, strong man who could slay dragons and protect from the boogie man under her bed.

Until she found out he couldn't. That he was just a man with feet of clay, falling victim to greed and cowardice like so many others.

They were silent as Cat drove down the hill to Fiona's. "Won't you stay for a bit?" Fiona invited as they pulled into the driveway. "I'll make tea."

"I'll make you some tea," Cat offered.

Part of Brenna wanted to stay, talk about Marcus,

enjoy Fiona's company. She remembered how Fiona had taken care of them after their mother died and wanted to do the same for her. But Seamus would be there, and everything in the house would only remind her of her past with him.

When she had been with Seamus, and still believed in her father's love. The love her father refused to show to her.

Maybe she was asking too much. His own father had just died. People dealt with grief in their own way.

Brenna had dealt with her own grief by shoving it so far down inside her that it was barely visible. She had almost convinced herself that she hadn't been the one to find their mother's body, almost believed it had been one of the others. But now it rushed back with the strength of a tidal wave, pushing everything else under.

The rough bark of the lilac tree against her hands as she had climbed; the coolness of the glass as she rested her forehead against the window. The sharp pain as the glass broke under her fist, falling into the room, the shards piercing her legs as she crawled to the bed. Shaking her mother, the sightless eyes staring up at nothing.

"Mom! Wake up, Mom. Please...please...it's my birthday. You have to wake up. Mommy..."

"Thanks, but I think I'll head back to your place," Brenna told Cat, pulling herself back to reality. "If that's okay?"

"She just needs some time," Brenna heard Fiona tell Cat.

Time was what she had too much of. Time to think, to remember, to mourn what she had lost.

The hours had crept painfully by at the hospital but now it seemed like the day had vanished quicker than a blink of an eye and Brenna was exhausted. She was tired of losing people.

Rationally, she knew it wasn't her fault that Marcus had died, but like her mother's death, she couldn't help but think she was somehow to blame. Maybe he had been so upset with her talk of her father that his heart couldn't take it. Maybe his heart broke with the guilt of denying her of her father...

Brenna had visited on Saturday. Even if he had been upset, it wouldn't have taken two days.

It was a quick walk through the woods. The house soon loomed before her, ghostly white in the near darkness. The chorus of barking dogs greeted her as she stepped onto the porch.

Home.

The word crept into her thoughts, easing some of the confusion.

After she let the dogs out, Brenna found herself in her mother's room on the second floor. She had never intended to go there, but entering the room was somehow a comfort. Switching on the lamp beside the bed, she sat gingerly on the bed, afraid of disturbing anything.

"Granddad's gone." She spoke aloud, feeling the tears prick her eyes like needles. "I don't know how you feel about that. I know there's always been bad blood there but Fiona seemed so happy with him. I think he changed. I talked to him about Dad..."

Brenna took a deep breath. If she was still alive, would she have welcomed Roger back? Accepted his excuses, his insincere apologies? Would she have gotten the help she needed?

Was he responsible for killing her? Not directly, but his abandoning them had certainly played a part.

Even in Brenna's conflicted state, she knew that was a stretch.

"He came back." Her voice was too loud in the

room. Echoing into the corners, out to the hallway. "I don't know if you know that...if you can tell..."

The first time she had experienced the sensation of her mother being in the room with her, the chill had been gradual, like her mother had been trying to prepare her. Now as she sat on the bed, the light of the lamp throwing shadows, Brenna felt as if she stepped into a freezer. The smell of lilacs filled the room, as a branch of the tree Brenna had climbed all those years ago scratched against the window in a gust of wind.

Goosebumps crawled up her spine. Maybe this was a bad idea. Could she handle a conversation with her mother's spirit? After everything that had happened? Brenna was tempted to leave it for another day. Crawl into her own bed with the hope that sleep would make her forget.

Instead, she stayed, pulling the quilt around her shoulders to block some of the cold, and talked to her mother.

"He was so rude to Fiona," she said, still bewildered by how her father had treated the woman. "Really mean. I probably shouldn't tell you that because it will make you mad, but I'm sure Cat will. She was pissed. Can I say pissed?"

"He told her to get her stuff out of the house and so we stopped and picked everything up. Cat's at her place with her now. I couldn't stay. I wanted to, but I just couldn't. With Seamus and...stuff. Did you know Fiona sent me a Christmas card every year? Every year. She never said anything about Cat and Seamus or her and Granddad though. I guess some things are better told in person."

Brenna knew it was silly and unnecessary but she waited for a response. It wasn't as if she was talking to herself—she knew her mother was in the room.

And it helped, like she knew it would.

"I'll miss him. Granddad, I mean. I know I haven't spent much time with him—any time at all—but since I've been back, I thought I was going to finally have the chance to get to know him. But now he's gone. You know what he did for me, don't you? I don't know if you can see everything from where you are, or just some stuff. Granddad helped pay for my school. He got me that scholarship and gave me money every year for it. He never said a thing about it. And you know..." She choked on a sob. The realization was a dam breaking, sending scalding tears streaming down her face. "I thanked him and I told him how he had changed my life, but he didn't really know...I didn't have time to show him the person I'd become..."

"He knew who you were. He would tell me - "

Brenna screamed, tripping over the quilt as she jumped off the bed. She gaped at the sight of Joss Ryan standing in the doorway.

"What are you doing here? Jesus, I think you gave me a heart attack!" She thumped her hand on her chest, before her shoulders slumped. "Oh, God, I shouldn't have said that! Granddad...he had a heart attack..."

"Sorry to scare you." Joss stepped into the room, looking sheepish. "Are you OK?"

"No!" Brenna gasped, hand at her throat. "You just about killed me. Jesus, stop making me say stuff like that! What are you doing here?"

"I stopped by to see...I saw the dogs were out so I let them in. The door was open, so I fed them. I didn't think anyone was home, and then I heard voices." Brenna didn't think it was possible for someone to look so uncomfortable and concerned at the same time. "I came to see if you were OK."

"Me?" Her heart had just resumed its normal pace when his words made it skip a beat. She frantically wiped away the tears from her cheeks.

"You." It was the same gentle tone he used when they shared the piece of pie, the same concern when he picked her up from the farm. He brushed his thumb against the wetness that remained.

"Why?"

"Why?" Joss echoed Brenna's question.

"Yes. Sorry, but I don't understand why you'd come and check on me." She pulled the quilt around her, even though the room had noticeably warmed up.

"I got that." He shuffled his dusty work boots, stared out the window, looking everywhere but at her. "I wanted to make sure you were all right. Your grandfather just passed away."

"I know that." She took a deep breath, unused to sympathy or concern from others, and burst into tears.

Brenna wasn't a crier. She tried to be strong, not show her vulnerabilities to others. Letting herself cry was opening herself to the pain of her childhood, and it had always been better for her to keep it all inside.

That was before. Now, all the emotions she had pushed down over the years seemed to be rushing out in a torrent. It felt good to let it all out. Let it all wash away.

"I'm sorry," Joss cried, his hands flailing like unable to decide to pat or hug, or stroke her back. "I didn't mean to make you cry. I thought maybe you might need someone."

"No one ever thinks I need anyone," Brenna choked through her sobs. The quilt fell from her shoulders as she covered her face with her hands. "No one. I don't have anyone, not since I left home. I didn't have anyone and when Toby was such a shit I didn't have anyone in Vancouver so I came home but I couldn't tell them it was because I've been so lonely and after Toby I couldn't stand it anymore and..."

"Brenna." Joss's big hands were gentle on her shoulders.

"I missed everything!" Her voice quavered with grief. "My sisters, finding out about Fiona and Granddad. He's gone! I can't tell him what he meant to me and what he did for me. I thought I had this great life and I wanted to have this great life, but now I found out that everything important to me was here, and I missed out on everything!" She rambled on and on, nearly incoherent through her tears.

"I didn't get most of that," Joss said with a smile

as he pulled her close, settling her on his lap on the bed. "But you're here now. I've got you." His arms tightened around her.

Brenna clutched Joss' shoulders like a lifeline, burying her head on his shoulder until the damp patch grew under her cheek.

She cried for the years she missed with her family, the end of her marriage, her career. She cried for the loss of her grandfather, the shock and disappointment of meeting her father. She cried for Seamus and the dreams of her youth. Brenna cried until there were no more tears, and her sobs quieted to halting breaths and the only sound in the room were her sniffles when she finally lifted her head.

"I got your shirt wet," she whispered.

"It'll dry," Joss said gruffly. Without shifting her off his lap, he reached for the box of Kleenex on the nightstand beside the bed.

"I'm sorry." Brenna tried to clean herself up with the tissues Joss handed her. There was no way to blow a nose discreetly, especially when sitting on someone's lap. She tried to move, but Joss still held her against his chest. "I don't normally do that."

"Cry after you lose someone?" How could he

sound so matter-of-fact? Look at how she acted, what she had turned into?

Brenna shook her head. “I never cry. I’m a mess.”

“I think you’re beautiful.”

She caught her breath and looked at Joss through wet, red-rimmed eyes. “Why?”

He touched her cheek, wiping a lone tear with his thumb. “Is that all you can ask?”

And then he touched her lips with his own.

Brenna was exhausted, spent from the tears but nothing had ever felt more natural. His touch was so gentle and delicious, his beard brushing against her chin, his big hands around her waist...

“We shouldn’t do this here,” Joss said, barely moving away from her mouth, his hands roaming across her back, pulling her closer.

“It’s okay.” Gone were her hesitations, washed away with her tears. Brenna suddenly felt alive and wanted.

“You sure?”

Instead of answering, Brenna tugged off Joss’ shirt. Fingers stroked bare skin, strong shoulders, broad chest matted with dark hair. And then she took off her own shirt, and pushed him back onto the bed.

"I didn't want this," Joss stammered, running his fingers delicately along her back. "I mean, I do, but I never thought..."

"Shh." She pressed herself against him, his arms tightening around her. She was surprised at how much she wanted him. It had come out of nowhere; she had been attracted to him, but nothing like this. For him to have found her here, when she needed someone...Brenna felt overwhelmed with gratitude.

But it wasn't gratitude that made her press her mouth against his again.

Chapter Thirty-Four

Cat

Of two sisters, one is always the dancer, one the watcher

—Louise Gluck

Cat felt her energy draining out of her, like a tire leaking air.

She and Seamus had settled Fiona in bed, called one of her daughters-in-law to stay with her. Made her tea, held her while she cried.

When they'd done everything they could, Cat finally allowed Seamus to drive her home. As Seamus pulled up in front of the house, Cat heaved a sigh of relief. She was glad this day was over.

The dogs greeted them from the porch, tails wagging happily. She pushed her way through them, opened the door. Beyond the scraping of their nails on the hall floor, Cat heard a cry from upstairs.

"What's that?" Cat asked as Seamus followed her into house. "Do you hear something?"

"I didn't hear anything. Maybe it's your mother."

Cat cocked her head towards the stairs. "It stopped. Sounded almost like..."

"That's Joss's bike out front."

Cat had been in such a daze she had walked right by it. "Brenna?" Silence, then a flurry of sounds. "Bitch! She's in mom's room!"

"What?" Seamus stared after her as she took the stairs two at a time. By the time Cat reached the door of their mother's room, Brenna was pulling the quilt around her but Cat was greeted with a view of Joss Ryan's bare ass.

"You didn't! In here?" Cat cried, arms outstretched against the door frame to prevent a quick escape.

"She wasn't here." Brenna scrambled on the floor for her clothes, clutching the quilt around her. Joss tried to cover himself with his jeans, turned to step in front of Brenna as though to shield her from view.

"It doesn't matter! It's wrong. It's gross!"

"It just happened."

"You could have used your own room. Nice ass, by the way," Cat told Joss. Brenna dropped the quilt and pulled her T-shirt over her head.

"What's all the yelling?" Seamus slid into Cat. "Oh God. I don't need to see that. Or that!" He covered his eyes.

"Oh, God!" Brenna cried, fumbling with the waistband of her shorts.

"I'd better go." Joss was clearly frazzled, hopping on one leg as he tried to pull on his jeans.

Cat couldn't help laughing. "Why? I'm sure our dead mother loves watching you jump around all bare-assed!"

Joss' scowl made her laugh even harder.

"Let them put their clothes on," Seamus suggested still covering his eyes.

Cat glanced sideways at him. "It's nothing you haven't seen before."

"Give them some privacy, Cat," he ordered, taking her hand.

Cat jerked it away and stormed down the stairs. "I can't believe she did that!"

"Better with Joss than Brady at least."

"But now? Granddad just died."

"It was probably his way of comforting her." Seamus headed for the fridge, pulling out two bottles of beer, handing one to her.

"Really?" A lascivious smile spread across her face. "Might be a good way to make me feel better, too."

"With Joss?"

Cat laughed again, this time at the look of horror on Seamus' face. "No, silly." She leaned forward, kissing him once, then again as she wrapped her arms around his neck. "We wouldn't use my mother's room, though."

"Well, that's a good thing." He pulled away as they heard steps on the stairs. "Can we wait for some privacy at least? I don't feel like giving them a turn at being an audience."

"Was that weird for you?" Cat asked, sliding around Seamus to wrap her arms around his waist from behind, leaning her head against his back.

"I think it was weird for all of us." He drank from

the bottle as if to punctuate his words

"I didn't know they were hooking up. Must be a new thing. She didn't say anything to me about it."

"Do you blame her? We've been together for three years and you never said a word to her about us."

Cat pinched Seamus in retaliation. As awkward as the sight of her sister and her friend together in flagrante had been, it had relieved some of the tension of the day.

It was a nice reminder that it was possible for life to go on.

"Joss," Cat called as the footsteps stopped outside the kitchen door. "Come have a beer. I won't laugh at you."

Joss scowled as he peered into the kitchen, which of course made her laugh again. She wasn't sure how to react, other than by laughing.

"I'm out of here."

"No, I promise. It's just—I've never seen my sister in that situation before."

"Well, neither had I," he said pointedly.

"Just take it to Brenna's room next time. And make sure you lock the door."

"Or go to my place," he muttered.

“Probably a good idea,” Seamus agreed. “The whole ghost thing kind of freaks me out sometimes. She’s pretty good about privacy, but you can just never know.”

“You never told me it freaked you out.” Cat glanced at him.

“Well, if you think about it...”

“Yeah,” Joss said. “Brenna said she was gone, so I figured...”

“It’s fine,” Cat told them, pulling two more beers out of the fridge. “Bee, want something?” Brenna had quietly padded into the kitchen in bare feet, with a similar embarrassed expression as Joss. Her shorts were wrinkled and her shirt—was it inside out? Cat smiled to see her so undone and passed her a bottle with a smile. “Want a drink?”

“I think I need it after that,” she said quietly. Cat caught her eye and knew she wasn’t talking about the recent commotion. They smiled conspiratorially at each other as Cat heard the front door open.

“Cat? Brenna?” Maggie called.

“In here,” Cat called.

The dogs ushered Maggie and Kayleigh into the kitchen, with Evie tagging behind.

"I didn't know if you'd be up at the farm." Maggie was red-eyed, as was Evie, but Kayleigh was stone-faced. "No, we got kicked out. Fiona, too."

"How is she?" Kayleigh asked, heading straight for the cookie jar.

"As well as to be expected, I guess. It wasn't pretty. The way they treated her..." Cat glanced at Brenna, wondering which of them should tell the story.

"Look," Kayleigh said before she said anything. "I didn't want anything to do with him—Marcus, our grandfather, whatever—but I never wanted him to die."

"Of course not," Maggie soothed.

"It's just that he never gave a damn about me so—"

"Actually, he did," Maggie interrupted. "Didn't you ever wonder why the rent is so cheap on the store? He owns the building." She gave Seamus a teary smile of gratitude as he passed her a bottle of beer.

"How do you know that?" Kayleigh demanded, twisting the bottle cap with the hem of her shirt to open it.

"Mike found out and then I asked Granddad. He's helping us pay for Evie's school."

"He is?" Kayleigh's face drooped, like icing melting in the sun.

Cat bit her lip. They had so much to thank their grandfather for and missed out on it. They could have shared so much, but because of their father...

"He helped me out too," Brenna cut in." "He paid for part of my tuition."

"And me. Only I didn't realize it," Cat confessed.

She stared into her bottle, gathering her thoughts. "Look, something happened at the hospital. Our father showed up." Her words were rushed, spoken so quickly it took a moment for anyone to understand her.

"You're kidding," Kayleigh breathed.

"Why?" Maggie asked rudely.

"His father just died," Evie said gently.

"Yes, but he hasn't seen him in thirty years, so why would he care if he was dead? Just like he doesn't care about us."

"I'm sure he still cares about us..." Brenna trailed off when she noticed the astonished expressions on her sisters' faces. "Deep down, somewhere. He is our father."

"He means nothing to me," Maggie said briskly, as if she was washing her hands of him. "I stopped giving him any consideration the day he walked out."

"We came to see if you were OK," Kayleigh said to Cat. "I'm not going to be a hypocrite and pretend he meant anything to me but I know you're close to Jamie and Cara. And Fiona." She glanced at Seamus. "She'd always been like a mother to us. We're here for her."

"Our father kicked her out of the house so he could stay there." Cat looked pointedly at Brenna. When Brenna didn't try and defend him, Cat let out the breath she'd been holding.

"Of course he did," Maggie said bitterly.

"Look," Joss interrupted. "This is family stuff so I'm just going to go."

"Me too," Seamus jumped in. "I've got to check on Mom."

"Chickenshit," Cat said, masking the word with a cough. Seamus caught her smile.

"Damn straight!" He dropped a kiss on her forehead. "Call me if you need anything. I'll be back later?"

"Are you asking permission?"

"I'll be back later," he said, with mock sternness. "Pam said she'd cover your shift tonight."

"I could probably go in," Cat began but he shook his head.

"As your boyfriend, I say don't and as your boss I say I don't want you there. Bar maids need to be happy and smiling and trust me, you're no good at faking. Love you, babe. See you later."

"Let me know if you need anything," Cat heard Joss say to Brenna. "If you need me, or anything from me..."

"I bet she'll need something from you," Cat said sotto voce and grinned as Joss flushed.

Brenna gave Cat a dirty look. "I'll walk you out," she said, following him out of the kitchen.

"What's going on there?" Kayleigh hissed, not even waiting until they were out of earshot.

"I can still hear you," Brenna called.

"What's going on with them?" Kayleigh said loudly.

"I came home and found them all naked like," Cat said with delight. "He's got a great ass!" she added, loud enough so Joss could hear.

"Still in the room," Seamus said mildly.

"I had no idea..." Kayleigh said with amazement.

Maggie shook her head. "Mike told me he'd been sniffing around."

"Sniffing?" Seamus asked painfully. "Is there another door I can leave from? Hey, Bren, coming through. My eyes are closed," he called.

"Were they really going at it?" Maggie wanted to know. "Again?"

"That was the first time apparently."

"But she had...on Friday..." Maggie trailed off and all eyes turned to Evie standing quietly, munching a cookie.

"Good for her," Evie said mildly.

"I'm really out of here now." With a wave at Cat, Seamus fled the room.

"I don't believe it! Who is she?" Maggie demanded. "First Brady—in my kitchen, apparently—and now Joss Ryan? She was never like that."

"She just broke up with her husband, Maggie. Give her a break," Kayleigh said mildly.

"I don't think she's a bad person, Mom," Evie put in quietly. "It just happened."

"Things like that don't just happen. At least not to

Brenna," Maggie insisted.

"Why shouldn't they?" Cat asked. Once again, she was feeling the need to defend her sister from Maggie's wrath. This time, she knew it was unwarranted. "She deserves to have some fun. Brenna's changed but it's not a bad thing. Brady might have been a bad choice considering the circumstances and location, but Joss is a good guy. I'm thinking it might not be a one-time thing."

"I don't know what's going on with us." Brenna stood defiant in the doorway. "But you're right about Brady. I regret it, but at the time it felt like a good move to get back at Toby. I don't sleep around. You may not believe it but I've only slept with five men in my life and three of them happen to be from here."

Maggie and Cat stared at each other. Maggie's hands were on her hips and she was chewing the inside of her cheek. Never a good sign.

"She apologized to me," Evie said loudly. "Not that she had to. Brady doesn't mean anything to me."

Cat didn't bother to hide her snicker.

"Not anymore! And there's nothing between us! Besides, Aunt Brenna didn't even know I liked him."

"I don't want that behavior in my house," Maggie

said stoutly.

"Then maybe you should talk to Addison. And I've caught Kady and Mac making out in the kitchen," Evie informed her.

"Kitchen seems to be a popular place," Cat mused. "Sexy. Just the other night, Seamus and I—"

"We're not discussing your sex life!" Maggie sputtered.

"I think it's a helluva lot more interesting than Bee's."

"I don't know...lately..." Brenna had a big smile on her face and Cat hoped for his sake, Joss had left the building.

"We could discuss that," Kayleigh offered.

"They were in Mom's room," Cat supplied helpfully. "I walked in on them!"

"That's gross!" Kayleigh grimaced.

"Did you at least use the bed this time?" Maggie said huffily.

"I did," Brenna told her, meeting Maggie's gaze with a hard look of her own. "Maggie, my behavior in your home was inappropriate and for that I apologize. But my intent was never, ever to hurt you or your family, and I hope you realize that. I've apologized to

Evie and I've apologized to you. You asked me to leave and I did. And I'm the one who has to live with the embarrassment. What more do you want from me?"

Maggie finally stopped chewing at her mouth. "I suppose that's enough," she conceded.

"Are you sure? Because I'd really like to put this behind me, put it behind all of us."

Maggie gave a brief nod. "They're your family, too."

"What?"

"My family. They're your family, too."

"Thank you. That means a lot."

"And I hope you stick around long enough to get to know them."

"Will you just hug it out and get it over with?" Kayleigh cried. "So we can find out all about Brenna's sex life? I'd be interested in hearing about Joss."

"Brady's a good kisser, too isn't he?" Evie said. Cat whipped around to see a wicked grin on her pretty face.

"What?" Maggie and Brenna cried in unison, wrenching away from each other.

"You didn't think there was a reason I kept him around when he's such a jerk?"

They were laughing so hard Cat barely heard the dogs barking. "Somebody's here," she said. "Anyone else expecting a booty call?"

"Oh, please – me," Maggie pleaded, hands clasped as in prayer.

"I think I might have to call you a hypocrite," Brenna laughed.

"My mother's not supposed to talk like that," Evie moaned, covering her ears.

"And you think it's easy for me hear about you kissing that boy?" Maggie demanded.

Cat headed for the front door, wading her way through a pack of excited dogs and wagging tails. They were always so excited when the doorbell rang, mainly because no one ever rang it. A quick knock and a come-right-in worked for most visitors. Whoever was at the door didn't know the protocol. Peering out the window, she saw a dark gray Audi sat in the drive, a car she didn't recognize.

"You gotta see this," she called.

The trample of feet joined her at the window as the bell rang again.

"Bloody hell," Kayleigh breathed.

"What the hell is she doing here?" Maggie cried.

"I can hear you," Dory called from behind the closed door. "Now, will you let me the hell in?"

Chapter Thirty-Five

Brenna

Sisters may share the same mother and father but appear to come from different families

—Author Unknown

No one wanted to let Dory in the house.

The four sisters blocked the front door, hands on hips and arms crossed. They stared with various degrees of hostility at Dory on the porch.

“What are you doing here?” Kayleigh demanded.

“Can’t a girl pay a little surprise visit to her sisters?” Dory replied with an even bigger smile.

Kayleigh snorted, joining Cat’s eye roll of disgust.

Brenna sagged with exhaustion at the sudden appearance of their sister. All she had wanted to was hide away from her sister's prying smiles and think about what had happened with Joss.

Joss. His gentle touch and kisses had been a revelation. She couldn't believe what had happened.

Brenna shook her head with resignation at the antagonism of her sisters. Now with Dory showing up, there was no doubt she was going to have to play referee. The way Cat was standing with her hand on the door, Brenna was convinced she was about to slam it in Dory's face.

"Let her in, Cat," Brenna said mildly, moving forward to hold open the door.

"You've been here two days and already you're like the queen of the fucking palace," Cat muttered but she stepped aside.

"Thank you, Brenna." The Dory of old would have been sullen and rude when faced with such a non-welcome. But here she was, full of magnanimous smiles and cheerful demeanor.

It made Brenna nervous.

"How are you?" Brenna asked as Dory pulled her into a hug.

Brenna might be as confused as the others, but Dory was their sister. The teenage rebel was gone, along with the harsh, artificial black hair. There were no visible piercings or tattoos and her clothes were stylish and sophisticated. She looked well put together in her slim pants and fitted jacket. She looked expensive, Brenna decided, glancing at the little sports car out of place beside Maggie's tired van and Cat's banged up truck.

Wherever Dory had been, she seemed to have done well for herself.

"I'm good," Dory said, pulling back. "We flew in from Montreal this morning."

"We?"

A man stepped onto the porch with a kindly expression on his pale face.

"Great. You brought a friend," Cat said under her breath.

"This is my partner, Callum." Dory indicated the short man, dwarfed by the huge shoulder bag he was holding. He was colourless, save for his clothes; bright blue pants paired with a lavender shirt and a purple paisley vest, with white and navy, vintage duck shoes.

"You shouldn't walk around town like that," Cat

warned, stalking to the end of the hall to give Dory's partner room to enter.

Maggie gave a little sigh and gently pushed Kayleigh out of the way. "Come in, Dory."

"Thank you, Maggie," Dory said magnanimously. She bent to give Maggie a brief hug, her heels adding height to her already tall form. "It's good to see you. All of you."

"This is Evie," Maggie motioned to her daughter hovering behind with a wary expression on her face.

"Oldest—no, that's Addison. She's the one going to university in the fall. It's nice to finally meet you," Dory smiled warmly at Evie. "I'm sure you've heard all about evil aunt Dory."

"Yes—I mean, no, not that you're evil," she said in a rush.

"Well, I'm sure they didn't say very nice things about me. No one was really happy with me, including me, when I left." Dory moved to hug Kayleigh, but Kayleigh's folded arms and set face stopped her. She settled for nodding at Cat, her smile fading as she took in the bruises on Cat's face. "What happened to you?"

"Brenna showed up unannounced," Cat said coolly.

"You were fighting?" Dory asked with a gleeful smile. "Things never change." She stepped into the hall and moved into the living room. "This place sure hasn't. A little faded but still home."

"It's my home now," Cat growled.

"You live here alone?"

"Bee's with me. For now."

"What are you doing here?" Kayleigh demanded, continuing her attempt at blocking Dory's progress into the house.

"Why don't we go sit down, see what's going on?" Maggie suggested, shouldering in front of Kayleigh.

"I need a drink," Kayleigh muttered from the doorway, still preventing Callum with his bag from entering.

"Me too," Cat agreed.

"Why don't I open a bottle of wine?" Brenna offered. Cat stopped her before she could make a welcome escape to the kitchen.

"I'm the waitress; I can do it. Besides," Cat said quietly to Brenna. "Don't leave Kay alone with Dory. I don't think Maggie would stop her from trying to kill her."

Brenna wasn't sure if Cat was joking or not.

“Nothing’s changed here,” Dory said with a satisfied smile, surveying the living room as she sank into one the squishy green chairs. Maggie moved to switch on the lamps and the dim light hid the fading wallpaper and sun bleached furniture. The room was spotless; not a hint of dust or picture out of place.

Brenna saw how Dory’s eyes flicked over them, appraising, evaluating, the less-than warm welcome never deflating her self-confidence. She looked at the room like Dory would; it looked less lived in than the rest of the house, formal and very un-Cat like with her grandmother’s crystal in the case by the fireplace, the pictures hanging on the walls.

Why hadn’t she ever noticed the pictures before? Brenna’s attention flipped back to the art. Were they original? Galvanized by the thought, she walked across the room to inspect the landscape hanging over the fireplace.

It looked like...it couldn’t be...Brenna had taken a Canadian art course as an elective in university, learning about the famed Group of Seven. The picture looked like a Thom Thomson, but why was it here, in her mother’s house?

She turned to look at the one beside it. Could that

be a Jackson?

No. Not here. She turned back to her sister. Dory was surveying the room, as if she was seeing it for the first time, eyes narrowed and calculating.

Dory noticed Brenna watching her. “I heard you were home. That’s too bad about you and Toby. He seemed like a nice guy.”

“How would you know?” Kayleigh demanded.

“I met him, what, was it about four years ago?” At Dory’s words, Maggie’s head whipped around to Brenna. “I looked Brenna up when I was in Vancouver. We had dinner.”

“You never told me that,” Maggie accused, eyes narrowing at Brenna.

“No, but I told Kayleigh,” Brenna said wearily. “No big secret.”

“Why are you here?” Kayleigh asked, sounding as sullen as the Dory of old.

“I heard about Granddad.” Dory patted the arm of the chair and silent Callum obediently perched beside her, like a parrot on the arm of a pirate.

“How’s that possible? He just died.” Kayleigh blustered. Brenna thought Cat’s warning about her had been right – the tension emanating from Kayleigh towards Dory was almost tangible.

"He's dead? But Dad said he only had a heart attack." Dory's face fell. "Dad said it didn't sound good but I don't think he expected him to die. Did he make it home in time to-?"

"Dad?" Dory's casual reference to their father was a bucket of cold water dumped over Brenna. "You've been in contact with our father?"

"Haven't you?"

"You know where he's been?" Brenna held her breath, pictures forgotten. Finding him had been as important to Dory as it had been for Brenna, but knowing she succeeded sent a jarring vibration through Brenna.

What would have happened if Brenna had found him? Would he ever have known her? If she'd walked up to him on the street – would he have even recognized her as one of his own?

Dory glanced at them in turn as she took the glass of wine Cat offered. Her smile had a tint of smugness. "I talk to him all the time. He's been in Toronto for about six years now."

Brenna's heart sank. He had been so close – not to her, but to Maggie and Kayleigh and Cat, never once reaching out to them.

"Really?" For a moment Cat's expression was wistful, eager before snapping closed. "Doesn't surprise me."

Kayleigh said nothing, her face stoic, eyes never meeting her sisters'.

"Bastard," Maggie said under her breath. "Never once..."

"Contacted us," Brenna finished. "Never got in touch with us."

"You'll have to talk to him about that." Dory's tone was self-righteous, proud of her connection with their father. Brenna felt a sudden surge of hatred towards her, surprised at the severity of it.

"But you were trying to find him." Dory looked earnestly at Brenna. "You told me that was your plan. Remember we would talk about getting him to come back, looking after us. It must have been so hard on Maggie." Her smile looked artificial, pasted on.

What was Dory after? "I didn't find him. Today at the hospital was the first I'd seen him since he left."

And he'd confused her with Cat.

Maggie shook her head. "You always gave him too much credit, Bee. He left us, which meant he didn't want to be found."

"I needed to know why."

"You don't know why he left?" Dory asked in bewilderment. "Uncle Peter made him leave, turned Granddad against him because Peter wanted the farm for himself."

"That's not what Granddad said." Brenna was quick to pick up on the disparities in what Marcus told her and what Dory believed. "It was nothing about the farm. Peter had nothing to do with it. It was our father's choice to leave."

"They made him leave!" Dory insisted. "He loved us. He told me."

"Well, he never told me." Maggie glanced at Brenna for confirmation. "You talked to Marcus. And Granddad is dead now, so there's no asking him."

"I can't believe he's gone," Dory mused sadly.

Callum put a hand on her shoulder. "I'm so sorry," he said in a voice barely above a whisper.

"You didn't even know him," Cat accused as she came back into the living room, a bottle of wine and two beers dangling from her fingers. "None of us did. Stupid feud." She pulled glasses out of the cabinet in the corner of the room, beside yet another landscape picture, and set them on the table before Maggie, who poured the wine.

"That was Peter as well," Dory said knowingly.

"So that's why you're here?" Cat demanded. "Because of Granddad?"

"I thought I should come back if he was so sick. He's family." It was her tone that sent off warning signals for Brenna. Dory had never been proud of her family, even when she lived with them. She had been quick to tell, to tattle, to complain about the others. To tell Dory a secret was to have it used as a weapon.

"You have a funny definition of family," Cat spat.

Dory looked at her, with the identical hard, stubborn green gaze. Brenna considered Cat to be a tough, strong woman, but she suspected Dory was the more dangerous. Looking back at their childhood, Dory had been manipulative, but being on her own would have brought out the sly and the sneaky, the crafty and the careful, especially under their father's influence.

Dory had an agenda and they needed to figure out what it was.

"I didn't see you extend an olive branch to me over the years." Dory shrugged lightly but her eyes were cold and calculating.

"Why would I do that?" Cat demanded.

"If family is that important to you, why wouldn't you? You never once tried to contact me."

"How would I do that when no one knew where you were?"

"Fiona knew. Brenna knew. And Kayleigh knew, too, didn't you big sis?"

Heads whipped around to Kayleigh's direction. Her face flushed, but still retained the stone-like expression.

"Is that right, Kay?" Maggie was the first to ask.

"Why didn't you say anything?" Cat wanted to know.

"I didn't see the need." Kayleigh turned to Dory, her voice cold. "You snuck out of here in the middle of the night, without a word, without even a good-bye. You didn't care enough to let us know you were even alive. You took something from each of us. Why would I want to bring you back? So you could do the same thing all over again?"

"It was easier for all of you after I left," Dory said, sadness apparent under her words. "You didn't have to deal with my problems. You never wanted to. The three of you were always so tight and cozy here. I always felt like an outsider, and so did Brenna."

"Brenna can speak for herself," Maggie said harshly.

"I'm right, aren't I?" Dory turned to Brenna.

Brenna knew Dory was trying to separate her from her sisters, keep them off balance, but she didn't know how to prevent it.

"A little but—"

"That's not fair! Brenna, we never—"

"Your definition of family therefore depends on who you're talking about." Dory raised her hand to interrupt Maggie. "I don't want to do this now. It's been a long drive, and a very long day. I think I'd like to go upstairs to my room now."

"You're staying here?" Cat growled.

"If it's not too much trouble," Dory said with a sweet smile.

Brenna watched as Cat continued to stare at Dory, neither moving, even blinking, like a Mexican stand-off.

"Is my bed still here?" Dory finally asked.

"Yep."

"Would you be able to provide sheets, maybe a

blanket?"

Without another word, Cat turned and left. Brenna heard the stomp up to the second floor.

"So domestic," Dory said. "She looks after this place for you, all by herself."

"This is her home," Maggie said evenly.

"I think it's our home, really. Don't you?"

"No. I have my own house, with my husband. Kayleigh lives over the store. This is Cat's home."

"Mom left it to all of us," Dory insisted.

"Actually, she didn't," Maggie said evenly. "She didn't leave a will. They never got divorced so this is the marital home. Legally, our father still owns it."

Dory never glanced at Callum still perched on the arm of her chair, but when Dory rose to her feet, he was right there with her, like they were communicating with a strange telepathy. "You know, I think we'd be more comfortable staying at the farm with Dad," she said. "I wouldn't want to put Cat out."

No one raised an argument as Callum followed Dory to the door. Brenna was the only one to say good-bye.

"What the hell was that all about?" Kayleigh wondered.

“I have a really bad feeling about it,” Brenna said.

Chapter Thirty-Six

Cat

The best thing about having a sister was that I always had a friend

—Cali Rae Turner

"She just left?" Cat demanded, thundering down the stairs. She still clutched a pillow, which she promptly threw at Brenna. "What the hell was that shit about you feeling like an outsider?"

"It doesn't matter now." Brenna looked hollow, like her insides had been scraped out. Cat felt a pang of sympathy for her. Out of all of them, Brenna had held on to the loyalty towards their father. What had seeing him been like for her?

"What was that all about?" Cat asked with a shake of her head. "Dory, just showing up like that."

"She wants the house," Kayleigh said quietly, staring at the beer bottle in her hand.

Cat's heart gave a sickening lurch at Kayleigh. Feeling weak, she sat quickly down on the couch before her legs gave out. "Well, she can't have it."

"How do you know that's why she's here?" Maggie asked, settling beside her.

Kayleigh heaved a sigh and sank into the chair. "She said as much to me when she called ten years ago. She wanted to know about what we were doing with it, who was living in it, what condition it was in. Look at the way she ran out of here when we told her it was still Da—our father's. She's gone right up there to whisper in his ear about it now." She glanced around, a guilty expression on her usually serene face. "I'm sorry I didn't tell you."

"I wouldn't have wanted to know," Cat said.

"It was so weird seeing her again—going to the door and she's suddenly there." Maggie's glass of wine was empty, unlike the others. Cat plucked Dory's untouched glass off the coffee table and passed it to

Maggie. “Just popping up out of nowhere.”

“She was always unconventional,” Brenna said, curling her legs under her beside Maggie.

“Is that what you call it?”

“I was trying to be tactful.”

“She looks good,” Evie offered, perched on the arm of the chair beside Kayleigh. “I didn’t know what to expect. I’ve only ever seen pictures of her when she was younger, with all the fake black hair…”

“Do you remember when she ripped up all those pictures of Mom after the funeral?” Maggie interrupted. “Smashed all the wedding pictures. She even tried to burn one of the photo albums until Kayleigh tackled her.”

“It was the only time I’ve hit someone in anger,” Kayleigh said with a faint smile. “And that was only because she bit me.”

“Did you fight with her, too?” Evie asked Cat.

“Why do you assume I was the fighter?” Cat wore an offended expression. “Your mother had the nastiest right hook of us all.”

“She kicked your ass that one time, ‘member?” Maggie recalled with a smile.

“I was ten!”

"You deserved it," Kayleigh added.

"I thought you were on my side!"

"Always, which is why I would have stopped her if I'd been at home." Kayleigh smiled at Cat. Cat knew Kayleigh was trying to reassure her, but it wasn't working. All she could think about was walking out the door of her house and never coming back.

But she had her sisters. They would take care of each other – always.

The loud sigh of one of the dogs sinking onto their bed in the kitchen was the only noise in the house. Cat waved the wine glass at Maggie. Her sister must be as exhausted as Cat, judging how quickly she'd finished the second glass. At Maggie's nod, Cat emptied the last of the bottle into her glass.

Across from her, Kayleigh stared into the mouth of her beer bottle like it held the secrets of the universe inside.

"What a shitty day," Cat finally said. "Granddad, our fa—Roger Ebans showing up, what they did to Fiona. Then Dory."

And it would only get worse if Dory got her way. Why did Dory even want the house? There was no sentimental value for her. Just a house; rambling, tired house that needed a paint job and a full-time plumber.

It was Cat's house.

"It hasn't been the best of days," Brenna agreed.

And like a lightbulb going on, Cat had her solution. Brenna would fix it. She was a lawyer, the closest of all of them to Dory. Brenna would make sure Dory didn't get away with this.

Cat laughed giddily, partly at the relief washing over her as well as the memory of the sight of a naked Joss. "At least you got laid!"

Maggie started to laugh. "And we're back to sex."

"It's the only thing we're not going to fight about," Brenna said with a rueful smile.

"You're probably right." Cat leaned forward. "So - what's going on with you and Joss?"

Brenna's embarrassment sent a flush of colour to her cheeks. "I'm not really sure. He showed up to see how I was—I started to cry—"

"You never cry," Kayleigh interrupted.

"Except for when I'm here and with a man who wants to -"

"You cried with Brady?" Evie demanded incredulously.

"No." Brenna dropped her head in her hands. "Can we please forget that happened?"

"Oh, no!" Cat laughed. "It's too good. Little Miss Perfect shows her dirty side."

"You seem a little too interested in my sex life," Brenna said.

"It's sort of like Bigfoot," Cat mused. "You hear rumors, you think maybe it's possible but until the proof is in your face, you don't really believe it!"

"You're comparing me to a mythical, hairy monster? Thanks." Brenna held her glass close to her chest like a shield.

Kayleigh and Maggie's laughter filled the room. This was just what she needed to put this day behind her, shake off the cloud Dory had brought through the front door. "Do you know Joss compared you to a pure-bred dog the first time he met you?"

"He did not!"

"I'm not sure that information needs to be shared," Kayleigh said wryly.

"In a nice way," Cat assured Brenna. "I guess he liked you from the get-go, although you could have fooled me."

"So what does this mean?" Maggie asked Brenna.

"Is this a trend? What about your marriage?"

"No. And no. My marriage is over. I talked to Toby—I guess that was today?" She glanced at Cat, who nodded. "This morning. It seems like a week ago. He called this morning."

"He called you? To apologize?" Maggie wanted to know.

"No. Although he did ask if I really wanted the divorce."

"And do you?" Evie asked.

Brenna nodded. "I don't think I love him enough to forgive him. And that's a problem right there. No, we'll get a divorce, quick and easy. Actually, he called to tell me about a law firm in Austria who was looking for an associate."

"Austria!"

"I worked there a few years back."

"I should have known that," Maggie said sadly. She turned to Kayleigh. "Did you?"

Kayleigh nodded. "I mentioned it to you. I think it was right before McKenna was born."

"And it didn't register. My little sister goes across the world and I don't think to be worried about her?"

"Why would you need to worry about me?" There

was no resentment in Brenna's voice this time, only affection.

"I'm your big sister! It's my job to worry and take care of you and I've done a crap job of it."

"You've done a great job," Brenna argued, touching Maggie's knee. "I'm a big girl. I don't need taking care of. And I didn't make it easy for you to take care of me when I was younger."

Maggie looked at her thoughtfully. "You made it difficult for anyone to get close."

"I think maybe I was protecting myself. First Dad left, and then Mom died, I was afraid you'd leave me too. So I left you first, so it wouldn't hurt as bad." She looked at Cat with a grim expression on her face. "Being here with Cat helped me realize that."

"We can blame our father for that," Maggie said, putting her hand over Brenna's.

Brenna blew out a deep breath. "I don't want to blame anyone. I just want to move on with my life."

"By going to Austria?" Cat couldn't help the condescending note in her voice. What right did Brenna have to pop in and out of their lives?

"I don't know. I never said I was here for good," she reminded Cat.

"You never said you weren't! You never said anything at all!"

"You're right, I didn't. To anyone, about anything and I'd like that to change. I need you—all of you—in my life. I feel horrible I've missed out on so much."

"We can make up for it now," Maggie told her with a sniffle. She stood and wrapped Brenna in a hug.

Bitterness crept over Cat like a chill. Brenna wasn't just back, she was back to being the favourite sister. And the smart sister, too. Smart enough to learn from her mistake and come back to their loving arms. Cat was going to lose her place with Kayleigh and Maggie. She'd be replaced; booted out. Again. They'd always loved Brenna best, she'd always been the favourite. Childish jealousy crept over her like a fog, replacing the warm glow of wine and sisterly love.

Kayleigh interrupted Cat just as she was letting the green-eyed monster take root. "We have to stick together," she said, leaning over to speak into Cat's ear. "Don't go trying to find trouble when there's none there. We love you both equally, but in different ways. We always have."

The air suddenly chilled. Kayleigh shivered and

rubbed hands over her arms. Cat lifted her head and sniffed. Lilacs.

Maggie kept her grip on Brenna as her eyes darted around the room. “Did someone open the door? Who’s here?”

“That’s just Mom dropping in for a visit,” Cat smiled.

Kayleigh stiffened on the couch, clutching her beer close to her chest. Maggie swept an arm open for Evie to come to her as Brenna wriggled free.

“She’s not going to hurt you,” Brenna said.

“What does she want?” Maggie demanded, pulling Evie close.

“To say hello,” Cat said. “To see what’s going on in our lives.”

“Well, I don’t want her to! She has no right! She lost any right to be a part of our lives when she let herself die!”

“Maggie, she didn’t let herself...she was sick...”

“She died! She could have gotten help and she could have gotten better, but she didn’t. She let herself die because she didn’t care enough about us.” Maggie’s voice lifted, and one of the dogs barked in response.

"It's okay, Mom," Evie said quietly.

Maggie ignored Evie's gentle words. "She left me with you—left me four sisters and a crazy grandfather to take care of! Didn't I have enough on my own? I thought when I got pregnant she'd see I couldn't do it all myself, but she didn't. I wasn't your mother – she was! She was the spoiled child, locking herself in her room when she had a tantrum. I had to deal with that! Me! I was a kid too!"

Cat was horrified. This surge of rage wasn't Maggie. Maggie was the responsible sister, the dependable one, the one who always took care of them.

Maggie was the sister who never got her own life because she was saddled with taking care of four sisters, a crazy grandfather and a mother with enough problems to write a book about.

"She was sick," Cat whispered. Would she have defended her mother if she hadn't sensed her in the room? Cat knew Maggie had every reason to feel the way she did. "She couldn't help it."

"She could! She knew what it was like!" Maggie insisted. "She grew up with Grandpa Earl and him trying to kill himself every other day. She knew what it was like to have a parent like that, and still she did nothing to help herself. And our father knew, and never tried to help her." Maggie had stepped free of Evie's arms and stood in the center of the room, hands flailing as if she was confronting an invisible foe.

Cat watched in shock as Maggie's face crumpled. Kayleigh stepped forward, reached out for her sister. "Maggie..."

"No!" Maggie pushed her away, whirled away from her like a tempest. "It wasn't right. Don't tell me it's okay, because it's not. Granddad, and Fiona—everybody knew what she was like! But no one did a damn thing because they thought it was OK because I could cope! Well, what if I didn't want to? What if I wanted to check out, just fuck off and leave like Dory and Brenna. What then? What would have happened?" Maggie heaved, tears streaming down her face. "She left me to do everything!"

"Mom? Mom, you're scaring me."Cat reached for Evie's hand. Maggie was scaring her, too.

"Maggie, don't," Brenna begged.

"Don't what? Don't tell you what it was like for me? Don't admit there were days I didn't know what the fuck I was doing? Days I just wanted to run and hide, or leave because I just wanted to be away from everything? But I couldn't because I loved you! I loved you so fucking much..." She sank to the floor, sobbing, and Cat's heart followed her down. She'd had no idea Maggie felt this way. Maggie had shouldered the burden of surrogate mother to them all and Cat had taken it for granted.

Kayleigh lowered herself to her knees, grabbed Maggie and held her through the heart-rending sobs. Evie and Brenna were beside her in an instant, crouched, arms reaching for any part of Maggie they could touch. Kayleigh looked at Cat over Brenna's bowed head and held out her hand.

Cat dropped to her knees with her sisters, wrapping one arm around Kayleigh, smoothing Maggie's hair with her hand. "It's okay," she said, for lack of knowing what would help.

"I'm not even...she's not..." Maggie sobbed.

"I know," Kayleigh soothed. "But it doesn't matter. It never has."

The air turned bitterly cold. Goose bumps racing along Cat's arms. They hugged each other for warmth as well as comfort.

"She's really in here," Cat said softly.

"I know," Maggie said through her tears. "Doesn't she know it's fucking freezing?"

"I think she's trying to apologize." Brenna's voice filled with wonder.

Cat's nose was cold, her fingers numb, like being outside in the winter without gloves. She shivered in her T-shirt, huddled closer to Brenna. The air filled with the overpowering scent of lilacs. "Should we tell her we accept her apology so it can warm up?" Cat's teeth were chattering. "It's really cold in here..."

"I think she's left it a little too late." Maggie said.

Slowly, the icy chill dissipated, as if the sun was chasing away the cold of the night. Cat breathed a sigh of relief. Her teeth stopped their chatter and she released her grip on Brenna. It seemed only fitting that their mother would find a way to practically freeze them in order to tell them she was sorry.

Cat had to believe their mother felt remorse at what she had done to her daughters. It was enough their father hadn't cared; she couldn't live with knowing their mother hadn't cared either.

Maggie finally shrugged them off. One by one they backed away, still on the floor but no longer huddled on top of her.

“She was sick,” Kayleigh said, nervously glancing around as if their mother was about to appear.

“She was wrong,” Maggie countered.

“She was,” Brenna agreed. “And we shouldn’t have taken you for granted. You should have been able to have a life outside us.”

“Thank you,” Cat said to Maggie quickly, not wanting Brenna to get all the credit of soothing her. “For raising us like you did. I know it wasn’t easy.”

“I loved you,” Maggie told them, wiping away the tears. “I still do.”

“You’re everything to us,” Kayleigh said simply. “You always have been. I don’t know what we would have done without you.”

They sat quietly, wiping tears, passing around Kleenex that Maggie found in her sweater pocket. The room warmed, leaving behind the faint hint of lilacs.

“Is she gone now?” Evie finally whispered.

“I think so,” Cat said, stretching out her long legs. “But I’ve never felt it that cold before.”

“That was intense.” Brenna looked at Maggie. “You okay, now?”

Maggie nodded. Evie kept her arm around her mother.

Cat couldn't resist. "I told you she was still here. You never believed me, but I told you." Her smile was smug as she passed it to her sisters.

Maggie groaned, and shook her head. "Only you, Cat. Only you."

Brenna chuckled.

"Don't you ever vacuum?" Kayleigh wondered as she picked up a hunk of dog hair from the carpet beside her.

"I have three dogs," Cat cried.

"I need more wine," Maggie sighed.

"I'll get another bottle." Evie scampered to her feet, obviously eager to help.

"Look what you made me do," Maggie groused.

Cat suspected she was talking to their mother and braced for another round. Luckily, her hostility had vanished. "I had a freak out in front of my kid and scared her. What kind of mother am I?"

"The best kind," Cat assured her. "To all of us. Always have been."

"We wouldn't be here if it wasn't for you," Kayleigh added.

"Seriously," Brenna added with a laugh. "I never would have come back if it hadn't been for Addison's wedding."

"The wedding," Maggie moaned. "I've still got so much to do and here I am crying on the floor."

She pulled herself to her feet, leaving her sisters with a new and fervent appreciation for Maggie.

Chapter Thirty-Seven

Brenna

Our siblings push buttons that cast us in roles we felt sure we had let go of long ago—the baby, the peacemaker, the caregiver, the avoider...It doesn't seem to matter how much time has elapsed or how far we've traveled.

—Jane Mersky Leder

"That was fun." Brenna's cheeks hurt from laughing as she helped Cat carry the empty glasses into the kitchen. She carefully rinsed each glass before putting it into the dishwasher.

Spending time with her sisters, Brenna realized how much she'd missed the musical sound of

Kayleigh's laughter, Maggie's rude snorts of amusement, Cat's sarcasm, the comfortableness of being with those who knew her best. She had no idea the hole was there until it was filled.

"It was nice of Seamus to take Maggie and Kayleigh home," she said to Cat. "I'd be worried about them getting there in one piece."

"Uh huh. Did you have any idea Maggie felt like that?" Cat asked as Brenna piled the empty wine bottles into the recycling bin.

"No," Brenna shook her head, a ball of remorse growing in her stomach. "She always seemed ready and willing to do whatever we needed. And we took her for granted."

Cat slumped against the counter. "She looked after us all, even when she was just a kid herself. Anytime Mom had one of her—whatever they were—we all turned to Maggie. She was like a mother to us. She was our mother."

Brenna took a handful of potato chips from the bowl Cat had put out earlier. "I couldn't have done it. Even if you had needed me, I don't know if I could have stayed."

Cat grew quiet, her expression thoughtful.

"What are you thinking?"

She took a deep breath, looking sheepishly at Brenna. "I was just thinking how I did need you. I had Maggie and Kayleigh to take care of me, and Dory to fight with, but you? You should have been my best friend." She shook her head. "We let everything get between us."

The lump in Brenna's throat hadn't been there moments before. "We let anything get between us. Anyone."

"It was stupid," Cat said after a long pause. "You know, you should call Joss."

"What?" Was it the abrupt change of topic or the mention of Joss that made her heart race? "Why?"

"Did I walk in on the two of you or not?"

Brenna giggled at the exaggerated way Cat swayed as she pushed herself away from the counter to reach the bowl of chips. She wasn't the only one feeling a little tipsy.

"Yes. I'm not sure," Brenna said with a foolish grin. "It seems a little surreal."

"Well, his ass in the air looked real enough to me. Pretty nice, too. You should call him."

Brenna pointed to the glasses Cat had loaded into

the dishwasher. "After how many of those? Not tonight."

"You were drinking when you first met him."

"And look how good that turned out."

"I think it turned out pretty good."

Brenna reached for another chip, realizing just how much she'd had to drink. Her thoughts of Joss were fuzzy, and seemed to be coated in pastels, like a baby's blanket. "I had sex with him," she giggled softly.

"Am I finally getting details?" Cat demanded, her mouth full of potato chips.

"No. No details." She had been the recipient of loose lips and wouldn't do that to Joss. "I'd need a lot more wine for that."

"That can be arranged."

"And pass out beside Evie?" Brenna shook her head a little too firmly and sent the room spinning. "I'd never live it down."

"It's not like you're going to live the other stuff down either," Cat said matter-of-factly. "After the scene Joss had to go through, I definitely think you should call him. It was pretty funny."

"Embarrassing, maybe?"

Cat waved away her protests. “We’re family: he’ll be ready for the next time, now.”

“I don’t know if there will be a next time. What if there isn’t? What if there is?” Brenna wasn’t sure which possibility frightened her more. “I’m not even divorced.”

“You can’t possibly feel guilty.”

She gave a more gentle shake of her head. “My marriage was dead anyway.”

“Plus, you already slept with Brady. Does Joss know about that?” Cat didn’t wait for Brenna to respond. “Probably. Everyone does.”

“Great.” It was Brady she was never going to live down.

“Do you like him?”

“Joss?” Did she like Joss Ryan? She found him attractive and intriguing, sexy and sweet. Did that mean she liked him? “It’s been a long time since I liked a man,” she admitted.

Cat grinned. “Feels good, doesn’t it?”

“It does. But the timing is all wrong. With Granddad and our fath- Roger and Dory...”

“That’s what makes it so good,” Cat said eagerly. “He’ll be the perfect distraction for all the other shit.”

"I don't know if I want him to be a distraction."

"Right. The new job." Cat's face closed. Lips pinched, she slammed the bowl back on the counter. "I guess you wouldn't want to be distracted by anybody here if you're taking off for that job all the way over in Europe. On second thought, Joss a good guy. Don't call him. I wouldn't want you to lead him on." Turning on her heel, Cat stormed out of the kitchen.

"Wait, that's not what I meant," she said to Cat's retreating back. She didn't want Joss to be just a distraction, but did she want it to be more?

Brenna sighed as Cat's footsteps pounded up the stairs. Maybe it was too much to hope that they could be friends.

*

The next morning as Brenna was making her way downstairs, she saw Dory pulling into the drive.

It was a good thing Cat was still in bed.

Despite the bright smile she pasted on, a tight ball of apprehension grew within as Brenna opened the house for Dory. They had been close once; Dory had confided her dreams to leave Forest Hills, Brenna provided an ear for her litany of complaints and rages.

Looking back, Brenna realized their relationship had only been one way. Dory hadn't give Brenna the attention she craved, never asked about her dreams, her desires. She was self-absorbed, solely concerned with herself.

Dory was one more person Brenna had been wrong about.

As she followed Dory into the kitchen, Brenna appraised her. She was well-dressed for so early in the morning. Her appearance was sleek and polished, like the delicate crystal glasses in the dining room. Out of place in Forest Hills.

"Does Cat keep any coffee in this place?" Dory asked, searching through the cupboards. "There's still no Starbucks, or even a Tim Horton's. This place is such a hole."

Brenna had unearthed the ancient coffee maker the day before and set about making coffee. "It has its charm."

"I still haven't figured out what that is yet." The scent of coffee quickly filled the room, the dogs venturing in to discover the new aroma. "Get away!

How many dogs does she have?" Dory cried as the border collie jumped up, pushing her nose rudely between Dory's legs.

"Just three," Brenna said, shooing them out the back door.

Brenna didn't want to admit she still didn't know the names of the dogs yet.

Dory brushed off her pants, an expression of disdain on her thin face. "I've never liked dogs."

"Good thing you're staying at the farm then," Brenna said lightly, careful not to let one iota of the bitterness she felt colour her voice. If Dory knew how hurt she was about Dory's relationship with their father, she'd find a way to use it against her.

Dory stood at the counter across from Brenna and watched the coffee drip into the pot. "Why'd you come back?"

"It was time."

"Because of your marriage? I don't understand why you'd bother coming back here. You were never cut out for this place, Brenna, we both know that. You would have been miserable if you stayed. It was a good decision to leave."

Brenna only shrugged. What was Dory after?

"Did they make you feel guilty about leaving?" Dory continued.

"No, no one ever did that. Just about not visiting."

"At least you talked to them."

"I left on better terms than you did," Brenna pointed out. She found a plate of butter tarts in the refrigerator and offered one to Dory. The red KitchenAid mixer still stood at attention on the counter, a reminder for Cat that she still had cakes to make.

Brenna hoped there wouldn't be another food fight when Cat found Dory in the kitchen.

Dory bit into the tart. "Mm. Homemade?"

"Cat made them."

"I don't picture her as the Martha Stewart type. I can't understand why she would want to stay here." Dory spread her arms. "Probably because no one realizes there's a whole other world out there that doesn't revolve around this tiny blip on a map! Everyone who lives here has this small-town mentality and it drives me crazy."

"Cat seems happy. So do Maggie and Kayleigh."

Dory snorted. "Don't they want more? Cat has nothing but a waitressing job and probably a fuck friend that sneaks in to her bed at night. Kayleigh owns a tiny little store that will never amount to anything. And Maggie! Well, she doesn't have a chance because of all those kids she was stupid enough to have—"

"Maggie loves her kids. She's a great mother," Brenna protested. "You don't know anything about their lives."

"Obviously Maggie didn't take after our mother."

"Kayleigh is happy with her store. She's done great. People come from all over to visit. And Cat..." Brenna paused, unsure of what she wanted to say about Cat. "Cat has kept this place going for years by herself, on just her waitress salary and Cat's Cakes."

"What's that?" Dory scrunched her nose with disgust.

Brenna fought to keep her temper. She pointed to the second tart in Dory's hand. "She makes cakes and things like that. She sells to The Sandwich Shoppe and - "

Dory laughed. "You're kidding. She's so small town."

"She likes it that way. They all do. They're happy here," Brenna said firmly.

"But you're not." Dory narrowed her eyes at Brenna, her voice suddenly calculating rather than condescending.

Brenna was caught off guard. "I don't know what I am. I didn't think I could be happy here, no, but since I've been back—"

"Oh, God, Bren, you've been back too long!" Dory laughed. "They're starting to warp your brain!"

"It's not that. It's relaxing here. In Vancouver, I was always so busy with work that I never had time to do anything. You know, it took me almost seven years to get up to the mountains? I never once went skiing or whale watching or things that people do when they come to British Columbia. I never had time and I never had anyone to do them with."

"And whose fault is that? It's because our mother was a freak, Bren! And because you spent the first eighteen years holed up in this hellhole that you didn't understand how to interact with real people!"

Brenna frowned "I don't think it's because of that at all."

"Look around you, little sis. These people are nothing. Best thing you ever did was walk away. And you should start running as soon as they put

Granddad in the ground because if you don't, you're going to get stuck here and ten years will go by before you know it, and you'll be living here with Cat with a houseful of animals and nothing else!" Dory's laugh had a hard, nasty edge to it.

"I think you should probably go," Brenna said quietly. The last thing she wanted was for Cat to walk into the kitchen and hear Dory talking like that. Cat didn't need Dory's cruel words.

"OK, look, maybe I was too harsh. It's been a while since I've been here." Dory quickly backpedaled. "I thought we were on the same page about things."

"I'm not into badmouthing our sisters or the people who live here."

"Fair enough." Dory brushed the crumbs from her fingers briskly.

"Why are you here, Dory?" Brenna demanded.

Dory raised one perfectly groomed eyebrow. "Our grandfather just died. Where else should I be?"

Brenna folded her elbows, leaned them on the counter. "That's the thing. We have no idea where you've been or where you should be. Do you have a family? Who's this Callum guy?"

Dory checked the clock on the stove, as though

Brenna hadn't spoken. "I'd better get going before Cat gets up and kicks me out. Dad's heading up to Elliot Lake to talk to the funeral home this morning and I told him I'd go with him for moral support. Uncle Peter's taking this pretty hard so Dad's taken over the funeral plans."

"It's nice you have such a good relationship with him," Brenna said stiffly. It was impossible for her to keep the resentment out of her voice this time.

"It is," Dory said blithely. "You shouldn't have given up looking for him. Turns out he's a pretty cool guy."

"I was under the impression he didn't want to be found."

"Well, I'm not the type to take no for an answer. I just kept poking away and finally he just gave up and was like—whatever!" She threw up her hands dramatically again. "I think it helps that I wasn't looking for a daddy figure. We're more friends than anything."

"Nice for you."

She smiled, a toothy, completely insincere smile."Look, I've got to run. I think the funeral's being planned for Friday. You still going to be around?"

“I don’t know what my plans are yet, but I’ll be here. There. At the funeral.”

“Great. Later.” And without another word Dory was gone, leaving Brenna shaking her head with confusion and disgust.

“What was that all about?” Cat’s said.

Brenna whirled around, peered up the stairs. Cat was crouched by the railing, in the same spot Brenna used to eavesdrop when people stopped by. “Were you listening?”

“To the last bit. What’s she doing here?” Cat started slowly down the stairs, as if the events of the previous day were weighing heavily on her.

“She’s not saying,” Brenna admitted. “Not the real reason anyway.”

“I have a bad feeling about this,” Cat said, echoing Brenna’s words from last night.

Chapter Thirty-Eight

Cat

A sister shares childhood memories and grown-up dreams

—Author Unknown

The rest of the week flew by. Marcus' funeral was planned for Friday, the same day as the rehearsal dinner. Addison's wedding was on Saturday.

Cat had never been so busy. With Brenna's help, she cleaned the house, supervised the painting of the porch, the repairs on two of the bathrooms and cooked enough food for an army. She had offered to host the rehearsal dinner for Maggie and with both families in attendance, as well as an extensive wedding party, she expected a full house.

"I have no idea why I agreed to this," Cat grumbled to Brenna on Thursday afternoon. The kitchen was full of enticing smells, the counters strewn with herbs and vegetable and sharp utensils. "Because it's Maggie," Brenna said.

No other reason was needed. And after Maggie's outburst on Monday night, which frightened Cat more than she cared to admit, they treated her with kid gloves.

"Here, cut them like this," Cat barked, snatching the potato out of her sister's hand. Brenna had eagerly agreed to help in the kitchen, but Cat was beginning to think she would have been better off doing things herself. Brenna's knife skills made her nervous and the last thing she needed was another trip to the hospital. "Don't you know how to do anything?"

"I told you I wasn't good in the kitchen," Brenna warned, stepping back to allow Cat to demonstrate.

"But it's a potato. How difficult can it be?"

Brenna scrambled for the rehearsal dinner menu tucked under a cookbook. "Maybe if you weren't making difficult recipes. I've never even heard of duchess potatoes."

"Mashed potatoes with whipping cream, piped into shapes," Cat retorted.

Brenna's mouth dropped open. "It sounds involved. Are you forgetting the funeral is tomorrow?"

"That's why we're making them today. And the mini gratins. I just need to heat them up here. The chicken breasts are stuffed; I pull them out of the freezer tonight and it's ready. The vegetables will be roasted – Seamus is going to do that for me at Woody's." Because she was so busy, Cat had managed to keep her mind off the funeral. "I'll have to make the salads, set out the appetizers and that's it for Friday. Desert is finished."

Brenna turned back to the list. "There's a lot of food here. How many are coming?"

"Thirty-four."

Brenna blew out her breath. "Do you think you have enough?"

"I really hope so." She took the list from Brenna. Normally so confident, Cat had her doubts about the menu, the amount of food, how it would all work out...

"Everything sounds so elegant. Chicken breasts stuffed with ricotta, spinach and walnut, roasted beets and kale topped with goat cheese, honey roasted carrots."

"But. You're thinking but. It's too fancy for Forest Hills, isn't it?"

"Of course not." Brenna spoke quickly, too quickly.

Cat slumped against the counter. "For my first wedding, Tommy's father barbequed burgers. There were ten of us in his backyard and I was so drunk I smashed a piece of cake in Tommy's face. The second time, Perry's mother insisted on an afternoon tea, so we ate cucumber sandwiches and scones. I had no choice but to stay sober for that one. The third time -"

"With Alex," Brenna prompted when Cat paused.

"Alex." She shook herself, reminded herself to think about the happy memories, not dwell on the grief. "He was already in the hospital by then. I fed him red Jell-o."

"You're giving Addison the wedding dinner you wanted," Brenna said, with an understanding smile.

Cat shrugged. "I don't know why I bother. It's Maggie who wants the rehearsal dinner. Addison couldn't care less. Do you know what she's having for the wedding meal tomorrow night? Ribs and pulled pork sliders."

"For a wedding. That's...messy."

"It'll be a fucking disaster. Sauce everywhere..." Cat shook her head. "The girl won't listen to reason. She insisted on that red velvet wedding cake, too. Thank God I finished that yesterday."

Brenna smiled. "It's a beautiful cake and tomorrow night will be amazing. The food will be perfect."

"Hope so." Cat pushed away from the counter. "Time to get back to work. Keep cutting."

Brenna obediently picked up her knife. "Are you going to marry Seamus?"

"Would you mind asking that when you're not holding a knife?"

Cat had been dreading this conversation since she heard Brenna was coming home. It was one thing to have the townsfolk discuss her relationship with Seamus; some thought a Todd/Skatt union, regardless of what sister, was inevitable and some thought it a recipe for disaster.

Cat didn't want to know what Brenna thought about it.

"I don't know," she said carefully. "I've been

married three times already."

"That wouldn't matter to him," Brenna told her. "He's always wanted a big wedding, lots of flowers and food and friends. We used to plan who we'd invite."

"We've never talked about it." And that was her fault. Every time Seamus brought it up, she changed it, or distracted him with a kiss, or even an argument so she wouldn't have to listen to his dreams.

Because his dreams should be her dreams and what was wrong with her if they weren't?

Cat resumed peeling potatoes before Brenna could continue the conversation. It hurt knowing she couldn't give Seamus what he wanted. The look on his face when she said she wanted his baby, not him, still haunted her.

What was wrong with her? She had a man who loved her, who wanted to spend the rest of his life with her, regardless of her past. Most men would have run scared, but not Seamus.

Never Seamus.

"I think I'd be okay with it."

Cat glanced over but Brenna was focused on the knife on her hand, cutting the potatoes into tiny cubes. "Really?"

Brenna only nodded and Cat felt a bloom of relief spread through her chest.

Maybe that was what was wrong with her...

Chapter Thirty-Nine

Brenna

Lord help the mister who comes between me and my sister.

-Irving Berlin

They worked until late at night, with fragrant smells of butter, garlic, and fresh thyme filling the kitchen. Brenna had lost track of time when the dogs announced Kayleigh's arrival.

"I saw the lights on," she called from the front door. "You still at it?" She waved a six-pack of beer as she trouped into the kitchen.

"Almost finished." Cat's tongue stuck out as she

carefully piped mashed potato into a delicate mound. “These need a quick roast tonight.”

“What time is it?” Brenna wondered as she gratefully accepted a cold bottle from Kayleigh. Her entire body ached – legs, back, feet. Even her little toe throbbed where she had dropped a pot. There was a blood-soaked bandage around her finger and a blister on her palm.

She had never enjoyed a day more.

Spending the day with Cat; talking, creating, sharing, not fighting; was like nothing she'd ever experienced. And while part of her felt exhilarated by the tentative friendship that was developing between them, another part of her regretted that it had taken them so many years.

They had wasted so much time.

“It's after ten,” Kayleigh said, wrenching Brenna back into the reality of the kitchen. “Do you have anything to eat? I'm starving.”

Cat met Brenna's eyes and laughed. The refrigerator was filled with julienned vegetables and cooked potatoes, bags of washed lettuces and bowls of dip. “There's stuff for a sandwich or cookies. I think there's a bag of chips somewhere.”

"Chips," Kayleigh decided. "I ate too many of those little sandwiches after the visitation tonight."

"You went - " Brenna began.

" – to the visitation?" Cat finished.

Kayleigh glanced between them. "Do you think you might be spending too much time together? In fact, I kind of expected the house to be ready to collapse if you had another one of your fights. What's going on?"

"Once Bee started to do what I told her, I didn't feel the need to slap her around anymore," Cat drawled. "But enough about us. I didn't think you were going tonight. You're still going to the funeral?"

"Maggie wanted to go tonight," Kayleigh admitted, rummaging through cupboards until she found the bag of chips. Brenna shook her head when Kayleigh waved the bag at her. After today she doubted she'd be able to get the potato smell off her hands and had no desire to eat anything made from the vegetable.

"Anything exciting happen?" Cat asked, head bent over her task.

"About what you'd expect. Peter never said a word to us. Da – our father - avoided eye contact. Dory was stuck to him like glue."

"Maybe we shouldn't bother going tomorrow."

Brenna frowned. "We'd be going to show our respects to Marcus and support Fiona, not for anyone else."

"I thought you were still mad at Marcus?" Kayleigh asked.

She sighed, thinking of the web of emotions brought on by Marcus' death. "It's complicated."

"Isn't it always with you?" Cat grumbled.

*

Brenna was quick to see Fiona as she followed Cat into the church the next day. Standing at the back of the church, Fiona's eyes were puffy and red but her chin held high.

Seamus was standing protectively next to his mother. "They won't let her speak." His jaw was clenched as he stared at Peter across the pews.

"I don't know what to say," Brenna said sadly. Marcus Ebans had forgiven the feud but it was obvious his sons would never be able to.

"There's nothing for you to say," Fiona insisted.

"This is between me and your uncle."

"More like our father," Cat said darkly. "Let's find a seat."

The Skatt and the Todd families made up the first three pews, sitting close together so no one would have to cross the aisle to where Jamie and Cara sat with their children, Dory sat with Callum in the row behind.

Brenna met Dory's eyes as she sat between Kayleigh and Cat. "You don't want to sit with your family?" Dory invited, waving at the nearly empty pew.

"This is her family," Cat barked in return.

Dory raised an eyebrow. "How long will the truce hold? You'll be scrabbling over something soon enough."

Brenna put her hand on Cat's knee, a wordless request to ignore Dory. She watched her father speaking quietly to his brother at the front of the church, the minister nodding beside them.

"It doesn't seem right that he's here for this and wasn't around for Mom's," Kayleigh said in a low voice.

"Nothing about this seems right." Their father not

speaking to them, their sister cutting herself off from them, Marcus dead... "It's all wrong."

"I don't think it's fixable."

Brenna grinned at Kayleigh. She'd had clients and deals that others had deemed impossible, and had learned to look at it as a challenge. "At work, I could fix anything. I was like an Olivia Pope gladiator."

"A what?" Kayleigh's expression was one of bewilderment.

Brenna sighed. "You've never watched Scandal? I think you need Netflix."

"I have Netflix. I watched all seven seasons of Gilmore Girls."

Both she and Kayleigh looked up when the shadow fell over them. "Brenna," Joss said gruffly. "Sorry for your loss." His eyes seemed to have a question when he looked at her, and Brenna flushed under his gaze.

"Hi." It was the first time she'd seen him since Monday, the first time she'd seen his hands after they had roamed over her naked body, the first time he'd smiled at her after kissing her lips... "Do you want - ?"

"Sit with us," Kayleigh interrupted, shoving Brenna over with her hip. "Lots of room for you to squeeze in here."

Joss smiled and Brenna wondered if it was relief she saw in his eyes. "Doesn't look like much room for me. Besides," he nodded across the aisle. "My sister."

"Of course," Brenna nodded, and kept nodding until she felt like a bobble-head. Kayleigh elbowed her.

"She'll see you after this is all over," Kayleigh assured him.

"Sounds good." And with a smile that warmed Brenna's heart, Joss moved to sit behind his sister, on the other end of the pew from Dory.

Dory leaned across aisle, a calculating smile on her lips. "Who's that tall drink of water?"

"None of your business," Kayleigh snapped.

As if he sensed trouble brewing, Seamus leaned over Cat. "There's a lot of redheads in here," he said in a low voice. "Too bad it wasn't kick a ginger day!"

Kayleigh and Brenna laughed, and Dory retreated with a sulky expression on her face.

Brenna's smiled faded as she watched her sister. She hated there was an aisle separating them. Dory should be with them, crammed into the pew, talking about inconsequential things like television shows so they wouldn't dwell on the casket before them.

They needed to distract each other so they wouldn't think of another funeral, so many years ago.

Dory seemed to have forgotten their promise to always be there for each other.

The organ swelled to life, masking the laughter. Fiona glanced down the row with a frown, but her face softened when she saw them together.

At least three of them were together, with Maggie close by.

Cat pinched her arm, jerking her head towards Seamus fighting sleep as the minister spoke extensively about Marcus, how his death was such a loss to the community. Despite the somber circumstances, Brenna grinned as she watched Seamus' dark head bob, then jerk upright several times.

Brenna let her mind wander, formulating her own eulogy, what she knew about her grandfather.

He was a stubborn man, who neglected his grandchildren.

He was generous, proving those same grandchildren with a means to educate themselves.

He found love with Fiona Todd, her mother's best

friend.

He hated her mother's family.

The man was a quandary; it was no wonder that she still couldn't decide how she felt about his death.

After the burial in the cemetery behind the church, a convoy of cars headed up the hill to the farm.

"I'm not going," Kayleigh said firmly. "No one wants us there."

"We have every right to go," Brenna told her. "He was our grandfather."

"Just because you feel some connection doesn't mean you have to drag the rest of us along with you," Kayleigh snapped. It was uncharacteristic of her speak so harshly and those grouped around stared at her in shock.

"We're going for Fiona's sake," Maggie cut in, in her best older sister voice. "Go for a half an hour and then you can leave. God knows I have enough to do to get ready for tonight."

Despite her convincing tone, Brenna felt more than a twinge of apprehension about what awaited them at the farm.

Chapter Forty

Cat

We know one another's faults, virtues, catastrophe's, mortifications, triumphs, rivalries, desires and how long we can hang by our hands on a bar. We have been banded together under pack codes and tribal laws.

—Rose Macaulay

Cat had been to countless funerals over the years, but as she stepped out of Seamus' truck, she couldn't help but remember the day her mother was buried.

There had been a gathering after her mother's funeral as well, but without the crowd Marcus Ebans' commanded. Cat remembered how she had huddled with Brenna and Kayleigh, watching an overwhelmed Maggie make sure the food was set out perfectly, everyone had enough to eat, and every guest had been thanked for coming.

The twenty-three year old Maggie, pregnant with her second child, had collapsed with exhaustion that night. Fiona had threatened to take her to the hospital if she didn't stay off her feet the next day.

As she had that day, Cat waited and watched for her father to make an appearance. Cat was torn between fight or flight – confront him, demanding answers, or avoid him like the plague.

She had no idea which urge was stronger.

"Jeez, it's like the whole town is here," Seamus said as he fought to find an empty space for the truck along the long driveway.

"They came for the party," Cat said distractedly as she double checked her lipstick in the side mirror. It was too red for a funeral, too garish. She quickly blotted it with the palm of her hand.

"This isn't a party," Seamus frowned as he hopped out of the truck.

"Even if it was, we still wouldn't be invited," Cat

murmured, rubbing the trace of lipstick into her hand. She slid out of his truck, tugging at her tight-fitting skirt.

"Should I say something to him?" Cat demanded as Seamus took her hand, steadying her. The high heels were too much for a country funeral but like the lipstick, they were only ones she had.

"Who?"

"My father." As grateful as she was for his hand, there was still exasperation in her voice.

"I thought you didn't want to talk to him."

As they walked up the gravel drive, Cat caught sight of the red hair of Brenna and Kayleigh together under a tree on the lawn. In her businesslike suit, Brenna looked as out of place as Cat felt.

She never thought she'd be comforted by the sight of Brenna.

"Cat?" Seamus tugged at her hand. "What's wrong?"

"My father is here. Dory is here. No one on that side of the family will acknowledge we have a relationship to the Ebans so they're all wishing we'd stay the hell away. I don't like feeling I don't belong."

"You belong here as much as anybody," Seamus

said with a squeeze of her hand. “But we can go. We don’t have to be here.”

Cat saw the challenge in his eyes.

“We can leave them in peace,” he added. “Is that what you want?”

“Not really.” She grinned and he laughed. Fight was apparently the stronger urge. A surge of adrenaline raced through her, like she was going into battle.

“It’ll be fine.” With another squeeze, Seamus led her across the lush, green lawn.

“Not if I don’t get rid of these shoes,” Cat muttered, off-balanced as her heels sank into the grass.

They joined the crowd outside the house at the tables of food.

“I should have brought something,” Cat fretted as they joined the line.

“You don’t want to be here and yet you want to help out?” Seamus asked with wonderment.

Joss slipped behind them. “Hey,” he said, without his customary scowl. “Sorry for your loss.” He scanned the crowd, his height making it easy for him.

“Brenna’s under the tree with Kayleigh,” Cat said

helpfully.

"Who says I'm looking for her?"

Cat handed him a plate. "Stop looking and get her some food. I don't think she eats enough."

Balancing two plates, Joss followed them over to Brenna and Kayleigh. "Cara did a nice job," Maggie greeted Cat. She held up a brownie. "These are yours, aren't they?"

Cat easily recognized her baking handiwork. "She must have got them from Sara at the Sandwich Shoppe. I would have made her fresh ones."

She watched as Joss offered the plate of food to Brenna, saw how her sister flushed, smiled shyly at him. With everything that had gone wrong lately, at least here was a possibility of something right.

But then Cat recalled Brenna's job offer and frowned. Brenna hadn't said anything since her announcement and Cat pictured her busily making plans to leave them again.

"What a cozy sisterly gathering."

Cat hadn't noticed Dory sauntering up, the silent Callum by her side. "Shit," she muttered under her breath, feeling a sense of foreboding as dark as Dory's dress. "This is a nice turnout," Brenna said politely.

Cat shook her head at Dory's uncanny ability to block out the sun.

"Thank you for coming." Dory smiled magnanimously at each of them.

Kayleigh responded with a rude snort. "He was our grandfather, too. Of course we came."

Dory eyes took on a bemused gleam as her gaze flew to Seamus standing between Brenna and Cat. "Isn't that nice. The two of you have finally learned to share." She smiled sweetly at Seamus.

"What's your point, Dory?" Cat demanded.

"Nothing. Just making conversation."

"Well, don't," Kayleigh said bluntly. "Or if you want to talk, why don't you tell us why you're here? Granddad was a handy excuse. What is it you really want?"

"Isn't it time that you did some talking, Kayleigh? I'm sure you have a lot of secrets you're not sharing, either."

Cat flicked her gaze to Brenna and frowned.

"Is that what you're trying to do?" Kayleigh laughed, but Cat noticed the uneasy expression cross her face. "You threatening to spill my secrets?"

"I'm not threatening anything."

"I think we all know better than to trust you with anything," Cat said angrily. "There's nothing about Kayleigh that would make us think any less of her."

"It doesn't matter," Brenna spoke up. "The only thing that matters is that we're here together and -"

Kayleigh threw up her arms, sending a leftover piece of lettuce flying off the plate. "Fine. I'll tell them. Would that make you happy?"

"I didn't say anything -" Dory protested, still with the bemused smile on her face.

"But you're going to. So look, everybody – I'm gay." Kayleigh glanced around, not meeting anyone's eyes, her face set, as if waiting for the blow.

There was a pause.

"Yes, we know," Maggie said impatiently.

"It's about time you said something," Cat added.

"And again – it doesn't matter," Brenna said.

Cat almost laughed at Kayleigh's expression; her sister's expression of fear and defiance magically transformed to wonderment and amazement. "Really?" Her shoulders seemed to sag with relief. "You knew?"

"Why else was Erica at the funeral today?" Cat drawled. "It's sort of been obvious for a while now."

Laughter bubbled out of Kayleigh as Maggie drew her into her arms. “Idiot,” she murmured. “You should have told us years ago. It wouldn’t have mattered then, either.”

“Nothing matters as long as you’re happy,” Brenna said, her hand on Kayleigh’s back. “That’s all we want for you.”

“Not everybody wants that.” Cat turned to Dory, her eyes hard. “Anything else you’ve got? Any other secrets you want to spill? I told you I used to like Kirby Conlin and then you go and convince him to leave town with you. Brenna tells you she wants to find our father, and you go and do it, then keep him to yourself. What are you trying to prove?” Cat’s voice rose in volume and she stepped closer to Dory. “We’re supposed to be sisters. There’s nothing -”

Dory’s hand covered her mouth. “You don’t know?” she whispered.

“Know what?” Cat snapped, even as the dread rose within her.

“What the hell are you talking about?” Brenna snapped. “I’ve had enough of this, Dory?”

“The four of you were always so special.” Dory’s face twisted into a sneer. “Dancing around, always looking out for each other. Never me. Never cared about me."

"That's not true," Kayleigh said in a low voice.

"Always promising to always be there for each other. But you never share the most important things. Kind of hypocritical, if you ask me."

Was this the whole reason for Dory coming home? To show the flaws in their relationships? Because even as angry as she was, Cat knew Dory had a point. They had all kept secrets from each other.

Dory shook her head. "All that sisterly love was such a good act. Especially when Maggie's not even your sister."

What? Cat turned to Maggie, the question on her lips.

Maggie looked pale and frightened. "I can't believe he told you," she said with a sigh.

"Oh, she's your half-sister," Dory continued in a breezy tone. "But not the half you care about."

Cat stepped back, losing her balance as her heel sank into the grass. Seamus grabbed her arm, steadying her. She shot him a look of gratitude.

"Explain," she pleaded to Maggie but it was Dory who answered.

"Turns out our father was a bit of a rascal in his youth," Dory began, a disapproving smile on her face.

"Carly Skatt was not my mother," Maggie interrupted, her face white and set. "My mother gave me up and our father convinced Carly to raise me as her own."

"How did we not know?" Brenna breathed. "You can't cover that up."

Maggie shrugged. "But they did. They pretended Carly was already pregnant when they got married. Five months later they had a baby. If anyone suspected different, they kept it quiet."

Cat stared at her sister – half-sister – seeing the resemblance to their father with her blue eyes, and long face. Maggie had been the only one without their mother's quick temper.

"Who else knows?" Cat asked in a strangled voice. She turned to Seamus, who frantically shook his head.

"It doesn't matter," Kayleigh said stoutly. "Just like you said to me. You're still our sister; you're more Skatt than Ebans." She reached for Maggie's hand, clutching it tightly. Maggie smiled tremulously at her, her chin trembling with the effort of withholding her tears.

"You raised us – for a woman who wasn't even your biological mother," Brenna whispered. "How?"

"You were still my sisters." Fat tears began slowly trickling down Maggie's face.

"Whoever your mother is doesn't change a thing. See?" Cat turned to Dory, eyes furious. "It doesn't matter what you've got on us. It won't change a thing."

Dory sighed. "It will when Maggie gets your share of the house. You really should have kept looking for him," Dory said to Brenna. "Then you wouldn't be in the same boat as them."

"He wants the house, doesn't he?" Brenna said in a quiet voice. "Not you."

"It's the marital home, they never divorced. You're a lawyer, you know how it works."

"He can't have the house," Cat declared but the waver in her voice announced her fear.

"Of course he can't," Kayleigh soothed.

"He can," Brenna told them sadly. "Legally, it's his house."

How could they be so calm? This was their house, her home! Her dreams.

"We can buy it from him!" Cat leapt on the idea, prepared to ride it. "Why would he want to live here?

It's worthless to him."

"Cat, you know I can't afford it," Maggie said softly, giving her arm a squeeze.

"He wants the money." Brenna turned to Dory. "Doesn't he? And I'm guessing you -" She nodded at the silent Callum, "- know exactly what it's worth."

"I'd say it's worth close to two million," Callum offered in a polite voice.

"Million?" Cat swayed, her heels embedded in the grass again. She angrily kicked her shoes off. "You're telling me that house is worth two million dollars?"

"It's a beautiful home, early 1900s with what, at least six bedrooms? The hard wood floors are gorgeous and original crown moldings. It's tired and needs some work but if you clean it up, you could get at least that for it. Maybe more."

"Callum's in real estate," Dory explained unnecessarily.

"Of course he is," Maggie said drily.

Cat stepped forward, filled with an undeniable urge to hit Dory. Brenna stepped between them, her hand gentle on her shoulder. Cat brushed it off. She couldn't bear to be touched, to be patronized. Her father was going to take her home...

"Bee, will you help?" Maggie pleaded. "We need a lawyer. He can't do this."

"She's not going to help," Cat said scathingly. "She's looking to get out of here anyway and if she plays her cards right, maybe she'll get a couple bucks out of the deal. It'll smooth her way when she moves to Australia."

"Austria," Brenna corrected. "But it's not like that. This isn't right. He shouldn't be allowed to do it. We'll fight it -"

Cat saw the expression on Joss' face out of the corner of her eye. Apparently Brenna's opportunity was news to him as well. Just like Brenna to think she could do it all herself, didn't need anyone.

"Why fight it?" Dory laughed. "If Dad sells the house, the money is ours when – you know. Eventually."

"When he dies?"Kayleigh demanded. "That's why you're here?"

Dory raised her hand. "You can't tell me you haven't thought about that. This farm is worth a fortune. The house is only a drop in the bucket. And to be honest, our father isn't getting any younger." She touched her hand to her mouth. "Oh...but I'm assuming you're included in Dad's will. I've been close to him for years, and Maggie - well, considering the circumstances of her not being a Skatt, I would assume she's included. I really don't know about the rest of you."

Pieces of the puzzle fell into place.

"Is that why you went looking for him?" Cat accused Brenna. "Because you knew all this? You went looking for your share, just like Dory?"

"Cat, no! I had no idea -" Brenna looked shocked at the allegation, but Cat was suddenly tired of giving her the benefit of the doubt.

She was tired of everything.

"Whatever! You want out, Dory just wants her money—no one gives a damn about the house but me! What about our mother? She's there too! Did any of you think of that? Did you think if we sell the house we're going to lose her all over again?"

"She's dead, Cat," Kayleigh said, touching her arm. Cat shook her off as well. "Maybe it's time for you to move on. You're holding on to her too tight. It's not healthy."

"And what do you know about healthy? Keeping your relationship with Erica secret for all these years?

What's your problem telling us about being gay? I couldn't care less and it pisses me off that you would think that."

Cat regretted the words as soon as they left her mouth. Kayleigh's face drained of color as she took a step back. Then she turned and walked away.

"Kayleigh, wait! Cat," Maggie breathed. "This isn't the time or place for this."

"Well, it's not the time for me to lose my home either, and you're making me deal with it."

"This isn't just about you."

"Whatever. Why can't you just leave things alone?" Cat rounded on Dory. "You never gave a damn about us until you thought there might be some money to get out of us." She didn't realize her voice was steadily rising until she felt Brenna's touch on her arm again. "Don't you try and stop me! You're the same as her. You don't give two shits about us and you never have!"

"Cat," Seamus soothed.

"It's true! She only came back because she had no other place to go. No one else gave a damn about her, so she thought she'd hide out here. And now she's going to fuck right off again, without even a good-bye.

Dory's as bad as she is—worse because at least she comes right out and says why she's here. 'Oh, I'm here for the wedding,'" Cat mocked. "Bullshit! You're a coward, Brenna Skatt. Ebans! And a bitch. And so are you." She turned to Dory. "It's my house," she shouted for all to hear. "Mine! Because no one else gave a damn about it!"

Chapter Forty-One

Brenna

Sisters are doin' it for themselves

—Eurythmics

Brenna watched Cat storm across the lawn in her bare feet. She was torn with running after her and finishing things with Dory.

She had never seen Cat so upset. This was about fear. Fear of losing yet one more thing that she loved.

Fear was something Brenna understood very well.

"She hasn't changed one bit." Dory smiled. "Still so dramatic."

Brenna held up a hand, conscious of Maggie

swelling with fury beside her. She'd been the recipient of her anger and didn't want to deny Dory the experience. But she needed to find out a few things first.

"How bad is his financial situation?" she demanded of Dory. "What's he told you?"

"I didn't say anything about that," Dory hedged.

Brenna gave a brisk nod. "And the pictures? The art in the house? I'm assuming he knows what they're worth?" She turned to Callum. "Are you an art dealer too?"

"What art?" Maggie asked, bewildered.

"Cat's sitting on a fortune and no one realized it. Those pictures in the living room? They're Group of Seven. I have no idea how much they're worth. But there's no way he's getting his hands on them." Brenna's eyes flickered to Seamus, who slowly backed away. She hoped the closeness she once shared with him would allow him to understand exactly what she needed.

"No way!" Dory shouted, noticing Seamus' quick retreat.

"What? He should check on Cat, make sure she's okay. As for me, I think I'll go have a chat with our father." She pushed her way past Dory before her sister could say another word.

Joss fell into step with her before she had gotten very far. "Hold on a sec." Because Brenna hadn't stopped walking, Joss put a hand on her arm. "What's this about some job? In Australia?"

"Austria. Now's not the best time, Joss."

"I don't really care. You can take a minute, tell me where I stand, can't you?"

Brenna stopped, looked up at him. She'd been both dreading and looking forward to seeing Joss all week, unsure of what to say to him. She had thought of him often, confusing thoughts jumping around her mind, like popcorn kernels.

What they shared had been intense and it hadn't just been the sex. He had seen Brenna at her most vulnerable and it frightened her.

"Things have been hectic," she began.

"I'm not in the mood for excuses," he growled. "I get that there's been a lot going on, and I've kept my distance this week, to give you space, let you be with your family. But I thought there was something between us. Was I wrong?"

"No." She looked down to see Joss's feet clad in a

pair of black leather shoes rather than his dusty boots. She remember how it felt being pressed against him on his motorcycle, the way he fed her pie, the way he listened to her.

"Are you leaving? Did you know about this job before or after we hooked up?"

His anger happened so fast and furious that Brenna stepped back. "Joss, there's nothing to tell. There's an opportunity for me—"

"In Australia?"

"Austria. In Vienna. I worked there when I was getting my degree. I found out about it just before Granddad passed." She shrugged. "I haven't had a chance to say anything yet."

"Don't you think you better?"

"This really doesn't have anything to do with you," she said slowly. Brenna could see her father in the distance, holding court with a group of people. As much as she wanted to sort things out with Joss, her family had to come first.

She had pushed them aside for too long.

"It has everything to do with me if you're planning on leaving." Joss' statement grabbed her attention and he leaned forward, his eyes blazing. "We made love, Brenna, and that means something to me. Maybe it's different from where you stand, but I think that gives me a say in things. At least to be told. Do you agree?"

"I..."

Joss shook his head with frustration. "Enough with the scared little girl act. You're a grown woman. You can't go running away every time you get into a fight with your sisters. You're an amazing woman, and I want you in my life. I need to know if you're leaving. Because I don't want you to go."

His words peppered her like bullets but instead of causing injury, they created a warm sensation within her chest, spreading through her body, down to her fingers and toes.

"I'm telling you this right now. I think we'd be good together. I could make you happy, better than anyone in Austria, or even Vancouver."

This man, someone she barely knew, was fighting for her.

He wanted her to stay.

Speechless with emotion, Brenna reached on her tiptoes to press her lips against his. She meant for it to be brief, but Joss grabbed her arms, pulling her against him.

"Stay," he murmured against her mouth.

Brenna wanted nothing more than to stay right there in his arms, but she pulled away. Eyes shining, a giggle of happiness bursting from within. "You've got to give me a minute."

"Brenna," Joss warned.

"I'll be right back," she promised, backing away and hurrying over to where her father stood.

She was amazed by Joss' declaration, excited, scared...and happy.

So happy that she could barely remember why she left him standing there.

Cat. She had to stop their father from taking the house from her. She wasn't sure what she could do, but there had to be something.

Roger stood with a group of people Brenna didn't recognize, but she had no qualms about interrupting. "I need to speak with you, please."

"Brenna," he said with no more than a moment's hesitation. "Thank you for coming."

She shook her head, her smile fading. "Did you actually think I wouldn't be here?"

"Yes. Well, will you excuse me?" With a nod of

farewell, he moved a few feet away.

They stood staring at each other for an awkward moment.

“How are you?” Roger asked, finally

“It’s been thirty years and that’s all you can say?”

Roger’s blank expression reminded Brenna of a salesman forced to deal with an upset customer. “What would you like me to say?”

“I’m not sure right now. But I want to talk about the house. Mom’s house.” He raised an eyebrow. “Cat’s house now. I’m staying with her.”

“And how long are you here for? You’ve done quite well for yourself in Vancouver.”

His words surprised her. “Have you been keeping track of me?”

“Yes.”

Her heart sank. “Were you in B.C. when I was there?”

“For a time. Then I moved on to Seattle, and then back to Toronto.”

“Why did you let Dory find you but not me?” Brenna could hear the hurt in her own voice, knew it wouldn’t make a difference to her father.

“Because I knew she wouldn’t make me come

back here. She hated this place as much as I did. My father told me you were a smart girl, Brenna, and you proved it by leaving home just as quickly as you could. There's nothing here. It's a place with no future. I always felt stifled and trapped. I always planned on leaving, but then your mother -"

"You got her pregnant and you were stuck," Brenna said flatly. "Or rather, you got someone else pregnant."

"There were circumstances you don't know about."

She held up her hand. "No need for excuses. I know enough."

And she did. Suddenly, all of the energy she'd spent searching, wondering about him, imagining the worst, the best, seemed worthless. She didn't want excuses, carefully worded lies.

"What do you want, Brenna?" Her father's voice was tight with anger. Maybe if they had a normal father daughter relationship, she might have been wary of the tone, of the coldness flashing in his hazel eyes, so like her own.

Brenna didn't want anything to be like him.

He spread his arms wide. "I've made a life for

myself, away from here."

"And Dory gets to be part of it. You shouldn't get to pick and choose your daughters, you know."

Roger gaze flickered around them, as if wondering how many were watching, listening.

"What's the matter? Are you afraid of everyone hearing what I'm saying? Some of these people are your family. Don't you think they already know what kind of man you are? They don't think you're the prodigal son, rushing back home in the nick of time to say good-bye to your dying father. They haven't forgotten how you've been gone for thirty years! They know you never once contacted your father, or your brother, or your daughters! You left your children!" Brenna voice rose as years of anger and loneliness crashed to the surface.

"Brenna, this isn't the place."

"I think it's the perfect place. You left us! He left us!" she shouted, making sure everyone could hear clearly. "And you are all swooning over him. Oh, Roger, so good to see you! Oh, Roger, what a good son to come back! I know what they're saying, because that's what it was like for me a week ago. But I had a damn good reason to leave, unlike you! Oh, Roger, what a shithead you are to have left your family. That's what I'd be saying!" she finished, tears of frustration threatening.

"That's what I'd be saying," Joss' spoke from behind her. Brenna glanced over her shoulder to see him standing with her sisters.

She took a deep breath, felt their strength boosting her.

Maggie stepped forward and took Brenna's hand. "We did fine without you," she said calmly.

"She's just saying that," Cat interjected. "I've been married three times and I'm sure as hell blaming you for that!"

"I believe I'm a lesbian because I didn't have a suitable male influence in my life," Kayleigh announced calmly.

Brenna's jaw dropped until Kayleigh gave her a wink.

Cat leaned across Brenna. "I don't think that can really be his fault," she whispered to Kayleigh.

"You're blaming him for everything in your life—why can't I?"

Brenna hid her smile. "We could stand here and tell you about the mess you made of our lives," Brenna pointed out. “But you know what? It’s not worth it. You’re not worth it. You’re not worth enough to know anything about our lives. Because you left, we became the strong, amazing women that we are.”

“That’s right,” Kayleigh cried.

“And you know what?” Brenna continued. “I was coming over here to ask you, to beg you not to take the house away from Cat, but now I’m not.”

“You’re not?” Cat said in a strangled voice.

“I don’t want to ask you for anything. We’ll fight you in court if we have to.”

Brenna turned; Maggie, still holding her hand, moved with her. As one, they walked away, Cat and Cayleigh right behind them.

“That felt good,” Cat said. “You lost me my house, but still, cool. You’re kind of an ass-kicker, you know, Bee.”

Brenna smiled at her sister.

Chapter Forty-Two

Cat

An older sister is a friend and defender—a listener, a conspirator, a counselor and a sharer of delights. And sorrows too.

—Pam Brown

"But what do we do now?" Cat's voice was plaintive. "Nothing has changed. He still owns the house and he's going to kick me out. Pretty fast, considering we just finished carving him a new one."

"As long as Seamus got the pictures out -"

"What did Seamus do?" Cat demanded, her voice

chilling.

Brenna stopped her march across the lawn, and Cat heaved a sigh of relief. She had had no idea where they were going, and while she didn't mind being barefoot, if she kept at it, there was no way she was going to be able clean the grass stains off her feet.

"The pictures in the living room that no one pays attention to? They're all paintings by famous Canadian artists. Some have been missing for years. I have no idea where they came from, but they're worth a fortune."

"But they're part of the house," Kayleigh frowned.

Brenna smiled. "Not anymore. As long as Seamus figured out what I wanted him to do. I think he did."

"He ran out of here fast enough," Maggie mused. "Is that where he went?"

"I've been looking into it all week," Brenna said. "I didn't want to say anything until I was sure. I talked to someone in the McMichael Gallery outside Toronto who's interested in seeing them. I'll take them there this week before our father realizes they're gone."

"But Dory..." Cat wondered.

"Our word against hers." Brenna said with a shrug.

“Spoken like a true lawyer,” Cat laughed.

“I don’t know if it’ll be enough to buy him out,” Brenna warned. “But I was thinking – I’ve got some money saved up.”

“We could buy him out,” Cat said in a rush, leaping onto another idea, a better idea. “The house. Buy it from him together.” Her voice faltered as she realized what she’d said to Brenna. “If you want to, that is...”

“What are you asking, exactly?” Brenna frowned. Cat could picture her in a courtroom, professional to the core. Why would she want to give that up? The career that she worked so hard for.

But Cat had never been one not to go after what she wanted. And suddenly, she wanted this very much.

She took a deep breath. “Open a B & B with me. In the house. Cat and Bee’s B & B.”

“Or Bee and Cat,” Brenna mused, fighting the smile.

“Unless you’re still planning on going to eat schnitzel in Germany.” Hope bloomed within Cat at the sight of the hint of the smile.

“Austria.”

“It sounds so far away,” Kayleigh said, sounding wistful.

“It’s not that far -”

“We’d never be able to call you. It would take forever to figure out the time difference.”

“It’s not that difficult -”

Cat rolled her eyes. “I thought you were supposed to be so smart. We want you to stay!”

“This time we’re telling you. Don’t go away again, Bee,” Maggie pleaded.

“Stay with your sisters,” Kayleigh added, holding tight to Maggie’s hand.

Brenna glanced at each of them, unable to contain the smile bursting at the corners of her mouth. “I turned them down two days ago.”

Cat was the first to hug her.

Chapter Forty-Three

Brenna

How the hell do you sum up your sister in three minutes? She's your twin and your polar opposite. She's your constant companion and your competition. She's your best friend and the biggest bitch in the world. She's everything you wish you could be and everything you wish you weren't

-M. Molly Backes

"Hey! Wait up." They were almost at the cars when Jamie caught up with them.

"I'm sorry we can't stay," Maggie apologized. "We've made a bit of a scene, and I think it's best if we slide out of here."

"That's why I'm here," Jamie said, puffing for breath. "My dad sent me over."

"Oh, shit," Cat groaned.

Jamie grinned. "No, it's good. If you want to keep the house, I know how you can buy out your father." He paused for a moment. "Granddad left everything to us. The five of you and me and my brother."

"What?" Maggie and Cat chorused.

"Dad told me – it was the only way he could make sure your father didn't get his hands on the farm. After talking to you, Brenna, he realized he made a mistake telling Roger to leave. He said he shouldn't have interfered. And he knew that everything he tried to do would be worth nothing if Roger inherited. So he changed his will, just the other day. Neither of his sons will get any part of the farm."

"Your father...?"Brenna asked, holding her breath.

"Nothing. He'll be fine. The farm is for us. And with the money, you could buy the house. "

"Are you serious?" Cat asked. Her hand covered her mouth, eyes full of hope.

"But the farm...?" Brenna's mind was racing, thinking of the details. Already looking for loopholes, making sure all the t's were crossed.

"There are already negotiations underway to sell. There's a company who wants to build a summer camp. It'll take a while to settle..." he glanced at Brenna. "We could use a good lawyer."

Brenna smiled. "Who put you up to that?"

She glanced towards Joss, who had a hint of a smile on his face. "You still owe me a beer. The one you knocked out of my hand that first night."

"You were in my way," Brenna said. "Besides, you owe me a slice of pie."

"It's a date. Our first date. Beer and pie," Joss promised.

Brenna looked at each of her sisters, turning last to Cat. "I'm back," she said simply.

"Welcome home," Cat said.

The End

Dear Readers,

Thanks for reading Coming Home!

This book has been a long time coming.

Coming Home was first published in 2013 by Etopia Press. When I retained the rights this year, I had planned on making a few changes before republishing it with Three Birds Press. A few weeks, max.

Four months later and Coming Home has been practically rewritten, thanks to a suggestion by my wonderful writing partner, Nita. The story is the same, with minor changes, and the characters are all the same, with a few name changes. But Coming Home 2.0 is definitely the improved version. I'm so proud of what it's become that if you have an original, please let me know and I'll send you this new version. Ebook or print, your choice.

Writing is a solitary pursuit, but there are a lot of people involved in getting a book released and I have a few people I'd like to thank.

First, my family, for putting up with living with a writer and ignoring the fact the house really needs to be vacuumed!

Second, huge thanks to Nita Collins for her neverending support and encouragement and amazingly awesome suggestions and critiques. I couldn't have done it with you, Nita! Her novel Holding Space will be available soon and trust me, you'll want to read it as quickly as you can!!

I also need to thank Pat, for being the last set of eyes on it; Donna Chabot for yet another beautiful cover, and Lisa and Maria, for their incredibly helpful suggestions.

I'd also like to thank the ladies (and gents) of ChickLit Chat for all their support and retweets!

I really appreciate that you took time to read, spent $ buying and basically took a chance on me. I might be a new author for you. I might be one of your favourites (yay). But writers need readers, so I need you!

So let's keep in touch. I'd love it if you visited my website and signed up for my newsletter. I send it out monthly, full of things going on with my books, new releases and events I'm involved with. I'd also love it if you could tell others what you think of Coming Home, either on Goodreads or the retailer where you purchased the book. I write because I love it but it's fun to sell books too, and reviews help with that.

Plus, being in touch will mean you'll be among the first to find out more about my next books! I'm writing a sequel to The Secret Life of Charlotte Dodd called Best Worst First Date. It will be available Summer 2017. Visit my website to find out more.

Thanks again!

Holly
xo

www.hollykerr.ca
www.threebirdspress.ca
www.Facebook/HollyKerrAuthor
@hollykerrauthor

Holly Kerr
Books
Put your feet up. Enjoy
unexpecting
Holly Kerr
Coming Home
Holly Kerr
ABSINTHE
Doesn't Make the Heart Grow Fonder
THE DRAGON
Under The Mountain
Holly Kerr
The Secret Life of
Charlotte Dodd
Holly Kerr
The Missing Files of
Charlotte Dodd
Holly Kerr
COMING SOON
The Best Worst First Date
Holly Kerr
THE DRAGON
Under The Dome
Holly Kerr

ABOUT THE AUTHOR

Holly Kerr loves watching Buffy the Vampire Slayer, old episodes of Alias and calls herself the mother of dragons because of her son's pet bearded dragon. Deep down, she'd like to be a superhero.

Visit her at www.hollykerr.ca

Made in the USA
Columbia, SC
19 April 2017